Treasured Christmas Brides

6 Novellas Celebrate Love as the Greatest Gift

Treasured Christmas Brides

AMANDA CABOT, REBECCA GERMANY,
CATHY MARIE HAKE, COLLEEN L. REECE,
MARYLU TYNDALL, MICHELLE ULE

BARBOUR BOOKS
An Imprint of Barbour Publishing, Inc.

The Christmas Star Bride ©2014 by Amanda Cabot
A Token of Promise ©2003 by Rebecca Germany
Band of Angel's ©2003 by Cathy Marie Hake
Winterlude ©1996 by Colleen L. Reece
Christmas Bounty ©2014 by MaryLu Tyndall
The Gold Rush Christmas ©2013 by Michelle Ule

Print ISBN 978-1-64352-181-7

eBook Editions:
Adobe Digital Edition (.epub) 978-1-64352-183-1
Kindle and MobiPocket Edition (.prc) 978-1-64352-182-4

Published by Barbour Books, an imprint of Barbour Publishing, Inc., 1810 Barbour Drive, Uhrichsville, Ohio 44683, www.barbourbooks.com

Our mission is to inspire the world with the life-changing message of the Bible.

ecpa Member of the
Evangelical Christian
Publishers Association

Printed in the United States of America.

Contents

The Christmas Star Bride

by Amanda Cabot

The LORD redeemeth the soul of his servants:
and none of them that trust in him shall be desolate.
PSALM 34:22

Chapter 1

November 27, 1885
Cheyenne, Wyoming Territory

There had to be a way. Esther Hathaway punched the dough with more force than normal. A good kneading was just what her trademark pumpernickel needed. She could—and would—provide that. If only she could find what *she* needed as easily.

Four weeks from today was Christmas, the day to celebrate the most wonderful gift ever given. It was also the day her niece would become Mrs. Lieutenant Michael Porter. Esther sighed as she gave the dough another punch. Susan's dress was almost finished. They had chosen the cake Esther would bake. Michael's parents had their train tickets and hotel reservations. Everything was on schedule with one exception: Esther's gift.

With the kneading complete, she slid the ball of dough into the lightly greased bowl and covered it with a towel to let it rise. The sweet white dough that would become cinnamon rolls for her early morning customers had already completed its first rising and was ready to be rolled out and filled with the rich butter and cinnamon filling.

Esther's hands moved mechanically, performing the tasks they did each morning, while her mind focused on the problem that had wakened her in the middle of the night. Susan claimed it didn't matter, but it did. Four generations of Hathaway women had had their Christmas stars, and Susan would too.

A smile crossed Esther's face as she thought of the stars, now carefully wrapped in soft flannel, waiting for their annual unveiling and placement on the tree. Each was as different as the happy brides and grooms whose portraits were highlighted by the star-shaped frames: Esther's great-grandparents, her grandparents, her own parents, and her sister and brother-in-law. Having each couple immortalized in a Christmas ornament had become a Hathaway family tradition.

Esther, of course, had no star-shaped portrait to display on the mantel or hang on the tree. Her hopes for that had died on the blood-soaked fields of Gettysburg more than twenty years before, but Susan—the niece she loved as dearly as if she were her daughter—would carry on the tradition. If only Esther could find a suitable artist.

Once the filling had been spread over the dough, she lifted one of the long edges and began to form it into a log that would then be cut into individual pieces and baked in one of the large, round cake tins that did double duty for cinnamon rolls.

Esther's smile turned into a frown as she thought of her search for someone capable of painting Susan and Michael's portrait. Quality. That's what she sought. When she'd taken over running the bakery, she had insisted on using nothing but the highest quality ingredients and the best pans she could find. Susan's portrait deserved the same high quality.

Esther had interviewed every portrait painter in Cheyenne, but none of them had been right. Some were too busy to take on her commission. Others lacked the talent she sought. Still others admitted they'd never painted a miniature. Though they were willing to try, Esther wasn't willing to take a chance on failure. She had found the perfect frame, a simple gold star, the only embellishment being Susan and Michael's initials engraved in each point. Now she needed an artist.

Bowing her head, Esther sent a prayer heavenward. Though she knew the good Lord had many more important things to do, she prayed that He'd send her the painter she sought. There was no answer. Of course not. It was silly to have expected an artist to knock on her door this early in the morning. She would wait.

Once the rolls were in the oven, Esther poured herself a cup of coffee and retrieved the morning paper from the front step. Settling into a chair at the kitchen table, she began to peruse the news, turning the pages slowly as she learned what had happened in Cheyenne yesterday and what events were planned for today.

Her gaze stopped and her eyes widened. The ad was so small that Esther almost missed it, but there it was, buried deep inside the paper. *Jeremy Snyder, artist. Portraits, landscapes, oils, watercolors.*

Her heart singing with happiness, she reached for a piece of stationery and an envelope. This was no coincidence. God had answered her prayers.

⬡

Cheyenne was a fine city, Jeremy Snyder reflected as he headed past the train depot on Fifteenth Street. Some might complain about the noise when an iron horse chugged and whistled its way to the depot, but Jeremy wasn't one of them. He recognized the trains for what they were: the lifeblood of the city. Thanks to President Lincoln's vision of a transcontinental railroad and the Union Pacific's part in turning that vision into reality, Cheyenne existed.

Jeremy crossed Hill Street. Just one more block and he'd be able to rest his legs. Though the doctors had told him that walking was good for him, even after more than two decades it remained a painful experience if he went too far or too quickly. He'd done both today, searching for work.

Other end-of-the-rails towns had disappeared, but Cheyenne had flourished. In less than twenty years, it had grown from a rough-and-tumble tent town to one of the wealthiest cities in the country. That was why Jeremy had come. He'd reasoned that all those cattle baron millionaires would want family portraits or pretty landscapes to hang on their walls. He'd been right. They did want artwork, but not from an itinerant painter like him. They could afford artists who'd gathered a following in the East. Some had even commissioned work from famous European painters.

Jeremy winced as pain radiated up his left leg, but the pain was not only physical. As much as he enjoyed living in Cheyenne, if he didn't get work soon, he'd have to move on. Though he'd hoped to stay until spring, that was beginning to seem unrealistic. The boardinghouse where he stayed was one of the cheapest in town, and he'd arranged to eat dinner only three nights a week to save money. But even with those economies, his small reserve would soon be depleted and he'd have no choice but to leave.

He climbed the five steps leading to his boardinghouse, deliberately ignoring the peeling paint and the squeaking boards beneath his feet. At least the roof did not leak, and his room had enough light that he could work there. . .if he had a commission. Lately all he'd been able to afford to paint had been watercolor landscapes. Though they filled his heart with joy, they did nothing to fill an empty stomach.

"Mr. Snyder." As Jeremy entered the boardinghouse, his landlady emerged from the kitchen, an envelope in her hand. "This just came for you."

It was probably rude, but Jeremy ripped the envelope open and withdrew the single sheet of paper, his eyes scanning the few words. His heart began to thud, and he grinned at the kindly woman. "Thank you, Mrs. Tyson."

"Is it work for you?"

"I hope so."

Back in his room, Jeremy buffed his shoes, then studied his reflection in the small mirror over the bureau. No one would call him handsome, but at forty, that was no longer important. What mattered was what he was able to create with brushes and paint. He pulled his leather case from under the bed, trying to decide which items to take. Since Miss Hathaway hadn't specified whether she wanted oil or watercolor for her niece's portrait, Jeremy included a watercolor landscape along with the oil portrait of his father that he'd done from memory and the miniature of his mother.

Sitting on the one chair the room boasted, he tightened the straps that held his left foot in place. Wood didn't flex like flesh and sinews, but at least it allowed him to walk without crutches or a cane. There was nothing he could do about the limp. That was a permanent reminder of what had happened at Antietam, but it was also a reminder that he'd been fortunate. He had lived, and now, if Miss Esther Hathaway liked his work, he would be able to spend Christmas in Cheyenne.

Mindful of the leg that protested each step, he walked slowly east. Instead of retracing his steps, this time he took Sixteenth Street, heading for the Mitchell-Hathaway Bakery on the corner of Sixteenth and Central. Jeremy had passed it numerous times on his walks through the city and had been enticed by the delicious aromas that wafted through the air each time the door opened, but he'd never been inside. The few commissions he'd obtained had barely covered room and board and the cost of supplies. There'd been nothing left for treats.

There it was, a small brick building on the southeast corner, facing Central. One plate-glass window held a display of tempting baked goods, while the other revealed four round tables that encouraged customers to enjoy a cup of coffee or tea with a pastry. Jeremy saw a second door on the Sixteenth Street side and suspected it led to the proprietor's living quarters. He'd been told that many shopkeepers lived either behind or on top of their establishments.

As Jeremy opened the front door, he was assailed by the smell of freshly baked bread and pastries, and his mouth began to water. He took another step inside, carefully closing the door behind him, thankful there were no customers to hear the rumbling of his stomach. Fixing a smile on his face, he turned. An instant later the smile froze and Jeremy felt the blood drain from his face. Instinctively, he gripped the doorframe to keep his legs from collapsing.

It couldn't be. He blinked once, twice, then a third time to clear his vision, but nothing changed. There was no mistaking that light brown hair, those clear blue eyes, and the patrician features that had haunted his memory for so many years.

"Diana, what on earth are you doing here?"

Chapter 2

Esther stared at the man who was looking at her with such horror in his eyes. Close to six feet tall, he had medium brown hair with only a few strands of gray, and brown eyes that under other circumstances might have been warm. His features were regular, almost handsome; his clothing well made; his shoes freshly polished. He might have been a customer, but the leather portfolio he held in his left hand told Esther otherwise. Unless she was sorely mistaken, this was Jeremy Snyder, her last hope for Susan's portrait.

She took a step forward, seeking to defuse his tension by introducing herself. She wouldn't ask about Diana. Indeed, she would not. That would be unspeakably rude. "I'm Esther Hathaway," she said with the warmest smile she could muster, "and I suspect you're Mr. Snyder." Before she realized what was happening, the question slipped out. "Who is Diana?"

So much for good intentions.

The muscles in Mr. Snyder's cheek twitched as if he were trying to keep from shouting, but his voice was level as he said, "No one important."

It was a lie. Esther recognized the expression in his eyes. The shock had disappeared, only to be replaced by sorrow and longing. It was the same expression she'd seen in the mirror too many mornings, but there was more. Mr. Snyder's face had the pinched, gray look of a man who hasn't eaten well. Esther had seen that look on countless faces as men made their way home after the war. The Union might have won, but the soldiers who'd filed through town had shown no sign of celebration.

"Please have a seat, Mr. Snyder." Esther gestured toward one of the four tables that filled the right side of the store. "I'll be with you in a moment."

Fortunately, this was a quiet time at the bakery, and with no customers to wait on, she could devote her attention to the man who might be the painter she sought. A slight shuffling sound made Esther glance behind her as she walked toward the kitchen, and she realized that Mr. Snyder was limping. Hungry and lame. The poor, poor man.

As she sliced and buttered bread, Esther wished she had something more substantial to offer him, but there was nothing left from her midday meal. Fortunately, two cinnamon rolls remained. She placed them on a separate plate, filled a mug with coffee, then positioned everything on a tray.

"I thought that while I was studying samples of your work, you could sample mine," she said as she arranged the plates and mug in front of him.

Though his eyes brightened momentarily, Mr. Snyder shook his head. "This isn't necessary, ma'am."

"Oh, but it is," she countered. "I can tell a lot about a man from his reaction to food. I insist."

He nodded slowly before opening his portfolio and extracting three framed pictures. "I wasn't certain whether you wanted oil or watercolors," he explained as he laid them in front of her.

Esther's eyes widened at the sight of a landscape, a man's formal portrait, and a more casual painting of a woman. "I had thought oil," she said as she picked up the watercolor landscape, "but this is magnificent. The flowers look so real I want to pick them. It's excellent work, Mr. Snyder."

"And this is the best pumpernickel I've ever eaten. There's

something unique about it—a hint of coffee, perhaps?"

Esther didn't bother to mask her surprise. "You're the first person to identify it."

He shrugged as if it were of no account. "I've drunk a lot of coffee over the years, and I've learned to recognize good brews." Raising his mug in a toast, he added, "This is one of the best."

It was a simple compliment, no reason for color to rise to her cheeks, yet Esther's face warmed at the praise. To hide her confusion, she lowered her head and studied the three paintings. Each was wonderful in its own way. There was no question about it: Jeremy Snyder was the man she wanted to paint Susan and Michael's portrait.

Fearing that he might stop eating if she spoke again, Esther kept her eyes focused on the miniature of a woman she suspected was the artist's mother, waiting until he'd finished the last bite of cinnamon roll before she spoke.

"These are exactly what I was looking for. Mr. Snyder, you're the answer to my prayers."

∞

"That's the first time anyone's called me that." Jeremy took another sip of coffee, as much to avoid having to look at the woman who sat on the opposite side of the table as to wash down the last bite of that incredibly delicious cinnamon roll. She didn't sound like Diana. Her voice was firmer, a bit lower pitched than Diana's, but there was no denying the resemblance. This woman could be Diana's twin, and that hurt. Every time he looked at Miss Esther Hathaway, memories threatened to choke him.

"Tell me more about this portrait you want me to paint." Though he had every intention of refusing the commission, Jeremy had eaten the woman's food. He owed her at least a few minutes' consideration. And the truth was, other than Miss Hathaway's unfortunate resemblance to Diana, he was enjoying being here.

The bakery was warm, clean, and filled with tantalizing aromas. A pressed-tin ceiling complemented the pale blue walls and the dark wooden floors. The tables were made of a lighter shade of wood than the floor, the chair cushions a deeper blue than the walls. Though the room was not overtly feminine, Jeremy suspected it appealed to a mostly female clientele.

"I'll do more than tell you," Miss Hathaway said in response to his request. "I'll show you."

She returned from the back of the bakery a minute later, a large flannel package in her hands. Unwrapping it carefully, she withdrew four star-shaped frames and laid them on the table. To Jeremy's surprise, though he'd expected each to hold a woman's portrait, two people had their likenesses painted in each one.

"It's a family tradition," Miss Hathaway continued, "to have the bride and groom's portrait painted for their first Christmas together. My niece will be married on Christmas Day, and this will be my gift to her." The woman who looked so much like Diana gazed directly at Jeremy, not bothering to hide the eagerness in her expression. "Will you do it, Mr. Snyder?"

I can't. The words almost escaped his lips, but then he reconsidered. As painful as it would be to spend days in the company of a woman who looked so much like Diana, there was no denying that he needed the money. He needed to be practical.

Jeremy nodded slowly. "My fee for a miniature portrait is . . ." As he quoted a figure, he studied Miss Hathaway, his eyes cataloging the simple gray dress that skimmed her curves, the white collar and cuffs giving it a festive look without seeming too fancy for a shopkeeper. Though she was as beautiful as Diana, Jeremy suspected that Miss Hathaway deliberately underplayed her looks, perhaps not wanting to compete with her customers.

"You're selling yourself short, Mr. Snyder," she said with a small smile. "The other artists I've considered would have charged considerably more than that and for only one portrait. Since you'll be painting two people, it seems only fair to pay you twice that amount."

Diana would never have said anything like that, but then again, Diana would not have thought to offer a hungry man food.

"I'm not looking for charity."

Miss Hathaway gave him a piercing look. "I didn't think you were. I'm looking for excellence, and I'm willing to pay well to ensure I receive it. Now, do we have a deal, Mr. Snyder?"

There was a challenge in her voice. It was almost as if she'd read his doubts and was daring him to conquer them. They'd only just met. The woman had no way of knowing that Jeremy Snyder was not one to back down from a challenge, and yet. . .

More intrigued than he'd thought possible, Jeremy nodded. "We do."

∽

"I tell you, Susan, the man is the answer to my prayers." It was several hours later, and Esther and her niece were seated at the kitchen table, their supper laid out before them. Though many shopkeepers had totally separate living quarters, when Esther's sister, Lydia, and Daniel had built the bakery, they'd seen no need for two kitchens. The apartment had two bedrooms and a sitting room but shared the bakery's kitchen. That arrangement had worked for Esther's sister and brother-in-law, and she'd seen no need to change it.

"Mr. Snyder's work is outstanding." Esther gazed at the girl who'd inherited her father's dark brown hair and eyes but her mother's delicate features, wishing Lydia and Daniel were here to share the joy of Susan's wedding plans. "You and Michael will be proud of your portrait."

Susan smiled as she buttered a piece of rye bread. "I'm glad you found him. I know I told you it didn't matter if Michael and I didn't have our star, but. . ."

"You really wanted it." Esther finished the sentence.

Blinking in surprise, Susan stared at her. "How did you know?"

"I've lived with you for the past ten years. I'd like to think I've learned a bit about you in that time." It had been a joy and at times a trial, watching Susan change from the bewildered eight-year-old whose parents had died of a cholera epidemic into a poised young woman of eighteen, but Esther did not regret a single moment.

Susan's smile softened. "Then you also know that as much as I'm looking forward to being Michael's wife, I hate the idea of leaving you." She reached across the table and touched Esther's hand. "Won't you reconsider? Michael and I want you to live with us."

Trying not to sigh at the fact that this was far from the first time Susan had raised the subject, Esther shook her head. "I appreciate the offer. You know I do. But I don't want to give up the bakery. People depend on it." Perhaps it was wrong, but Esther couldn't help being proud of the way she turned her sister and brother-in-law's struggling enterprise into one of the most successful bakeries in Wyoming's capital.

"There are other bakeries in Cheyenne."

"But none that feed the hungry." Knowing that it was sometimes the only food they'd have, at the close of each day, Esther took bread to the boardinghouses and cheap hotels where the poorest stayed.

"I know others might not consider it a mission, but I believe I'm doing God's will. I can feel His approval in the way He's blessed me with a home of my own and you to love."

Susan had no way of knowing how important that home was to Esther. Esther had lived with her parents, caring for them until their deaths ten years ago, and then she'd moved to Cheyenne to live with Lydia and her husband.

Though she would have given anything to have had Lydia and

Daniel survive the cholera and be able to raise Susan to adulthood, Esther could not deny that she had flourished in the ten years since their deaths. Forced to make her living, she'd discovered that she had a flair for both baking and attracting customers. And for the first time in her life, she had a home that was hers and hers alone. A home and independence. She couldn't—she wouldn't—give that up.

"This is my place," she said softly. "I can't leave."

Chapter 3

They were an attractive couple. Jeremy took a step to the right, studying the subjects of his next painting. Michael's golden-blond hair and blue eyes provided a pleasing contrast to Susan's darker coloring, while her yellow dress shone against the dark blue of his uniform. But what impressed Jeremy the most and what he planned to capture in their portrait was the love they shared. He took another step, wanting to see them from every angle. That love was evident in the way their smiles softened when they looked at each other and the way Michael kept Susan's hand clasped in his.

Jeremy paused, wondering whether he and Diana had been so deeply in love before the war. Though he wanted to believe they had, the way their love had ended said otherwise. But there was no point in dwelling on that, even less in envying this young couple their happiness and their bright future. While it seemed unlikely, it was still possible that God's plans for Jeremy included a wife and the kind of happiness Michael and Susan shared. In the meantime, he had work to do. Jeremy settled onto a stool and began to sketch.

He'd been sketching for the better part of an hour when the clock chimed and Michael rose. "I'm sorry, Mr. Snyder," the young man said, his voice ringing with regret, "but I need to return to the fort."

Trying not to smile at the realization that Michael's regret was over leaving his fiancée rather than the portrait session,

Jeremy nodded. "That's not a problem. Miss Hathaway explained your schedule. I've spent most of today making sketches of you. Those will be the foundation. I can fill in the details after I've finished Susan's portrait."

The truth was, Jeremy did not need to have his subject in front of him when he painted a portrait. Once he'd made the preliminary sketches, he could work from them, but since most people were accustomed to posing while the artist painted, he continued with what was almost a charade.

As Susan rose to accompany Michael to the door, Esther approached the corner of the store where Jeremy had set up his easel. Esther. Jeremy smiled. He wasn't sure when it had happened, but he'd ceased to think of her as Miss Hathaway. Of course, he wouldn't presume to address her that way, but in his mind she was Esther.

"Are you certain it's all right to work here in the main room?" She'd removed one of the tables to give Jeremy space for his equipment and the high stools that Michael and Susan had used. "Our sitting room is more private, but it just wouldn't be proper. This way Susan is chaperoned."

Esther smiled, a sweet smile that made Jeremy pause. While it was true that she resembled Diana, their smiles were not at all alike.

"I have to confess that I had a mercenary motive too," Esther said with another smile. "I thought having you here would be good for business."

"Yours or mine?" Though he'd been in the bakery for less than two hours, Jeremy had noticed that several people had lingered to watch him. They'd bought a cup of coffee or tea and a cookie or pastry to give them a reason for sitting at one of the tables.

Esther's smile broadened. "To be honest, both. I can't compete with the variety of goods Mr. Ellis's Bakery and Confectionery offers, but at this point, I run the only bakery in Cheyenne with its own artist-in-residence."

Though she looked at the easel, she made no comment. Jeremy appreciated that. Preliminary sketches were exactly that: preliminary.

"I haven't had additional customers today, but some of those who've come have stayed longer and spent more money than usual. Monday will be different, because word will have spread. That'll be good for me."

Jeremy grinned. "And it's free advertising for me."

"Exactly. I wouldn't be surprised if you got several commissions in the next few days."

"I won't complain if that happens." This could be the boost his career needed, a way to stay in Cheyenne until spring, maybe even longer. "I appreciate your help, Miss Hathaway."

Those lovely blue eyes twinkled with what appeared to be amusement. "We're going to be seeing a lot of each other over the next month. Please call me Esther."

Jeremy blinked in surprise. The woman was amazing. Had she read his mind and known that he no longer appreciated the formality society demanded?

"I'd like that...Esther."

∽

Esther bit the inside of her cheek as she tried to control her reaction. It was silly how the sound of her name on Jeremy's lips made her feel all tingly inside. The last time she'd felt that way had been before the war, and that had been a long time ago. She was no longer a girl of less than twenty pledging her love to her dearest friend; now she was a confirmed spinster with a business to run.

As Susan returned to her stool, her smile a little less bright now that Michael was no longer with her, Esther returned to the kitchen to prepare a tray with coffee and cookies. She didn't want to embarrass the man, and so she'd decided to wait until tomorrow to add a sandwich or two to the plate. She had it all planned, how she'd claim that she'd cooked too much beef and that she was afraid it might spoil. Always a gentleman, Jeremy wouldn't refuse to eat it.

"I thought you might like a break," Esther said a few minutes later as she placed the tray on the empty table next to Jeremy's easel and darted a glance at his foot.

Though Esther had always thought artists stood while they painted, Jeremy perched on a stool, undoubtedly to rest his leg. She wouldn't ask about the limp, but she had studied the way he walked and sat and had decided that he had lost his left foot. The wooden replacement allowed him to walk, but since it did not flex like flesh and bones, it couldn't be comfortable to stand for long periods.

Susan rose, her expression once more eager. "Are we done for today? I promised Pamela I'd help her choose a dress pattern."

Jeremy nodded. "I've got enough to work with tonight."

Esther raised an eyebrow. She hadn't expected him to work nights. Didn't artists need good light? Before she could ask, Susan clapped her hands like a small child.

"Good. Aunt Esther can keep you company." Susan kissed Esther's cheek and hurried to their apartment for her hat and cloak.

"I hope you like oatmeal cookies." The words sounded stilted, but somehow with the buffer of Susan removed and the store momentarily empty of customers, Esther felt awkward sitting across from Jeremy. She hadn't been alone with a man since the day Chester had donned his uniform and left for what they'd believed would be only a few months of fighting.

Jeremy took a bite of the cookie, chewed thoughtfully, then washed it down with a slug of coffee. "It's delicious," he said, his brown eyes serious as they met her gaze. "You added nutmeg as well as cinnamon, didn't you?"

Esther nodded. Perhaps it was foolish to be so pleased that this man appreciated the special touches she put into her baked goods, but Esther couldn't help it.

He finished the first cookie and reached for a second. "I noticed the bakery's name is Mitchell-Hathaway. Is Susan a part owner?"

This time Esther shook her head. "When I moved to Cheyenne, my sister and her husband were running it—Lydia and Daniel Mitchell. After they died, I took over. People kept calling me Miss Mitchell, so rather than explain every time, I decided to add my name to the sign."

"But you kept theirs too."

Esther wondered why Jeremy was so interested in the bakery and its name. "They were the ones who started the business."

"From what I've heard, it was struggling, and you're the one who made it the success it is today."

"Who said that?" As color rose to her cheeks, Esther tried to tamp down her embarrassment. She shouldn't be blushing simply because this man had called her a success.

He shrugged. "Does it matter if it's true?"

"I suppose not. I am proud of the way the business has grown. I hadn't expected it, but it's very rewarding—and I don't mean only monetarily—to create a new recipe and watch people enjoy it. I feel as if I was called to do this."

The instant the words were out of her mouth, Esther regretted them. Why was she confiding her inner thoughts to a man who was practically a stranger? The answer came quickly: for some reason, Jeremy didn't feel like a stranger.

"Have you always been a painter?" she asked, determined to turn the focus away from herself.

A brief shake of the head was Jeremy's response. He was silent for a moment before saying, "Only since the war. Before that I was a farmer." He took another sip of coffee, and Esther suspected he was corralling his emotions. Mention of the war had that effect on many.

"The war changed my life," he said, confirming her supposition. "At night, after we'd been marching all day, men would play the harmonica or sing. I couldn't do either, so I started making sketches for them to send to their mothers or sweethearts. They liked the results, and I realized that I enjoyed sketching. It was one good thing that came out of the war."

The way he said *one* told Esther there was at least one other. "What were the others?"

"There's only one. I discovered the joy of traveling and exploring new places. Before the war, I had never been more than ten miles from my home. Now I've seen almost every part of this great country."

It was a life Esther could not imagine. She hadn't particularly enjoyed the trip from Central New York to Cheyenne, and now that she was here, she had no desire to travel farther.

"So you don't have a permanent home?" That was even more difficult to understand.

"No. I haven't yet found a place where I wanted to stay."

And she was firmly rooted in Wyoming Territory.

It didn't matter that Jeremy was the most intriguing man Esther had ever met. He was like the jackrabbit that had fascinated Susan one winter when it had apparently taken residence under one of their lilac bushes. Susan would check each morning and every afternoon when she returned from school, giggling with delight when the rabbit was still there. And then one day it had disappeared, leaving Susan feeling bereft. Like the rabbit, Jeremy was merely passing through Cheyenne and Esther's life.

Chapter 4

Five days. It had been five days since he'd met Esther, five days since his life had changed. Jeremy couldn't claim he understood the reason, but he found himself dreaming of her every night. And now he was here, in the warm, aromatic building that had become his studio as well as her bakery.

"I'm so excited about having my own home." Susan's smile turned into a grin. Though she was good about remaining motionless while Jeremy captured her likeness on canvas, the instant he lifted his brush, she began to speak, her words as effervescent as the fizzy drinks he'd enjoyed as a boy.

"Michael showed me what officers' housing is like," she continued. "Did you know that families have to move if a higher-ranking person comes to the fort? Sometimes they only get a day's notice." Susan shuddered in apparent dismay. "I don't imagine that'll happen to us, though. We're going to be in one of the smallest houses at the fort. That doesn't matter, though, because it'll be ours."

To Jeremy's surprise, the corners of Susan's mouth turned downward. "I only wish Aunt Esther was going with us."

Jeremy doubted any newlyweds really wanted company, but Susan seemed sincere. "You'll still be able to see her."

"It won't be the same. I don't know what I'd have done without her. She's been like a mother to me ever since my parents died." Susan continued talking, repeating the story Jeremy had heard about how Esther had revived the bakery at the same time that she'd adopted her orphaned niece.

"She's a remarkable woman." That must be the reason Esther dominated his thoughts. The only reason.

⁂

"Mrs. Bradford is here for your fitting, Susan." Esther smiled at Jeremy as her niece rose from the stool, shaking her arms and legs as if to relieve a cramp. "It shouldn't take too long." Pointing to the wall that divided the bakery from her sitting room, she smiled again. "Just knock on the wall if a customer arrives."

Jeremy shrugged as he swirled the tip of his brush on the palette. "I have plenty to do. You needn't worry about me."

But she did worry about him, Esther admitted as she followed Susan to their apartment where Mrs. Bradford waited with the wedding gown. Though she couldn't explain it, Esther dreamed about Jeremy every night. When she awakened, all she could remember were fragments, but they were enough to convince her that Jeremy Snyder's life had not been an easy one. It wasn't only his limp or the painful thinness that worried her. More important was the sadness she saw in his eyes when he didn't realize she was watching.

"You're a good Christian woman, Miss Hathaway," Mrs. Bradford said as they waited for Susan to slip out of her daytime dress. She smoothed the hair that had once been a bright auburn but was now fading and threaded with silver, and gave Esther a look that could only be called patronizing. "I admire you for taking pity on that poor man. It's such a shame that he's been afflicted with that limp, but it explains why he's not married. No woman would want to be shackled to a man like that."

How dare she say that! Esther felt her hackles rise. "You're wrong, Mrs. Bradford." What she wanted to do was slap the woman who'd insulted Jeremy, but good manners kept her hands at her side. "There is nothing pitiful about Jeremy. He's a strong man and a very talented artist. Any woman would be proud to be seen in his company."

The seamstress raised an eyebrow, her expression calculating. "Jeremy, is it? Just what is going on here?" Her tone left no doubt she thought the worst.

Esther took a deep breath, exhaling slowly as she corralled her anger. "What is going on? Simple. I've employed Jeremy"— she stressed his name—"to paint my niece's portrait, just as I've employed you to sew her gown." She stared at the woman who was one of Cheyenne's premier seamstresses. "I can see that you don't believe me. That's your prerogative, but if I hear any scurrilous gossip, you may be certain I will tell my customers that, although you are skilled with a needle, you are less skilled at minding your own business."

The woman's eyes widened, and a flush stained her cheeks. "I didn't mean I thought anything wrong was going on."

Esther let the lie slide. There was nothing to be gained by continuing the confrontation. As Susan emerged from her bedroom, Esther forced a bright smile to her face. "What do you think about adding another row of ruffles to the skirt?"

Though anger still simmered, by the time she and Susan had made a decision about the ruffles, Esther felt calm enough to face Jeremy. She hadn't wanted to do that when she feared her face would reveal her fury with the outspoken seamstress, but a quick glance in the mirror told her that her color had returned to normal.

"I wondered if you could start coming earlier, perhaps around eleven," she said as she approached Jeremy. He was cleaning his brushes, the pungent smell of turpentine mingling with the more pleasing aromas of yeast and chocolate. When he raised a questioning eyebrow, she continued. "Susan and I would like you to join us for our midday meal. That will give us an opportunity to discuss the portrait."

It was an excuse, nothing more, to ensure that he had at least one good meal a day. If it also gave her the opportunity to spend more time with him, well. . .that was an added benefit.

Curiosity turned to surprise, and Jeremy raised one eyebrow. "I can certainly arrange that, if you think it's wise." The way he phrased the acceptance made Esther suspect he'd overheard Mrs. Bradford's comments and her response through the thin walls.

"I do." Oh, that hadn't come out the way she had planned. "I do think it's wise," she amended, lest his thoughts had turned the direction hers had, to wedding vows. "Michael will come whenever he can, but you realize the army has first call on him."

Jeremy's eyes crinkled as he smiled. "That I do. And that leads me to something I wanted to discuss with you." He gestured toward his easel. "I studied the other portraits, because I know you want this one to be similar. I'd like to suggest one change, though. Their backgrounds are all plain. I wondered if you might want something different for Susan and Michael."

Esther hadn't thought about backgrounds. Her focus had been entirely on finding an artist talented enough to convey the young couple's likeness onto canvas. "What would you suggest?"

"Perhaps some aspect of Fort Russell. After all, that's where their married life will begin."

As happiness bubbled up from deep inside her, Esther gave Jeremy a warm smile. In all likelihood, the men who'd painted the other family portraits hadn't been skilled at landscapes. Jeremy was. "What a wonderful idea! That would make Susan's star even more special."

He nodded, obviously pleased by her enthusiasm. "There's only one problem. I haven't seen the fort, and I don't know which location they'd prefer."

Esther doubted either Susan or Michael did, either. "If you

can wait a few days, we can all go together. I can't leave the store, so that means Sunday." She took a shallow breath before she continued. "Would next Sunday after church and dinner be a good time for you?"

"Perfect. I'm looking forward to it."

So was she.

Chapter 5

It was the perfect day for a ride. The deep blue Wyoming sky accented by a few puffy cumulus clouds always brought a smile to Esther's face. Though at this altitude the sun made the air feel warmer than the thermometer claimed, the presence of the man at her side warmed her far more than the sun. It had been so long—half a lifetime—since she'd gone for a Sunday ride with a man.

Susan had taken the backseat, insisting that Esther sit in front with Jeremy, and though they had tried to involve her in the conversation, she had closed her eyes as if she were dozing. Esther knew it was feigned sleep. Susan was playing matchmaker, wanting her aunt to have time alone with Jeremy.

More pleased by her niece's ploy than she wanted to admit, Esther shifted slightly on the seat and gazed at the man who'd captured her imagination. They talked about everything and nothing. Jeremy told her how grateful he was to be painting in the bakery, because he already had three new commissions. Esther confided that her business had improved since he'd been there. They spoke of the weather, of the harsh beauty of the Wyoming prairie. They discussed the relative merits of pumpernickel and rye bread and the different uses for watercolors and oil paints. The one thing they did not discuss was Diana.

Esther took a deep breath, exhaling slowly as she unclenched her fists. Ever since the day she'd met Jeremy, she had known that Diana—whoever she was—was an important part of his life. While Mrs. Bradford might claim otherwise, Esther believed that Jeremy had chosen to remain unmarried, that Diana, and not his wooden foot, was the reason he was a bachelor. Though she longed to know the story, Esther wouldn't ask. That wouldn't be polite, and if there was one thing Esther had been raised to be, it was polite. But she couldn't help wanting to learn more about Diana and her role in Jeremy's life.

⌘

Jeremy smiled and loosened his grip on the reins. The horses seemed content to amble along. Perhaps they recognized that he was more than content to continue riding, so long as Esther was at his side. He took a deep breath as he gazed at the woman who'd captured his thoughts. She was remarkable, the kindest person Jeremy had ever met. Look at the way she'd invited him to have dinner with her every day.

The need to discuss Susan's portrait had been only an excuse. Jeremy knew that. What Esther really wanted was to ensure that he was well fed. Perhaps he should have refused, but he hadn't, for there was nothing he'd wanted more than to spend time in Miss Esther Hathaway's company.

The food wasn't the attraction, although she was a superb cook. No, the simple fact was that he enjoyed being with Esther. He admired her quick wit, her friendly smile, the obvious love she lavished on her niece. Even more, he enjoyed the way she made him feel almost as if he were part of the family.

Perhaps he was mistaken. Perhaps this was the way she treated everyone, but Jeremy did not want to believe that. What he wanted to believe was that she had begun to harbor some of the tender feelings that welled up inside him every time he was with her, every time he thought of her.

It was too soon to ask her that, and so Jeremy posed the first question that popped into his brain. "Do many of the officers' wives visit your bakery?" Though the answer affected his plans, what he really wanted to ask was why a woman as wonderful as Esther had never married. Susan chattered about almost everything else, but that was one subject she had never mentioned, and Jeremy hadn't wanted to pry.

"A few. Why?"

For a second he wondered what Esther was saying. Then he remembered the question he'd posed. Clearing his throat, he said, "I was hoping some of them might be interested in my paintings. I thought perhaps they'd want a landscape to remind them of their time in Wyoming Territory." And if they did, he would have a little more spare cash to do some of the things he'd begun to dream of.

Esther tipped her head to the side, as if considering. "I don't know any of the wives well, so I can't predict their reaction. Why don't you bring the landscape you showed me to the store? That way we can see if they're interested."

We? Jeremy felt a bubble of hope well up deep inside him at Esther's casual use of the plural pronoun. It might mean nothing, and yet it could mean that she'd begun to feel the way he did. "I have other landscapes finished," he admitted, pleased that his voice did not betray his excitement. "Portraits are easier to sell, but landscapes are what I enjoy most."

"Then you should focus on them. Life is too short to do things you don't enjoy."

Jeremy couldn't agree more. Though part of him wanted the ride to last forever, Fort Russell was only a few miles northwest of Cheyenne, and they soon reached it. The collection of mostly frame buildings around the diamond-shaped parade ground caught Jeremy's eye, and he could envision that as the background for the portrait, but after touring the whole fort, looking for possible sites for their portrait's background, Michael and Susan chose the house they'd share.

Though it wouldn't have been Jeremy's choice, he understood their reasons. Pulling out the folding chair Esther had insisted they bring, he began to work. While Jeremy sketched the simple building with the modest front porch and the young couple strolled along the walkways, he couldn't help noticing that Esther was deep in conversation with two women who'd come out of neighboring houses.

"You're right," the taller of the women said, her voice loud enough that Jeremy had no trouble distinguishing her words. "A painting would make a wonderful Christmas gift. I'll come into town tomorrow to see which one I like best."

"And I'll be with her." The second woman's giggle made Jeremy think she was no older than Susan. "My husband deserves one too."

Jeremy grinned. Unless he was mistaken, Esther had just sold two of his landscapes. She was a truly remarkable woman.

∞

"I'm so glad we went to the fort." Susan smiled as she drew the brush through her hair one last time. "My star will be the most beautiful of them all."

If there was one thing Esther could count on, it was her niece's enthusiasm. "Jeremy's very talented," she said.

"He's handsome too. . .for an older man," Susan added, the corners of her lips turning into a grin. "Don't shake your head, Aunt Esther. I know you've noticed, and *I've* noticed the way your eyes sparkle when he's around." She started to braid her hair, then turned back to look at Esther. "I think you're harboring special feelings for him."

"Nonsense!" Esther glared at her niece. It was true Jeremy was never far from her thoughts. It was true she treasured the time they spent together. It was true she had begun to dream of a future that somehow included him. But Esther wasn't ready to admit that to Susan.

That night she dreamed of Jeremy again. The dream began the way it always did, with him walking down a deserted lane. Then it changed, and it became clear that this was no aimless strolling. His stride was purposeful, the purpose soon apparent. A beautiful woman was waiting at the end of the lane. Diana.

∽

"Who's Diana?" Taking advantage of the momentary lull between customers, Esther was sharing coffee and dried apple pie with Jeremy when the words popped out of her mouth. She hadn't intended to ask, but now that the question was in the air, she did not regret it.

Jeremy did. That was apparent from the way he shook his head, his lips tightening and his expression darkening. He stared at the pie on his plate as if the answers were there, and Esther suspected he would not speak. Then, after a few seconds, he raised his eyes to meet her gaze. "I don't like to talk about her," he said softly, "but you deserve to know." He took a sip of coffee before continuing. "Diana is the woman I wanted to marry."

Is, present tense. That meant she was still alive. "What happened?"

Gesturing toward his left foot, Jeremy scowled. "Antietam is what happened. I lost my foot and my fiancée the same day. I just didn't know it at the time."

He ran his finger over the rim of the cup in a nervous gesture Esther had not seen before today. "I wasn't much good to the army with only one foot, so they sent me home. Despite the pain, I was glad. You see, all the time I was traveling, I pictured a joyful reunion with Diana. Instead, she stared at me, horrified. Three days after I returned, she gave me back my ring, telling me she wanted to marry a farmer and that I couldn't be a good farmer with only one foot."

Esther gasped, horrified by the evidence that Diana's love had been so shallow and by the realization that although more than two decades had passed, Jeremy was still suffering from Diana's rejection.

"I can't believe anyone would be so cruel." Though she'd known Jeremy less than two weeks, Esther knew he was a good, honorable man, the kind of man who made dreams come true. But Diana had thrown his love away.

"The war destroyed so many dreams," she said softly.

∽

Jeremy stared at Esther, more touched than he had thought possible by the sheen of tears in her eyes. She'd cared—really cared—about what had happened between him and Diana all those years ago. And now, if he read her correctly, she was opening the door to her past.

"Is that what happened to you? Your dreams were destroyed?"

She nodded. "We weren't officially betrothed, but Chester and I had an unspoken agreement that we'd marry when the war was over." A bittersweet smile crossed her face as she said, "I'd known him my whole life."

As her eyes darkened at the memory, Jeremy felt a twinge of jealousy at the evidence of a love far stronger than what he and Diana had shared. Esther and Chester had been fortunate.

"Everyone joked that we were meant to be together because our names were so similar," Esther continued. "We thought we were invincible, but we weren't. Chester was killed in the first day of fighting at Gettysburg."

"And you've never married."

"No."

"Why not?" Jeremy couldn't imagine that she'd lacked for suitors, especially here where men far outnumbered women.

Esther's eyes were somber. "No one else could compare."

It was what he'd feared.

Chapter 6

"You look happy, Mr. Snyder." Jeremy's landlady wiped her hands on a towel as he entered the kitchen looking for a cup of coffee to keep him awake while he painted.

"I am happy," he admitted, though he was surprised it was obvious. "I'm beginning to think I might settle down in Cheyenne."

Though he had felt a moment of despair when he'd heard the story of Chester, the last few days had given him hope that there might be a future for him here and that Esther might be part of that future.

Mrs. Tyson nodded, her eyes narrowing as she studied him. "It's a good place to live. When Abel went to heaven, my sister wanted me to move back to Illinois. I was tempted for a day or two, but then I realized that Cheyenne's my home."

Like Esther. The difference was Esther had never had a husband. Jeremy felt his heart clench at all that she had missed. Anyone could see that she would have been a wonderful wife and mother. All you had to do was look at how she'd raised Susan and the way she treated her customers to know that she had an abundance of love to share. And then there was the way she'd dealt with him, paying him more than he'd asked, serving him dinner each day, helping him find new clients. That was wonderful, but there was more. Jeremy sighed softly, remembering the glances Esther had given him, the sparkle in her eyes, the sweet smile that accompanied those looks. It was enough to make a man dream. And so he had.

"I guess you'll be looking for a permanent place to live once you marry." Mrs. Tyson's words brought him back to the present. "I'll miss you," she said, "but it's plain as the nose on my face that you've changed in the last few weeks. You're wearing the look of a man in love."

Jeremy hadn't realized it was so obvious. It was true that he'd never felt like this, not even with Diana. Everything seemed different. Colors were brighter, sounds sweeter, even his painting was better. When he sat by the easel, he felt as if his ideas were being translated into images almost without conscious effort. He'd completed two new landscapes in less time than ever before, but the quality had not suffered. To the contrary, this was the best work he'd ever done.

He smiled as he pushed open the door to his room and set the carafe of coffee on the bureau. If this was what love brought, he never wanted it to end. And maybe, just maybe, it wouldn't have to.

Opening one of the drawers, he pulled out his money sack and counted the contents. It would be a stretch, but this was something he wanted to do.

∞

"He's courting you."

"Nonsense!" The idea was appealing—very appealing—but Esther knew better than to assign too much importance to the invitation. "He simply wants to thank me for all the meals I've cooked."

Susan shook her head and returned to brushing Esther's hair. Though Esther had protested the extra effort, saying she could wear her normal hairstyle, Susan had been adamant that a special evening demanded a special coiffure and a special dress.

"That might be what he said, but I have eyes." Susan shook her head again. "I've seen the way he looks at you, and it's not like you're a cook. Besides, if all he wanted to do was thank you, he wouldn't have invited you to the InterOcean. There are plenty of other restaurants in Cheyenne, but he chose the most exclusive one."

"I know." And that had bothered Esther. Though she'd never eaten there, she knew that the hotel's dining room was renowned for both its fine cuisine and its high prices. "I told Jeremy it was too expensive, but he insisted."

Susan wrapped a lock of Esther's hair around the curling iron. "It's what I told you. He's courting you, and only the best will do." She released the curl and studied the way it framed Esther's face. "Perfect. Jeremy will like this."

When he arrived an hour later, it appeared that Susan had been correct, for Jeremy was speechless for a second. Clearing his throat, he said, "You look beautiful, Esther."

As color flooded her cheeks, Esther tried to control her reaction. It had been many years since she'd dressed to please a man, and she hadn't been certain she would succeed. The fact that Jeremy's eyes gleamed with admiration set her heart to pounding.

"It's the dress," she said, running her hands over the purple silk. "I had it made for the wedding, but Susan insisted I wear it tonight." The gown had been beautiful when Mrs. Bradford had finished it, but unbeknownst to Esther, Susan had spent countless hours embroidering a row of lilacs around the hem. The delicate flowers captured in floss had turned a beautiful gown into one that was truly spectacular.

Jeremy shook his head. "Your beauty is more than the dress. I'll be the envy of every man at the hotel." He reached for Esther's heavy woolen cloak and settled it over her shoulders. "And now, if you're ready. . ." He bent his arm and placed Esther's hand on it. "I hope you don't mind walking."

Esther did not. Though Jeremy had proposed hiring a carriage, she had insisted that she was capable of walking the one block to the InterOcean. Her initial thought had been to save him the expense, but now that they were on their way, she realized how much she enjoyed walking at Jeremy's side, having her hand nestled on his arm, feeling as if she was part of a couple. This was the stuff of dreams. And when they entered the hotel and were ushered to the dining room, the pleasure only increased.

"This is even more beautiful than I'd expected," Esther said when they were seated. With its polished dark wainscoting and coffered ceiling, the dining room exuded elegance, while the white table linens and shiny wallpaper brightened what could have been a dark room.

"You mean you've never been here?"

She shook her head. There were so many things she'd never done, and dining with a handsome man was one of them. "A woman alone doesn't eat in places like this. It would have been awkward." There were no tables for one.

"Then I'm doubly glad we came." Jeremy smiled, and the warmth in his expression made Esther's pulse begin to race. Was Susan right? Could Jeremy be courting her? Was it possible that her dreams of marriage and happily-ever-after might come true?

"I feel honored to be the one who introduced you to this restaurant." Though his words were matter-of-fact, Jeremy's tone caused her heart to skip a beat. Truly, this was the most wonderful evening imaginable.

When the food arrived, Jeremy bowed his head and offered thanks for the meal, then waited until Esther had tasted her trout before he picked up his fork.

"The food is delicious," she said, savoring the delicate sauce. Perfectly prepared food shared with the perfect companion. She could ask for nothing more.

Jeremy cut a piece of his meat and chewed slowly before he

said, "It's not as good as yours."

Esther did not believe that. "There's no need for flattery."

"It's not flattery. It's the truth. The stew you served on Wednesday was more flavorful than this bison."

It couldn't be true, but Esther appreciated the thought, just as she appreciated everything Jeremy was doing to make the night so special. "I enjoy cooking," she told him, "and I'm more than happy to share it with you." It felt so good—so right—having Jeremy at her kitchen table. His presence there made her heart pound and fueled her dreams.

He nodded, as if he'd heard her unspoken words, and Esther blushed. "Your cooking is superb," Jeremy said, "but the company is even better. I've enjoyed these past few weeks more than any I can recall."

And then the bubble of happiness burst. Though his words touched her heart, Esther heard the finality in them. Tonight wasn't simply a thank-you. It was an early goodbye. Jeremy was reminding her that he would soon be leaving Cheyenne.

Mustering every bit of strength she possessed, Esther smiled. "I'm the one who's grateful. If it weren't for you, my dream of giving Susan her Christmas star would have remained just that—a dream. Thanks to you, she will have something she can treasure for the rest of her life."

And Esther would have memories of these few sweet weeks when Jeremy was part of her life. He filled the empty spaces deep inside her. He made ordinary days special. He brought color to what had been a gray life. Esther lowered her eyes and pretended that the trout demanded her attention. She didn't want Jeremy to read the emotion in her eyes.

Just being in the same room with him lifted her spirits, and when he smiled at her, Esther's heart overflowed with happiness. She placed a piece of trout on her fork and raised it to her lips. She could deny it no longer. She loved Jeremy. He was the man who'd put a spring in her step. He was kind, talented, and generous. Oh, why mince words? Jeremy was everything she'd dreamed of in a man. If only they had a future.

But they did not. He was leaving, and she was staying. That was the way it had to be. Even if Jeremy had asked her to go with him, Esther would have refused. If there was one thing she knew, it was that she would be miserable sharing the itinerant life that was so important to him. And misery was the quickest way to destroy love. Esther wouldn't take that risk, for it wasn't only her heart that was at stake. Jeremy had been hurt once. She would not be the one to hurt him a second time.

Chapter 7

"I don't understand it." Jeremy muttered the words under his breath as he sat on the edge of the chair and unstrapped his left foot. He'd believed Esther would be pleased by dinner at the InterOcean, and for a while it had seemed that she was enjoying not just the food and atmosphere but also his company. Her eyes had shone with what he thought was genuine happiness, and her cheeks had borne a most becoming flush. Then suddenly the lovely glow had faded, and only a blind man would have missed the sadness in her eyes. Esther had said all the right words, but Jeremy could tell that she wasn't happy, and that had spoiled the evening for him.

He wanted Esther to be happy. Oh, how he wanted her to be happy. But she wasn't, and he wasn't certain why. Though he'd replayed the evening a dozen times, trying to understand what had caused the change, the only clue he had was that she'd looked sorrowful when she spoke of the Christmas star. Perhaps Esther's thoughts had returned to the past and she'd wished she'd had her own star, that Chester had survived the war and given her the life she'd dreamed of.

Jeremy rubbed petroleum jelly into his stump as he did each night. Though that eased the pain in his leg, it did nothing to assuage the pain in his heart. He hadn't been lying when he told Esther that he enjoyed seeing new parts of the country. What he hadn't told her was that the itinerant life was lonely. For years,

Jeremy had prayed for a home of his own and a woman to share it. And now when it seemed that his prayers were close to being answered, he feared that once again they'd be dashed, unless he could find a way to make Esther happy. Jeremy couldn't bring Chester back to life, but surely there was something he could do to make her eyes sparkle again.

All he had to do was find it.

⌒⌒

What a fool she was! Esther winced as the brush tangled in her hair, but that pain was nothing compared to the pain in her heart. She had spoiled a perfectly wonderful evening by worrying about her future. Hadn't she learned anything in her thirty-eight years? She knew she couldn't control the future. Only God could. She knew she needed to trust Him. He'd healed her heart after Chester's death; He'd brought her here and shown her the way to succeed. He would guide her to her future, if only she would let Him.

Her hair needed to be braided, but that could wait. There was a greater need right now. Esther reached for the Bible on her bedside table and opened it to the book of Jeremiah. Chapter 29, verse 11 had always brought her comfort, and it did not fail her now: "For I know the thoughts that I think toward you, saith the Lord, thoughts of peace, and not of evil, to give you an expected end."

Esther closed her eyes, letting the words sink into her heart. When she felt the familiar comfort settle over her, she read the next verse. "Then shall ye call upon me, and ye shall go and pray unto me, and I will hearken unto you." The promise of peace was there, but if she wanted it, she needed to ask for it.

Kneeling beside her bed, Esther bowed her head. "Dear Lord, help me find joy in each day. Show me the path You have prepared for me."

Though the future was still clouded, that night she slept better than she had in months.

∽

From her vantage point behind the counter, Esther watched as Jeremy put the final brushstroke on the painting.

"We're finished, Susan."

"Can I see it?" Susan asked as she slid from the stool. "You've been so secretive."

Jeremy shook his head. "Your aunt told me that's part of the tradition. Although others can see the portrait, you need to wait until your wedding day."

Susan's pout drew Esther to her niece's side, and if that meant that she was near to Jeremy, that was all right too. Though she'd tried her best to regain the special feeling of closeness they'd shared at the InterOcean, Esther had failed. It seemed as though a barrier had been erected between them, and nothing she said or did demolished it. Jeremy seemed preoccupied. He'd even stopped eating with her and Susan, claiming he had work to do and couldn't afford the time. The worst part was that although Esther suspected she had created the barrier, she had no idea how to make it disappear.

"Jeremy's right. It's only eight more days." A quick glance at the canvas confirmed what Esther had thought: the painting was magnificent. Turning to Jeremy, she raised an eyebrow. "When will you have it framed?"

"Two days. It needs to be completely dry first. If it's convenient for you, I'll bring it Saturday afternoon on my way back from Mrs. Edgar's house."

This was what Esther had feared. Today would be the end of her time with Jeremy. Oh, she'd see him occasionally while he was still in Cheyenne, but those wonderful days of sharing meals and conversations with him, of having only to look across the room to see him, were over.

"The offer of using the bakery as your studio is still open," she said, hoping she didn't sound as if she were pleading.

He nodded as he dipped his brush into turpentine. "I appreciate that, but Mrs. Edgar doesn't want anyone to know she's having her portrait painted. Apparently her husband has been asking for a miniature to put in his watch for years. When Mrs. Edgar heard about Susan and Michael's portrait, she decided this would be the year Mr. Edgar got his wish."

"Will you have enough time to finish it?" Susan's portrait had taken almost three weeks to complete.

Jeremy nodded again. "I just won't be sleeping very much." Or sharing meals with her.

"I'm sure it'll be as wonderful as Susan's portrait." Esther darted another glance at the finished work. Jeremy had captured more than Susan's and Michael's features; he'd captured their love. Though the other Christmas stars were beautiful, this one was spectacular. "I can never thank you enough."

"It was truly my pleasure." For the first time since the night at the InterOcean, Jeremy's smile seemed unfettered. As the clock chimed, the smile turned into a frown. "I'm sorry to rush away, but I have another appointment this afternoon."

A minute later he was gone, leaving Esther with an enormous void deep inside her.

 ∞

Jeremy pulled his watch from his pocket, trying not to scowl when he realized that the store would close in five minutes. If he were able, he'd run, but running had not been a possibility since Antietam. When he opened the door to Mullen's Fine Jewelry, the clock was striking five, and the proprietor seemed on the verge of locking the door.

"Thank you for waiting for me. I'm sorry I'm so late." Jeremy brushed snow from his coat. "Were you able to find one?"

As the jeweler shook his head, his elaborately waxed and curled mustache wiggled. "I sent telegrams to my best suppliers, but no one had what you want."

Though he'd feared this would be the case, Jeremy could not disguise his disappointment. "I know I didn't give you much notice."

Mr. Mullen stepped behind the main display case. The assortment of gold and silver pieces, many decorated with gemstones or pearls, was the best in Cheyenne, yet it held no appeal for Jeremy. There was only one thing he wanted.

"That's true," Mr. Mullen agreed. "You didn't give me much notice. On top of that, it's a busy time of the year for every jeweler. I was afraid I would not be able to find it. That's why—"

Jeremy had heard enough. This was one dream that would not come true. "There's no need to apologize, Mr. Mullen. I know you did your best. The fault is mine."

The jeweler fingered his mustache, almost as if he were trying to hide a smile. That was absurd. There was no reason to smile.

"If you'd let me finish, you'd know that I wasn't going to apologize." Mr. Mullen's words came out as little more than a reprimand. "When you first approached me, I knew it was unlikely anyone would have what you need. That's why I took the liberty of making one." He reached under the counter and brought out a cloth bag. "Is this what you had in mind?"

Jeremy stared in amazement at the object in Mr. Mullen's hand. It was everything he'd dreamed of and more. "It's perfect."

⌒

"Is something wrong, Aunt Esther?"

Startled by her niece's approach, Esther dropped the rolling pin. As she bent down to retrieve it, she frowned when she saw the amount of flour she'd spilled onto the floor. This wasn't like her. But then the way she'd been feeling for the past few days wasn't like her either. Despite her prayers, the future was still unclear.

"Nothing's wrong." Though Esther had hoped that her indecision hadn't been obvious, Susan had seen behind the mask she'd been wearing. "I'm simply extra busy this year." That wasn't a lie, but it also wasn't the whole truth. Esther had spent far too much time dreaming about a future that would never happen.

Susan perched on the edge of a chair. "It's my wedding, isn't it? I should never have planned a Christmas wedding. I know how busy the bakery is during December."

After rinsing the rolling pin, Esther resumed her work on the piecrusts, grateful that the task kept her back to Susan. She didn't want her niece to see the confusion she knew was reflected in her eyes. "It's not your fault, Susan. This is the perfect time for you and Michael to marry. I wouldn't have it any other way." Being busy should have kept her mind focused on happier thoughts than Jeremy's absence.

"But something is wrong," Susan persisted. "I can tell."

Esther hadn't planned to say anything to Susan until she'd made her decision, but the girl's obvious concern made her admit, "I've been thinking about my future. I'm trying to decide whether I should sell the bakery."

"What?" Susan jumped up from the chair and put her arm around Esther's waist, turning her until they were facing. "You said this was your home. Your life."

Esther nodded slowly. "That's true. You and the bakery have been my life for the last ten years." She laid a finger under Susan's chin, tipping it upward. "They've been wonderful years, but it feels as if they've been a season in my life and now that season is ending."

Susan was silent for a moment, her eyes searching Esther's face as if she sought a meaning behind the words. "If you do sell the bakery, you can live with Michael and me."

Her niece's generous offer did not surprise Esther, but there was only one possible answer. "Thank you, Susan, but I cannot do that. You and Michael are starting your life together. As much as I love you, I know it would be wrong for me to be part of that life."

Susan looked bewildered. "But what would you do?"

"I'm not sure." That was the reason Esther hadn't slept last night. "I know what I want to do, but I'm not sure that's possible." If wishes came true and prayers were answered, she would spend the rest of her life with Jeremy, but he'd never spoken of love or of wanting her to be a permanent part of his life.

Bewilderment turned to a calculating look as Susan stared at her, and for the briefest of moments Esther feared her niece had read her thoughts. Impossible.

"Aren't you the one who told me Grandma Hathaway said Christmas was the season of miracles?"

Esther nodded, remembering the number of times her mother had said exactly that. "Yes, but. . ."

"Then start praying for one."

Esther did.

Chapter 8

Three days until Christmas. Jeremy peered into the mirror as he wielded his razor. No point in nicking sensitive skin. They'd be a busy three days, but he wasn't complaining. No sirree. If everything went the way he prayed it would, if he had enough courage to do all that he planned, this would be his best Christmas ever.

The first part was easy. He would finish Mrs. Edgar's portrait this afternoon, frame it tomorrow night, and then deliver it early on Christmas Eve morning. The second part was more difficult. Laying down the razor, he studied his face. No whiskers visible. He rinsed the bits of shaving cream from his face, then toweled it dry. Those were all mechanical tasks, things he did every day. What he was contemplating was far more difficult.

He'd completed the other painting last night so that it too would be ready for delivery on Christmas Eve or perhaps Christmas morning. The question was whether he could muster the courage to do that. While it had seemed like a good idea when he'd first considered it, now he wasn't so certain. But there was no need to make a decision this morning. He had three more days.

Dressing quickly, he descended the stairs for breakfast. First things first. He'd put the final touches on Mrs. Edgar's portrait, then think about the other one.

"You have a letter, Mr. Snyder." Mrs. Tyson grinned as she

handed him a cream-colored envelope. "A young woman just delivered it."

Jeremy hadn't been expecting mail, and he didn't recognize the handwriting. Carefully running his finger beneath the flap, he opened the envelope and withdrew the heavy card, his eyes widening in surprise when he realized it was an invitation to Susan's wedding. Why had she invited him? Susan had said it was going to be a fairly small wedding, with only her and Michael's family and a few close friends. Jeremy didn't fit into either category.

Uncertain how to reply, he slid the card back into the envelope, then realized there was a second piece of paper inside it. That was ordinary stationery, not the heavier vellum of the invitation. Curious, he unfolded the sheet and read:

> *Dear Mr. Snyder,*
>
> *I hope you will join us on Christmas Eve. We attend services at 11:00 p.m. Afterward, Michael's parents have invited us all for supper at their hotel. I know this is short notice, but it would bring me much pleasure to have you as part of our group. You need not reply, but if you can come, please arrive at our home at 10:30 p.m.*
>
> *Sincerely yours,*
> *Susan Mitchell*

Jeremy sank onto the hallway bench, trying to regain his equilibrium in the face of this extraordinary missive. By rights, the invitation should have come from Esther, not Susan. By rights, Jeremy should refuse it. Yet what if this was the answer he sought, the impetus he needed to gather his courage?

Jeremy nodded. When he'd read Susan's note, he'd envisioned himself walking to church with Esther at his side, sitting next to her, sharing a hymnal with her, and afterward. . .

This was one invitation he would not refuse.

∽

"Now, aren't you glad I convinced you to wear this gown?" As Susan slid the last button into its loop, she turned Esther toward the cheval glass. "Look."

Esther stared at her reflection in the mirror, not quite believing what she saw. The burgundy silk with the elaborate bustle and the double box pleats circling the hem was the most elegant garment she had ever owned, and the intricate hairstyle Susan had insisted complemented the gown left Esther feeling as if she were looking at a stranger. An elegant stranger.

"Are you sure this is me?"

Susan nodded. "The new you. You want to make a good impression on Michael's parents, don't you?" Though Esther had had more than a few minutes' worry over her first meeting with the elder Porters, Susan's almost secretive smile made her think her niece had something else in mind. That was silly, of course, for what else could Susan be thinking of?

"It's very kind of Michael's parents to host supper tonight." The couple had arrived in town only this morning but had made all the arrangements in advance, telling Esther they wanted to thank her for the many meals she had given Michael over the course of his courtship.

It was the same argument Jeremy had made when he'd invited her to dine at the InterOcean, but tonight would be far different from that evening. Though Esther had no doubt that the meal would be enjoyable, she was not filled with the same anticipation she'd felt before. The reason was simple: instead of being half of a couple, tonight Esther would be part of a group, a group that did not include Jeremy.

A firm knock on the door broke her reverie. "The Porters are early," she said, glancing at the clock on the bureau.

"Do you mind going?" Susan gestured toward the lock of hair that had somehow come loose from her coiffure.

Knowing her niece wanted everything to be perfect, Esther headed toward the door. When she opened it, she stared in amazement as the blood drained from her face.

"Jeremy! Is something wrong?"

∽

His heart sank. This was not the reception he'd expected. Though he'd suspected that Susan had sent the invitation without consulting Esther, he had assumed she would have told her before now. The shock on Esther's face made it clear that she had not expected him.

"As far as I know, nothing's wrong," Jeremy said, trying not to stare at the woman who held his heart in her hands. "Susan invited me to join you tonight. I thought you knew."

Though she was clearly flustered, Esther looked more than usually pretty tonight. It might be the fancy dress or those loose curls that danced against her cheeks. It could simply be the flush that colored her face. Jeremy didn't care about the reason. All he cared about was whether or not this beautiful woman would allow him to share Christmas Eve with her.

"Come in," she said, ushering him into the sitting room. "We'll be ready to leave in a few minutes."

Though the words were ordinary, Esther's voice sounded strained. It could be nothing more than the shock of an unexpected guest, but Jeremy feared the reason was more serious. Perhaps he'd misread her earlier friendliness. Perhaps it had been nothing more than charity that had made her be so kind. Perhaps she saw him only as the man who'd painted Susan's portrait. All of that was possible, but Jeremy refused to believe it. He wouldn't give up so easily.

"I can see that my coming is a surprise. I should have

considered that, but to be honest, since the day I received Susan's invitation, all I've thought about was being with you again."

Esther's eyes darkened, and her lips turned up in a sweet smile. Before she could speak, Jeremy continued. "If you'd rather I leave. . ." He had to make the offer, though he hoped against hope that she would refuse.

"No, of course not." The color in her cheeks deepened. "I'm so happy to see you again." Though Esther started to say something more, Susan rushed into the room, her brown eyes twinkling with what appeared to be mischief. "Aunt Esther and I are glad you're here."

"Yes, we are." The warmth in Esther's expression sent a rush of pleasure through Jeremy's veins. It appeared that coming here tonight had not been a mistake.

∞

Perhaps it was a mistake, but if it was, Esther would have all her tomorrows to regret it. No matter what the morning brought, she intended to enjoy the simple pleasure of being with Jeremy tonight. Perhaps she should have chided Susan for issuing such an inappropriate invitation and neglecting to tell her about it, but Esther could not, not when that invitation had brought her what she longed for: time with Jeremy.

There was no time for private conversation, for the once-quiet sitting room felt as crowded and noisy as the train depot when Michael and his parents arrived. Though the Porters appeared to be as charming as their son, Esther barely heard a word they said. Instead, her gaze kept meeting Jeremy's, and she found herself wishing they were alone. The opportunity came sooner than she had thought possible.

"Esther and I can walk," Jeremy said when Mr. Porter explained that he had hired a carriage but that it might be a bit crowded with six passengers. "If she agrees."

Esther did. Minutes later they were walking down Sixteenth Street. It felt like the night they'd dined at the InterOcean as they strolled along the street with Esther's hand nestled in the crook of Jeremy's arm. But tonight would be different. Esther was determined to do nothing to spoil the evening. Tonight was a night to celebrate the wonder of God's love and the greatest gift the world had ever received. Sharing that joyous message and the hope that accompanied it with Jeremy only made the night more special.

As happened each year, the church was crowded, the scents of perfume and Macassar oil mingled with the pungent odors of candle wax and wet wool. Yet no one seemed to mind the crowding or the smells, least of all Esther. Even if it was only for a few hours, she was with Jeremy.

When the first hymn began, she discovered that his voice was as off-key as her own, but that didn't matter. What mattered was that they were worshipping together. Judging from the expression on his face, Jeremy was as moved as she by the minister's reading from the Gospel of Luke.

"'Fear not: for, behold, I bring you good tidings of great joy, which shall be to all people.'"

Esther felt the prickle of tears in her eyes as joy filled her heart. Even if her prayer for a miracle was not answered, this was a Christmas she would never forget.

"Are you certain you want to walk again?" Mr. Porter asked when the service had ended and they'd filed outside. "We could let the young people do that."

Jeremy turned toward Esther. "If Esther's willing, I'd prefer to walk. It's a beautiful night."

It was indeed. The wind had subsided, leaving a star-studded sky with a few lazy snowflakes drifting to the ground.

"I'd like to walk." And to share more of this night with the man who had captured her heart.

They strolled in silence for a few minutes. When they were

two blocks from the church and the crowd had dispersed, Jeremy stopped.

"The beautiful night wasn't the only reason I wanted to walk." He reached into his greatcoat pocket and withdrew a cloth bag. "I have a gift for you." His voice sounded almost hesitant, as if he were afraid of her reaction.

Esther stared at the dark green velvet sack, her heart leaping at the thought that this wonderful man had brought her a gift. "I didn't expect anything." Just being here with Jeremy was more than she had expected.

"I know you didn't, but I want you to have this." He placed the bag in her hand.

As her fingers reached inside and touched the familiar shape, Esther gasped. It couldn't be, yet it was. Gently she pulled out the star-shaped frame. Similar in size to the one she'd bought for Susan's portrait, this frame was more ornate, with open filigree decorating each of the points. And in the center. . . Esther took a deep breath, hardly able to believe her eyes. All her life she had longed for her own Christmas star, and now Jeremy had given it to her. Looking back at her from one side of the painting was her portrait. The other side was nothing more than blank canvas.

"It's beautiful, Jeremy, but I don't understand. I didn't pose for this." What Esther really didn't understand was what he meant by the gift. He knew the tradition.

He gave her a smile so sweet it brought tears to her eyes. "You didn't need to pose. Your image is engraved on my heart. All I had to do was close my eyes, and I pictured you."

Esther nodded. Though she was not an artist, she had no trouble picturing Jeremy when they were apart.

His expression sobered. "I wanted to give you a finished star, but I couldn't, because I wasn't certain what you wanted on the other side." He paused for a second. "I can paint a landscape there. That may not be like the others, but it's important to me that you

59

have your own star. I know you've dreamed of one, and I want to make your dreams come true."

Esther looked at the star, marveling at the way Jeremy had portrayed her. It was her face, yet it wasn't. She had never seen herself looking so beautiful, so in love. Was this how Jeremy saw her?

He took a shallow breath before he continued. "I know how I want to finish the portrait. In my dreams, it's my face next to yours." Jeremy's voice rang with emotion. "More than anything, I want to be part of your Christmas star and part of your life."

Esther stared at the man she loved so dearly, the man whose words were making her heart pound with excitement. He said he wanted to make her dreams come true, and he was doing exactly that. When she opened her mouth to speak, he raised a cautioning hand.

"I know I can't take Chester's place, but I want whatever place in your life you can give me." Jeremy paused for a second and took her left hand in his. "I love you with all my heart. Will you marry me?"

Her heart overflowing with love, Esther nodded. Susan had been right. All she needed to do was ask God for a miracle, and He'd granted it. "Oh Jeremy, there is nothing I want more than to marry you. It's true that I loved Chester and that he'll always have a place in my heart, but my love for you is stronger than anything I've ever known." The words came tumbling out like water over a falls as Esther tried to express the depth of her love.

She squeezed Jeremy's hand, wishing the cold night hadn't dictated gloves. "I think I fell in love with you that first day when you walked into the bakery. I had never felt that kind of instant connection before, but it was there, and it's only grown stronger since then. Marrying you will make my life complete."

"And mine." Jeremy's eyes shone with happiness that rivaled the stars' brilliance. "Oh my love, you've made me happier than I dreamed possible."

When Esther smiled, he drew her into his arms and pressed his lips to hers, giving her the sweetest of kisses. His lips were warm and tender, his caress more wonderful than even her wildest dreams, and in that moment Esther knew this was where she belonged: in Jeremy's arms.

When at length they broke apart, she smiled at the man she loved, the man who was going to be her husband. "It may take awhile, but I'll sell the bakery so we can travel wherever you want."

His eyes widened, and she saw him swallow, as if trying to control his emotions. "You'd do that for me?" Jeremy's voice cracked as he pronounced the words.

Nodding, Esther explained. "A month ago, I felt as if the bakery and Cheyenne were my home. Then I met you, and I learned that home is more than a building or even a city. Home is the place you share with the person you love."

Jeremy matched her nod. "Will you share your home with me?" Esther's confusion must have shown, for he continued. "I've learned a few things too. One is that I want to stay here. Cheyenne will be my home as long as I'm with the woman I love."

"Oh Jeremy!" Esther raised her lips for another kiss as snowflakes drifted past them. "You've made all my dreams come true."

"And so have you, my Christmas star bride."

 **Amanda Cabot**'s dream of selling a book before her thirtieth birthday came true, and she's now the author of more than thirty-five novels. Her romances have appeared on the CBA and ECPA bestseller lists, have garnered a starred review from *Publishers Weekly*, and have been finalists for the ACFW Carol, the HOLT Medallion, and the Booksellers Best awards.

A popular speaker, Amanda is a member of ACFW and a charter member of Romance Writers of America. A Christmastime bride herself, she married her high school sweetheart who shares her love of travel and who's driven thousands of miles to help her research her books. After years as Easterners, they fulfilled a longtime dream when Amanda retired from her job as Director of Information Technology for a major corporation and now live in Cheyenne.

You can find her at www.amandacabot.com.

A Token of Promise

by Rebecca Germany

Dedication

To all those family members who came before me
and left not only wonderful heirloom reminders of their lives
but an unshakable faith upon which I could build
my own Christian faith. I thank God for you.

Chapter 1

October 1897
San Francisco, California

Red! He appreciated the color in a sunset, in a strawberry pie, and in a woman's blushing cheeks, but tomato red did nothing for Gabe Monroe's freshly polished top boots. Would the beaver cloth forever be stained?

He looked from the mess of seeds and tomato pulp up the length of long skirts in front of him. *She must be the one. Yes, she'll do nicely.* With her slight frame and golden-flecked brown hair, she favored his late sister-in-law.

"Oh!" The young woman's market basket dropped to the ground as she knelt and swiped at the mess with her hands.

Gabe touched her shoulders, coaxing her to stand. "It will wash up."

"I'll get you a rag."

"Don't worry about it. I'll clean up back at the hotel."

Her gaze darted toward the well-tended yard until she braved a look into his eyes. He returned her study of him with his head tilted to the side, admiring her blue eyes and blushing cheeks.

"I really. . .am. . .am sorry," she stammered in apology.

"Are you Reverend Chiles's ward?"

"Umm, yes."

"Well then, I'll return for you on the morrow next. Good day." He touched his hat and strode to a fine carriage and horse that waited in the shade of a tree. *What luck! It is a most uncanny resemblance.*

Charlotte Vance hurried in the side door of the large home of the Rev. and Mrs. Chiles. Weaving between several barrels of packed china, she willed her racing heart to return to normal. What business could a handsome man of some obvious wealth have at the reverend's home? She didn't recognize him as a parishioner, and if she understood him correctly, his visit seemed to have something to do with her. . .and two days hence. Questions and possible scenarios vied for attention in her mind.

From the kitchen came the high-pitched voice of the lady of the house. "Charlotte, where have you been? Oh, there is so much to be done, and my poor legs are already weak with the tension."

Charlotte took a deep breath as she rounded the doorway to the kitchen and placed her groceries on the table. "The market was busy today, ma'am, with the last of the harvest having come in. I saw Mrs. Morgan, and she sends her regards and prayers for your health."

Mrs. Chiles rummaged through the basket, seemingly ignoring Charlotte's words. "Is this all you got? The reverend specifically asked for tomatoes."

"Yes, ma'am, those—"

"Tsk. I'd send you back, but there is too much to do here." The woman thumped her cane against the polished floorboards. "You must get things packed and ready for the movers. Now that you are leaving, the reverend says we will start for my niece's home in just four days—after Sunday's church picnic of course."

"Leaving?"

"Get the lunch together, then I believe you should start with the parlor knickknacks." The old woman sank to a kitchen chair. "Oh, how I ache. I so look forward to settling in Phoenix. Retirement must be a lovely thing. No more ridiculous expectations placed on an old woman. . .and man." She sighed.

"But Mrs. Chiles, about where I am to go in two days. . ." Charlotte choked on the fear that suddenly rose in her throat. For two years she had relied on the Chileses' generosity to give her a home in exchange for her work as a housekeeper. She had no means to support herself.

Raising a frail hand as if shooing a fly, the old woman said, "Oh child, the Lord is blessing you with a ready-made family. Though love escaped you when your dear Oliver was killed, you are going to be comfortably provided for all in perfect timing for our departure."

Charlotte's heart went back to race speed. "Family?"

"Why, yes. A man with a child is in need of a wife." She smiled. "And he's a Monroe. I met his grandmother Aggie back some thirty years ago. What a dear lady." Mrs. Chiles's body slumped against the chair as she seemed to tire of the topic. "The man will be here on Friday to take you to the boat."

Arctic blue eyes and wavy, dark brown hair rushed to her memory. She covered her warm cheeks with her hands and asked, "Boat?"

"Girl, must you persist with these one-word questions? Of course a boat. You will be living in Alaska with half the rest of the country who have been struck with gold fever." Mrs. Chiles rose to her feet, aided by her cane. "I must survey what needs to be done. Oh, so much work remains."

Left alone with still more unanswered questions, Charlotte quickly found a chair to drop into. Though she was twenty and without parents, did that give others the right to decide her future?

This couldn't be happening. She knew she would need to find a home and a job when the Chileses moved to Arizona, and she had been praying for an answer to her problem. But this didn't seem natural—marrying a stranger, mothering a motherless child, moving to Alaska.

Still, what choice did she really have? If Reverend Chiles had approved of the man and the marriage plan, it must be worthy of her trust.

Four and a half years ago she had promised to marry Oliver McKnight, but could she really be ready to be a wife—and mother—in two days?

∞

Alaska. It seemed like another world to Charlotte. A place of wild and sensationalized stories. But it was where she was bound with all her worldly possessions stuffed into two large trunks along with new purchases of wool-lined boots and fur-lined gloves.

She sat on the edge of the berth, happy to have a small sleeping compartment to herself away from the three other women onboard who were rumored to be adventuresses. She could feel the stress along her shoulders, the consequence of the morning's rushed activities.

With all the shopping, packing, and goodbyes to be done in two short days, there had been no time for Mr. Monroe to come to dinner and give Charlotte a more clear idea of what to expect from her new home. She still didn't know if the man's child was a boy or girl. And worse, she didn't know exactly when her nuptials would be performed.

She didn't know if she'd ever learn to demand answers from her elders. It wasn't in her upbringing. She just assumed that Reverend Chiles would perform the wedding vows Friday morning when Mr. Monroe came for her.

He arrived while she finished the breakfast dishes, and her trunks were promptly loaded into his carriage. When Charlotte ventured to ask about the wedding, Mrs. Chiles made her feel like a child.

"Don't slow the man down, you have a boat to catch. Mr. Monroe has all the marriage fixings worked out for when you reach Alaska. Don't you, sir?"

Mr. Monroe only frowned at the old woman and stepped closer to Charlotte. He towered over her, and she had to look up into his eyes. Eyes the color she could only guess an Alaskan glacier might reflect.

He cleared his throat. "Miss Vance, please accept this locket as a token of your engagement."

As he placed the fine, oval-shaped locket in her hands, she noticed his own hands were rough—not the hands of a high-society gentleman. They were strong hands, testifying to honest work.

No more was spoken on the subject as goodbyes were said, and Charlotte left the fresh flowers she had gathered for a bouquet in a vase for Mrs. Chiles. Mr. Monroe had remained quiet all during the drive through the long, steep streets to the wharf, and Charlotte had concentrated on keeping her tears behind a dam.

She fingered the gold locket that hung around her neck. Though heavy and ornate, its beauty charmed her.

Oh Lord, give me strength to do as Thou wouldst lead. I've done as my elders have told me, but, Lord, if I should get off this boat now and fend for myself, I will. I'm scared of the unknown—but mostly of being alone. Oh, dear Father. . .

Suddenly Charlotte felt the need to get out of the cramped room and go on deck to view the docks and city. She threw her cape over her shoulders and made her way to the top deck. Rushing to the railing, she clung to it as she felt the small steamer shift and pull away from the dock. She scanned the crowds of people on the wharf who cheered on the Klondike stampeders even as they hurried back to work in preparation for another boatload to leave. A few dozen men lined the *Dawson Belle*'s decks to wave back, but the hull of this boat mainly carried supplies to sustain those already living in the northern regions.

"Wouldn't you be more comfortable below deck and away

from the chill wind off the bay?"

Charlotte already recognized the deep baritone voice as Mr. Monroe's. She closed her eyes and tried to relax. This mellow voice would greet her every morning.

"Miss Vance?"

Slowly she turned to face him. She couldn't explain how, but she already liked him. He exuded confidence yet with a bit of bashfulness. "May I ask your name, Mr. Monroe?"

"My name?"

"Yes, don't you think we should be on a first-name basis now?"

He cleared his throat and leaned against the rail. "Well, it's Gabriel, but friends just call me Gabe."

She liked it and couldn't stop a grin, but as she looked up into his face, she saw something in his expression. A question? A regret?

He looked away. "Would you like me to walk you to your room?"

"No, thank you. Not just yet. Please tell me a little about Alaska."

"Well. . ." He cleared his throat again. "It is large and wild. Majestic mountains tower around the little valley where Dyea sits with only a small opening out to the ocean. It rains a lot."

"Is Dyea a large town?"

"Sure. It's been fast doubling in size. It's located just south of Chilkoot Trail, which so many are using to get to the Klondike."

"But there is gold in Dyea too, right?" The reports she heard made it sound like gold was all over the ground in Alaska.

"Nah. You gotta get over the mountains to start looking for gold." He crossed his long legs, throwing more of his broad weight on the rail. "I'll be heading there before long myself—after you're settled, of course."

Suddenly it seemed like her lungs couldn't draw air. "You mean. . .you are going to leave me in Dyea. . .alone?"

He stared at his boots. "Philip will take good care of you. You'll know that as soon as you meet him. He has a real prosperous store there. In fact, he leases this steamer for hauling his goods." He smiled at her; though as she kept staring at him, his brows began to pucker.

"Who is Philip?"

He drew himself up straight. "What? He's my brother. . . younger brother." He began to relax. "I'm sorry if I forgot to give you his name in all the rush and excitement of finding you. I know you'll like him fine, and everyone can't help but love his little Sarah."

Charlotte swallowed hard against the tightness in her throat and chest. "His daughter?" she whispered.

"Yes, that's Sarah." His tone warmed at the mention of the child. "She just turned two. Her mother died of a fever."

She turned back to the rail, clinging to it for support. *Lord, it was bad enough that I have no other option than to marry a stranger, but to marry a man I haven't even set eyes on is. . .*

Charlotte gazed out at the shrinking harbor. Her heart sank as she knew her destination had been confirmed. She would go to Alaska and become Mr. *Philip* Monroe's wife.

∽

The silence of a woman could be such a deafening noise. What had he said to stifle her questions and dim the light of interest in her eyes?

Gabe lifted his hand. He wanted to touch her shoulder. He wanted to offer her comfort and reassurance, but. . .this was his brother's bride. Right now his feelings weren't very brotherly.

She drew him like a moth is drawn to candlelight. It was a crazy sensation. Gabe had had his one true love and watched her be taken from him. He knew Charlotte had also lost her fiancé. Love like that didn't strike twice.

He sat down on a nearby crate. The deck had cleared of all but a few men who were smoking together. He gazed at Charlotte's back, so stiff yet so delicate.

Gabe swallowed hard and searched for something to say. . . anything. "Lottie, would you like to sit down?"

She turned her face toward him. "What did you call me?"

"I thought since you asked for my first name that I could call you Lottie," he mumbled.

"Charlotte is my name."

"I know. I just thought Lottie was fitting." He looked up to gage her mood.

She sighed and moved to sit beside him. "I've never had a nickname. My father always called me Charlotte, and I was always the proper preacher's daughter."

"You don't think Lottie is a proper name?"

She gave a laugh as she leaned back against the steamer. "It's fine."

"When did your father die?" he asked, enjoying the relaxed tone the conversation had taken.

"About two years ago."

"And your fiancé?"

She turned pain-filled eyes to him. "Four years ago, in Colorado while mining for gold." A tear suddenly sprang down her cheek, and she dashed her fingertips against it.

"I'm sorry. I'd. . .um. . .offer you a handkerchief, but I don't carry anything decent for a lady." Silence cloaked them for a couple of minutes as they gazed at the water around them, then he offered, "I can understand your loss. I lost my fiancée."

Charlotte looked at him, and somehow he relished having a connection he could offer to her pain.

"She died?"

"Well, no. She. . ." How could he explain such a painful event? "Aileen's father and mine did business together. My father has full or part ownership of a lot of businesses in and around San Francisco—even Philip's business in Dyea. He got the bulk of my grandfather's wealth that came out of the '49 gold rush."

Gabe took a focused breath. "Anyway. Aileen's father got into a tight business situation, and my father initially helped him. But then my father withdrew all his money when the Panic hit, and Aileen's family went broke. They lost everything, and her father has even been under question of the law. He refused to let us marry and made her marry another wealthy man. Someone who wasn't Blackie Monroe's son."

He chanced a look at Charlotte. Her blue eyes reflected his pain. Her soft features held understanding and sympathy. It gave him strength to continue.

"If I make money in the gold fields, I can pay back what my father owes the family. . .and do it without my father's money supporting me."

She nodded. "It's not your debt, but I understand."

"I can accept now that marriage isn't for me with the loss of Aileen," he continued. "Just as you have resigned yourself to marry someone you have never met after losing your love."

She stared at him with her mouth agape. Then seeming to shake herself, she closed her mouth and looked away. She pulled her cape closer around her neck.

Again he felt like he had not worded things right. "Lottie?"

She shook her head but turned to him. "Do you think God would allow love to be stolen away from us and never give us something to fill the hole?"

"I don't know if God gets all that involved in how we feel."

"Oh, but if you believe in Jesus Christ and the Holy Spirit, you must believe that God wants us to know His love and cares about even the smallest part of our lives. Only through His comfort have I managed my grief over losing Daddy and Oliver." Her eyes pleaded for Gabe to understand her faith.

"I believe and all, but. . ."

An icy wind whipped around the steamer. This conversation weighed on his soul more than talking about Aileen. It took too much effort to ponder God's role in his daily life, and he just wasn't ready to think that deeply about it.

"Perhaps we should go below deck and get settled in before the lunch hour," he suggested.

She gave a resigned nod and rose. He tucked her arm around his. She fit comfortably alongside him. He knew he could get used to her presence. This woman and her role in his life must be handled with care.

Gabe spent the next several days both trying to avoid the feelings Charlotte sparked in him and reminding himself of why he was taking her to Alaska. A man—his younger brother— needed the comforting presence of a woman, and an adorable little girl needed a mother to hold and love her. Still he was drawn to Charlotte's company and lured into more talks about relationships with others and God. He didn't want to think about these things, yet the conversations seemed to come naturally when he was with her.

For two days he found enough excuses to stay away from her, hoping the time and space would clear his thinking. Then they entered the Inside Passage. The waters were calm, protected by islands to the west. Rocky, forest-covered shorelines stood sentinel on the east. Occasionally she pointed out to him a bald eagle, a sea lion, or a pod of black-and-white killer whales. He took excursions off ship at Victoria, British Columbia, and Mary's Island.

One day, though, four kegs of beer fell and broke in the hold, and crates of goods had to be shifted, sorted, cleaned, and dried. He smelled like a brewery, and he couldn't understand why his brother agreed to supply the foul stuff to numerous saloons.

Then just north of Fort Wrangell a storm churned up the waters and blew rain and seawater in against the small vessel.

Chapter 2

Charlotte lay on her bed trying to keep as still as possible. The steamer tossed back and forth on the waves, up and down, back and forth. With each dip of the boat, the walls of her room seemed to bend closer to her. Her cape and dressing gown swung away from their hooks. Her trunks slid into her small walkway.

She had never experienced seasickness or claustrophobia before, but the combination of motion, illness, and enclosure tore at her sanity. She threw back the blanket and searched for a means of escape. The room had no window to open, only a glass-covered hole for light, and no storage areas in which to contain the shifting items on every inch of space.

It seemed to take several minutes for her to pull herself off the bed and secure a footing on the floor. She tried to straighten her skirt and blouse, then reached for her cape. The pitch of the ship hurled her against the door, and she knew she would be sick. As soon as the ship settled again, she threw her door open and stumbled into the passageway. Gripping the handrails, she tugged herself up the stairs to the deck level.

Water ran everywhere, from sky to deck, from sides to sea. Charlotte shuffled to the railing, and the sight of rolling sea brought her sickness out. She clung to the railing with each pitch of the boat. Then someone slid into her back, and his long arms came around her.

"Lottie, what on earth are you doing out here?" Gabe nearly yelled against her ear.

He smelled like fermented yeast, and she became sick again. He held her as she recovered. "I'm so sorry you're sick, but you have to go below. The storm isn't safe."

Only a moan could get past her throat. He pulled her tightly against him and moved them away from the rail. Getting her back to her room took several minutes of zigzagging their path with the roll of the steamer. He not only smelled like a drunk, he walked like one.

Finally he helped her ease down to the edge of her berth, removed her wet cape, and wrapped her blanket around her. He brought her washbasin to the bed and rearranged some items that had been tossed askew. Then he went to the door. "I'll come back in an hour or so and check on you."

"Nooo," she whined. "Don't leave. I. . .hate to be sick. . . alone."

Slowly she moved her aching head to look at him. He drew his hand across his face and into his wind-tossed hair, seemingly deep in thought. In time, his shoulders relaxed, and a smile tugged at his mouth when he looked at her clinging to the edge of her bunk.

He tried to help her lie down, but she resisted. "I n–need to sit up." She tugged at his arms. "Sit down. . .hold me."

He jerked back. She couldn't look at him. Her head swung like a weighted pendulum. She plucked his arm again, and he eventually settled down beside her.

"You stink," she said.

Sharp laughter filled the small space, and his body shook. "I got caught in a spill—not a binge." He removed his jacket and tossed it to the far side of the room, sending the majority of the smell with it. Then he leaned back against the cold wall of the steamer and tucked her against his side.

Gradually she felt herself begin to relax. The heat radiating from him soothed her battered body. She even felt sleep teasing her senses. Perhaps the storm would pass.

When she awoke, she was alone and cold. The boat had ceased its erratic pitching, and with it, her stomach had settled; but her heart beat a dangerous staccato rhythm of unwarranted emotion. She missed Gabe, missed their conversations. *Oh Lord, how can I marry his brother with these feelings warring in me?*

∞

Gabe took his breakfast coffee to the deck. Through the morning fog he could see chunks of ice on the water and land to his right. The familiar sight of Haines Mission brought welcomed relief. They should reach Dyea's tidal flats before sunset, which came ever earlier as fall deepened.

Though silent, he felt Charlotte come to stand alongside him before she placed her hand on his arm. She had recovered well from her bout of sickness, but his attraction to her still threatened to drown all his good intentions and determined goals.

Her simple touch reached his heart. He took a deep breath. "We'll be home by dinnertime."

"Home. . ." She stood pensive, taking in the mountainous view. "What will be there for us?"

The word *us* echoed through his mind. It seemed as if she had asked if their friendship could have a future beyond that of the brother and sister they would be once she married Philip.

He forced himself to ignore it. "Dyea isn't much, but it's home for now. Sarah will be shy at first to meet you, but she'll warm up quick." He purposely left out mention of his brother's welcome.

"We live in a small room and lofts at the back of Philip's store," he continued. "Dottie created a homey little space back there—"

"D–Dottie who?"

Dread rose in Gabe's chest. "Sarah's mother."

Charlotte withdrew emotionally and physically from him, backing toward the door to the stairs.

"She has been gone well over six months," Gabe said, reaching out toward her. "Lottie, I'm sure Philip will let you make your own home out of the place and with Sarah."

"Don't!" she snapped. "Don't ever call me Lottie again!"

Gabe was taken aback, but as he quickly reviewed what he had just said, he realized his late sister-in-law's name was similar to Lottie's. "I'm—I'm sorry. I never meant to use the name to change you into someone you are not."

"Yes, you did!" she gasped. "You wanted me to replace Philip's wife. You changed my name so you wouldn't forget—so I wouldn't forget—what I'm intended to be." She shivered. "Another man's wife."

She disappeared into the ship before he could offer another word. Her statement held truth. Something as simple as a nickname had become a wall between them—a sobering reminder of their individual places in the pattern of life.

❧

When the *Dawson Belle* anchored in Dyea's deeper waters, Gabe dreaded finding Charlotte. He wouldn't blame her if she refused to go ashore and demanded to return to California. Much still lay ahead of her, not the least of which was the unpredictable way Philip would react to her.

After stalling long enough with preparations for going ashore, Gabe found Charlotte's room empty. She already waited atop deck with her luggage, watching the scow being loaded with other passengers.

"Let me go first to help you aboard," he offered.

She raised her chin and stared straight ahead, but she allowed him to guide her down the ladder onto the other boat that bobbed in the gathering dusk.

The trip to shore seemed to pass too quickly. Gabe felt confident that he had done the right thing bringing Charlotte here as Philip's wife, but still a nagging sensation made him uncomfortable and edgy.

He stepped off the scow and helped Charlotte onto the beach. Around them lights shone from windows of unpainted wood-planked buildings, tents, and combination wood-and-canvas structures. The streets flowed with people, horses, and dogs. In the mix of noise, music rang out from numerous businesses of entertainment even at this early hour.

Charlotte tried to take in all the activity, but her mind nervously focused on the introductions yet to come. She took a few steps and promptly stuck her shoes in mud.

Gabe immediately acted upon her plight. "Here. Let me carry you?"

"What?" Barking dogs, shouting men, chopping axes, and now this ringing in her ears as Gabe swooped her up into his arms and against his broad chest. She gasped and wiggled in an attempt to loosen his grip.

"Stop it," he said, clenching down on his jaw. "Just don't. . . just rest."

Charlotte obeyed. His touch calmed her and created a shelter amid the ruckus all around them. Gabe gripped her close to him as he walked through the wharf area. Men leered at her, and she tucked her face into his neck, focusing only on the leather and musk scent of him.

Soon she felt him take a step up, and she looked above her to read a large sign painted in bold blue letters—MONROE'S GENERAL MERCHANDISE.

She thought of putting her feet against the doorframe and begging Gabe for more time to prepare herself. No time, though, could erase the fact that her heart wanted one brother while her words and actions had pledged her in marriage to another.

The door swung open, and Gabe strode into the middle of a large room filled from floor to ceiling with every imaginable type of saleable goods. He proceeded with her to a back corner where a small table sat beside an imposing stove and the walls were covered with shovels, rakes, picks, and all manner of long-handled tools. Here he finally let her settle onto her own feet. She eased away from Gabe toward the heat from the stove.

A tall man with a dark head of thick hair came out from behind a long counter. "Well, my brother," his voice boomed, "I hardly recognized you with that lovely piece of jewelry draped around your neck. Welcome to Monroe's, ma'am."

Gabe frowned and offered his brother a somewhat reluctant hug. "Philip."

Charlotte removed her cape in the heat from the stove and tried not to stare as she considered the man named Philip. He looked much like Gabe, though leaner with darker eyes of gray blue.

"How was ol' Californy?" Philip asked.

Gabe cleared his throat. "Just fine. Much the same."

"And Father and Mother?"

"I saw them only briefly, but they are the same as always."

"Gabe..." Philip held in check what would likely have turned into a rebuke of family affairs. Instead he smiled at Charlotte. "Where did you meet this fine lady? Whoa now...what's this?"

Philip stepped closer to her. "Why, Gabe, she has a locket like. . . Gabe. . . This *is* grandmother's locket. *Dottie's* locket!" He swung around to face Gabe with an unspoken demand for answers.

Gabe shuffled his feet. "Yes. Well...Miss Vance." Gabe sighed. "Philip, this is Miss Charlotte Vance."

Charlotte recognized the stress he put on her full name.

She held her breath.

"She has come to. . ." He rushed on. "Well, she has agreed to marry you and be a mother to Sarah."

Philip looked like Gabe had struck him as he took a step back and shook his head. "What on earth. . .have you done?"

"Now, Philip, Charlotte—I mean, Miss Vance—comes upon the recommendation of Reverend Chiles. She is a preacher's daughter, orphaned, and in need of a home."

Charlotte reached for the back of a nearby chair, nearly burning her hand on the stove in the process. She took a tight hold on the arched wood.

"I don't care who recommended her," Philip spat.

The conversation had drawn the attention of customers in the store. Gabe lowered his voice. "You said it didn't matter who you had for a wife as long as Sarah had someone to raise her well."

"Hah! Sure, I could use a wife. Yes, Sarah needs a mother. But I was talking out of my grief. I didn't expect you to go snatch a woman off the streets—pardon. . .church pews."

Gabe looked like he wanted to hit him.

Philip gave a short, bitter laugh. "Don't go trying to fix my problems, big brother. My problems are bigger than even you can manage. Stick to your own issues."

The brothers stared at each other.

Quietly an older man approached. "Perhaps you gentlemen would like to take this out back and air it away from your customers."

Gabe raised an eyebrow.

Philip shrugged. "This is Michael Stanton. I've hired him to help out around here—since you're never around." He spun on his heel and stomped through a rear door through which Charlotte glimpsed a smaller room and another door that seemed to lead outside. Gabe followed.

Charlotte took a tentative step, but Mr. Stanton held out a

deterring hand. "You best let them handle this."

"But. . .but it's my future they're debating," she whispered.

"Oh, I believe it is much more than that." He pulled a chair out from the table. "Can I get you anything, ma'am?"

Charlotte didn't know what to do, so she sat down. "I don't think so."

∽

Philip leaned against the back of the wooden building, facing a row of tent houses. Gabe stopped on the bottom of three narrow steps.

"You know it's funny, Gabe. When I saw you with that woman, I thought you had finally gone and put the past behind you, accepted things that can't be changed, and found someone to love."

"You know there was only one love for me," Gabe choked as his heart thumped. "I'm not going to up and marry someone else—especially when I've got so many wrongs to right."

"If—and I mean *if*—Father has wronged Aileen's family, then it is his place to confess the corn."

"Hah. And you think he would. The man barely spent two days with us while we were growing up. We don't know half of the business he's cooked."

Philip glared at him. "You could have jumped in there and found out for yourself. Father offered you half the business."

"I'm not going to let him put a leash on me and lead me around. He's got enough puppies in his holdings. He doesn't need me, and I don't need him."

"Is that what you think of me because I took his money to set up this place?" Philip asked.

Gabe sighed. Arguing about their father never got them anywhere. "Can we just keep to the issue at hand?"

"I am!" Philip snapped. "You're so much like Father, yet you won't admit it. You want everything to go your way. You make a rash decision and expect everyone to fall in line with your idea. Well, I won't!"

Gabe paced the rain-soaked patch of yard. "Just give Charlotte a chance. Look at her. Talk to her. You'll like her. I promise."

Philip just stared at him.

"She's pretty. She's a good listener."

"If she really knew us, she'd run far away from us blokes," Philip said with the first hint of a smile.

"She already knows most of the important things about us. Even about Father."

"You told her about your clash with our father?"

Gabe nodded.

Philip seemed stunned. "Then you told her about Aileen?"

"She seemed to understand. She was once engaged herself." Gabe suddenly felt warm and clammy despite the brisk wind.

"Well, my brother, I think you should marry her if she got you to say that much about yourself."

"I can't."

"And I won't—so I guess you'll have to send her home." Philip turned to take the steps back inside.

Gabe grabbed his arm, looking up at him from ground level. "Just give her a chance. She doesn't have a home or job to return to. Just take a few days to get to know her. Let her help you with Sarah."

Philip sighed and leaned back against the doorframe, studying him. "You really do care what happens to this woman."

"I feel responsible for her."

"And you care."

Gabe started to protest.

Philip raised a hand. "Don't bother. We'll see how things go."

"Where can we have her stay?"

"She'll stay here."

"But. . ."

"What do you think this is, high-society San Fran? This is lawless Dyea. Her situation will hardly draw notice, and we'll, of course, treat her like a *sister.*"

Sister, for certain.

Chapter 3

Charlotte wandered the narrow aisles of the crowded store. Goods of all varieties lined shelves and tables or were displayed in open crates and barrels. Large piles of gold pans sat in one front corner. Above them hung several hooks full of snowshoes, which looked like misshapen tennis rackets. Hooks also hung from beams under the peaked roof, suspending large items like sleds and even a small bathtub. One little table boasted sturdy Indian moccasins, while another exhibited the best in factory-made, dual-buckle, rubber boots.

Sleeping bags, camp stools, fishing tackle, and knives awaited the outdoorsman. Nothing much held feminine appeal. Even the foodstuffs were practical. The basics filled shelves behind the counter, including odd-looking squares of dehydrated vegetables. Sacks of carefully weighed miner's rations formed a low wall down the middle of the store.

Several men crowded the counter, attempting to dicker with Michael for the lowest prices and arguing among each other about the best ways to navigate the treacherous Chilkoot Trail. No one paid Charlotte any heed, and she soon meandered back to the corner stove. A Sears, Roebuck, and Company catalog lay open in the middle of the table, and she sat down to flip through it. If she were staying, there were some things she might need to have ordered.

A breathy whisper soon caught her attention. "Daddy."

Where the rear door had not been tightly shut, a small pixie face peered out. Near-black ringlets dangled over dark eyes that were lined with long lashes. A pink gown in rumpled state hung down to tiny stockinged feet.

Charlotte's heart twisted at the angelic sight.

"Daddy." The child rubbed her eyes.

Charlotte stood and stepped toward her. "Come here, child." The little girl's eyes widened. She looked behind her, then around the store at the men, who paid her no notice. Charlotte knelt down to her level. "My name is Charlotte. What's yours?"

Stepping tentatively from the doorway, she said, "Sarry."

Charlotte smiled. "Is that Sarry or Sarah?"

The adorable child just nodded and stepped within arm's length of Charlotte. She studied the adult before her, then reached out. "Pwetty." Her tiny hand clasped the locket at Charlotte's neck.

"Oh honey. . ." It had been the child's mother's. Could she possibly remember?

Charlotte scooped up the lightweight tot and took her to the chair by the stove. She combed her hair with her fingers while the child continued to turn the locket over and over in her hand. "You got more pwetties?"

"Hmm, no, I guess I don't have any other jewelry." Charlotte leaned toward the child's ear. "This is very special, and I promise it will be yours one day."

Heavy footsteps came from the back room, and soon Gabe and Philip entered the store, filling the room with their presence. Charlotte sought Gabe's gaze for a hint to the outcome of the brothers' conversation. She didn't know what to expect. She didn't even know where to place her hope.

Gabe's eyes widened when he saw her with Sarah. He smiled warmly, then quickly turned away.

Sarah spotted her father and squealed, "Daddy!"

She reached up to him, but Philip seemed frozen. He stared at Charlotte and Sarah for a long moment. Gabe scuffed his boots against the wooden floor and coughed.

"I hold you, Daddy." Sarah reached for her father.

Philip propelled himself to pick up his daughter. He smiled as she hugged him and swung her around. "See, your uncle Gabe is back. You wanna give him a hug?"

The child pulled back bashfully, then suddenly she flung herself toward her uncle with arms wide open. Gabe deftly caught her in a big hug. "How's my big girl? Well, I do believe you've grown while I was away."

Charlotte enjoyed the family scene. It touched her to see grown men making such a fuss over a child.

Philip stepped away from Gabe and Sarah, approaching Charlotte. She stood.

His guarded look appraised her. "I apologize for my rather rough greeting earlier. Welcome to Alaska."

Charlotte dipped her chin and waited.

"Gabe will give you a tour of the accommodations while Sarah and I dish up the stew I have simmering." He gave her a curt nod, then retrieved his daughter.

As the two entered the back room, Gabe gave Charlotte a rather sheepish look. She would have laughed if her situation hadn't seemed so serious.

"Sorry. I have a way of acting on some things before I fully think them through."

She drew back. "So it would seem." What did that mean for her?

He looked at the floor. "Philip is mad that I've tried to push him to move on for Sarah's sake. He'll get past it and come around soon enough."

She raised her brow, waiting.

"You'll stay. You can sort of be Sarah's nanny while you and

Philip get to know each other." He turned his blue eyes to her. "It'll work out. Trust me."

Trust him? He had dragged her hundreds of miles on a whim, caused her heart to hope for love with him, and now would leave her future dangling until who know when.

"Perhaps I should go back to California?"

"Back to what? Reverend Chiles told me you have no family, and he had not been able to secure any position for you in these hard times. Just give Philip a little while. It won't take him long to lo—like—you as I. . .as I know you deserve."

Charlotte searched his expression, but any emotion hid behind a stoic face. He extended his arm, allowing her to precede him into the back room.

Lord, hast Thou taken me into this remote land and put me through tortures of the heart just so that Thou canst use me here? I want to be able to help that child, but I so long for some of my own happiness.

Over the next several weeks, Charlotte developed a morning routine. She put the oatmeal on the stove to simmer and checked to make sure Sarah was contentedly playing at dressing her rag doll for the day. Then Charlotte took her Bible to the kitchen table that had been fashioned from a large crate and drew the rocking chair up to it. The living quarters were tight with the makeshift table and chairs taking up most of the space the small cookstove and cabinet didn't occupy.

Oddly enough, she had gotten out of the habit of daily readings while living with the reverend and his wife. Still she knew her source of true strength could only come from praying and reading God's Word.

The month of November had passed, and with it Thanksgiving Day. No one had made any noticeable effort to celebrate the American holiday.

Dyea had seen a few snow flurries the first two weeks of December, but then it rained, making the ground a treacherous mixture of mud and slush. Snow pummeled the mountain passes, and no trail over the peaks would be navigable until the snow packed. The town teemed with men who were putting together their Yukon outfits and taking in a lot of amusement before their trip. Even some from points along the trail like Canyon City and Sheep Camp had come to enjoy Dyea's culture for a while.

Charlotte rarely ventured out into the lawless streets—and never alone. Just last week a man had been murdered in the street two buildings away from Monroe's. Shots were heard any time of day, be it for celebration or dispute.

Charlotte kept to herself and out of the way of the Monroe men. Gabe headed into town every day on what seemed to be missions to learn more about the trail and what lay beyond the mountain range from those who were headed there and from some who had returned. He had even taken overnight trips to Skagway four miles away at the base of White Pass. He brought back a few hair-raising tales that made Dyea's troubles seem tame in comparison.

Philip spent his days in the store on the other side of the wall from her, but they rarely spoke. He always treated her kindly, but she had no indication that he thought about her becoming his wife.

She spent her days preparing meals, reading to Sarah, and tending to the living area and laundry. Everything was as neat and orderly as possible in the tight quarters—not that she had a compulsion for neatness. The idle days dragged on, long and tiresome. Though she gratefully accepted the roof over her head in such foul weather, shouldn't a maid get some pay?

She pulled her shawl snug to her as she rose from her readings. It was hard to concentrate on the writings of Solomon, who lived in grandeur yet wrote about dissatisfaction in his life.

The damp cold seemed to seep clear through, keeping her shivering all the time. At night she would climb the ladder to the loft at the rear of the store. Crates of supplies lined the low walls, and a mattress just fit under the eaves. She would tuck herself between Sarah and the stovepipe, but still she could find no warmth. If the cold bothered the child, she didn't show it.

"My, it's warm in here," Gabe remarked as he and Philip came in from the store where they kept their sleeping pallets near the heating stove. "I didn't know that little cookstove could put off so much heat."

"I'm sorry. I—I hadn't noticed," Charlotte stammered.

Philip chuckled. "You'll get used to the damp cold here soon enough. Though I can't promise it will get any better until at least April."

Charlotte served up the oatmeal with thick slices of toasted bread.

Sarah pushed her bowl back toward Charlotte. "Mine sweet, Lottie."

Gabe came to attention on his stool. "What did she call you?"

Charlotte felt blood rush to her cheeks. "S—she's just taken to shortening my name. I—it's easier for the child."

"Ahhh, well. . .I never. . ." Laughter rumbled from deep in Gabe's chest, and Sarah clapped her hands, giggling.

His brother just stared at him.

Gabe quickly sobered. "Oh, I'm sorry."

Philip's brows came together. "For what?"

Gabe shot a look at Charlotte. She waited for Philip to display outrage at the nickname, so like his wife's. His grief had ways of surfacing unexpectedly in conversations or routine tasks.

Then Gabe relaxed. "Well, if you don't mind. . ."

"I mind that you're keeping me from my breakfast."

Charlotte sprinkled Sarah's cereal with a small amount of brown sugar, then she silently blessed the food while the men dug right in. It bothered her that the Monroes didn't make giving thanks a part of each meal, but it didn't seem her place in the household to point it out. She just continued to pray for God to make Himself real to each man in every area of life.

"Does anyone realize that Christmas will be here in three days?" Philip asked as he sipped his coffee at the end of the meal.

Gabe shrugged.

"A man came in yesterday asking about Christmas decorations." Philip laughed. "With so many real necessities to haul up here, why would I give thought to stocking such baubles?"

Heaviness settled on Charlotte. "Don't you celebrate Christmas—Jesus' birth and all?"

"Oh, sure," Philip responded casually. "Back home Mother would deck the whole house in Christmas finery, throw parties, and give out grand gifts. But up here, what's the use?"

Charlotte bristled. "Christmas is a reminder of how Christ came so humbly to redeem us. Lavish or not, wherever we are, we should do something to show thanks for what the Lord has done for us."

"He hasn't done much for me lately," Philip muttered.

Gabe interjected, "He's just saying that up here without parlors and families, there's little call for all the fuss, but we can still have Christmas." He pushed his stool back from the table and stood, his large frame dwarfing the others and filling the small room. "In fact, I'll go into the forest today and see if I can't find a small tree and some spruce boughs for you to liven up the place with. How would that be, Charlotte?"

His face held such childlike expectation that she had to smile, and her heart did a flip. She truly appreciated his efforts to give her a Christmas celebration.

"I'd like that very much."

She watched as Gabe bundled himself into his heavy brown duck coat, admiring his muscular shoulders and strong hands.

His big heart seemed to extend to those hands as he ruffled Sarah's curls and tweaked her nose on his way out the back door into the dark, misty morning.

Charlotte sighed.

When she turned back to the table, she was surprised to see Philip still sitting on his stool. He leaned against the wall with his hands clasped at his waistline, watching her. His eyes held a new sense of curiosity. Could this be interest?

She couldn't return his odd look. She had tried not to worry about her future or pine for solutions to her awkward situation. But she would rather be a maid in Philip's home than his wife. When she gave him any real thought, he reminded her of what a brother should be.

"Charlotte." He waited until she looked at him. "I've failed to say thank you for all your work around here and the attention you give to Sarah. You are appreciated more than you may know."

He rose and flashed her a grin as he went into the store to open for the day.

She slumped back against the simple rocker she always sat in at the meagerly furnished table. She fingered the locket that still hung around her neck. Maddening emotions battled for her attention, but the day wouldn't be long enough to sort them out.

Chapter 4

The next afternoon, Philip stuck his head into the rear room and asked Charlotte to help out in the store while his assistant, Michael, went across town on an errand. Charlotte had spent her whole morning arranging pine branches on the two windowsills and cabinet top. Gabe had left them at the back door along with a skinny little spruce tree he had cut down. She would wait to bring it indoors tomorrow—Christmas Eve.

Grateful for another diversion from her mundane days, Charlotte followed Philip into the store. Smoky lanterns lit the room even in the middle of the day.

She arranged Sarah near the stove with some playthings, then eased behind the counter, awaiting instructions. He asked her to start by unloading a small crate of canned fruit onto a low shelf behind the counter.

The flow of customers seemed to be extra heavy for this wintry day.

A large woman with a manly frame leaned over the counter. "Ma'am, would you help us? Your man doesn't seem to know nothin'."

Charlotte straightened from her task and glanced around for Philip. He had moved to the end of the counter to help a man weigh a purchase.

"Umm. . .certainly, if I can," she replied.

"I need spices for cookin' a goose, and he"—she jerked her

bony thumb toward Philip—"says he stocks no rosemary. Then he tells me there is no pure white sugar. What then do you have so I can make a proper Christmas dinner?" Her voice rose with exasperation.

Charlotte searched her mind. She knew very little about what Philip stocked.

"Well, I'm cooking a roast with lots of onions and baking a butterscotch pie. Can I show you our onions?"

The woman clucked her tongue like a hen that had lost an egg. "I must find some rosemary or sage or thyme, something worthy of the Christmas palate. We can have onions any day here. I thought this was supposed to be the best-stocked store in town. I have been sorely deceived," she stated with gusto.

Charlotte sighed and looked toward Philip. Should she interrupt him? But what more could he offer the woman? He would still lose a customer, and she wouldn't go quietly.

Then Charlotte had a sudden thought. "Please wait a moment, ma'am. I may have something that will do."

Charlotte wove her way to the kitchen area of the back room and opened the small cabinet. She took out a little cloth packet she had noticed before. Pockets of muslin were sewn together along one side like a booklet. Each pocket had a button flap and stitched labels that read *oregano, parsley, thyme, sage, rosemary,* and *chives.* They looked like they'd never been used. Philip's wife might have received the packet of herbs as a gift.

Charlotte fingered the beautiful packet for a moment, then strode back to the store and handed it across the counter to the gruff woman. "We don't stock herbs and spices, but you may have this."

The woman seemed shocked. She took it and read each label. "I never. . ."

Another woman, dainty with a pointed nose, approached the counter. "Don't take it, Mrs. Sheever." Then barely lowering her voice, she added, "You don't know what that Jezebel has been using those for."

Charlotte lurched backward against the rows of shelving.

Mrs. Sheever dropped the packet and turned to the other woman. "Do tell."

"This may well be the most popular store in town because of the men who come just to catch a peek at the woman Mr. Monroe and his brother generally keep locked in the back room. She lives there with them. . .*both,*" the woman hissed with a twitch of her sharp nose, "but she's not the sister or wife of either one, and God is surely disgraced."

Unshed tears threatened to choke Charlotte. "How dare you make accusations about my situation when you know nothing about me. There are plenty worse things. . .and *people.* . .in this town who need *your* kind of god's attention more than me and my. . .family. Merry Christmas!" she spat as she turned on her heel and raced past Philip, who apparently had given the incident his full attention.

She would have slammed the door behind her if Sarah hadn't followed her.

If Charlotte had been back in any small town in the States, the women of the church probably would have given her an old donkey and told her to load up and be gone by dawn. Her father had told her of just such a happening in the Illinois town where he first pastored.

Charlotte dropped into the rocker as tears came like a tidal wave. Sarah wiggled up onto her lap and sat patting Charlotte's cheek. "It be okay, Lottie. Chwistmas is comin'."

It hurt to smile, but Charlotte finally did.

Lord, help me be more like a child and trust Thy protection and guidance.

Later as she began to put supper fixings together, Charlotte heard

Michael's voice in the store. Soon Philip came into the kitchen. He paced a bit before saying, "I'm sorry, Charlotte, about that scene. I personally escorted the ladies out."

Charlotte kept her back to him as she worked at the little stove. *They were no "ladies."*

"I know things are hard for you, and you must get frustrated wanting things to come together." He became quiet for so long that Charlotte thought he must have slipped back to the store. She glanced over her shoulder.

Philip stood rubbing his chin while Sarah silently clasped her father's leg in a bear hug. The child must have sensed the tension.

"Perhaps I should move out," she suggested. "Is there a minister and his wife in town who'd take me in?"

Philip gave a half chuckle. "There are no churches in Dyea. We do have one minister who lives in Bailey's Hotel and preaches hellfire and brimstone down at the waterfront. You're much better off staying put. Just give it a bit more time," he said; then kissing his daughter on her head, he returned to the store.

Time. Time for what? If Philip knew he planned to marry her, why didn't he just do it and give her his name? Time could be dangerous. More time to soil what name she had. More time to worry. More time to fall deeper in love with Gabe.

In a town that had no churches and barely took time to sleep even under nearly eighteen hours of darkness per day, Philip kept his store open on Sundays. While the men treated Sundays like any other day, Charlotte used the time to teach Sarah hymns. She missed being in church and gathering with other believers.

So it rather surprised her when Philip announced that he would keep the store closed on Christmas Day. Her joy quickly faded when she wondered what the four of them would do all day cramped into the tight quarters.

After a breakfast of flapjacks, Gabe and Philip went outside together. Charlotte started the roast and rolled out her piecrust. She had little gifts for each of them, which she would give at dinnertime.

The sun had already begun to wane when the men returned. Philip set something covered with a blanket on the table while Gabe placed a small cradle on the floor. Sarah sprang to his side. "What's it? Mine?"

Gabe coaxed her to pull the little blanket out of the cradle. Sarah tugged at the blanket like something underneath it might bite her. But her face filled with delight when she saw a new porcelain doll lying in the cradle. It had lovely long brown hair and a painted face with brown eyes.

"Hello, Mary!" Sarah exclaimed.

"Who's Mary?" Philip asked.

Sarah gave him an exasperated look. "My dolly, Daddy."

Gabe chuckled. "Well, I wonder where she got that name."

Charlotte hesitated. "Probably from the Bible stories I've been reading her this week."

Gabe nodded approval, and Philip just shrugged.

He turned to the object on the table. "This is for you, Charlotte."

Charlotte stepped tentatively to it and pulled the blanket away. There sat a new china pitcher and bowl set. "Oh, why thank you." She knew Philip didn't stock such breakables in his store, only special ordered them for some hotels.

"I figured you and Sarah might be tired of washing with the pail," he mumbled.

Charlotte almost wanted to laugh. The gift was thoughtful, yet practical.

"Let me get your gifts." Charlotte opened the cabinet, glanced at the herb packet that had mysteriously returned to its place, and pulled out three small packages she had hidden on the bottom shelf. She gave one to each person.

Sarah tore right into the brown paper. She squealed over her new knitted slippers and tugged them on over her shoes. Philip thanked her for his wool mittens. Gabe took his time opening his package, unnerving Charlotte. She gripped the back of the rocker as his package revealed two hand-stitched and monogrammed handkerchiefs.

"Oh." He met her gaze. "Thank you very much," he said, adding softly, "Lottie."

Charlotte felt the blush flame her cheeks and turned to the oven to peek in at her pie.

As she cleared the table, she noticed that Philip had sat down on the floor with his daughter to play with her. Again, Charlotte marveled at what a good father he was, and she could understand how he didn't want to be separated from his child.

Gabe stepped to Charlotte's side, trapping her in the small area between the table, stove, and cabinet. "I, uhh. . .well, I have something for you. Just something little." He practically shoved a paper envelope into her hands.

Charlotte's fingers shook as she unfolded the paper. A necklace lay in the center. On the chain a tiny charm was attached—a rough-edged heart.

"Oh my." Charlotte looked up into his eyes, and she could barely breathe under the tenderness in his gaze.

He seemed to shake himself then. "It's a real gold nugget that came shaped that way. Some old geezer had it, and I traded him for it. Think of it as a souvenir."

His words held a chill, but she wanted to believe some of his heart came with the tiny gold charm.

Across the room, Philip rose from the floor and stared at them. Gabe turned around, and Philip's eyebrows rose in an unspoken question.

Gabe glanced away. "I'm going to wash up for dinner."

Charlotte slid her necklace into her apron pocket, but she fingered the heart shape a moment before she went back to setting the table.

If someone asked her to define love, she wasn't sure she could. She had loved her father with the devotion of a daughter. It was a love that had always been with her. She had loved Oliver with all the excitement of a young woman who at every step was being pursued by a love-smitten young man.

Oliver had always been attentive. They met in school. He escorted her to every school and church function. He came by her home several nights a week to sit and converse with her and her father. She relished being the center of his world.

When he suddenly announced that he was going to Colorado to seek gold, it nearly froze any feelings of love she had. But when he asked her to marry him, promising to return with riches that would set them up for life, she promised him her undying devotion. She believed him to be investing in their future, so that must mean he would always love her.

The feelings she experienced now were so different. She rarely saw Gabe. He seemed to avoid time alone with her. Yet often she thought she could see past his rough exterior and guess what he might be thinking inside. The briefest of smiles from him could make her heart sing, and just having him sit across the table from her made her feel like everything fit into its place.

"Dinner is ready," she called. Sliding into her seat directly across the table from Gabe, she looked into his eyes alone and asked, "May we bless this meal with prayer?"

"I will," Gabe said.

Chapter 5

Gabe surprised himself with the offer to pray. He had been giving God a lot of thought lately. He knew his parents and Aileen's parents claimed to be Christians. He also knew he couldn't judge who God was from a handful of people, not when he saw God's goodness in everything Charlotte did and said.

She lived a genuine faith. He rarely saw a hint of question from her about her status in the household and how her future would work out. She trusted the brothers. . .but more so, she trusted God.

Gabe prayed, asking special blessing on the food and the hands that had prepared it.

When he looked up, Charlotte's gaze met his with a hint of tears on her lashes. He shifted in his seat. He hadn't meant to make her cry.

Philip shoved a pot of mashed potatoes at him, and he tried to give his full attention to Charlotte's good cooking.

He didn't understand his brother. Charlotte was a wonderful person. She clearly loved Sarah and gave her wonderful care. What more could Philip need to see before marrying her? Philip needed her, and she needed him.

Gabe had heard about the incident in the store, and it frustrated him that Philip's stalling would bring such reproach upon Charlotte. Something had to be done. Maybe Philip just needed a push.

Gabe looked across the table. Charlotte smiled at him. His meat stuck in his throat, and his heart did a funny little dance. He looked away and grabbed his mug of coffee.

Yes, something needed to change. These tight living arrangements were getting to him.

Alaska's long night of darkness and a fresh layer of snow cloaked the town, yet every building seemed to dance with the usual nighttime revelry of drinking, gaming, and carousing. Gabe stood on the back stoop of the store and couldn't think of sleeping or bringing this holiday to an end.

A flash of light streaked above a distant mountain range. Gabe watched as it came again and flickered like a flame taking hold of a wick. The light spread out, displaying fingers of blue, green, and pink.

Why would God go to the trouble of painting the night sky like that?

Gabe felt the answer deep inside him. *For me.*

"Charlotte should see this." Gabe opened the door and stepped back inside.

Charlotte sat alone in the room with a book. "Philip is in the loft, putting Sarah to bed," she said. "She was getting very cranky."

"Well, good. Come outside. I have something you should see."

She gave him one of her electrifying smiles. She took the blanket on the back of the rocking chair and wrapped it around her shoulders like a shawl. He held the door for her, and they stepped out onto the top step together.

She looked up at him expectantly. Her eyes sparkled in the light from the barely closed door. She sucked her lower lip in as she waited. . .waited for him. He nearly forgot why they were there. He turned to the night sky.

"What do you think of that?"

"Oh. . ." Her breath sang past her full lips. "I've never seen anything like it. What is it?"

"It's unique to the North Country. They are called the northern lights."

His gaze returned to her. She stood with her hands clasped at her breast, holding the blanket yet appearing to be in worship. Her face seemed to take on the colors from the sky, radiating with childlike wonder.

"Gabe, do you ever wonder why God went to all the trouble of making even the smallest thing in nature beautiful?"

He smiled. "Sure. I guess He pays attention to details."

"He even counts the hairs on our head." She touched his sleeve. "Gabe, God wants to share every detail of life with us—all our joys and all our pains. Do you know you can talk to Him about anything?"

Her touch was poignant, even through his coat. His thoughts slowed. He wanted to believe like she did. He wanted to trust God like that.

Yet he also wanted to touch her cheek and see if it felt as soft as it looked. He wanted to pull her close and draw strength from her faith.

No, he couldn't. He had to get away.

"Why are you letting the cold in?" Philip asked from the doorway. "Oh, excuse me. . . ."

"No." Charlotte suddenly seemed terribly nervous. "I was just going in. Take a look at the lights for yourself." She rushed past Philip, her blanket slapping at them both.

Gabe admired her rigid stride, then turned to his brother. Frustration that had been simmering in him erupted. "When are you going to marry that woman?"

Philip laughed. "I should be asking you that."

Gabe glared at him. "I brought her here for you. She's been waiting weeks for you to get used to the idea of marrying her. She has been nothing but patient with you and loving toward your daughter. What more do you need?"

"I care for Charlotte. . .like a sister, and I wouldn't think of marrying her."

The word nearly exploded from Gabe. "Why?"

"I couldn't marry any woman my brother looked at in that way." Philip raised his chin as if he enjoyed holding something over his older brother. "What kind of *brother* gives a woman a golden heart necklace? Of course, you are in love with her."

"What. . . ?" A disturbing emotion clawed for Gabe's attention. "No, you are mistaken. You don't know anything. You *have* to marry her."

"No." Philip stood with his feet planted firmly apart, and he looked at Gabe like their father did when he waited for his son to confess to a mistake.

"Yes. Yes you must." Gabe felt a panic rise in his chest. "I can't!"

∽

Charlotte strode across the room before she realized the door still stood ajar, and she could hear everything the brothers said. She didn't want to draw attention to herself by moving to close the door. She turned to the ladder that went to the loft.

The men's conversation became distinct, and she froze with one foot raised to the first rung.

Philip refusing to marry her lifted a feeling of dread that she had been carrying from the boat, even before she knew him to be a kind and decent man.

When Philip challenged Gabe's attraction to her, Charlotte's heart soared. She was right. Gabe didn't look at her as a sister and friend. His heart spoke in those tender looks.

"I can't!" Gabe's voice thundered in the room.

Charlotte slumped against the ladder.

Philip grated a response. "Give it up, man. Can't you see—"

"No. You don't see. There's Aileen."

"She's gone, Gabe. Married."

"But. . .our father. . ."

"When are you going to stop looking at him through that situation?" Philip asked. "Aileen's father ended your engagement, not our father. And if Aileen had loved you enough, she would have found a way to change her father's mind. Don't let Aileen and her father put this wall between you and your father. Stop fighting. The battle is over, and the girl is gone."

Gabe tromped down the steps. Charlotte could hear him grumbling, then his voice became more distinct.

"Don't tell me what to do, little brother. We're talking about your future, not mine. Go ahead and marry Charlotte. It's for everyone's best."

A tear trickled down the side of her nose, but she didn't move. She couldn't even breathe.

Gabe continued, "Next week I'm starting up the trail, and you won't have to worry about how I look at Charlotte."

Philip made a noise.

"I'm gone," Gabe seemed to add for clarity.

Charlotte caught a sob behind her hand. She clawed her way up the ladder as tears clouded her eyes. Not giving thought to her best dress, she flung herself onto the mattress beside the sleeping child and curled into a ball.

Not even at the deaths of her father and Oliver had she felt such searing pain. Rejection. It must be worse than death.

Why is this happening, Lord? Did I do something wrong? Should I have kept my heart locked up tight and ignored this love for Gabe?

Just when a new and special kind of love had blossomed and she felt hope to carry into the years to come, it had been cut off—severed as completely and painfully as if she had lost a limb.

What am I to do, Lord? Where can I go?

Sobs shook her body long into the night. Relief would not come in answers, only in exhaustion.

⌒⌒

Before anyone else stirred the next morning, Gabe left the store with a pocketful of money. He had worked more than a year for two of his father's business competitors to finance this trip into the Yukon. The first order of business would be to buy a tent. He would make his purchases in other stores in Dyea and Skagway. He wouldn't ask his younger brother any favors. Besides, he needed to stay away from the store.

Hopefully, if he stayed away, the time alone would help Philip, Charlotte, and Sarah to form a family bond. He'd only go to the store to sleep once in a while. He'd need to start getting acclimated to the cold. He'd be sleeping in a tent for the next six months to a year.

He headed to the Yukon Outfitters building, hoping to meet up with the three men who just a month ago had agreed to team up with him for the trip up the Chilkoot Trail. His steps were slow. He tried to concentrate on his goals, but they seemed hazy. Getting down to the business of preparations would surely clear his mind.

But before he entered the large warehouse building, he found himself talking to God. *I know if I get a ton of that gold, it isn't going to bring Aileen back. Maybe I don't care for her anymore.*

And I know that no amount of gold is going to fix what my father has done. I don't think I could impress him with gold I dug with my own bare hands.

Sometimes I don't even know why I'm still going to Dawson. I just know I can't take Charlotte. The Yukon is no place for a woman like her.

Philip is stubborn. He needs Charlotte. She'll be good for him. God, can't You just make it all work out?

Trust.

Yes, I've trusted them to Thy care, God.

Trust.

But have I trusted myself to Thy care as well?

Gabe stood with his hand on the knob of the door until someone asked him to move. He stepped inside and was promptly greeted by two of his trail partners.

Chapter 6

January 20

Charlotte moved this and dusted that in the confined kitchen while Philip and Gabe talked at the back door. Sarah hopped in front of her uncle, begging to be picked up. She hadn't seen him for a month and demanded his attention now. Gabe swung her up into his arms as if she weighed no more than a feather.

"We've finished stashing our outfits at Finnegan's Point. We'll camp there now and pack up trail. There should be no reason for me to return to Dyea, so I'll say goodbye now." He squeezed Sarah. "Take care of this little one. I trust you to do right by our girls, Brother."

Charlotte looked up. Gabe kissed Sarah's ear, causing the child to laugh, but if he glanced at Charlotte through lowered lashes, he gave no indication. Her heart tugged her toward the door, but she kept her feet firmly planted by the stove.

Gabe handed Sarah to her father. With a quick pat to Philip's back and the briefest of nods to Charlotte, Gabe turned and walked down the alleyway between buildings.

She had been dreading this day ever since Gabe had announced his leave at Christmas. She had held on to some hope that he might say something to her—anything that might tell her he loved her and couldn't let her go.

It seemed now that leaving came easy to him, and his gold fever—coupled with fever for retribution—was greater than any affection he might hold for her.

Philip returned to the store, Sarah pulled her doll cradle into the middle of the floor, and Charlotte surveyed her home. She lived here, but this wasn't *her* home. She didn't belong here. She didn't want to be here if she couldn't be with Gabe.

She slapped at the table with her rag. She felt trapped.

It was Gabe's fault that she was here. He charmed the Chileses, and he charmed her too with his good looks, good manners, and tenderness to boot. Why couldn't she see this dead-end road before she took it?

Gabe wanted things his way, but she and Philip weren't his puppets. They would lead their own lives.

A week later she had an announcement for Philip at the dinner table.

"I've been composing some letters. I haven't sent them yet, but I'm hopeful that someone in Reverend Chiles's church or in one of my father's last two congregations will help me find a worthy position. I just may have to ask to borrow money for my passage. I—I will repay you."

Philip leaned back, studying her. "What's all this? I owe you more than I can ever give you. If you must return to California, of course I'll pay your way. But wait until the weather is more amicable for travel."

Charlotte relaxed.

Philip pulled a sheet of paper from his pocket. "Perhaps you would be interested in this." He spread it out on the table. "I've been drawing up plans for a house. I hope you like them."

Charlotte felt her guard rise again. Could he be thinking marriage *now*? It was much too late for even the most congenial arrangement between friends or business partners.

"Philip, I. . ." She reached behind her neck and unclasped the oval locket she still wore. "It's not right for me to wear this. I release you from any promises Gabe made on your behalf. He shouldn't be telling either of us what to do."

She laid the locket on the sheet of paper.

Philip said nothing, just looked at her.

Charlotte clasped the other chain still around her neck and unconsciously fingered the heart-shaped nugget.

"Dear Charlotte, if I could have ordered a sister from Sears and Roebuck, she would have been just like you. You are a remarkable woman." He smiled at her. "Hold on to that nugget like a promise. I know your heart belongs to Gabe...and his heart belongs to you. He just hasn't admitted it yet."

Charlotte gasped.

"I want you to stay and make this your home for as long as you wish. He'll eventually come back."

She tried to choke back a sob. "Gabe has been such a dolt, but...I miss him so."

Philip reached out and awkwardly rubbed her shoulder. Sarah looked up from her plate of barely touched food. "I eat, Lottie. Don't cry, dear."

Philip tried to hold back a laugh. Charlotte giggled even as tears trickled down her cheeks. Sarah rolled her shoulders toward her chest and grinned.

When Charlotte had dried her tears, Philip said, "I got something in the mail yesterday and haven't known what to make of it." He pulled another paper from his pocket.

"This is a letter from my wife's aunt. May I read it to you?"

Charlotte nodded.

Dottie,

Please excuse my lack of communication. Life does have a way of rushing by. My dear Henry had been sick so long and I was so consumed with taking care of him that I lost touch with you and your brothers. I was appalled—yet strangely thrilled—to hear you had taken up residence in Alaska. Your father would be proud of your adventuresome spirit.

*Henry passed on this fall, and I find myself looking for
a diversion from the emptiness of this big old house. I fear I
could go insane with nothing to do.*

*Please write back and let me know if there is space
enough in your home to have me visit. I would so like to see
you and the child you named after your mother.*

Yours truly,
Bessie Aldredge
Portland, Oregon

Philip looked up. "What would you tell the woman? Dottie spoke fondly of this aunt. She reportedly is quite a lively one. How do I tell her of. . .of Dottie? Should I let her come?"

Charlotte felt sorry for Philip. What a place to be in to have to tell a person of her loved one's death—especially when the pain was still so fresh for himself.

"She will have to know, and I can help you compose the letter."

"But should I let her come? Would she still come?" Philip stared at his daughter. "I could use someone like her. And. . ." He looked at Charlotte. "You could feel comfortable staying with another woman around."

Charlotte laughed. "What would you do with two women and a child underfoot? I'd still be in the way."

She reached across the table and patted his hand. "Write her, Philip, and see what she says. Maybe she'll be able to come and take my place once I've found a position."

Philip nodded slowly. After a moment, she tentatively added, "If she doesn't come, I could take Sarah back to California with me. To your parents or to your wife's parents—"

Philip's fist hit the table. "No!"

His anger stunned Charlotte.

"I—I'm sorry. My parents can't handle a toddler. D–Dottie's folks are gone." Philip buried his face in his hands. "There is no other way. Sarah and I stay together."

Charlotte swallowed the lump in her throat that responded to his visible pain.

No easy answers—and certainly not a new wife—would fix Philip's grief and bitterness.

∽

Gabe plodded uphill. He shifted his heavy pack and bent into the wind. Snow whipped at his cheeks, and the cold burned his nostrils. The weather was getting worse. He could barely see where to place his next step, and some spots along this part of the trail could be tricky.

He let out a moan. No one would hear him over the wind. Wilderness surrounded him, and he didn't even know why he insisted on putting himself through this torture. Did he want to anymore? Where had all that driving purpose gone?

He tripped against a rock, but he kept moving. The goal for the moment was to reach the cache and unburden himself of this load.

Awhile later with the goods stashed, he and his partners headed back down the trail, sliding and sometimes almost running when the trail smoothed out. They would only pack one load this day.

Gabe shivered as he all but hugged his camp stove. The snowstorm raged for a second day, blinding and confining them. They could only cut wood and sit in the tents.

His companions became irritable when no progress up trail could be made. They griped at each other and argued over the fall of their card hands. Gabe stayed away from the games. He'd had little card experience; besides, he could hardly sit still long enough for one round.

Twice before when they had encountered downpours that made the uphill climb treacherous, Gabe had gone back down the trail into Dyea on errands for mail, newspapers, and supplies. He didn't stop in Monroe's store, but he found ways to learn that his family fared well—and that Charlotte still lived at the back of the store. . .unmarried.

He craved diversion. The nearly six weeks of twice-a-day trips up and down the trail kept him too busy and too tired to think. They each packed fifty- to one hundred-pound loads on their backs and could transport even more if a sled could be used. The trail wound sharply around boulders, and often ice hung down from ledges above, requiring one to duck under it. More often strong headwinds barreled through the Dyea River Valley, drifting snow over the trail.

They would pack their outfit sometimes only a mile up trail, then they would move their camp to the new cache and start packing again. Stacks of supplies lined the trail, and even without sufficient law enforcement, everyone knew that to steal from someone else's cache meant to risk death.

Gabe stretched out on top of his sleeping bag, which lay on top of a row of crates and sacks of supplies. He estimated it to be nearly noon, yet the sun barely reached him through the snow and trees.

Gabe dug through his clothing bag and found a small Bible. Though not often read, it had been with him since childhood. He would read a psalm. He opened to the Twenty-Second Psalm and heard David cry out to God in his agony. Pursued and scorned by enemies, David always seemed plagued by trouble. Even animals circled him, tearing at him. No strength was left in him, and he pleaded to be saved.

Closing the book after skimming the end of the psalm, Gabe wondered about the things that followed him. He felt pressured, shadowed, hunted by unseen aggressors.

Oh God. . . He knew that only God would listen to him, befriend him. His trail partners didn't know the real Gabe

Monroe. He only let them see the surface. No one made an effort to dig deeper. He was a fair and hardworking partner, which satisfied them.

He stared at the Bible, trying to shake off the weight on his soul. What did he fear?

He couldn't seem to keep thoughts of Charlotte away. Her brown hair, blue eyes, and comely figure were admirable; but he especially appreciated her quiet grace and strong faith. He could never be worthy of such a woman. His brother was much more settled as a respected businessman and father. Eventually Philip would see it too.

Did he fear that Philip wouldn't get around to marrying her? Could he be worrying about Charlotte's security? Or. . .was she more dangerous to Gabe if she remained unattached?

He stood up, shivering. The shaking hurt his muscles, and he couldn't control it. He moved around the small space, flapping his arms and stamping his feet to generate warmth.

But the motion couldn't drive away his nagging fears. *Okay, Lord, what if my plans fall apart? What if none of the things I've been reaching for mean anything?*

But I have to repay what my father took from Aileen's family.

Though it is not my debt.

Who am I trying to impress? Who is left?

Would giving up the gold hunt be more painful than this present agony?

But what is my purpose, and what is there to go back to?

Charlotte.

Gabe shook his head as he leaned over the stove.

But I don't know that she cares for me. She should despise me for taking her to this country where she can be the target of gossip and improper advances from some of the men because she doesn't have the protection of being a married woman.

He picked up the Bible again. He desired to read about a

godly woman. He considered the stories of Mary, Ruth, and Esther, then decided on Ruth. She lived in a foreign country and relied on God to provide her needs. God did so through a man named Boaz.

Philip was Charlotte's Boaz, wasn't he?

Chapter 7

Sarah sat on the floor by the heating stove in the rear of the store methodically removing small items from a box, then putting them back in. Philip and Charlotte shared cups of coffee at the table while they watched her. The furniture was much nicer than what they used in their living quarters, and she had long wondered why Philip didn't use the table and chairs in his kitchen.

Traffic through the store had virtually halted. Most stampeders who wintered in town were now up on the trail making a push for the pass before the spring thaw.

Philip suddenly cleared his throat. "Michael has told me that he had a couple businessmen mention seeing Gabe in town once, a week or so ago."

Charlotte's heart suddenly dipped. "Why didn't he stop in?"

"Isn't it obvious?" Philip stared at his coffee mug. "He loves you, and the pain of not being with you is eating at him. Still he is too stubborn to admit to not getting his way. He found out he couldn't manipulate things. He couldn't control his heart."

She felt heat pulsing in her cheeks.

"Sooner or later he's going to realize that he has to give up trying to change the past and grab on to the future."

Charlotte looked at Philip with his head still bowed. He could also be talking about himself.

They sat in silence, each lost in their own thoughts. Philip sipped at his coffee, but Charlotte ignored the now cold brew in her cup.

"I finally received a letter from Aunt Bessie," Philip said.

Charlotte sighed. She herself had received a couple of letters in response to her job search. Though polite, kind, and sympathetic, no one could offer her work while times were still financially precarious. What could she do?

"She'll come within a week or two, assuming the ships are running, and she sounded positively thrilled by the invitation. Though, I'm afraid she may try to play mother hen." Philip slumped in his chair like a youth.

Charlotte laughed in spite of her circumstances. "I have a feeling that the woman will be just what you and Sarah need."

"And you," Philip offered.

She waved away the comment. "It's time I think of moving on."

Philip scowled at her. "And where do you think you're going?"

"I—I could. . ." Her thoughts spun, and she almost spoke the first silly notion that came to mind.

He continued to study her, even though Sarah tried to hand her father a block of wood that she had been playing with.

"See Uncle Gabe?" the toddler asked.

"Maybe so," Philip replied as Charlotte turned away from his scrutiny. "Maybe so. From what I can gather, Gabe and his group should have reached the Scales about now where their outfits will be weighed and redistributed before the climb up the pass."

"He's been gone two months. That's only around seventeen miles," Charlotte said. "Are you sure that's all the farther he's gone?"

"No, not positive, but they're each packing at least a thousand pounds without horses and without hiring any packers. And then there are the storms we've been having," Philip said, beginning to smile.

Charlotte shifted in her chair and spilled some of her coffee.

"That's all very interesting."

"And you want to go," Philip stated. "You want to go after him, but you'll need to do it before he crosses the summit."

It seemed as if Philip had plucked the crazy idea out of her own mind. She coughed. They had to be crazy to even mention it.

"You can't get past the summit's customs check without the required supplies," Philip continued enthusiastically. "So you need to go as soon as possible. The store is slow, and Michael's free now. He's been up that trail many times with a cargo company that hauls loads for a penny a pound. He knows it well, and I fully trust him to get you through. You could be there in two—maybe three—days."

Charlotte shook her head even as she let herself imagine what she might have to endure on a trek up that trail.

"Leave now before Aunt Bessie arrives, or she might try to talk some sense into us romantics."

Charlotte burst out with laughter. "But. . .but how are you going to manage everything—the store, the cooking, Sarah? She's become more energetic these days. The walls can barely contain her."

Philip contemplated his little girl. "Guess I can't tie her to my back like a papoose, but we'll survive until Bessie comes."

Sarah leaned against Philip's leg and smiled up at Charlotte with her dimples flashing.

Charlotte couldn't believe this crazy idea suddenly looked doable. Was Philip right? Did Gabe really care for her? Could a little push make him admit those feelings?

This would take some prayer, but finally she said, "Let me cook up some extra food for you."

Philip smiled. "That would be appreciated."

∽

The last day of March didn't give any promise of spring's arrival.

The cold morning air bit at Charlotte's face, and she adjusted her scarf to better cover her nose and cheeks. She carried a light pack of clothing on her back, while Michael walked beside her with a heavy load of food supplies and sleeping bags. They had been hiking at least an hour, even though darkness still cloaked the valley.

Charlotte's body ached this second day on the trail. Her routine at the store didn't require a lot of exertion, and last night's hotel accommodations did nothing to live up to its grand name. A large tent displayed the sign for the Palace Hotel and Restaurant. It had a dining area and a sleeping area. Charlotte had to lie fully clothed on a cot in an open room with other cots and endure the snores of a dozen men. At least the meal had been hot and filling.

Her boots slid in the snow, and again she was grateful for the skirt she had shortened for the hike. It rained the day they started out, but not far up the trail, they encountered snow.

Trying to conserve her energy and focus on the snow-covered trail, Charlotte rarely spoke to Michael. He seemed to understand her need for silence and left her to her thoughts. And they were many.

Where would they find Gabe? How would he receive her? What if he rejected her? Was this love she felt worth the risk?

She pictured Gabe on the day they met, tomato covering his boots. She recalled how she'd admired his light blue eyes—the kind of blue that peeked out of a snow pack.

He appeared strong and determined, yet boyish, when he had stood on the steamer's deck with wind whipping his dark hair. Was it then she began to love him?

He showed kindness toward her when they shared about their lost loves. Their many chats aboard ship had sealed their friendship.

Even though she was intended to be Philip's wife, it was Gabe's tenderness toward Sarah that tugged at her heartstrings.

The way she felt for Gabe couldn't be controlled, and it scared her. She didn't know what to do with such emotions when he seemed so unattainable. She tried desperately to ignore things he did and said that seemed to show his heart, but no one could ignore the gift of the heart-shaped nugget.

Now she was free to offer her love to Gabe, but would he be ready to accept and return that love?

After a late lunch of cold fried bacon, corn bread, and ice water, Michael said, "We'll stop at Sheep Camp tonight. I feel a storm brewing."

By morning—after another night in humble conditions—Charlotte heard the snowstorm howling and knew they would make no progress on the trail that day.

∽

Gabe and his partners had managed to haul about half of their goods to the summit by March 31. Then two days of very foul weather set in, paralyzing their progress again.

Moving at a snail's pace, it had taken more than two months on the trail just to reach the summit. Then they had a boat to build and miles of lakes and rivers to navigate before they'd ever reach Dawson and stake a mining claim. With all the people on the trail—sometimes one right after the other climbing the "Golden Stairs" to the Chilkoot Summit—he wondered if there still could be any gold left in the Yukon.

Gabe drifted through the camp town, seeking someone who could make a better pot of coffee than he could master. Most of the thousands who called this their temporary home chose to keep inside due to the foul weather.

He made for a tent that served as a mercantile and postal exchange. He'd been checking for mail nearly daily with no results.

The shopkeeper sorted mail beside the stove as Gabe asked if there was anything for him.

"Monroe? Seems like I did see that name." The bald man dug into a large canvas bag. "Ah, yes, I was just about to send this on to Lindemann. It's been here awhile."

"But I check mail regularly."

The older man just shrugged.

"Never mind," Gabe grumbled, then added a thank-you as he took a small bulky package from the man.

He stopped inside the store's door to open it. The return address read Monroe of San Francisco, California, and he hesitated. Pulling paper open revealed a letter and a pocket watch.

Gabe turned it over. This belonged to his father. The golden design was unmistakable.

He slowly unfolded the letter.

Dear Gabe,

I write this to you while flat on my bed. It has taken a wrenched back to make me stop and take notice of what things are most important in life. I've raged at the Lord a lot while staring at the ceiling. Even your mild mother knows to stay away.

Gabe could picture his father's anger at being confined.

I need to tell you that I'm sorry I wasn't totally open with you about my dealings with Miss Aileen Mayer's father. I was trying to protect my family and business. I thought I was involved in legitimate business with Mr. Mayer, but when I learned of illegal trafficking of goods between here and China, I pulled out. I've paid fines to the city and confessed my poor management of this situation to your mother and God, but I need you to understand. Mr. Mayer is shady, and he was, and still is, using his daughter as a business pawn.

Gabe felt his stomach twist. It was true.

Please accept this watch. It was your grandfather Monroe's. The nuggets in the cover are from his gold strike. My father taught me about good business, honesty, and faith. I've not always done well to take the time and care to instill those lessons in you boys. Praise God you turned out fine, thanks to your mother.

If you should see fit, there is a position in the company for you. I would enjoy sharing my father's teachings with you.

Sincerely, [scratched out]

With love,

Your father, B. Monroe

Relief flooded Gabe. His father's forgiving and contrite tone soothed him, and the need to continue fighting the man seemed to disappear.

Gabe stuffed the paper and watch into his coat pocket and started walking. The snow whirled down the mountain in heavy flakes, clouding his vision. Then he bumped into a signpost. "We buy and sell outfits," it read.

Chapter 8

April 3 dawned feeling almost warm despite the altitude. Charlotte was eager to leave camp. Sheep Camp had little to boast but tents and dirt and hordes of people. Even if Gabe had a tent in the town, she felt most confident of meeting him on the trail or at the Scales.

Michael came to her as she fastened her backpack on. "The natives are saying we shouldn't go any farther up the trail due to avalanches," he said.

"Avalanches? But. . .but Gabe is up there."

"He'll take care of himself, but I'm not taking you anywhere today." He turned and left, striding between tents.

∞

Charlotte parked her belongings back in the canvas hotel, then she strolled through the camp town. Melting snow crunched under her feet, and she was grateful for the warm sun.

Two women sat on crates of provisions just outside a small, privately owned tent. Charlotte stopped to chat with them about where they were from and where they were going. She unwound her scarf under the bright morning sun.

A muffled boom, followed by a roar, barreled down the trail from the summit. The camp came instantly alert. Some men scrambled down the trail away from the noise while others started climbing toward it.

Charlotte's heart pounded. Avalanche.

She left the other women and wove through rows of tents, looking for Michael.

Before noon another, louder roar filled the valley. She caught a sob in her throat as she thought of Gabe possibly trapped by a wall of snow.

Tripping on a tent stake, she rounded a corner and came upon Michael talking to a group of men.

"Miss Charlotte, now don't fret." Michael put his hands on her shoulders and looked in her eyes. "Don't lose hope."

Charlotte looked up at the kind man through her tears.

"I'm heading up the trail with a group to. . .help," he said, then pointed to one of the men. "This man has a wife in camp, and we'll take you to her."

In a tiny tent that seemed to lean against the mountainside, Charlotte met a petite woman and her equally small daughter of about ten years. The woman looked peaked. They huddled by their camp stove and seemed to have no energy for chitchat. Charlotte had enough to think about without making conversation. The waiting tore at her nerves, and she soon left the tent.

The camp swarmed with people. Many came down trail from the Scales. Charlotte started asking men if they knew Gabe Monroe. She made her way through camp, working toward the trail's incline. Just past the horse bridge, she met a group of m a sled. Two bodies lay on the sled, twisted and frozen.

She turned back to camp. She couldn't see any more ᴄ ᴜɪs. She lost what remained in her stomach beside a large tent. She looked up only to see men hauling avalanche victims inside that very tent.

Hurrying away, she sought refuge in her mind as she repeated the Twenty-Third Psalm. "Yea, though I walk through the valley of the shadow of death. . ." Shadows couldn't hurt her, but the dread they brought with them stifled her hope.

She stumbled into the hotel. The smell of hot coffee wafted

from the stove, and though the proprietor didn't seem to be around, Charlotte helped herself. She sat down at one of the plank tables, resting her head in her hand.

Sometime later, Michael came through the main tent opening, dragging two backpacks. A man who looked vaguely familiar followed him. Michael set the packs down before he noticed her.

"Dear Miss Charlotte, I didn't expect to find you here," he said. "This is Mr. Jarvis, who is with Gabe's party."

Charlotte nodded at the men but didn't voice any of the questions that most pressed her.

Michael moved around the table to her side and cleared his throat. "Mr. Jarvis believes Gabe left camp before dawn to pack a load to the summit before light. A Ken Davies of their party also went packing." Michael pointed to the pile of backpacks. "Some of this has been confirmed as belonging to Davies."

Charlotte felt numb from the tips of her fingers to the core of her heart. How could this be? Why would Gabe have taken that climb under such conditions?

She pushed past the tingle of tears in her throat and said, "When can we leave? I don't want to be here when they haul his body into that tent."

Michael pulled back. "We. . .we don't know Gabe will be among them. This town is full of men who came back from the Scales ahead of the last slide." He seemed to silently seek Mr. Jarvis's opinion. "Besides, I feel obligated to Philip to find out for sure."

Charlotte couldn't speak. She just nodded as the men excused themselves and returned to their duty.

What now? What was there for her to do?

She should pray, but the pain was so intense, she couldn't form legible words. So she laid her head in her arms and wept.

When she finally raised her head, the hotel proprietor quietly worked beside his stove, putting together food for the dinner hour. Looking up, he offered her some beef broth and potatoes.

After nibbling at the fare, Charlotte headed outside, steering clear of the morgue tent. She aimed for a sign that had caught her attention the day before.

With each footfall, she became more determined that Gabe could not be dead. She pressed her chest where the golden heart nugget rested between her blouse and coat. He must be at the top of that summit.

She stepped inside a small tent where a man sat at a desk made of two crates labeled as provisions. He raised his brow in question when he saw her.

"You sell outfits for the Yukon?" she asked.

"Certainly. That's what the sign says," he replied.

"I. . .how much?"

He frowned at her, then named an outrageous price.

She withered. If she had that kind of money, she would have returned to California by now.

Turning, she pulled back the tent flap to leave as a man stepped in. Tall and broad, he had a beard covering his face.

"Excuse me," Charlotte mumbled.

"Ma'am."

She glanced up into arctic-blue eyes. Though the skin around them appeared chapped and leathery and the bones looked more pronounced, she recognized him.

"Gabe!" She flung her arms around his waist and squeezed with all her might.

"Well. . .I. . .Charlotte." He stared at her as he pulled her away from him. "You're the last person I expected to see here."

Charlotte sobered as she gazed at him. Trail life had aged him, yet he looked so good in his rough garb.

"How did you get here?" he asked. "What was Philip thinking, letting you leave Dyea?"

"He blessed my trip and sent Michael with me."

Gabe shook his head. "What for?"

"To find you."

"But. . .why?" Gabe gazed at her beautiful face, tinged red by the wind. Her eyes nearly danced as she looked up at him. She had never looked more lovable, and a fierce need to protect her swelled within him.

"You can't stay here. This trail is much too dangerous for—"

She placed both of her hands on his chest and pushed. He back-stepped out of the tent and away from the shopkeeper's eyes. A determined look settled on her face.

"Gabe Monroe, you brought me to Alaska, and you will see me out. I'm not going anywhere without you."

He felt a grin twitch at his mouth even before his brain could register his thoughts. Her feisty attitude surprised him, but he knew he just loved her all the more.

He crossed his arms in front of his chest. "What will I do with you?"

She shrugged and glanced away, giving the first indication that she might not be so sure of herself.

He reached out just to touch her cheek, but he couldn't stop from pulling her into his arms.

"My dear Lottie." He cradled her head against his chest, and she wrapped her arms around him. "So much has happened to me in the two months on this trail. I discovered all that is really important is that I surrender my stubborn will to God. . . ."

She squeezed him.

"And that I can love again."

She pulled back and gazed up at him. "Truly?"

"For real this time," he whispered as he leaned down to touch her lips with his own.

The touch stirred the embers of his lonely soul to a flame. He clutched her tightly to him. If God put this woman in his life—as only God could—then he would never let her go.

They walked hand in hand through the camp town. Though still bustling with thousands of stampeders, a solemn attitude permeated the atmosphere. The highest risk taking had just been played out in front of them all.

Charlotte leaned into Gabe's arm. "Your partner said you made that climb this morning. Why?"

"Well, I went up before dawn to mark my cache and was at the summit when the avalanche let go. I hiked down the long way." Gabe glanced at her. "You see, I had already decided to sell my outfit. I was labeling it for the buyer, and. . .I was going back to Dyea. . .for you."

She looked up at him through her tears. "I couldn't wait long enough. I had to find you." Heat touched her cheeks.

Gabe threw back his head and laughed. "I love you, Charlotte Vance."

Her heart did a giddy dance, and a smile pushed back her cheeks.

"What's your middle name?" he suddenly asked.

"Uh. . .Ruth."

His laughter rang again through the valley, and people turned to stare.

"Well, Miss Charlotte Ruth." He stopped walking and pulled her around to face him. "I will be your Boaz, if you will be my Ruth."

He had never seemed so happy to her. Seeing him so did more to thrill her soul than the proposal she had for so long pined.

"Gabe, you. . ." How could she be at a loss for words now? "I. . .you are a wonderful man, and I love you so."

She rose on her toes and boldly planted a kiss of promise on his smiling lips. His arms engulfed her as he picked her off her feet and swung her around until they both turned giddy with dizziness.

He set her back on her feet. "What now, my dear?"

"Now?" She reached up to feel his short beard. "Well, my love, I've been wondering what the other side of that mountain looks like. In fact, I was in that store to price outfits. . .just in case I had to pursue you all the way to Dawson—seeing as how I couldn't accept the idea that you could be dead."

Chuckling, Gabe linked arms with her and started them down a grade. "I would have packed you up and taken you with me when I started this trip if I had thought gold country was any place for a lady. Now—though I'd love to see if all the grand tales are true—the real reasons for going don't exist anymore."

He pulled a watch from his pocket, and Charlotte admired the old design.

"It belonged to my father. He sent it to me with a letter that I just got yesterday."

Gabe stared down the valley, and Charlotte waited for him to finish his thoughts.

Finally, he said, "We can head back to Philip's store. Maybe I can help him out for a while, until. . .until I'm sure I'm ready to go home—back to California and the family business."

Charlotte patted his arm. "I'll go anywhere with you, Gabe. . . even to gold country." This hike up the Chilkoot Trail had flared a sense of adventure in her she'd never known she possessed.

"It's not necessary. . . ."

"I heard your grandfather was a gold miner. Don't you want to see what drove him?"

"Sure, that's what started this whole adventure. . .until I mixed in some of my lesser motives."

"Then let's go," she said, having made up her mind.

He looked down into her eyes. "But Philip will likely make more money in his store than I can dredge out of any creek bed."

She shrugged. "Let's just do it for the adventure," she stated, then stopped. "But I don't have an outfit."

Gabe thought awhile, then said, "Davies died in the slide. He didn't have a wife or anything. We'll use his supplies and mail his folks a fair price."

He put his arm around her shoulders and pulled her tight. "I'm not forgetting the risk we would be taking by continuing the trail. And it's a shame that kid had to die when his dreams were so strong."

"We can't know why things happen the way they do, but I'm so thankful God spared you."

They strolled along for a while, then Gabe said, "Now about the marriage business. Don't you think you've waited long enough to become a Monroe?"

Charlotte laughed. "Long enough to be sure I marry the right man."

He gazed lovingly down at her. "Think there might be a reverend in this unusual town?"

"We'll find one." Charlotte smiled broadly.

∞

Four days later, on April 7, 1898, Gabriel Black Monroe married Charlotte Ruth Vance on the summit of the Chilkoot Trail. The wind whipped at the little customs shack where a small party huddled together for the occasion. At first word of the upcoming wedding, Michael had returned to Dyea so Philip could make a quick trip up the trail to stand as his brother's witness.

As Gabe made his vows to her, Charlotte knew she had never felt so cool on the outside while so warm and content on the inside. She relaxed against the arm of the man she looked forward to being with for the rest of her life—a life full of promise.

Rebecca Germany considers herself an old-fashioned kind of girl who loves old-fashioned kinds of romance. She was hooked from a young age, and it was a natural progression when she chose to devote her life's work to books and writing. Heartsong Presents inspirational romance series and book club started in October 1992. Rebecca joined the Heartsong team exactly one year later and was named managing editor in 1995 and senior fiction editor in 2002. She has written several things, and her first work of fiction was a novella published in a collection from Barbour Publishing. She now has five novellas in print along with a few compiled gift books. Single, but contentedly enjoying life on the old family farm, "Becky" has several hobbies (like reading, singing, gardening, crafts, quilting, and so on) to keep her very busy.

Band of Angel's

by Cathy Marie Hake

Dedication

To Deb.
We went to countless museums and libraries,
toured a mine, and even panned for gold.
The real treasure of it all has been your friendship.

Acknowledgments

I'd like to thank Knott's Berry Farm in Buena Park, California, and Bill Jones at the Old Hundred Gold Mine in Silverton, Colorado. They generously provided guidance, information, and encouragement as I researched prospecting.

Chapter 1

Colorado, 1893

Gold!

Jarrod McLeod stared at his pan in disbelief. The very first time he'd slipped his pan in the creek, and he'd struck gold. Oh, this was no fool's gold. Then again, it wasn't a nugget or a few bright flakes. There, gleaming in his rusty, secondhand pan, was a small wedding band.

"Well, now I'll be!" he marveled aloud as he gently brushed away some silt and pinched the woman's ring between his fingers. He set aside the pan, carefully rinsed the ring in the icy stream, and squinted to take a closer look at the treasure. Plain it was—a wee bit lopsided from having been on the owner's finger for many a year. Sun glinted off the smooth surface of the band, making it sparkle all the more.

He read the inscription inside. "AW & JM."

A mule brayed behind him. Jarrod carefully tucked the ring into his shirt pocket, rose, and headed toward the beast. "You'll have to be forgiving me, Beulah. Prospecting fever, don't you know. A man stakes a claim, and he loses most of his sense."

The mule twitched her ears and danced to the side. The pack on her back held half of Jarrod's earthly goods. He quickly loosened a rope and relieved her of the burden. She waited as he unloaded Otto, and both mules plodded across the hard spring ground to the stream. After they drank their fill, Jarrod secured them to a line he tied between two sturdy pines. "You beasts behave yourselves, and I'll be giving you a carrot for supper."

The bundles on the ground made for a goodly sized mess. Jarrod toed one bundle out of his way and looked about his new home. After spending the last six hours trying to locate the right claim and dealing with prospectors who thought he was a claim jumper, he had little patience for sorting through his gear, but grit and a dream kept him going. Determination would get him through the next several months. Once he coaxed enough gold dust from the claim, he'd head off and buy himself a pretty little start-up ranch. Yes, a nifty place where a man could put down roots, work his back sore and his hands raw, and smile every last minute while doing it.

A means to an end. This plot along the creek was nothing more than a means to achieve his dream. With that thought in mind, the pickax, shovel, and pans looked mighty fine. He'd work himself morning, noon, and night. No foolishness, either—he'd seen his share of men drink away their hard work or get cheated out of it at a card table. Lonely miners and placers went to town and consorted with shady women or paid unheard of sums for a decent meal. Well, not Jarrod McLeod.

He'd walked the length of the creek bank first thing. Quartz rock along it hinted that the area held gold. So did the fine-grained black sand. An occasional greenish streak in the boulders spoke of copper—another good sign since he'd read copper and quartz often lay alongside gold. Hard work and a lot of prayer, and this claim might well yield enough to put him back in a saddle.

The saddest-looking lean-to a man ever threw together sat over on the west side of the camp. Jarrod scowled at it and muttered, "Looks like the keys on a burned harpsichord." The old fellow who sold this claim to him had boasted it held a solid structure. Solid? Ha. Two logs stuck out of the ground and stood just over four feet tall. Lashed between them was a single, thick, six-foot stick. The whole affair sagged under the weight of about two-dozen logs that sloped against it to form the one and only wall. A stiff gust would probably blast apart the pathetic pile.

The air smelled like rain, so Jarrod didn't spend time moaning. He'd not be able to take shelter under that—he'd best put his hand to fixing up something habitable. He stalked over to the lean-to's wall and gave the closest edge a few brutal kicks. Spiders and beetles scuttled away as three of the logs rolled and thudded into the dirt. The other logs jumped to and fro, completely unsecured to the rickety frame.

He stood back and looked at the mess, then felt the wind pick up. Another glance at the sky let him know he had just a few hours of light left, and the rain might well come before dark. "I'd best get down to business if I want to stay dry."

Jarrod tore it all apart, leveled the ground, and cut down two lodgepole pines. By notching and stacking the new logs and adding them to the ones from the lean-to, he built a tiny, three-sided hut. He made the side walls shorter, but the seven-foot-long back wall allowed him to lie full length and stack his viands in a place that ought to stay dry. So far, the dwelling—such as it was—barely measured four feet high. Jail cells measured bigger. He'd run out of light and logs, though.

Jarrod hastily draped canvas over a pole he stuck in the center of the floor and weighted it outside the walls with handy rocks as the first raindrops fell. He strode off a few paces to take a quick look at the results of his labor. His "cabin" didn't look like a jail cell anymore: it looked more like the circus tent he'd seen back East.

Back sore and hands blistered, Jarrod sat beneath his newly constructed shelter. Rain pattered off the canvas and slid outside the cabin. He warmed his hands around a cup of scorched coffee and stared at the flickering lamp. Other men might find it odd that a wee chain of daisies danced about the globe, but Ella had loved that lamp, and it was all he had left of her other than his memories. She'd shared his dream of the ranch, and he wanted to put her lamp on the kitchen table someday in her honor. Until then, with Ella's memory in his heart and God in his soul, he counted himself a rich man.

∽

Angel Taylor stood by the boiling pot and shaved one more curl of homemade lye soap into the water. She shoved four shirts into the water, thrust in a wooden paddle, and agitated the smelly contents of the cauldron. A few more pokes, and she set down the paddle. Mud caked the pile of britches at her side. She dragged them down to the river, rinsed the worst of the dirt from them, leaned over her corrugated washboard, and scrubbed stubborn dark spots on the seat and knees of each pair.

"I'm hungry, girl. What're you fixin' to do? Starve me half to death?"

Angel gritted her teeth to keep from snapping back at her stepfather. Not once had he asked how Mama was faring. Her cot had creaked all night because of her racking cough. Nothing Angel did seemed to lessen Mama's misery, but Ben's callous disregard certainly made it worse. At least he'd caught fish this morning, so they'd have something more than rice and beans to eat.

"Girl, I asked you 'bout dinner!" His pan clanged on the rocky ground as he tossed it down.

"Rice is boiling. Soon as I rinse out the shirts and hang them to dry, I'll fry up the trout."

"Shoulda seen to my meal afore you got them shirts started."

Wiping back a damp curl that fell on her forehead, she called, "It won't be long."

Half an hour later, several garments hung on the clothesline, and Angel handed a pie tin of rice and fish to her stepfather. If she changed into her other skirt, this one would have enough time to dry by nightfall; but she dismissed that fleeting thought. She refused to risk waking Mama by slipping into the tent. Besides, as soon as lunch was over, Angel would be knee deep in the water again. Days like today, she felt sure she'd never be warm again.

"Ten shirts, six pair of britches, and five balbriggans." Her stepfather spoke with his mouth full and pointed his fork at the laundry neighboring prospectors dropped off. "I reckon that'll barely keep us in beans and coffee for a week or so. Ain't you got a couple of flour sacks you can stitch into a shirt to sell? That'll give us some fatback."

They'd had this conversation two weeks ago. Angel's jaw hardened. "I need one more sack so I can make myself a new skirt. I only have two, and they're both ragged."

"Nobody here to see and court you. A new skirt's a waste. A man's shirt—well. . ." He drew out the word with relish. "A shirt, that could bring in enough to make a real difference 'round here. Gotta pull together, Angel. We're family."

"This wouldn't be a problem if you'd have grubstaked us for the winter."

"I ain't begging others for food, and I won't be beholden to any man."

Angel tugged at her wet sleeve. "Since today is the third day in a row that I've done laundry, we have money. You could take it to town and get Mama medicine. She needs tonic and a cough elixir, and we need—"

"Enough!" He stood and stomped toward the river.

Angel sand-scoured and rinsed the plates. The wind shifted, and she caught a faint whiff of coffee from a neighboring claim. The scent made her mouth water. She remembered how she used to have parties with Mama and Grandma where they'd set the table with fine linen and china. As a treat, they'd allow her to have coffee with plenty of cream and sugar. When she'd come to Colorado with Mama and Ben, she'd learned to drink it black. The next year, she'd watered it down to stretch their meager supplies. This past winter, they'd run out.

During the winter, folks didn't have laundry done—they wore every last garment they owned in an attempt to stay warm. As a result, her stepfather had run out of money, and they were perilously low on supplies. Now that spring had arrived and she was doing laundry again, it stood to reason they could spare some money for Mama's medicine.

Harvey Bestler and Pete Kane came back for their laundry. Pete paid her stepfather the laundry fee and wandered off. Harv went on into the tent, took off his only other pair of britches, and tossed them out. "Go on ahead and scrub those today. I'll just take 'em wet and hang 'em from a tree."

"I'd better not." Angel bit her lip and looked away. "The britches on the line need mending."

"I can wait."

She scrubbed the grimy pants and rinsed them, then hung them close to the fire in hopes that they'd dry a little while she mended the others. Her sewing box already sat on a stump because she'd had to stitch on a button. She sat down and applied her needle to the threadbare pants. As she jabbed the needle into the fabric, she promised herself, "I'm only staying to take care of Mama. I don't have to stay after. . ."

Chapter 2

"Angel, I've spent half the day here and given you good cash money. Now give me back my pants."

Jarrod heard the baritone from inside one of the two tents and turned to leave. He wanted nothing to do with a shady lady or her customer. The dainty wedding ring in his pocket couldn't possibly belong to this woman, whoever she was.

"A man's always glad to keep company with a pretty gal like you, but I really do got to go. A fella's gotta work."

"Here you go," a sweet voice said. "They're mended, but I don't expect that patch to hold for long. Next time you're in town, you'd better get some cloth. I'll stitch you a new pair for cheaper than you can buy them."

Jarrod stopped in his tracks. Guilt rushed through him. Maybe he'd been wrong in his assumptions, and if so, he'd been wrong to judge and condemn the woman. He tromped back around the stream side of the camp and spied several garments fluttering on a clothesline. From the variety in size, he deduced she did laundry as well as sewing. Yes, he'd been wrong. It was a good reminder not to judge.

Jarrod glanced around. The campsite rated as Spartan as his own. Two sun-bleached canvas tents sagged near a stand of trees—undoubtedly located there in hopes that they would provide a windbreak. An outdoor cook fire seemed to also double as the laundry site. Stumps served as seats, yet not a single felled tree lay about or formed a structure. They must have used the rest of the wood for fuel. They were panning at the creek side instead of using a rocker box. Perhaps these folks were new arrivals too. If so, this woman was quite enterprising to start up a business right away.

Jarrod patted his pocket and determined to see if this was the ring's owner. She'd probably be delighted to have it back. Women put stock in sentimental things like that.

"You need help, mister?"

Jarrod turned around and froze. An unkempt man stood all of four feet away, and he had the business end of a rifle aimed right at Jarrod.

"Just what're you doin', skulking around here?"

"I'm, um. . ." Jarrod cleared his throat. "I'm your new neighbor. I have the adjoining claim. Downstream."

"You take me for a fool? Pete Kane was here today already, and Charlie has the claim just beside us on this side of the creek. We don't want no trouble, and we don't cotton to claim jumpers, so you can just hike right back outta here."

"Hang on, Ben." A man came out of the tent, adjusting his suspenders. "Charlie told me he was cashing in. Could be this man's not trying anything fast."

"I have the deed." Jarrod didn't move an inch. Hostility shimmered in the eyes of the man holding the gun, and he hadn't lowered the weapon.

"Father," a pretty blond woman said as she rounded the tent and stopped next to the grouch. She cast a quick glance at Jarrod and pushed the barrel of the rifle toward the ground. "He's not armed."

"Could have a gun back behind his belt." The rifle jerked back upward, its aim directed at Jarrod's midsection. "Might be he has a knife strapped to his leg."

"A fella would be ten times a fool to go 'bout unarmed," the man from beside the tent agreed.

"So he's either a claim jumper or a fool. Some fine howdy you men give to a new neighbor." The tiny woman stepped directly in front of the weapon. "I'm Angel Taylor. Behind me is my step-father, Ben Frisk, and over by the tent is Harv Bestler. Sorry for the poor welcome. Folks here tend to shoot first and ask questions later—if they bother to ask at all."

Jarrod gave her a grateful smile and dipped his head in greeting. "Jarrod McLeod. It's a pure pleasure to be meeting you, Miss Taylor." He didn't lie and say he was glad to meet the two men. Neither seemed the neighborly type. "I came as far as the pine with my weapon but left it there as a sign of goodwill."

Harvey rose on the toes of his battered boots and craned his neck. "I don't see nuth—what in the world? A bow? You sound funny, but you don't look like no redskin I ever saw."

"You in league with them?" Ben asked. "We got these claims legal. You ain't takin'—"

"Now hold on. I'm a placer, just like the both of you. Bought my claim, aim to work it, and hope to make a go of things."

While he spoke, Jarrod noticed how Angel's jaw hardened. He didn't know what he'd said wrong, but he'd stepped amiss again. These folks were bristly as hedgehogs.

He shrugged. "I can see you folks are trying to settle in too."

"We been here three, almost four years now." Ben finally took his finger off the trigger.

Jarrod tried not to show his surprise. Other than the tents, no shelter could be seen. "So you're seasoned placers. It's good to have neighbors who know the ropes."

"Wasted 'nuff time jawin'." Ben swished his hand in the air as if he were swatting a bothersome gnat. "Git along."

Harv slapped a battered gray felt hat on his greasy hair, picked up a small bundle of clothes, and nodded at Angel. "You done a fine job, gal." He then tromped straight across the creek and into a tiny shack that leaned precariously toward one side.

Jarrod jammed his hand in his pocket and felt the smooth gold ring. He didn't want to waste a lot of time tracking down the owner, but he'd worn out his nonexistent welcome.

Ask. Just ask, a small voice inside urged.

He cleared his throat. "Um, I was wondering if you could be so kind as to tell me—are there other women upriver?"

Angel's cheeks went scarlet.

Horrified that she'd misconstrued his meaning, Jarrod yanked the ring from his pocket and held it out. "I found this. I'm wanting to return it to its rightful owner. I'm sure the lady is heartbroken at the loss."

For a brief instant, unmistakable recognition lit Angel's eyes. In a spontaneous move of joy, she began to reach for the ring, but Ben's growl halted her move. Every speck of color bled from Angel's face. Jarrod watched her flinch and immediately shoved the ring deep into his pocket. "If you hear anything, please let me know."

Ben turned to Angel. "Is that what I think it is?"

"I'm sure hundreds of women wear wedding bands just like it." Jarrod realized he'd managed to get the woman into trouble and strove to say something to let her off the hook.

Angel's stepfather wheeled back around and blustered, "Lemme see that ring."

Jarrod noticed how she folded her arms around her ribs and subtly shook her head. Her wide hazel eyes pleaded with him. He didn't understand what was going on, but he refused to act against the lady's wishes.

When Jarrod didn't hand over the ring, Ben Frisk banged the butt of his rifle into the ground in a show of rage. "Girl, that was worth money. Coulda had us coffee all winter if I'd pawned it."

"Miss Angel, if you're the rightful owner, I'm more than willing to return it."

"She's the owner, all right! Letters scraped inside it'll prove I'm right."

Angel shook her head. "It's not mine anymore. I don't want it."

"If you change your mind—"

"Oh, she's a-changin' it right this very minute!"

Angel shook her head again. Sunlight glinted off the strands of her hair, making her glimmer. "Mr. McLeod has rightful claim on that gold. Whatever a man finds on his claim is his."

Chapter 3

"Gal, yore stupid as you are stubborn."

Angel ducked her head and scrubbed the frying pan a little harder. Ever since her grandma's wedding band had come loose from where Angel tacked it to the hem of her ragged skirt, she'd been heartbroken. It took everything inside of her not to take it back when that new neighbor offered it to her—but the minute her stepfather found out she'd gotten it back, he'd take and pawn it.

Ben had been in a terrible mood since she refused to take back the ring. Three days of listening to his grumblings and rants left her nerves as tightly strung as a new clothesline. He cared more about gold than anything or anyone. Lung fever had hold of Mama; gold fever claimed Ben.

"Coulda had a nice hunk of fatback and coffee for weeks, but you ruint it all. Got yourself of a mind to have a conniption. I'm a-tellin' you, missy, yore gonna use them flour sacks to make a shirt. After what you done, you don't deserve no new skirt. Took the food right outta my mouth."

"I'm not making a shirt." She stared him straight in the eye. Standing, she spread out her skirt. "Take a good look. I've patched this as best I can, but the hem's ragged and it has dozens of little burned spots from embers. My other one is even worse."

"Ain't no fancy cotillion here. You got what you need."

"No, I don't. With Mama's help, we barely got everything

done and pulled in enough gold to keep going. She listened to your dream about striking it rich and said a woman had to follow her man. Well, look what your big plans did to her—she's deathly ill." She swept her hand toward the tent, then gestured toward the creek in utter disgust. "Instead of thinking about how to help her recover, all you can do is squat over there, lusting for more gold."

"Enough!" He bolted to his feet. "Your mama knows her place. Good thing she's not out here to see how yore behavin'." He snatched his hat off a stump, spanked it against a thigh, and slapped it on his head.

Tears obscured Angel's view of her stepfather's back as he knelt and began to pan for gold. "How could you say such a terrible thing?" she whispered. "If you loved her, how could you think it's a good thing she's so sick she can't even get up anymore?"

Smoke from the cook fire blew into her face, causing the tears to overflow. Angel didn't want her stepfather to witness her tears, so she plodded to the water's edge. She favored this spot because she could turn her back to her stepfather and let the wind blow his mutterings the other direction. A few deep breaths and a swipe of her hand, and all evidence of her teary moment was gone.

An eddy of water swirled into the tiny curve of the shore, and she plunged her pan into it. No matter how often she did this, the icy water came as a shock. Angel shivered as she agitated the pan. Neck, back, arms, and legs all cramped from working to coax anything of value from the creek. The weak spring sun rose higher in the sky, and she shifted a bit to lessen the glare from the water.

"Miss Taylor, you make doing that look easy."

Angel twisted to the side as she gasped.

"I didn't mean to startle you," Mr. McLeod said in his rich Scots burr. He gave her a rakish smile. "If you're of a mind to forgive the intrusion, I was hoping we might come to an agreement."

Angel set aside her pan, carefully covering the tiny dish containing the flecks she'd gotten during the long morning. A quiver full of arrows over his right shoulder reminded her of one of the tales Mama used to tell her. . .*Robin Hood*, she remembered. The brace of rabbits he held made her stomach rumble in the most unladylike way. "What kind of agreement?"

"Whilst building my shack, I ripped the knee on my britches. If you have a dozen nails, I could surely use them too."

"You've built a home?"

He chuckled. "Home is a fancy description. 'Tis a wee place, but it'll serve."

"I heard your ax biting through logs, but I presumed Charlie didn't leave any firewood."

Bootfalls announced they had company. Her stepfather came up, put a proprietary hand on her shoulder, and scowled. "What do you want?"

Mr. McLeod casually repositioned the beautiful bow on his shoulder. "I came to barter. I'd like Miss Taylor to mend the knee of my britches and would appreciate a dozen or so nails from you."

Ben squeezed her shoulder, telling her to stay silent. "Nails? They're dear out here."

Mr. McLeod nodded. "In town, they were seven cents a pound."

"It'll waste half a day, you going to town and comin' back. Even if I figgered two cents apiece on those four rabbits, you ain't got enough to trade for the nails and my gal doing your mending."

Angel choked back a cry and plastered a smile on her face. She wriggled away from her stepfather and clasped her hands behind her back. "But those look to be plump rabbits—especially for it being spring. Besides, Mr. McLeod isn't just anybody; he's our nearest neighbor. I think three rabbits, and we've struck a fair bargain."

"Four," Ben rasped angrily.

"Four," Angel repeated as she stepped forward and reached for the rabbits. "And Mr. McLeod joins us for supper."

Mr. McLeod's bright blue eyes twinkled. "Now there's a bargain made in paradise."

⁓

Jarrod hiked back over for supper after sunset. Ben had made it clear he wasn't about to waste any daylight with socializing. How pretty Miss Taylor managed to endure her stepfather's sour disposition rated as a true mystery. In the past few days, Ben's strident voice had carried in the crisp air, and most of what he said revolved around wanting meat and coffee. *And I made it worse by letting him know she lost that gold ring.*

Jarrod marveled at the fact that they were out of such essential supplies. Miners got paid an hourly wage; placers who panned their own claims didn't have reliable income, so they usually got the mercantile owner or a townie to grubstake them. He'd had two offers from business owners, and the man at the land office even offered the names of a few more. Though no one seemed to become rich overnight along this creek, the claims produced enough to keep merchants interested in a cut of the take.

Savory aromas wafted past him. So did the sound of someone coughing. Jarrod called ahead to keep Ben from grabbing his rifle. "Oh, something's smelling wonderful!"

"Pull up a stump," Angel invited as she stepped out of one of the tents. She held a spoon and tin mug. "Supper will be ready in just a few minutes."

"Go dip your mug in the creek, McLeod," Ben mumbled. "Ain't got nothing better or stronger to drink."

Jarrod collected the three mugs by the fire and filled them with bracingly cold water. He paused for a moment on the way back, then handed one to Ben. "Looks like you're starting a garden."

"Angel's messin' with it." He snagged the first plate Angel dished up.

Angel's cheeks went a beguiling scarlet as she gave Jarrod an apologetic look. He continued to stand until Angel had food on both of the other tin plates. "You're a clever lass to be gardening, Miss Taylor. Why, canned vegetables and fruits were higher than ten cats' backs. I bought me some seeds, hopin' to come up wi' sufficient to keep my slats apart."

She tried to give him his plate, but he still held a cup in each hand. Jarrod chortled as he turned his palm upward and held both cups in that one hand. "There, then. I think we can make a go of this."

Once Angel sat on an overturned crate, Jarrod perched on the tree stump and smiled at her. She lowered her lashes in an innately modest reaction, but it wasn't for prayer, because she grabbed her fork. Ben was already eating, so Jarrod came to the realization that they didn't bless their food. He quietly bowed his head and said a silent grace.

"These are the first dandelion greens for the year," he said in appreciation.

" 'Bout time we had something different." Ben scooped up a forkful of food. "Sick of eating this rice."

"To my way of thinkin', rice always tastes good—but this gravy on it makes it better still." Jarrod helped himself to another bite. "Looks like you used some kind of herbs on the rabbit."

"I had a little basil and rosemary dried from last year."

"The mercantile owner's wife insisted I take a packet of herbs," Jarrod said. "Only thing I know to do is use cayenne to keep animals from digging into the garden or henhouse."

"I could give you a few pointers on what herbs are suited to different things," Angel offered.

"I'd be much obliged. I figure since my cabin's finished, I'll pan for a few days, then put in the garden."

Angel leaned forward. "Did you hear that, Father?" Her voice sounded a bit strained. "Mr. McLeod has already built himself a fine little log cabin. It'll be so warm and safe."

"I tole you afore, no use wastin' time on those projects when we got us our tents."

Jarrod looked at the pair of tents. The canvas looked old and tired. He seriously doubted it could last through the sun and snow of another year without rotting clean through. "I'd be willing to spend a day or two to help you. If we gathered a few other men, we could have a wee place—"

"Not interested," Ben interrupted. "Satisfied with how things stand."

"Well I'm not." Angel clenched her hands in her lap. "Mama needs better shelter, and I don't want to be cold and hungry anymore."

"You ain't cold. You already changed into your dry skirt. Got plenty of blankets, don't you?"

Jarrod gave her a startled look. "Your mother is here?"

Angel stared at Jarrod pleadingly. "She's sick—terribly sick—and needs decent shelter. What could I trade you? I'll sew for you. I'll do your laundry forever—"

Ben raised his hand. "Hold on here. You git paid for them chores so's we can buy vittles. Cain't go givin' away valu'ble work."

"I'm making a fair barter."

Jarrod frowned. "I shouldn't think it would cause discord for me to lend a hand so your wife has decent lodging."

"It's been a sore point between us since the day we arrived," Angel said. "I'm sorry you're having to hear this—"

"You ain't sorry atall. You're stirrin' the pot so's it'll boil over and you can git what you want."

"I'm trying to make a fair trade so I can get what Mama

needs." Angel turned back to Jarrod. "Please—just tell me what you think would be fair."

Ben lifted the piece of rabbit and bit off a huge mouthful. His glower could start a bonfire. "Go ahead. Me? I don't need nothin' other than what I got. Build them somethin'. Mebbe then she'll quit her whining."

Chapter 4

"Ach! Now will you be lookin' at what I did?" Jarrod lifted his right arm and stuck his left forefinger through the rip in his sleeve.

Angel walked over toward the home he'd been working on alone. Never once had her stepfather offered a hand. Every log felled, notched, lifted, and fitted testified to Jarrod's kindness. Her father insisted he'd never step foot in such a folly and demanded it only be big enough for a bed for Mama and her. She'd agreed—all they needed was a warm place to lay their heads. Jarrod insisted that cutting the logs two or three feet shorter wouldn't save him any labor, so what she'd thought would be a bitty shack was turning out to be a sound little cabin.

Jarrod's callused finger wiggled through the ripped fabric. "I did a royal job of tearing this to kingdom come."

"It's not so bad." Angel inspected the damage. "Just a bit of stitching, and it'll be serviceable for a long time yet."

"Easy for you to say such a thing. You've needles, thread, and talent aplenty. Me? I'm beggared on all three accounts."

"It's my cabin you're making; it's only right I repair your shirt. I'll have it done in a trice."

"Nae, lass. We already struck a fair bargain for my labor."

She whispered emphatically, "It's far more than we agreed upon. I was to have a roof over Mama's head, and you're making me a—a—a rainbow!"

He chuckled. "If 'tis a rainbow, the both of you'll be swimming inside at the first rain if I don't get that roof on it." He pulled his finger out of the hole and moved the arm with the torn sleeve behind his back. "You'll not take a single stitch unless we come to an understanding. Just as your stepfather refuses to be beholden, so do I."

"Piffle! It's nothing!"

He pulled away and gave her an indignant look. "Angel, you need to value yourself and your work. God created a wonderful, talented lass in you. Modesty is a fine quality, but denying the value of one of His gems is pure silliness."

Angel looked up at him and felt an odd glow. How long had it been since anyone told her she was special? Long ago. . . back before her stepfather moved them here. Her cousins, Philip and Gabe, for all of their teasing, still treated her like a princess. When the day came for her to depart, each of them had managed to pull her away for a moment and say something dear to her. In the everyday scramble and hardship of settling and surviving here, the niceties of compliments disappeared.

Niceties. That was it. Jarrod McLeod managed to bring a touch of gentleness and decency along with him. His rich burr made each word sound important and sincere. Oh, and how he spoke! He'd gone in to meet Mama, and never once did his kind face reflect dismay or disgust at how sallow and frail she was. The big man no more than reached Mama's cot, and he'd gone down on his knees instead of towering over her. He'd paid his respects as if she were an important lady and the tattered tent were a fine mansion. He'd murmured quietly, given Mama a few sweet moments of pleasant company, then held up her head and given her a sip of broth. Touched to the core of her being at his incredible kindness, Angel barely managed to choke back her tears when he tucked the blankets up as if Mama were his very own.

Better still, each time he came over, he paid Mama a short visit. Ben refused to allow any Bible reading, but Jarrod got around that by quietly reciting a few verses he'd memorized, then he'd whisper a brief prayer that invariably left a smile on Mama's face.

Now. . .now he stood here, smiling at Angel and calling her a gem. She'd thought God had forgotten about her. In all of the ugliness of the past years, she'd let her spirits sink. Her relationship with the Almighty had practically dwindled away to nothingness. But here Jarrod stood, calling her a gem of God.

"I'm not a gem," she blurted out. "Mama and I sometimes pray together, but I don't think God even listens to us anymore." She hung her head and wished she hadn't ruined everything with that confession.

"Lass, our heavenly Father hears you." Soft as a breeze, Jarrod's voice reached her, but underneath the quiet tone was rock-solid certainty. "His children aren't spared hardship, but He stands beside them in their trials. Your faith might have withered a bit on the vine, but a bit of tending, and it'll flourish."

"I wish I had your faith."

"Faith is for sharing." He tilted her face up to his. The kindness in his eyes sparked something deep inside. "I'll gladly share mine with you."

The rip in his sleeve caught her attention again. "Then I'll share my needle with you."

Jarrod's brow furrowed and his eyes narrowed as he gave consideration to the matter. Suddenly his eyes brightened and he gave her a cocky grin. "I have it."

"What do you have?" *Oh, why did I ask? I wanted to mend his shirt as a favor—not for gain.*

"Well now, I'm hoping you'll not be offended by my paltry offer. Seeing as you're restoring wear to my shirt, what if I barter a used skirt for it?"

"A skirt?" What was he doing with a skirt? The very question made her cringe. She'd simply assumed he was alone and unmarried. Could he have a wife waiting for him somewhere?

"My Ella, God bless her soul, was sick a good long while. After she passed on, I just bundled her clothes up."

"I'm so sorry for your loss." *No wonder he's so good with Mama even though she's ailing.* "How long were you married?"

"Married?" He chuckled. "Oh, no. Ella was my sister. We had grand plans to start up a ranch."

"Then why are you prospecting instead?"

His face went pensive. "After payin' the doctor's fees, my pockets were pretty nigh unto empty. I'm not going to spend my whole life standing knee-deep in chilly water, Angel. My dream hasna changed one iota. I'll stay here only 'til I have enough to buy me a sweet plot of land."

"Plenty of men say that, but then they succumb to gold fever."

He positioned another nail, then hammered it in place with a single, solid whack. "The forefathers of this fine country might hae said all men were created equal, Angel, but that doesna mean they were all created the same. Money isn't wealth. It canna buy love or happiness or health."

She stared at him in silence as he worked.

"So?" He turned and looked at her. "Are you willing to accept the barter of a skirt? I've three shirts, and I canna afford to lose this one. Sure as the sun rises and the river flows, this rip will race all the way up my poor sleeve. I need the shirt; I certainly dinna have any use for a skirt!"

"Oh Mr. McLeod, I'm sure you could barter it for more than getting a small tear sewn back up."

His brows veed. "Miss Angel, you're the only lady hereabouts—excepting your mama, of course. I dinna know a single man who can sew worth sneezing at. Seems to me, since you're the only one who could barter for the skirt, you can set the price to suit your fancy, and I'd not complain a bit."

"Mr. McLeod, I don't believe I have yet to hear a single

complaint come out of you."

He shrugged. "God provides what I need. I've a roof o'er my head, clothes on my back, and my daily bread." He flashed her a smile that made her heart do an odd flip-flop. "And on top of all of those blessings, you're makin' that bread, and that means I see a beautiful woman each day."

"Flatterer." She knew from the heat that flashed from her bosom to her hair that she must be three shades of scarlet.

"Nae, lass. 'Tis the honest truth. A fact is a fact, e'en when the telling may cause a comely blush. Now tell me, where are you wanting me to set a wee window in this place?"

She blinked at him in surprise. "A window? I've no glass!"

"We can still make do, if you want. I'd just grease paper to fill the hole—it'll let in light and air on fair weather days, and I'll make a tight-fitting set of shutters to hold out the cold of winter."

Her stepfather stomped up. His scowl could scare away a bank of thunderclouds. "Just because he's here is no excuse for you to slack off. Get on down there and pan."

"But you said I could work on the garden today!"

"That was 'fore you wasted the whole mornin' simpering around this fool. We're gonna go hungry, and he'll not have a single grain of gold in his pouch if I leave you two together."

Angel whirled about and ran to the bank of the creek. Tears blurred her vision as she dipped her pan. Water and silt slopped over the edge as she gave the pan a savage jerk. *Thanks to that dreadful man, Mama and I have gone without a roof, wear rags, and skimp on food. Did he have to humiliate me too?*

∽

Lord, give me wisdom. I want to slug this man into next year for treating the lass that way.

"The fault was mine. I ripped my sleeve and—"

"She don't work for free." Ben glowered at the tear and a spark of greed lit his eyes. "She stitches that up, and you pay."

"I agree. We came to a fair price."

"Since when did you have my permission to conduct business with her?"

"You told us to come to an agreement about me building the cabin." Jarrod slapped the nearest log with the flat of his hand twice. "You can see I've been a man of my word."

"It's taken you long enough. Whole thing's foolish. We done just fine without no cabin. Dumb thing's takin' up timber I'm gonna need, come winter; and Angel's wastin' half her time, tryin' to fix up fancy vittles since you're eatin' with us. She ain't gotten that garden patch planted and ain't panning as much. I can't do all the work myself. We're gonna go hungry. All 'cuz of this. . ." He angrily waved his hand toward the cabin. "This dumb thing."

The man's a selfish lout. He's not caring for his dear wife as he vowed he'd do. He expects that poor lass to launder and garden and pan, but he won't even put a roof over their heads or give Angel a length of cloth for a skirt. Jarrod straightened his shoulders and clenched his hands into angry fists. He couldn't abide any man mistreating a woman. Then again, if he took out his temper on Angel's stepfather, there was always the possibility that Ben would turn on them when Jarrod was gone.

Turn the other cheek, my son. Walk the extra mile.

Jarrod slowly relaxed his shoulders and uncurled his fists. "I'd not want to have my help turn into a hardship. I'll turn o'er the rest of the gardening plot for you."

Spluttering in surprise, Ben backed up a step and quickly recovered. Tugging at the hem of his sleeve, he grumbled, "That makes us just about square."

As Angel's stepfather walked back to the stream, Jarrod turned back to work. *I've given my word, and I'll keep it, Lord. Give me patience and let me be a good witness. But God? I need to be working my own claim. I know I just told Angel that money isn't everything, and Thou knowest every word I spoke was sincere. But I'm never going to get enough gold to buy my ranch if I let Ben badger me into doing everything here.*

He glanced over his shoulder at Angel. Sunlight glinted off her tawny hair. *Father, I'd be thinkin' she's the real treasure here, and just about any man would be proud to take her to wife. I'm not any man; I'm Thy son. I'd spoil my witness by romancing her heart for myself instead of tending her spirit for Thee. Let me be a light to her and Ben, but don't let me forsake wisdom because I let my heart run away.*

Chapter 5

"Ready?" Jarrod's eyes sparkled as he gently scooped Mama into his arms.

"Mama, just wait and see." Angel hurriedly folded up Mama's cot and rushed out of the tent. A stone's throw away, the new cabin promised sound shelter, and she hastily set the cot in the back corner where it would be warmest and the sunlight could shine through the window to give Mama brighter days.

Jarrod followed along. Cradling Mama as if she were his very own mother, he murmured, "Here you are, now."

Mama rested her head on his shoulder and managed to whisper, "Oh, thank you, Mr. McLeod. God bless you." Those few words started her coughing and stole her energy.

"You're more than welcome, and God does bless me." He turned sideways to fit Mama into the doorway without bumping her and chuckled. "I've never carried a woman over a threshold before. I'm supposing you'd best start calling me by my given name."

Angel wanted to thank Jarrod again, but as soon as he settled Mama on her cot, he headed back to work his own claim. Maybe that was for the best. She and Mama spent a few moments of peace and joy together, and for the first time in ages, Angel took Mama's hand and said a prayer of thanks.

Ben hadn't bothered to offer his help with anything at all; he snorted and snarled the whole while from his place by the creek.

Bless his heart, Harv Bestler had crossed the creek and helped Jarrod lift the last logs on the walls and put on the roof. Angel didn't know whether to be thankful for the help of her neighbors or angry at her stepfather for his black-hearted ways. Though it didn't seem possible, he grew more surly with each passing day. He'd netted a fish for supper, but if it fed two children, they'd both leave the table hungry. Still, he'd declared he'd done his fair share and caught his own supper. To her mortification, he hadn't just said it, he'd bellowed every last word.

Harv looked across the stream at the little fish. His voice, rich with sarcasm, boomed back from the other side of the creek, "Now there's a nice change. I always like to hear good news."

Though Jarrod had gone back to his own claim, she knew he had to hear the selfish, mean-spirited boast too. All of an hour or so later, Jarrod returned. His knees and sleeves were wet, and a few wood shavings freckled his hair. Without saying a word, he set down a rope-handled bucket and left. The two modest-sized trout he'd brought now sizzled in the frying pan.

She crossed the creek and asked Harv to join all of them for supper, but he whispered, "Ask me some night when Jarrod isn't there. He's a fine man—don't get me wrong—but I'd rather you had one or the other of us with you at two suppers than both of us at once. That way, you don't have to get indigestion by eating alone with Ben."

So here she was, holding her new skirt off to the side, careful not to let it drag near the edge of her cook fire. The flames made the russet and gold leaves in the calico print glow, and Angel twirled a damp wisp of hair around her finger, hoping it would stay in a tendril to make her look soft and feminine. She wanted everything to be perfect tonight—as an expression of her deep gratitude.

"Ah, a pretty woman and a pan of fish." Jarrod stepped into the ring of firelight. He wore an endearingly crooked grin. " 'Tis a sight to warm the heart."

Her stepfather snatched the largest fish, dumped it on his tin, and plopped down on a stump. "It's gold I want in my pan."

Jarrod put a small bundle off to the side and sat on what had become the stump he usually used. "How is Mrs. Frisk?"

Her stepfather snorted, so Angel softly said, "I fed her earlier, and she's fallen asleep. She hasn't looked this comfortable in years."

He smiled at her, accepted his supper, then bowed his head for a quiet moment. He always did that—praying before he ate. At first, it seemed so oddly out of place. Soon, Angel expected it and it gave her a bittersweet flood of memories. Back home, Grandpa Monroe always said grace at meals. She scarcely remembered her own father, but one of the memories she held was of him holding her on his lap, his big hands enveloping hers to form a steeple, and the feel of his chest rumbling against her back as he'd pray.

Fork poised over his fish, Jarrod said, "Angel, I'm a mite thirsty. Could I trouble you for a mug of water?"

His request startled her. Jarrod always saw to the minor details for himself. Then again, what kind of hostess was she, expecting a guest to go stoop at the creek and fill his mug—especially since she had no coffee to offer? "I'll be right back with it."

The tin mug went cold at once from the water, and her fingers felt nearly numb in the scant minute it took for her to dip it and return. Angel handed it to Jarrod, then turned and stopped. He'd switched their pie tins and taken the smallest fish for himself. When she sat down, he calmly boned his supper and made an appreciative humming sound.

"What's in the parcel?" her stepfather demanded.

Though guilty of wondering the same thing, Angel wished he'd not be so rude as to ask—especially in that tone.

"A few traditional things." Jarrod finished his last bite and set his tin down on the ground. He lifted the cloth bundle and unknotted the corners. "I had to make a few changes, owing to what's on hand. The Scots usually give bread, wine, salt, and a candle when blessing a new home." He pulled out a small bag of flour. "So you never go hungry."

Angel accepted the flour and mentally calculated it would make bread for three days.

"Being that I dinna imbibe, I have no wine. I gathered some berries, though, in hopes that your life is always sweet."

Angel accepted the bowl and ignored Father's snigger. "We'll enjoy these as dessert tonight."

"Salt, so there's always spice in your life. . .and a candle, so you'll always have light." He gave her a paper twist that felt grainy and an ordinary tallow candle.

Angel looked at the four simple things and felt rich beyond compare. His sincerity in wanting good things for her shone through. He couldn't give her expensive, fancy things, but he gifted her with shelter, a pretty skirt, and blessings for her home. Safe and provided for— she hadn't felt either of those things for so long, yet both feelings flowed over her. Tears blurred her vision.

"Our family tradition is to bless a home with a reading from the Word. I brought my Bible, and I—"

"Put that away." Her stepfather shot to his feet. "You don't, and I'll feed it to the fire."

Jarrod rose and held the black leather book to his chest. He said nothing.

"I'd like a blessing," Angel dared to stand and say.

"Not out of that, you won't." Father pointed at Jarrod's Bible.

The rippling water and night sounds filled the air, but silence still crackled along with the fire. Jarrod finally broke it. "An Irish couple on the ship over gave my sister and me a blessing. 'Tisn't from the Bible, but I think it's fitting. I'll share it, instead."

"Please do." Angel moved a step closer. Why did her step-father have to spoil everything?

Still holding his Bible close to his heart, Jarrod looked over her shoulder at the cabin, then into her eyes. His delicious baritone filled the air. "May God grant you always a sunbeam to warm you, a moonbeam to charm you, and a sheltering angel so nothing can harm you."

"Oh, that is lovely."

"It's pure drivel. Supper's over. Time you left, McLeod. No reason for you to be coming back, either."

Angel watched Jarrod walk away. As he stepped past the illuminating circle the small fire cast and into the shadows, she felt like the only light in her life had been extinguished.

Days and weeks passed. Jarrod spent little time in his cabin. After surveying his claim with a pick and pan, he'd wanted to repair the dilapidated shaker box Charlie left behind. Using the shaker box would be far more effective than kneeling at the bank and panning. Pete Kane came upriver to have Angel do his laundry, and he'd helped Jarrod replace a few parts on the rickety-looking equipment so it worked like a charm. He'd taken a fistful of coffee beans in trade, and Jarrod set to work with the box at once. Afternoons and evenings, he prospected. Mornings, he tried his hand at a bit of gardening.

He'd put in a fair-sized garden, and some of the truck came up beautifully. He'd discovered if he asked Ben about giving or bartering some of it, he'd always be rebuffed. On the other hand, Angel and he managed to deal well. He'd planted more cabbage than he could eat; she traded him for lettuce. She had bush beans by the pint; he had radishes and onions. They'd each planted herbs, carrots, and different varieties of squash. She also had beets, butter beans, cucumbers, and tomatoes. Both gardens suffered from the wild animals' plundering, but Angel had warned him, so Jarrod planted far more than he'd need.

It wasn't long before prospectors would float messages down the creek or walk up it and want to buy or trade. Jarrod learned to give Angel his surplus. She could sell it for him, especially when men came to get laundry done. Most of the men didn't have cash money. They'd either come up with half a pinch of gold dust or something to trade. With winter over, a fair number of them had empty flour or sugar sacks. She'd accept them, then sew shirts from them. He'd never seen a more industrious woman. If she wasn't shaving lye soap into the wash kettle, she was scrubbing things on a washboard, sewing, gardening, or panning for gold.

Even with all of that to do, she cared for her mama with great tenderness. Jarrod slipped Angel some Rumford pocket soup so she could fix broth for her mama on days when she couldn't eat anything else. He'd tried to give her a bit of his Underwood deviled ham to share with her mama after a five-day rainy stretch where hunting and fishing hadn't been possible, but Ben pitched a fit.

Harv Bestler crossed the creek that night. He and Jarrod shared a cup of coffee and conversed in low tones. Harv said, "That God-fearing woman followed her husband here, only to have her health go as sour as Ben's disposition."

"Have things been this bad all along?"

"First year wasn't too bad. It's a hard life, but they managed. Second year, things took a bad turn." After gulping one last mouthful of coffee, Harv confessed, "I offered to send word to Mrs. Frisk's brother to come fetch her and the girl, but Mrs. Frisk feels a woman should stay with her man. She wanted Angel to go, but she was too weak to write; the gal refused to leave her mama, so she wouldn't pen the note and I can't write none."

Jarrod listened somberly. It galled him to think these women had been enduring this at all, but the sheer length of time they'd suffered made it even worse. He let out a deep sigh. "Let's make a pact to keep an eye out for Angel and her mama."

Not many days thereafter, a man slogged up the creek past Jarrod. Even from a few yards away, Jarrod could smell the reek of whiskey on him. Jarrod wasn't about to let things slide any closer toward danger. He grabbed his bow and an ax and hastened through a small break between the bushes separating their claims. Exaggerating his stride until he swaggered a bit, he walked straight up to Ben and announced, "I'm here, so we'd best go ahead and decide where to put that smokehouse we'll be sharing."

Ben gave him a baffled look.

Under his breath, he said, "You're about to have bad company."

Ben pivoted. He sized up the man coming out of the river and reached for the shotgun he always kept at his side. "Don't want strangers here. Be on your way."

"I got hard cash." The stranger craned his neck to look about the site. The tents partially blocked his view of the cabin. When he staggered to the side a bit and spied it, a lecherous smile lit his face. "Heard tell you gotta woman here."

"My daughter's busy." Ben waggled the business end of the shotgun at him. "Now git."

The stranger lazily sat down on the nearest stump. " 'S'okay. I'll wait my turn."

Footsteps sounded from behind them. Jarrod's heart sank. He'd hoped Angel would stay out of sight, but here she stood. Breathlessly, she said, "Jarrod?"

Jarrod shoved Angel behind his back.

"Hoo-ooey! She's got yaller hair." The stranger stood and started to yank one of his suspenders from his shoulder. "Purty thang."

Jarrod stepped forward. He gripped his ax in his right hand and slapped it back into his left hand a few times for emphasis as he growled, "There's no lightskirt here."

"Y'all kin share. I ain't had me a woman—"

"Ben, you wanna shoot him before or after I heft my ax?"

"I'm not patient. I'm givin' him to the count of three to be off my claim, else he's gonna have more holes 'n a harmonica. Nobody comes on my claim without my say-so."

"No use getting all het up." The stranger started to back up toward the creek.

"We'll consider it an honest mistake." Jarrod continued to thump the ax in his palm. "You don't come back, and we'll all forget this."

After the man left, Angel sank onto the ground. "Oh my."

"You're just fine." Ben shot her an impatient look. "No use havin' a fit of the vapors. He's gone."

Angel looked up at Jarrod with huge, frightened eyes.

He smoothed her hair back from her forehead. "I was just talking to Ben about a smokehouse. We ought to put up some meat for the winter, and we could build something right here, along the property line, to share. Why don't we work on that today? You can sit right there and pan by the bank, and we'll be right here by you."

"Smokehouse is a waste of time." Ben spat off to the side.

Angel raised a shaking hand to her throat. "Only because you don't have any ammunition for your rifle."

Chapter 6

"We're going to town tomorrow—the three of us."

The set of Jarrod's jaw made it clear he wasn't going to put up with any refusal. Angel watched as he stared down her stepfather.

Finally Ben kicked the ground. "I was already plannin' to go. If you wanna, you can tag along."

"Good. Be ready by sunup."

"But my mama—"

"I'll ask Harv Bestler to keep an eye on her for the day."

Ben spat off to the side. "You think you got everything all worked out, don'tcha, Scotsman?"

Jarrod made no reply, but from the way he stared at her stepfather, he clearly wasn't willing to put up with any nonsense. Finally he turned and met her eyes again. "Angel, pack up your extra truck. We'll tie it to my mules, and you can sell it." He spared her a smile, but his eyes still held fire. "Maybe you can get yourself a little something with that."

"She's buying coffee."

Angel allowed Jarrod to help her to her feet. The feel of his big hand wrapped around her arm, steadying her, made her long for more. She wanted to lean into him and absorb his strength. She hadn't been to town for two years. A day where she didn't have to plunge her chapped hands into the cold water—it was almost too marvelous to believe, and Harv would be gentle with Mama. Jarrod was responsible for this. He'd made it possible.

166

"Coffee sounds wonderful."

"Since we won't be panning tomorrow, we gotta do more today." Ben tugged Angel away from Jarrod's side. "Get busy."

Jarrod tacked on, "Bring your pan to the edge of the claim. We'll keep you betwixt us just for good measure."

Angel panned for the rest of the afternoon, but she did it reflexively. She'd dip her pan, swirl and shift it until all of the silt washed out and all that was left was the black, fine pay dirt. Until that color showed in her rusty pan, she didn't have to pay attention at all. Then, she'd rinse it carefully, shake and coax and wash off the last until the only things left in the pan were the few precious grains of gold. Pan after pan after pan...

She wondered how much gold dust they had. Her stepfather always took her findings for the day and hid them away. She had no idea precisely where he kept the hard-earned treasure. It never seemed right that he took it all. Then too, when he'd go to town and come back empty-handed, she'd swung between being irate and hopeless. Had he wasted it all, or had he only taken a portion? Tomorrow, he'd have her along. She'd be sure they went to a mercantile and bought staples first. If only Father would walk out of the range of hearing for a moment, she'd turn and plead with Jarrod to help her force Father into that plan. It shamed her, but she decided her pride wasn't half as important as the dire need to restock her empty larder.

How much does a bag of flour cost? A pound of coffee? Oh, and sugar. Beans and rice. They'll store well in the back corner of my cabin. She studied the little dish she kept fingering her gold dust into. *What will that much gold buy?*

⌒

Ben muttered under his breath, but Jarrod anticipated his attitude and took coffee to share the next morning. It served as a potent reminder of what they could get in town. After a cup,

Ben's penchant for the scalding drink made him stand up and smack the dust off the seat of his britches. "We'd best not wait all day. Get a move on."

Angel quickly handed two full sacks of her garden truck to Jarrod to tie onto Otto's back. While he secured them, she did one last check on Mama, then thanked Harv for the kindness he showed by staying with her for the day. Within minutes, Jarrod lifted Angel onto Beulah, and they'd all set out.

Jarrod held Beulah's halter and walked along at a fair pace. He wanted to get into town and back before the sun went down. Squinting at the horizon, he estimated if he kept up this pace, they'd make it.

"Are you sure I'm not wearing out Beulah?" Angel leaned toward Jarrod from her perch. "I'm going to want her to carry a lot of supplies back."

"You're just a dab of a lass." They'd barely finished crossing Pete Kane's claim, and Jarrod didn't want her to start fretting. They had a long day ahead of them. "Beulah's happy to carry you, and it'll keep your hem from gathering dust."

She let out a bit of rusty laughter. "Wouldn't that be a sight? Me telling the men they can bring me their laundry while I have eight inches of grime around my hem!"

The hair on the back of his neck prickled as Jarrod stopped dead in his tracks. "You're not going to tell them you'll take on business. 'Tisn't safe."

"I'm gettin' more ammunition," Ben growled. The bags of produce on Otto's back jostled as Ben led him ahead. "She'll be plenty safe."

Greed. Jarrod had a strong hunch gold was the one thing that motivated Ben. Jarrod unashamedly took advantage of that sad fact. "To my way of thinking, with the late runoff, this is the best time to be panning. Angel can keep her laundry business going to earn money from the locals, but if she does much more, you'll miss out on everything she's panning because she'll have to make more soap, spend more time scrubbing and wringing, and—"

"You're already wasting good pannin' time, gardening and such," Ben mused. "Cain't miss out on much more. I ain't goin' through another winter without coffee."

Relieved, Jarrod set a slightly faster pace. Colorado rated a close second to the most beautiful place on earth. Scotland headed the list, but a man couldn't live in the past, so he appreciated the fresh pine scent, the loamy earth, the birdsong, and the endless blue sky surrounding him now. Most of all, he appreciated the one piece of scenery that surpassed anything he'd ever seen: the sight of Angel smiling.

When they got to town, Ben licked his lips, dropped Otto's halter, and headed straight toward the saloon's batwing doors.

Jarrod reached over and caught his arm. "We'd best go to the mercantile first."

A soiled dove leaned over her balcony from the upstairs of The Watering Hole and called out with notable enthusiasm, "Benny! C'mon up and pay me a visit!"

Jarrod didn't turn loose. He gave Ben's arm a squeeze and said, "You have ammunition and coffee to buy."

"Sometimes a man's gotta—" Ben glanced at Angel.

Jarrod looked up at her too. Her face had gone white with shock. She stared at him with glistening eyes that ached with all of the betrayal she felt on her mother's behalf. She slowly turned her face to the other side of the street. Jarrod wanted to comfort her, but this wasn't the time or place. He directed a scalding look at Ben.

Ben lowered his voice to a raspy, man-to-man whisper. "You know. A man's gotta take care of things. Manly things."

Purposefully mistaking him, Jarrod started traveling down the rutted street with Ben in tow. "I agree with you. Taking care of supplying your wife and Angel is the manly thing to do. A man always takes care of his loved ones."

While Jarrod helped Angel off Beulah, Ben stomped into the mercantile. Jarrod didn't let go of Angel at once. Instead, he continued to hold her waist and gave it a reassuring squeeze. He refused to lie or to make excuses for Ben, so he opted for a different tack. "Take the opportunity to stock up. Beulah and Otto wilna be happy if they made this trip for a mere bag or two, and I'm not of a mind to deal with three stubborn mules on the way home."

"Three?"

He waggled his brows. "There's no changing Ben's disposition, so help me make Beulah and Otto happy."

A flicker of a smile let Jarrod know he'd managed to handle the awkwardness so Angel wouldn't feel ashamed around him. "I'd guess we'd best take our vegetables inside."

As Jarrod untied the first bag off Otto, a head of lettuce escaped. A well-dressed man bent and snatched it up. He cradled it to his vest and eyed the other bags. "Do you have more of this?"

"Yes." Angel went to reclaim it. "Beans and—"

"I want it all," he interrupted. "I'll pay cash money."

Jarrod chuckled as he hefted one bag. "I'm doubting you'll be wanting it all."

"But I do! I own Fancy Pans. I'm always ready to buy quality truck. If those bags hold anything similar to this, I'll be more than happy to snap it all up."

By the time he'd looked in the second bag, the restauranteur didn't even bother to inspect the other two. "Four dollars for all of it."

Jarrod felt Angel jump. She looked to him, and he shook his head. Staring at the man, he demanded, "How much is a meal at your establishment?"

By the time Jarrod held the door of the mercantile open, he couldn't help smiling at Angel. She positively skipped over the threshold. The bargain they'd struck and the promise of a free meal in a nice restaurant made Jarrod want to jig right alongside her.

They'd been paid in coins, and he promptly gave Angel her half. She hurriedly handed back one of the silver dollars and whispered, "Please keep it for me. It's not much, but I'll need it someday."

He'd slipped it into his pocket and added one of his own. When the time came, she'd need all he could spare her.

Chapter 7

Ben shot them a dirty look as they entered the store, then thumped a can of Wedding Breakfast coffee onto the counter and set three tins of chewing tobacco next to it. " 'Bout time you got in here. Bring in that truck so's the storekeeper can tell me how much credit I'll get."

"We already sold it," Angel said. "Jarrod and I each have three and a half dollars cash and lunch at a restaurant!"

The lass acted like a child at Christmas in the mercantile. Every last thing held her enthralled. The first thing she did was choose a cough elixir and a health tonic for her mother. Bless her soul, she didn't even look at the cost. Jarrod knew she'd sacrifice anything for the sake of her mother.

The most pressing needs seen to, she then agonized over which flour and sugar sacks she liked best, stood by the huge barrel of coffee beans and inhaled the aroma as if she were a bride appreciating the most beautiful bouquet a groom ever gathered.

Seeing how she relished each and every scent and item, Jarrod lollygagged as he selected things and formed a small stack of goods on the counter. The storekeeper's hair glinted oddly in the sunlight streaming in through the window. At first, Jarrod thought it was merely the pomade casting a reflection. Upon second inspection, Jarrod realized the truth. He was a sticky-fingered proprietor.

Oh, he'd read about such men—just never met one. Sure

enough, the storekeeper would run his fingers through his hair, then reach into a miner's poke to pull out a pinch of gold flakes as payment for something. Most of the dust went into the receptacle behind the counter, but some clung to the storekeeper's fingers—which he'd run through his hair or wipe off on his apron. By panning the wash water from his bath and laundry, the man undoubtedly pulled in as much gold dust as any of the local placers who worked by the cold streams.

A pair of Cornish miners played draughts over between the stove and the cracker barrel. "Smashed Oliver McKnight like a june bug," one said grimly.

The other shook his head. "He was always talking about coming to the mine to earn a nice nest egg so when his sweet little Charlotte was of age, he'd be able to 'give her the world along with his heart.'"

"Three-fifty a day sounded like a lot, but seein' Ollie all bloody and squished—" The first shook his head.

"Superstitious cowards," the storekeeper whispered disparagingly to Jarrod and Ben. "They had another cave-in—just a little one. Only killed one man. Still, the mountain's making some noise, so they're sure the tommyknockers are warning them to stay out of the mines."

Ben snorted. "Don't need pretend creatures to warn me off. Couldn't pay me 'nuff to crawl inside a mountain and haul out gold for another man."

"Your claim doing well?" The shopkeeper gave both men an assessing look.

Ben scowled, and Jarrod knew better than to give a direct answer. They'd be fools to admit anything, so he shrugged diffidently. "I just bought the claim off someone else. I'm supposin' it'll take me awhile to be any good at it. Came to stock up on some staples."

He specifically chose his flour sack to match Angel's. Truth be told, he'd look mighty silly to be walking down the street with his flour in pink fabric with wee daisies sprinkled all over it, but he didn't much care. The lass could use the extra fabric to make herself a frock instead of a skirt, and she'd be pretty as one of her blushes in this color.

Angel's stack of supplies at the counter nearly made Ben's eyes pop. "Now hold on. No use gettin' extravagant," he protested as she set a small box atop the bags and tucked a metal pail of lard beside them.

"Baking powder, baking soda, and salt aren't extravagances," she said quietly, but Jarrod detected the firm undertone. "I've stuck to basics: flour, sugar, beans, lard, and coffee. Did you get your ammunition?"

Ben rapped his knuckles on a box of bullets he set next to a slab of bacon and scowled. "Money we got from the truck ain't gonna be 'nuff."

Jarrod slipped a few last things on the counter with his selections. He drew his gold-dust pouch from his pocket. "Ah, but there's satisfaction in knowing we earned every speck of what we eat." When he'd finalized the transaction, he said, "Speaking of eating, I'm ready to go to that restaurant."

He and Angel spent time savoring the fine meal. Her gracious manners made it clear to Jarrod that though she'd never said much about her past, she'd obviously grown up in drastically different circumstances. Ben wolfed down his meal and plowed out of the restaurant so he could get to the saloon. Jarrod stayed behind and savored the food and company.

Ben ambled along next to Otto. He hummed under his breath—no doubt, the time he'd spent bending his elbow in the saloon was responsible for his uncustomary merriment.

Angel walked between him and Jarrod and daintily held up

her skirt a bit. She'd worn the one Jarrod had given her, and she fretted over the hem as if the dust wouldn't ever wash out. Every few minutes, she kept glancing at the burden on Otto's sturdy back. Each time, her smile grew. Jarrod had whispered to her to estimate generous quantities, and the packs tied to the mules gave her a sense of accomplishment and even a flicker of hope. *I'll be able to give Mama medicine and feed her well.*

Ben and Jarrod were discussing the smokehouse as if it were already built. That heartened her further. Ever since Jarrod arrived, things had improved. He'd shown her kindness and courtesy, seen the longings in her heart and bettered her life in every way. She and Mama had a roof over their heads, and after today, they had medicine, plenty of staples, and the promise of sufficient meat—if Jarrod continued to be as adept at hunting as he'd been thus far.

But for how long?

Jarrod said he would stay only as long as it took for him to pan enough gold to buy his dream ranch. She didn't know how much gold that would require—or how long it would take. Jarrod hadn't wasted a single cent in town. Every last purchase rated as a necessity. Some might consider that parsimonious, but she didn't. After her stepfather's previous forays to town where he spent everything—from today's events, Angel had a mortifying notion of just how he'd squandered their gold—she had a deep appreciation for a man who exercised self-discipline and frugality. A deep contentment radiated from him, making it clear he didn't need a lot of material things to keep him satisfied.

Her stepfather dragged her and Mama here and hadn't put himself out at all in any way for them. Even after Mama got sick, he'd not lifted a finger to ease things by getting medicine, chopping wood for heat, or providing adequate shelter.

For all others might say about love, Angel decided few people knew what it truly meant. They saw love as taking, not giving. In that light, love would prove to be vastly overrated and empty.

She'd turned down many a proposal out here—none of the men who asked cared a whit for her. She vowed to stay for Mama. She couldn't fool herself into believing Mama would recover because Mama had lost too much weight and slept most of the time. At least that was a blessed escape from her pain and cough. For now, they had food aplenty, clothes, and shelter—humble as it was.

She owed it all to Jarrod.

And he'd be leaving.

Chapter 8

Arms full of branches, Angel walked to the smokehouse. Her stepfather had agreed with Ben and Harv about building it, but when the time came to do the work, he balked. Jarrod and Harv decided to build it near the bank on Harv's side of the creek. Neither of those men said a word about why they'd chosen that location. They didn't have to: Angel knew full well why. Her stepfather wouldn't do his share of building or filling it, but he'd gladly help himself to whatever the smokehouse contained if it were on his claim. When Jarrod left, he'd not want to rob Harv of his fair share. Hardworking as Jarrod was, Angel knew he'd not be a placer for long.

Angel nimbly crossed the log bridge Jarrod had constructed, and she dumped off the wood. Though she couldn't hunt, she'd do her family's part by helping dress out and cure the meat.

Harv grinned at her. "Jarrod went a-huntin' this mornin'. Got hisself a passel of squirrels. I set out a sieve last night and netted 'leven fish. Pete brought over a few fish he wants smoke cured too."

Jarrod rested his hands on his hips and tilted his head to the side. "I was just telling Harv and Pete about what a good cook you are. Think we could talk you into making squirrel stew and dumplings? Then Harv will fillet and smoke the fish for us to have some other day."

"I'll bring coffee," Pete offered.

Warmth rushed through her. Jarrod had been complimenting her cooking to someone else? Angel smiled. "Squirrel stew and dumplings it is, gentlemen."

Jarrod nodded, then gave her a chiding look. "You'll not be carryin' wood again, lass. 'Tisn't fitting."

She shrugged. "I do it all of the time for the wash pot."

"We know," Harv grumped. "Makes me wonder which Ben uses less—his ax or his head."

All of them exchanged a glance, and the men burst out laughing as a smile tugged at the corners of Angel's mouth. Harv had a way of looking at life and speaking his mind that managed to lift the spirits.

"We're partners in this venture," Jarrod said, "and we men already agreed you're not responsible for any of the wood, so that's how the vote stands."

"But if you both hunt and dress the meat, I—"

"Will be filling the air with the aroma and our bellies with your fine squirrel stew." Jarrod took her arm and started back toward the bridge. When they reached it, he cupped his hands around her waist to help her step up. She didn't need the assistance, but his gentlemanly ways made her feel dainty and special, so she didn't protest.

He didn't lift right away. He stared down into her eyes. "I have the ring. I'll slip it to you, and you can stitch it back into your hem."

She cast a glance across the creek and shook her head subtly. "He'd find it. Every night, he searches to be sure I didn't keep any of the gold for myself."

A muffled sound of outrage rumbled in his chest.

"The day Ben gets his hands on my grandmother's ring, it'll be lost to me forever. My cousins, Philip and Gabe, are to receive Grandma Monroe's locket and get Grandpa's pocket watch. The ring is my one worldly treasure. Grandpa made it for her out of the first gold he ever mined. I trust you to keep it for me, Jarrod."

"You deserve better, lass."

Lass. He called her lass as if it were an endearment. His rich, deep burr made that word and her name both sound like caresses when he said them. Before she let him know where her mind was wandering, she shook herself free and scrambled onto the log bridge. "Bring the squirrels as soon as you can. I'll want them to simmer 'til tender."

She made it all of a few steps when he hopped up and fleetly followed behind her. "I've carrots aplenty. I'll pluck them up along with a turnip or an onion for the stew."

"No, no," she denied as she finished crossing. Relief flooded her that he'd left the sore subject behind and chosen to discuss something so practical and mundane. "Feed the carrots to Beulah and Otto. I have a bumper crop of carrots too."

"I've been thinkin' on digging a root cellar."

Angel spun around and looked at him. "For a man who said he'd stay only long enough to pan out enough to buy a ranch, you sure are putting down roots."

Lines around his eyes crinkled as he threw back his head and chortled. "The roots are already planted, lass. I'm just hoping to save me a fair bunch of them for when the harvest is over."

"If you keep hunting and gardening, it'll take you years to pull enough from the river to buy that ranch."

Jarrod's face took on a pensive air. "Whatever happens, it's all in God's time, according to His will."

She gave him a flicker of a smile. "Once I told you I didn't think God listened to me anymore. I was wrong. He took His time to answer my prayers. Because Mama and I had to do without for so long, it makes all I now have seem far more precious. It's as if He's showering me with blessings."

"Sure and enough, He is, Angel. Of that you can be certain."

"I need to go see to Mama."

"We'll talk more about this later."

She pressed her lips together and cast a surreptitious look to the side. Her stepfather would make Jarrod stop seeing her if he found out they discussed anything religious. She couldn't take that risk. "I have to go." Before he could say another word, she dashed off.

C"

The elixir really did help. Mama's breathing didn't carry that rasp if she had a dose four times a day. Maybe it wasn't as much the medicine as the company. Jarrod came over about noon each day and carried Mama to a pretty spot where he and Harv had slung a length of canvas to form a hammock. Fresh air, sunshine, and gentle companionship put the slightest tinge of pink into Mama's cheeks.

Jarrod and Harv made a show of having an argument over who got the privilege of feeding Mama lunch each day. Ben never sat with them—he'd grab his food and stalk off. While Angel sewed, one of the men would feed Mama and the other would gut fish or dress out whatever they'd hunted. The camaraderie between Jarrod and Harv reminded Angel of how her cousins, Philip and Gabe, used to act with one another. Some days, it made her homesick; other days, it was such fun, she'd lose herself in the joy of their nonsense.

"I've decided on a spot to dig my root cellar," Jarrod announced one day just as the air started to take on a decided nip that warned the season was changing. He pointed at a site.

"That spot is all rock. It's as hard as your head," Harv teased.

"It'll keep creatures from burrowing in and helping them-selves to my food." Jarrod nodded to himself.

"Everybody knows you have the second-best carrots around," Mama said in her shaky voice.

"Second best?" Jarrod gave her a look of mock outrage.

"Seems I'm the only impartial judge hereabouts." Harv swiped a part of a carrot Angel had been cutting to dehydrate and chewed it. He then wandered over, picked a carrot from Jarrod's garden, and rinsed it in the creek. He took a bite and made a wry face. "Hard to say. Maybe I ought to eat a couple more to make up my mind."

"What mind?" Jarrod asked Mama in a stage whisper.

They all laughed—Mama included. Later, as Jarrod carried her back into the cabin, she tapped his chest. "You've got a good heart, Jarrod McLeod. I prayed God would pour out His joy and love, and you're the answer to my prayer."

Jarrod decided prospecting for gold held absolutely no charm whatsoever. The sun glaring on the water hit his eyes and burned his skin. Hot as it was, he wouldn't remove his shirt out of deference to Angel's sensibilities. He'd used his pickax at a particularly promising black streak on his claim and fed it through his shaker box. Some days, he managed to find several tiny nuggets and a gram or so of little golden grains. Other days, he'd garnered nothing more than flakes that caught along the rusty spots in his pan.

Silver miners were paid twenty dollars a week. Most weeks, Jarrod knew full well he'd have made more working in the dark bowels of a mountain with other men, but the very thought of being closed in like that made him break out in a cold sweat. He'd spent almost all of the voyage from Scotland up on deck because he couldn't bear being crammed so tightly with everyone else in the dim steerage compartment.

He cupped his hand and scooped up a drink of cool water, then stood to stretch his weary back muscles. *Lord, I'm sorry for having a complaining spirit. Thou art showering me with sunshine and fanning me with a fresh breeze.* Just then, Ben shouted something unintelligible at Angel. *And Father, I'm thinkin' Thou hast planted me here for more of a reason than funding my dream.*

Angel broke into his prayer by marching straight across to his claim. Temper set her hazel eyes aflame and lent vivid color to her cheeks. She carried a gunnysack over her shoulder, but Jarrod knew it couldn't contain her belongings. She'd never leave her mother, and if death had come, Angel would be in tears, not in a roaring temper.

Angel didn't say a thing until she stood right before him. "I'm going to town. Mama's out of cough elixir, and she needs it bad. Will you keep an eye on her while I'm gone?"

Ben stomped up and made a grab for the gunnysack. "You ain't going nowhere, and this food ain't yours to sell."

"I planted and grew it!"

Ben thundered, "On my claim!" He yanked the sack from her grasp.

Jarrod steadied Angel so she wouldn't fall. He pursed his lips and looked up at the scudding clouds for a moment, then back at Ben. "So 'tis your claim, is it?"

"What kind of fool question is that? Of course it is!"

"Not your family's?" Jarrod gritted his teeth together so hard, he could feel the muscle in his cheek twitch.

"Mine." Ben thumped his chest with his free hand. "My wife's useless, and whatever Angel does, it barely pays the keep on the both of them."

"Families pull together to make ends meet," Jarrod said softly, but then he injected a steely undertone to the rest of his words. "A man's place is to provide for his kin."

"Ain't none of your business. Besides, Angel ain't my blood kin."

"No, she's not your family," Jarrod agreed with a steely glare. "You agreed Angel should work the land. She's sharecropping. Rightfully, a portion of the yield is Angel's to do with as she pleases."

While Ben dropped the sack and let out a bellow at that pronouncement, Angel took the next mental step. "Part of the money I earn with laundry is mine from now on too. And so is a portion of the gold when I pan!"

Ben shook his finger in her face. "You stop it right there, missy. You ain't got any call on nothin' of mine. You're workin' so's you and your ma can eat. You start challenging me and making fancy demands, and you can keep off my land."

Jarrod could feel her shudder and wilt. Everything within him railed at this cruelty. He tilted her face to his. "I'll let you and your mama live in my cabin."

"My wife ain't goin' nowheres."

The trapped look on Angel's face and the tears in her eyes nearly tore Jarrod's heart from his chest. He gently fingered an errant golden tendril back behind her ear and urged, "Go take care of your mama, lass. I'm needin' to go to town myself. You just tell me what to get."

"It's a waste of good money. No matter what you give her, she ain't gettin' better."

A wounded cry spiraled out of Angel. Jarrod clasped her to his chest as she shook with nearly silent weeping. He glared at Ben. "The elixir eases your wife's cough and gives both comfort and rest. 'Tisn't a waste at all; 'tis a necessity, and a merciful one at that."

"Ain't your business, and it ain't your money." Ben swiped the sack from the ground, made a sound of disgust, and walked off.

Jarrod continued to hold Angel as she cried. They'd never said a word about how her mother was losing ground and growing more fragile with the passage of each week. Ben had been cruel, and Jarrod despised that fact. But he knew he couldn't lie now and reassure Angel that her mama would improve.

Lord, help me get Angel away from that black-hearted man.

From behind him came the sound of a man clearing his

throat. Harv's voice broke in to Jarrod's thoughts. "Mrs. Frisk— she didn't. . .um. . ."

"No." Jarrod stroked Angel's back as he watched his friend circle around them. "We're concerned because she's worsening. I'll be going into town to fetch more medicine. I'll be askin' you to keep an eye out for Angel and her mama for the day."

"I'd be right proud to. I could use a thing or two, since you're making the trip." Harv's brows beetled in a dark, questioning frown as he tilted his head toward Ben's claim. When Jarrod nodded subtly, Harv gave Angel's shoulder a clumsy pat. "Maybe our missy can have a sit-down for a few minutes and write out a list for me."

Angel shimmied from Jarrod's hold, wiped her face with the backs of her chapped hands, and said in a small, choppy voice, "Of course I'll scribe your list."

"Be much obliged." Harv rocked from toe to heel a few times, and an impish twinkle lit his eyes. "First thing I want is the strongest purgative you can buy so's I can slip it into Ben's coffee."

Angel forced a pitiful excuse for a laugh and grabbed each of their hands. Squeezing them tightly, she asked, "What would I do without you?"

Jarrod cupped her jaw with his other hand and captured her gaze unwaveringly. "You've no need to ask the question, lass. You'll not be finding that out."

Jarrod stood in the mercantile and looked about. He let the storekeeper gather the items of Harv's list while he made careful choices for himself. He'd taken about half of his placer gold to the assay office and sold it, but for all his hard work, the financial results left his spirits flat and his pocket far too light.

Prices in town had gone up. Jarrod grimly determined to get the root cellar dug, dehydrate vegetables and berries, and hunt as much as he could. If the prices made him wince, they'd send Ben into a fury.

Angel had wisely been gathering berries and drying some of her vegetables. She even filled a big crock with a dill brine in which she'd been making pickles. At her suggestion, Harv donated a barrel, Jarrod gave her cabbage, and she'd made sauer-kraut that would be done curing in the late autumn. Truly, he'd never seen a more industrious woman.

The sales lithograph over the display of Dr. Jayne's expectorant that Angel told him to buy made Jarrod's heart lurch. Little Red Riding Hood huddled in a doorway in her cloak—it seemed oddly, sadly appropriate. His Angel and her mama had suffered far too much, and even if it took every last cent he had, Jarrod was going to make sure they were cared for.

He studied the other patent medicines. Supposedly, Seeley's Wasa-Tusa cured most anything, but he set it back on the counter when he read the boast "87 percent alcohol." Since Angel thought Dr. Jayne's worked well, he'd trust her judgment—but he didn't buy just one bottle.

The trip home in the dark was treacherous. Thanks to Beulah and Otto's surefooted walk and Harv's beacon-sized fire, Jarrod made it back. "Coffee smells good."

"Have a cup."

"After I take Mrs. Frisk her elixir." He took out what he needed and headed toward Angel's cabin. From halfway across the campsite, he could hear her mama's harsh cough. "Angel?"

The door flew open. A tiny flicker from the kerosene lamp glowed around her like a halo. "You're back!"

His nose wrinkled at an awful smell. "Sounds like your mama needs this." He handed her two bottles.

"I made an onion and mustard plaster for her chest. It helped a little, but this will make all of the difference. Thank you so much!"

He held out a crushed cone of paper. "Horehound drops."

Angel's jaw dropped and she blinked at him. "You bought candy?"

" 'Tis said it helps with coughs, but I want you to have a piece or two yourself."

"I don't need—"

"Life's not always about needs, lass. Sometimes, it's about little pleasures and tiny joys. Give me your word you'll have one tonight."

Tears misted her pretty hazel eyes and lent a throaty quality to her voice. "Yes."

"There now. That's a fine promise. The night's goin' chilly. You latch the door now and bundle up soon as you've given your mama her elixir."

"I put aside some supper for you. Harv has it."

"Then let me give you a scripture before I go." He looked at the beautiful, careworn lass as she clutched the medicine and candy to her bosom and felt a glow, knowing she'd still thought of his needs and set aside a meal for him. " 'Tis in Psalm 34, but I canna recollect the exact verses. 'The angel of the Lord encampeth round about them that fear him, and delivereth them. O taste and see that the Lord is good: blessed is the man that trusteth in him.' "

Angel watched Jarrod walk away, then latched the cabin door. She turned and set his offerings on the little shelf he'd built into the wall. She carefully set it so Mama could still see her carved wooden rose. Just as Angel treasured her ring, Mama cherished that rose Grandpa made when he'd courted Grandma. "Mama, Jarrod brought you some of Dr. Jayne's expectorant. Wasn't that nice of him?"

Once Mama swallowed a spoonful and caught her breath, she patted Angel's hand. "Good man."

Angel turned away from the meaningful look in her mother's eyes. Mama cottoned to Jarrod, and for good reason. He showered her with affection and respect. Harv did too, but in a different way. Harv was a sweet, bumbling jester of a man. He'd tried to help out when he could, but Jarrod—well, Jarrod had a way of stepping in and getting a lot done with a minimum of fuss. Angel didn't want Mama trying to play matchmaker just because Jarrod believed in putting his muscles behind his faith.

The brown paper drew her attention. Horehound. Just the thought of it made her mouth water. Grandpa used to slip her a chip of it in church when the preacher got a bit long-winded. She took the tiniest drop for herself and gave one to Mama. "Here. A special treat. I think you'll have sweet dreams tonight, Mama."

"Some days, you live on dreams. Some days, you live on blessings."

Angel stooped, gave her a kiss, then closed the shutters. She'd left them open in the hope that the dim light would help lead Jarrod home. When the sun set and he'd not yet gotten back, she'd been worried. It was her fault he'd gone to town. Now, with him back and a spoonful of medicine in Mama, relief poured through her. She curled up on her cot and sucked on the horehound. . .and the flavor lingered long after the candy dissolved—just like Jarrod's comfort lingered even after he went back to his own claim.

Chapter 9

The pickax barely made a chip in the hard rock. Jarrod broadened his stance and hefted the pick again. It came down in a mighty arc and made a small divot. Almost an hour later, he had a hole the size of both of Angel's fists. He leaned in an arc to ease his back and arm muscles, then waved at Angel. "How's your mama today?"

"She slept like a baby, thanks to you."

He chuckled. "Good thing. As much noise as I'm makin' now, she's probably thinkin' the walls of Jericho are tumbling down."

"What if you used a metal tent stake as a chisel? Would that help?"

"Why, yes, I do believe it would." Half an hour later, Jarrod grinned at his progress. By chipping away at the edges, he'd managed to almost triple the size of the opening. If he worked at this all day for the next three days, then the mornings for a few more, he'd have a nice-sized, secure root cellar. Grayish granite chipped away, and Jarrod halted. Green. He'd hit a streak of green. It meant he'd found some copper, and copper often ran alongside— *No. I'm not going to let my imagination run away with me.*

He struck again. More green. Then more. The stripe widened. Time passed, but he lost track. Finally thirst made him halt. He walked to the creek and took a big, long drink, then splashed the refreshingly cold water on his face and neck.

Ben glanced over at him. "Never seen a man waste as much time as you—wandering off to town, messin' with a garden, diggin' a root pit."

Jarrod shrugged. "Bible tells of Joseph setting by food for the lean times. From what I hear, a man gets hungry in winter here if he doesn't plan ahead."

"You sayin' I didn't plan ahead? You callin' me a fool?"

"I have no idea how you supplied your family. Rain might have spoiled supplies. Creatures might have gotten into the bags and barrels. I'm just saying I'm trying to exercise wisdom on my own behalf."

"Hmpf." Ben plunged his pan into the water again.

Jarrod stopped in his cabin for something quick to eat. He didn't want to waste time cooking. After eating a chunk of jerky and taking a quick glug of apple cider from a jug, he was back out at the root pit.

Curiosity made him want to dig deeper, but common sense told him to widen the opening. If all he did was drive straight down, Ben would suspect he was digging a sample core. Not wanting to give Ben any reason to get snoopy, Jarrod tamped down his own feelings. He needed to stay calm. *Might be, nothing is here at all. Even if I don't strike gold, I'll still have a fine place to store my garden truck.*

Light began to wane. Jarrod served a few more blows on the chisel. All day long, he'd carefully taken the coppery earth off and slipped it in the hollow of a rotting log. The secrecy of the action went against his grain, but safety demanded he do just that. He set a board over the opening and started to walk away.

"You've been busy today."

"No more than you, Harv. What do you have there?"

"That net you set out caught this beauty." Harv held up a sizable trout. He hitched a shoulder and added, "I didn't catch nothing today, and I thought maybe you'd feel like sharing if I cook."

Soon, the men sat by a small fire and ate the trout. Harv stretched out his legs and studied his boots. He bent over and thumbed a crack in the old leather. "These ain't gonna last me another winter. I'm of a mind to bag me a buck. Injuns wear buckskin boots. Figure I could too. Eatin' something other than squirrel, fish, or rabbit would suit me fine."

"For all of the berries, I haven't seen many deer."

Harv shook his head. "Thimbleberries this time of year. Deer don't favor them. They was fine, eating the whortleberries and bilberries in July, but whatever we didn't gather, the gray catbirds, quail, and squirrels ate. The back corner of my claim is part of a deer run. What say we stake it out at daybreak and try to get us one?"

Jarrod didn't want deer—he wanted gold. The pit called to him, drew him. In that instant, he understood the seductive, insidious pull of gold fever. He cleared his throat as a flicker of compassion for Ben kindled in his heart. "Harv, I'd be proud to hunt with you. Are you wanting me to leave my bow behind?"

He pursed his lips and pondered on the matter. "Bring it. May be that some other critter happens by. You can take it down all quiet-like, and the deer won't be spooked away."

"The smokehouse can handle a buck, no problem. I'd like to see us fill up on as much as we can. I've decided to start setting more snares—all of the beasts have been fattening up over the summer, so they're of good size."

Harv agreed and headed for the log bridge. After he left, Jarrod put some gravel in his shaker box and worked by firelight for another hour or so before turning in.

After he read his Bible and prayed, he stacked his hands behind his head and stared up at the roof. A realization struck him. *Even if I hit gold and have enough to go buy my ranch, I'm not leaving until I can take Angel with me.*

⟳

"Mama! You're the one who always told me to be grateful."

"I never served you deer liver."

"It won't keep. Jarrod and Harv are smoking almost all of the rest of the deer. They butchered it into pieces no self-respecting cook would recognize, but we'll have plenty of fine meals from it. Here. Eat some."

"Did Ben at least help them butcher it?"

Angel shook her head.

"I can help." Mama rose on one elbow. "I'll wash the tripe and we can make sausage."

"No, Mama. You save your strength. We'll do just fine. Truly, we will." Horror streaked through Angel at the thought of her mother doing anything at all. The minute she attempted even the smallest task, Ben would take that as a signal that she ought to be panning again.

As Angel gently nudged her to lie back down, Mama said, "Ever since Jarrod came, we've been eating better."

"He said Harv shot the deer. Harv's proud as a peacock. While they were waiting, Jarrod used his bow and brought down a wild turkey. It's months early, but we decided we're going to celebrate Thanksgiving day after tomorrow."

Mama's lids drooped, but a sweet, weary smile chased across her face. "Lord knows, we have plenty for which to be thankful."

⟳

Two shirts. The nip in the predawn air demanded Jarrod put on two shirts. Even working to go through solid rock, he'd not work up enough heat to keep himself warm if he wore but a single shirt.

His breath condensed in the air as he stirred the banked coals from last night's fire. While coffee and oatmeal cooked, he carried some of the gravel from the pit over to his shaker box. He'd begun to see little glimmers last evening, so he'd decided working it would be more promising than working the creek silt. Then too, it would quell any curiosity from Ben—as long as Ben didn't realize he'd carried the gravel from the area where he was digging.

Because he didn't particularly care to get in and out of the water all day, he'd taken to scooping a score or more of the sixteen-inch pans full of creek bottom and piling them by the shaker. He'd never dreamed when he started that habit would stand him in such good stead now.

A bowl of oatmeal and a cup of much-too-strong coffee later, Jarrod started to operate his shaker box. Pan after pan, he shook gravel through the grates.

Muscles heated from the hard work and the rising temperature as the morning sun climbed, Jarrod removed the outer shirt. He squinted at what he'd coaxed from the shaker box: several specks and flakes that amounted to about the size of his thumbnail. *Better than what I'd normally get, but still not much. I'll dig back there a bit deeper and see if there's more to be had.*

"Jarrod?" He looked over his shoulder and smiled at Angel as she picked up his shirt from the stump where he'd flung it. "I'm doing laundry today."

He nodded. They'd tangled over this a few times, but he'd finally relented. They'd made a deal—he made the cabin for her; she did his laundry and occasionally cooked for him. Just as he didn't want to be indebted, neither did she.

"We still have a bit of turkey left. I thought I'd make pasties for lunch."

He headed for his cabin. "Only if I give over some flour." When he came back out, he held a small bundle of laundry under one arm and a bowl of flour in the other and winked. "I'll carry this back so I'll have an excuse to visit your mother."

"You don't need an excuse. Mama looks forward to seeing you." Angel fell into step alongside him. "How are you doing on the root cellar?"

"It's taking a lot of time. I chose rock because I'm tired of creatures burrowing and eating the roots. I suppose I could have sunken a barrel, but being a hardheaded, stubborn Scot, once I started, I refused to change my ways."

They'd reached her fire. Jarrod set down his laundry and flour and wordlessly lifted the big iron wash cauldron. He carried it to the stream, filled it, and carried it back to the fire.

Harv and Pete were crossing the log bridge with their laundry. Pete dumped his sorry-looking pile of clothes and scratched his elbow. "That turkey you folks shared surely sat fine in my belly. Harv'll tell ya I make a purty fair corn bread. I even got me two eggs to make it, so how 'bout if I invite myself to lunch?"

"I got cornmeal," Harv offered.

Jarrod tucked Angel's braid behind her shoulder. "See there? You'll not have to cook at midday."

"I don't mind at all—"

"Laundry's hard work." He gave her a stern look. "You've got plenty to keep you more than busy."

"How'd you get eggs?" Harv asked Pete.

"Angel, get busy." Ben's interruption made them all turn around. He glowered. "You ain't getting anything done, standing 'round with this pack of lazy men. They might not have nothing to do, but you shore do. The rest of you, git."

"We'll eat at high noon, my claim," Harv whispered.

Just as the other two men headed toward the bridge, Ben swaggered back over. "You two best pay up now for your wash."

"Left my money over on my claim," Harv said.

"Me too." Pete gave Ben a look of owl-eyed innocence.

∞

Gold. Jarrod squatted down and reached in to touch the nugget he'd just chipped free. The front of it was copper, but the whole back gleamed with promise. Instead of lifting it, he paused and caught his breath, then shoved it aside and touched the rock face he'd just bared. Gold.

He chipped out a piece and placed it in his pocket. Someday, when he had a ranch, he still wanted a keepsake from this moment. *Lord, I prayed Thou wouldst help me get Angel away from that black-hearted stepfather of hers. My heart knows Thou hast placed this gold here. Let me be wise in what I do with it.*

Chipping away at the stone, Jarrod uncovered the colorful vein. He scraped the granite, quartz, and copper out of the pit to form a heap that would fill a lard bucket twice over. He stared at the widening yellow streak and wondered how deep it ran.

"Chow time!" Pete yelled from Harv's claim.

Jarrod crossed over to Harv's claim and sat next to Angel. She handed him a steaming pie tin. "Harv already fed Mama some. She said Pete's corn bread is so good, it'll be served at the banquet table in heaven."

"There's a fine recommendation." Jarrod took the food and frowned. "Your hands—"

"Washerwoman hands," she interrupted in a matter-of-fact tone. "I have my hands in and out of water so much, it's a miracle I haven't sprouted gills."

He wished he'd not said anything. The lye soap had her hands all red, and they'd been chapped already. Angel wasn't a vain woman, but she surely didn't need a man pointing out any of her flaws. He forced a chuckle, then took a taste of the corn bread and hummed his appreciation.

Secretly he kept thinking that the golden corn bread was disappearing fast, but the real gold of the day was just starting to make an appearance. That gold would buy Angel's freedom.

Chapter 10

Jarrod had gone to town again. Angel would have loved to accompany him, but Ben refused to let her go. In fact, Ben wouldn't listen to a word she said about supplies she wanted. He shouted that she'd spent far too much the last time she'd been in town, and he wasn't breaking his back every day down at the creek so she could squander his gold on foolishness.

Angel barely kept from asking him about *her* gold—the gold she slaved to get from the cold creek's bottom. He'd continued to take her findings each evening, and she'd seen him go through the hems of her skirts and her shoes before bedtime each night. He invariably muttered that she'd steal him blind if he didn't check. It had gotten worse since the men who paid for laundry started giving her the pay instead of handing it to Ben. Ben thought he'd take it back, but she'd entrusted it all to Jarrod, and that only made Ben more livid.

The paltry sum she counted as her very own wouldn't be much. She had no choice, though. Once Mama passed on, Angel knew she'd have to leave. Ben wouldn't give her a cent or a blanket when she left, either. If she could scrape together enough, she'd send a telegraph back home to Uncle Blackie and ask him to wire her enough money to buy a ticket on the stage. She should have thought to see how much a room in the boardinghouse cost. She'd need to stay there at least a few days. A telegraph would be three dollars for ten words, but she had a grand total of $1.81. Perhaps she could convince the owner of Fancy Pans to hire her for the time she'd be in town. He'd seemed nice enough.

The thought of Mama dying wrenched Angel's heart, but Mama often spoke of going home to be with Jesus and how happy the thought made her. Knowing Mama would be at peace softened Angel's grief, but it didn't take it away. On the other hand, the notion of leaving Ben filled Angel with nothing short of relief. Her mind skipped to Jarrod. He was rarely out of her thoughts these days. When she left, she'd be leaving Jarrod behind. The tremendous ache intensified inside of her—she'd lose Mama and Jarrod all at the same time.

At first, she'd been worried that Jarrod would strike gold and leave her behind when he went off to his dream ranch. He and Harv sometimes spoke aloud of ranching together—they'd make good partners. If they both left, she'd never survive here.

But now, she had come to the conclusion that even with them splitting the costs of buying a ranch, the men would have to stay at the creek for years—and Mama wasn't going to last that long. The irony of Angel leaving the men instead hit her. She couldn't laugh, though. The whole situation was just plain awful.

Jarrod had been wise to tell her to load up on supplies. Especially with the smokehouse full, she didn't have to worry that Mama and she would go hungry. Even so, she would have enjoyed the opportunity to walk along the path to town, wander past the storefronts, and watch the rich panoply of folks in town. She might have been able to take in a shirt and sell it. Chances were good, she wouldn't even reach town before she sold it—prospectors and placers were eager to stay on their claims. They'd be interested in bartering for a new shirt she'd made from some of the sacks she'd gotten in return for her produce and laundry.

Instead, she watched as Jarrod tied a small keg of sauerkraut to Beulah so he'd have something to barter. He'd set out at daybreak, and a terrible sense of loneliness lapped at her with every panful she swirled. From the day he'd come, Jarrod somehow managed to insert himself into her life—to extend his friendship, his help, comfort, and his strength. Just knowing she could look over and see him or call out if a problem arose had given her a sense of security.

Last night, he'd come over to spend a few minutes with her and Mama. He'd recited the fourth chapter of James. Some of the words spun in her mind over and over again in the same cadence as she revolved the pan. *"God resisteth the proud, but giveth grace unto the humble. Submit yourselves therefore to God. Resist the devil, and he will flee from you. Draw nigh to God, and he will draw nigh to you. . . . Humble yourselves in the sight of the Lord, and he shall lift you up." Humble yourselves. . . . Humble. . .*

Lord, how much more humble can I be? I try so hard not to sass my stepfather. My hands are chapped, and my hair is straggly, and I have nothing of value.

The pan held no gold whatsoever. She dumped it, scooped another panful, and continued to work. *God, I think I have the humility part down. How about Your part where You give grace and lift me up?*

Jarrod headed for the assay office. He wanted to be the first man there for the day. Along the way, he'd been stopped twice by thirsty, armed men who wanted the contents of his keg. They hadn't accepted the explanation that it contained sauerkraut until he pried out the large cork stopper and gave them each a whiff. Disappointed, neither of the men were further interested in the keg when they discovered it held no spirits.

Hitching Beulah to the post outside the assay office, Jarrod whispered a prayer of thanks. He'd worried he'd not make it here with his precious load. To be sure, he doubted anyone had ever hefted a keg of sauerkraut into the place; but once he entered the office, pried off the lid, and pulled out the lard can, he said in the quietest tone possible, "This isn't an ore sample with lots of rock. I believe it's what the fables say leprechauns guard at the end of the rainbow."

Sooner than Jarrod could sneeze, they'd locked the assay door and put up the CLOSED sign. He'd secretly hoped they'd do just that. If anyone discovered he'd struck gold, his life and dreams would be in danger...and the most important dream was for him to be able to sweep Angel away from here.

"Never had such a stinky sample." The assay man wrinkled his nose. His expression changed to open-mouthed astonishment when he accepted the lard pail from Jarrod. The weight of it spoke of an appreciable load. He quickly thumbed off the lid.

Jarrod grinned. "I know you don't normally let a fellow stay and watch, but it'll take dynamite to make me leave."

"Uh...yes, well..." The assay man choked, "Feel free to stay. Jimmy, forget the sledgehammer. Put this on the buckingboard and use the muller."

Jarrod watched him take several crucibles from a shelf and cleared his throat. "I've also brought a coffee tin that's full too."

The clerk and the assay man exchanged startled looks.

Quirking them a grin, Jarrod offered, "If we get hungry while you work, we can always eat some of the sauerkraut. Best you ever tasted. My Angel made it."

"Mister, if this turns out to be real, that angel of yours is going to be walking the streets of gold."

"We'll still want to do splits on this," the assayer said as he pulled a device to the fore that would divide the pulverized gold into three separate sample splits.

"Don't bother. When I leave, I'll be giving away the claim, so

I don't need to establish an average yield or prove the ore is high grade."

The assayer shook his head and put some of the pulverized gold into a crucible. He selected litharge as the flux and mixed it in to help the metal melt. The crucible went into the D-shaped upper door of the combination furnace and came out a half hour later. Carefully he poured the melt into pointed-bottom molds and whistled. "Hardly anything but color here."

While that cooled, he filled several more crucibles.

Jarrod knew he had to stay on the far side of the counter, but he leaned forward to watch the assayer empty the molds and shatter away the glass-like slag to get to the metal that had sunk to the bottom. He placed the metal into heated bone ash cupels and placed them in the other door of the furnace. The litharge burned away, leaving nothing but the metal button-shaped dore. Once freed from the cupel, the dore was painstakingly weighed, then dipped in nitric acid to remove any silver. All that was left was gold—which, of all things, looked like a black button.

The dore was weighed again, and the assayer murmured, "You're losing almost no weight here. Your sample is nearly pure gold."

The clerk and assayer listed each dore, added up the weight, and independently calculated the value of Jarrod's bonanza. They conferred and showed Jarrod their ciphering. "At $20.67 per Troy ounce, sir, you just struck it rich. Never saw anything like it. That is a vein of pure gold."

" 'Tis a miracle. God put it there." Jarrod shook his head. "I'm blessed."

⌒⌒

Angel tossed the hot potato from one hand to the other. Its warmth felt wonderful. Jarrod had brought back two gunnysacks of potatoes. "You're going to have to dig that root cellar even bigger now."

He grinned. "It'll be worth it."

Ben snorted. "Why bother? Weather's turned. It'll be cold enough to keep them in your cabin."

Jarrod ignored him. "I sold the sauerkraut. Since the keg was yours, Harv, and Angel did all of the work with my cabbage, I reckoned we all ought to get something out of it."

"Kraut's not worth much." Harv scratched the back of his neck.

"Worth plenty," Ben said as he leaned forward. "How much didja git for me?"

"Winter's coming." Jarrod gave Angel a smile that warmed her heart every bit as much as the potato warmed her hands. "I brought back kerosene and wicks for our lanterns."

Ben shot to his feet. "You had no right. Wasn't your money to spend."

"It was mine, and I'm delighted." Angel looked up at her stepfather. "You're in the tent with a lantern. Mama and I will need to use the other, so the extra kerosene—"

"This is your fault, Scotsman. Built that stupid shack, and now it's costing me."

Angel wanted to cry. Her stepfather was a miserable, selfish lout. Just yesterday, she'd seen him swipe the horehound candy, leaving none at all for Mama. Now he wanted to rob Mama of the comfort of a lamp.

Harv banged his plate on his knee. "Aw, pipe down, Ben. The way I see it, he did you a favor. Now you got an empty tent to work in all winter. Sure beats freezin' outside like you done last winter."

"This ain't none of your business."

Jarrod folded his arms across his chest. "The business was his, Angel's, and mine. Harv helped raise the uppermost logs and roof. The deal didna involve you at all."

"Forget dealin' with the man, Jarrod." Harv glowered at Ben. "He ate your taters and my venison, but he didn't put a morsel on our plates. Something for nothing—and even that's not good enough. Plain and simple, he's a leech."

Ben blustered, "Angel cooked that food!"

Jarrod nodded. "Aye, she did a fine job of it too. I doubt there's a harder workin' lass on the face of the earth. If you were her father, you'd have call to be proud."

His words of praise made Angel's heart sing. So did the fact that he stood up for her. Ben was the one who disavowed any blood tie to her. Jarrod simply underscored that now.

"Speaking of parents, Angel, is your mama feeling well enough for me to pay her my respects?"

"She'd love to have you visit."

"Sickly old women and root cellars," Ben sneered. "Never saw a man waste so much time."

"What a man counts as important is between him and God."

⟳

Two months later, Jarrod slipped the section of log back into place inside his cabin. He'd chiseled about a foot free, hollowed the core, and filled it with more gold. Once mortared in place, it made a perfect hiding place.

The vein of gold had narrowed to a mere thread, but he didn't care at all. He had more than enough now to take Angel to a modest ranch and provide for her. God had blessed him with all he needed in a material sense. *Lord, open the lass's heart fully to Thee. The bloom of her love took a bad frost. Winter's here, and yet Thou canst make a flower bloom at any time. Tend her spirit, and then let me tend her heart.*

He put on his jacket and tromped through the snow to Angel's cabin. "I chinked a few places between my logs and have extra mortar, Angel. Do you have a few areas that need a wee bit of attention?"

"You built it soundly, Jarrod."

"But there are bound to be a few spots." He walked around and dabbed a few places here and there. Angel accompanied him, and he waited until Ben's back was turned and handed her a bottle.

"Boveril?"

He nodded. "If you get snowed in, you and your mama can dilute it and heat it over the kerosene lamp to have beef soup."

His eyes narrowed as her hands shook when she slipped the bottle into her skirt pocket.

"Lass, I've an early Christmas present for you. 'Tisn't much, but I'd rather you have it now. Come with me."

"Jarrod! You don't need to give me a thing!"

He ignored her protest and took hold of her elbow. As soon as they reached his cabin, he let go. She'd not come inside, and he'd not have it any other way. He ducked in and reappeared. "Close your eyes."

A beguiling flush filled her cheeks as her lashes fluttered shut. "This isn't right, Jarrod. I don't have anything for you."

"Hush." He unfolded the fawn-colored cloak and draped it about her shoulders. The thick wool swept around her. He was sure the cloak would match the brown and golden shards in her eyes, as he fumbled to fasten the button at her throat. "Merry Christmas."

Her eyes opened. A glistening of tears turned them into molten gold. "Jarrod, it's so beautiful!"

"The woman who's wearing it is beautiful." He pulled up the hood and gently tucked strands of her soft hair inside the dark fur trim. "There."

She slipped her hands out and clasped his. "Thank you."

Pete wandered up. He chuckled. "Now will ya get a gander

at that. Our Angel's wearin' new duds. I was in town yesterday. Came by to drop off a letter and pass on the word: Sunday, they're holding a Christmas tent meeting. Circuit rider's scheduled to be here."

Jarrod's heart jumped. He smiled down at Angel. "I'd be pleased to take you."

"She ain't going nowhere with you, Scotsman." Ben's bellow split the cold air. "Least of all to church!"

∞

"I want you to go with Jarrod," Mama said. "I'm giving you my permission."

Angel sat on her cot and stared at her mother in surprise.

"I heard Ben shouting. I made a terrible mistake marrying him, Angel. I was so lonely, and he was the first man who paid me any attention after years of widowhood. I knew he wasn't a believer, but I ignored God's Word and married him anyway. Foolishly I was sure I could change him. All it did was cause you and me both misery. I won't have him ruin your life anymore. Go. Go to church. I'll tell Ben I'm letting you."

Ben's dark mood couldn't ruin Angel's excitement. The beaming smile on Jarrod's face when she gave him the news warmed her every bit as much as the cloak. Harv volunteered to come over to feed Mama stew for lunch, and for the next three days, Angel thought of almost nothing other than the fact that Jarrod would be taking her to church.

Saturday night, she boiled water, bathed, and washed her hair. After it dried, she sat on the floor, and Mama helped her roll the back of it in rags so she could arrange her hair in a suitable style for Sunday. When they were done, Angel went to the shelf to get Mama's medicine.

It was gone.

Chapter 11

Jarrod heard Mrs. Frisk's cough as he walked to the cabin. Angel opened the door, but she wasn't ready for church. Pale faced and red eyed, she stepped outside and shut the door. "I can't go."

"Not with your mother sounding like that," he agreed. "What happened? She was stable."

Tears spilled down Angel's cheeks. "Her elixir is gone—there was still almost a full bottle yesterday afternoon. I know it's Sunday, but when you're in town, could you see if the storekeeper would open just long enough for you to buy some?"

Jarrod wrapped his arms around her. "No need to weep, lass."

His jacket muffled her whisper. "Use the money you're keeping for me."

He dipped his head and brushed a kiss on her temple. The dear woman in his arms was willing to sacrifice her own escape for her mother's sake. "There's no need. I've two bottles of Dr. Jayne's at my cabin."

"I still want you to go to church without me."

He cradled her face and said in a soft growl, "We'll be havin' our verra own church right here."

"Oh, I'd like that. Mama would too."

"Go on inside and keep warm. I'll be back in a trice."

Jarrod went to his own cabin and quickly collected several things in a gunnysack. Just as Angel opened the door for him, they heard a loud roar and looked just in time to see Ben fly through the air and splash into the nearly iced-over creek.

Harv stood at the bank where Ben had been. He wore a thunderous scowl as he stared at the hole in the ice a good four feet away and waited until Ben surfaced. "Served you right," Harv bellowed as Ben started to climb out of the frigid water. "I shoulda done that months ago." He stomped up to the cabin and demanded, "How's Mrs. Frisk?"

"Jarrod brought her some elixir." Angel pulled them both inside and latched the door. "There's not much space. Please take a seat on the other cot."

Harv ignored her. He stood over Mrs. Frisk and nervously rubbed his knuckles. "Don't like how you're a-coughin'. I aim to lift you a tad higher so's to ease your breathing. Angel, stick something 'hind her shoulders. That ought to help a mite."

It took but a few moments to situate and medicate Angel's mother. By then, the poor woman was exhausted. Harv waited to be sure she'd fallen asleep, then growled to Jarrod, "That no good varmint met me at the bridge. Said I didn't need to come check on her. Bragged he'd made sure Angel wouldn't be going no place. Know what he did then? Poured out Mrs. Frisk's medicine."

Angel went white and turned away. Jarrod longed to speak with her privately, but he didn't want to leave her mother alone, and Harv needed to be calmed down. Then again, Jarrod wasn't sure he was the man to pacify anyone at the moment.

"I shouldn't have planted him a facer; I shoulda filled his hide with buckshot." Harv rocked back and forth in agitation.

"The Bible says to do good to them who hurt you." Jarrod shook his head. "Right about now, that's about the furthest thing from my mind."

Harv snorted. "Yeah, well, I was thinking of another verse. Told me just where to aim my buckshot: Turn the other—"

"Enough!" Jarrod silenced him.

"Sorry, Angel," Harv said. "I have a bad habit of letting my temper get ahead of my sense."

Angel reached up, but from his vantage point, Jarrod couldn't tell whether she was rubbing weary eyes or wiping away tears. He softly said, "We're not going into town, but that doesn't mean we can't have our own Christmas service right here. Why don't you nap a bit, Angel? Harv and I'll go fix a nice meal. When you and your mama wake up, we'll all break bread and worship."

"Could we?" She turned around, and a tiny bit of hope glimmered in her sad eyes.

"Absolutely."

Harv cleared his throat. "I'm not 'zactly a Sunday-go-to-meetin' kinda fella, but I'd be proud to join you."

"There you have it then. We'll be back after awhile." Jarrod gently turned Angel to the side and smiled at her baffled look. He reached up and teased free the knot holding a length of rag. A satiny soft ringlet unwound and curled about his fingers.

"Oh!" Embarrassment colored that small sound.

"A woman's hair is her crowning glory, and I'm thinking you're quite a princess." He lifted her off her feet, laid her on the cot, and as Harv luffed a blanket over her, Jarrod brushed her curls on the pillow. "Rest, lassie-mine."

"Make up your mind," Harv teased. "Is she a princess or is she a mere lass?"

Jarrod walked past him and waited until the second he was shutting the cabin door to say, "My lass is a princess."

~

"Do good to them who revile you for My name's sake." The instruction played through Jarrod's mind. He didn't have a right to welcome Ben into the women's cabin. Yes, Angel's mother was Ben's wife, but his neglect and outright abuse gave ample cause for the women to be insulated from him. Even so, Jarrod tried to do the

right thing. He dished up a portion of the meal and took it to Ben's tent.

"Ben?" The tent flap was loosely tied back, so Jarrod stepped inside.

"Get out!" Ben wheeled around and roared.

Jarrod stood rooted to the ground. The dirt bore an arc-shaped scrape from a small chest having been pushed aside. In the earth beneath where the chest had stood was a hole—and in it were stacked several of the small leather pouches placers used to hold their flakes.

"You've starved your kin and wanted to pawn off a family treasure, yet you have more than sufficient to provide for them?"

"Ain't none of your business." Ben shoved the chest back over his stash.

"I'm making it my business."

"Not a week after I married what was s'posed to be a rich widow-woman, I found out the house she was a-livin' in belonged to her uncle and she only had fifty stinkin' dollars to her name. I figgered to leave her a-hind with the excuse that I was going prospectin', but she took a mind to tag along. Said a woman belonged with her man. You got no call to be judgin' me. She made her bed, and she's lyin' in it."

With painstaking care, Jarrod set down the plate. "Esau sold his birthright for a meal. I'm thinking you sold your soul for gold."

Ben rose and stood toe-to-toe with him. "Then I'll sell my family too. You keep yer mouth shut about my stash; I'll leave them alone and let you come on my claim to provide for them."

∞

Angel smoothed the russet shirt, took a deep breath, and reached for the door. She'd slept hard; so instead of forming orderly ringlets she could style, her hair spiraled in an impossible commotion she'd tried to contain in a ribbon at her crown. *Mama's in her nightdress, I'm a mess, and we're entertaining for Christmas. I didn't even cook or—*

"Let them in, dear," Mama whispered. "It's cold outside."

"Happy Christmas." Jarrod smiled at her with enough warmth to melt every snowdrift in Colorado.

"Yeah, Merry Christmas. Now git inside afore I drop something." Harv nudged Jarrod inside.

In a matter of minutes, the men dragged in a small bench, tossed a towel over it as a tablecloth, and set several dishes on it. Harv sidled between the "table" and Mama's cot, scooped her up, and sat down with her on his lap. "Beggin' your pardon, Mrs. Frisk, but I want you to have a good meal; and you'll waste all of your strength trying to sit up on your own. I mean no disrespect."

Jarrod sat next to Angel. "I'd like to say grace." He said a simple, heartfelt prayer, then lifted the Dutch oven's lid with a flourish. "M'ladies, Christmas dinner is served."

Angel smiled at Jarrod. "Roast duck and baked apples—you and Harv put together a wondrous feast."

Awhile later, Mama said, "I can't eat another bite."

Jarrod wiped his hands and reached into a bag. He pulled out his Bible. "I thought to read the nativity from Saint Luke. 'Tisn't just a fairy tale or a birthday story. The King of creation sacrificed His Son to ransom us—each one of us—back into His family. Divine love paid the price."

Grandpa used to read this passage, then Uncle Blackie did. Angel hadn't heard it for years. She closed her eyes and listened to Jarrod's rich, deep voice as the words of Christ's birth filled her tiny cabin.

"We oughtta sing a carol or two," Harv decided aloud when Jarrod shut the Bible. They sang "Hark! The Herald Angels Sing," then managed to mix up all of the gifts in the "Twelve Days of Christmas," and ended with "Silent Night."

Mama glowed with joy, but her weariness was unmistakable. They tucked her in, then cleaned up the supper mess. Angel insisted, "I'm doing the dishes."

Harv chortled. "Won't hear me complain. I hate that chore."

As they worked together, Angel quietly confessed to Jarrod, "Hearing the Bible does something deep inside of me. Until you came, Mama and I had gone years without the Word or church at all. I'd nearly lost faith, thinking God forgot us."

"God never forgets His children."

"I suppose not, but this child sure lost sight of Him. You tell me I'm a princess, but—"

"No buts. You're the daughter of the King of kings. Might be that your faith got weak, but that happens when you don't have the Bible or any Christian fellowship. God's here with you, and His arms are open wide. He's glad to have you run to Him."

"When you were reading the Christmas story, I was thinking about what you said. Divine love—God ransomed me back with His sacrifice of love."

"That He did. I'm leaving my Bible in your cabin so you can read from it for yourself each day."

"Jarrod! You can't do that. You treasure your Bible."

They'd finished the dishes. Jarrod cleared his throat and folded her chapped hands in his. "We need to have a talk, lass. Things are changing."

She dipped her head. *He's leaving. I should have known.*

"I told you from the start that I didn't plan to stay here for long."

Lord, I've started to lean on Thee again, and with Jarrod leaving, Thou art the only way Mama and I will make it.

"But your mama's doing poorly."

Give me strength, God. I'm not just losing my mama. I'm about to lose the man I've come to love.

Jarrod watched the color drain from Angel's face and slid his arm around her waist. He drew her into the shelter of his arms. "I know losing her will grieve you. I'll miss her too. She's a dear woman."

Angel remained silent. She nodded, and tears slipped down her cheeks.

Jarrod tenderly brushed them away. "I'll be staying 'til she goes home to be with the Lord." His heart wrenched when Angel let out a small sob. He cradled her head to his chest but used his thumb to tilt her jaw up so she'd still face him.

Somewhere in the span of months he'd been here, the time that he was ministering to her in God's name had also become a courtship. At first, he'd been wary of that fact because he didn't want Angel to think he'd used God as a tool to work his way into her heart. She'd needed spiritual restoration, and he didn't have a doubt in his mind about the strength of her faith. Love had blossomed alongside faith—and that boded well for marriage. He looked at her and knew the time had come to speak from his heart.

"I'm wanting you for my wife, Angel. Will you come away with me on that day? We've a future waiting for us together. I've fallen in love with you, lass. I'll cherish you as the Bible tells me to."

"You love me?"

He chuckled softly. The dazed look in her eyes might have hurt him, but the wonder in her voice and the hope in her smile charmed him. "Heart and soul. Will you be my wife?"

She clutched his jacket with both hands and burrowed close. "I kept telling myself not to fall in love with you because you'd leave. I couldn't help it, though. I prayed God would send someone to help, but I never thought He'd really hear me. You're the answer—not just to my dreams, but to my prayers too."

Jarrod finally allowed himself the kiss he'd waited and longed for. He sealed their engagement with a kiss that held the promise of a bright future.

When they parted, Angel took a few moments to catch her breath and gather her wits. "But Jarrod, you were going to stay until you'd have enough gold for a ranch."

"Lass, I've had enough gold for a ranch now for a whole season. God blessed us with a sweet little pocket here on my claim. We've gracious plenty to meet our needs."

"Then why did you stay?"

"Because the gold in your eyes was more precious to me than anything else. The real treasure wasn't what the current of the river swept my way. It's what the path of God brought."

"You sacrificed your dreams to stay with me?"

"No, dearling. I realized my heart's desire when God set me down here next to you. 'Twas no sacrifice—'twas a joy." He pulled her ring from his shirt pocket. It sparkled in the weak winter sun. "This band was a token that God used to bring us together. It even had my initials inscribed inside—see here? JM. I want you to wear it now as a symbol of our engagement. Your grandpa made this band for your grandma from gold he found, and I thought it was a fitting tradition. I've had gold from my claim made into a band of your verra own. 'Twill fit alongside this the day we take our vows."

"Ben will take it from me."

"Nae, lass. Ben willna ever bother you again. You and your treasure are safe at last."

Epilogue

Christmas morning brought no more than a light dusting of snow. Jarrod stopped by the root cellar that he'd emptied. Once it held God's gift of gold for him to ransom Angel from this place. Now a cross stood over it. Angel's mother had been delighted with the news of their engagement. She'd given her blessing and said a sweet prayer for them. The very next day, she'd simply failed to awaken from her midmorning nap. Jarrod rested his hand on the cross and promised softly, "I'll be takin' your daughter to a nice little place, and she'll be cherished. God keep you until we meet again at His banqueting table."

He nodded at Pete and Harv. They stood off to the side. Jarrod's things took most of the space on Otto and Beulah, but one gunnysack held Angel's things. Ben had blustered last night about Angel trying to steal his supplies, but she'd packed nothing but her clothes and the little wooden rose her mother passed down to her. All of Harv's possessions formed a haphazard lump on the back of a placid-looking mule. He'd been happy as could be when Jarrod and Angel asked him to join them on the ranch Jarrod bought.

The men each held the halters of a trio of horses. Pete and Jarrod had gone into town yesterday so Jarrod could quit claim his place over to Pete. Jarrod then bought the horses so they could travel on to the ranch he bought.

The day he'd heard of the Christmas service, he'd been sent

a telegram from a widow whose ranch he'd admired. They'd kept in contact, and with the silver panic and the devaluation of land, she'd decided to sell. Now, that spread would belong to him and Angel. He didn't want his wife having to walk out of here—he wanted her to ride like a queen.

Jarrod crossed Ben's claim one last time. The hour had come for him to collect his bride. He patted his pocket. Angel's band nestled there. Soon it would glitter on her hand, always to remind her she was his true treasure. He knocked on the cabin door and called out from the second chapter of Song of Solomon, " 'Arise, my love, my fair one, and come away.' "

Cathy Marie Hake is a southern California native who loves her work as a nurse and Lamaze teacher. She and her husband have a daughter, a son, and two dogs, so life is never dull or quiet. Cathy Marie considers herself a sentimental pack rat, collecting antiques and Hummel figurines. She otherwise keeps busy with reading, writing, and bargain hunting. Cathy Marie's first book was published by Heartsong Presents in 2000 and earned her a spot as one of the readers' favorite new authors. Since then, she's written several other novels, novellas, and gift books. You can visit her online at www.CathyMarieHake.com.

Winterlude

by Colleen L. Reece

Chapter 1

Early November, mid-1930s

Ariel Dixon gazed into the shadowy image reflected in the mirror on her bedroom wall. Dread of the coming interview with her aunt showed in the sea-green eyes. An inner voice taunted, *You have to tell her.*

Ariel turned from the mirror, but the accusing voice went on. *Where is your Dixon courage? You've faced raging seas, been chased by wild animals. How hard can confessing to Aunt Rebekah be? You don't want her to hear what you've done from someone else, do you?*

"No! Please, God, give me strength," Ariel prayed. She sat down on the fluffy green bedspread that matched the brocaded draperies at her window. Peace gradually crept into her troubled heart. God would not desert her. She took her well-used Bible from the bedside stand. A tiny envelope rested inside the front cover. Ariel's fingers trembled when she opened it. Even after twelve long years the dusty remains of a single forget-me-not brought pain. Why had her girlhood companion vanished without a trace? Why did Jean Thoreau's memory still have the power to stir her?

Oh, for those long-ago carefree days! The excitement of life in San Diego had pushed precious memories aside. Now they returned full force, along with contempt for herself. "How could I have fallen prey to the lure of fool's gold after knowing Jean?" Ariel whispered.

A tap at the door interrupted her. "Yes?"

"Madam would like to see you in the library," the Patten

butler announced. "She seems dreadfully upset, Miss Ariel."

The troubled girl's heart sank. She should have told Aunt Rebekah the minute she got home instead of cowardly hiding in her room. Heart pounding, she rose and followed the butler downstairs into the library.

Rebekah Patten, hair as fair as Ariel's except threaded with silver, occupied a throne-like chair beside the fireplace. Ariel marveled at how little the beauty that captured a wealthy husband and elevated Aunt Rebekah to the top of San Diego society decades earlier had faded.

Blue eyes snapping, her aunt demanded. "I've just learned you threw a tantrum and broke your engagement because Emmet Carey refused to let you browbeat him into taking you to Ketchikan for what he called a 'winterlude,' whatever that is."

"Breathing space to get away from San Diego."

"What triggered this off? And why at this particular time?"

Ariel stared at the ring finger that felt strangely light without the Carey heirloom betrothal ring. "I saw a snowflake."

Rebekah gasped. "A *snowflake*? Have you taken leave of your senses? Snow seldom falls in San Diego and never at this time of year."

With a rustle of skirts, Ariel rushed across the room and flung herself onto the priceless Oriental rug by her aunt's chair. "I really did see a snowflake. It was on the windshield of Emmet's car, as out of place here as I am." She grasped her aunt's well-cared-for hand. "Will you do something for me? Something I want more than anything in the world."

Rebekah's eyebrows rose. "That depends on what it is."

"I want to go home. I know I promised to stay a year, but I miss Ketchikan so much—and Dad." Scalding tears escaped.

"Then your break with Emmet is final? Does it have anything to do with his mother? I never could stand her."

Relief flowed through Ariel. At least Aunt Rebekah wasn't

chastising her without hearing her side of the story. "His mother is only part of it. It's Emmet. And the Carey cook." A nervous giggle escaped. "Would you believe that Emmet checked his watch and was more concerned about offending the cook by our being late for lunch than taking me home so he could meet Dad!"

Rebekah's hand tightened on hers. She said nothing, but Ariel detected the beginning of sympathy in the watching eyes.

"The snowflake made me realize I could never promise, as Ruth did in the Bible, 'whither thou goest, I will go. . .thy people shall be my people.' Another scripture came to mind: 'Be ye not unequally yoked. . . .' Who could be more unequally yoked than an Alaskan fisherman's daughter and a pillar of California society?" Ariel sprang to her feet. "Emmet had the nerve to tell me it was a good thing you rescued me from life among uncivilized fishermen, except it was too bad it wasn't sooner, and that—"

Rebekah interrupted. "Didn't you tell him your father is the uncrowned king of the Alaskan salmon industry? Unlike the Careys, he inherited nothing but built an empire."

"It didn't impress Emmet. Not even that in the fish famine of 1927 when fish failed to come to Dixon Industries, Dad pursued them. He kept the business afloat, although thirty other canneries went broke."

Ariel choked back indignation. "After Mother died, Dad told me, 'It's just you and me now, mate. Our Father in heaven will see us through. God loved all the people in the world enough to send Jesus to die so those who believe on Him can live forever. He will make sure your mother's happy until we go to her.'" Her voice dropped to a whisper. "It was the only time I ever saw Dad cry."

Rebekah sniffed and Ariel brushed away her own tears. "How did I ever think I could abandon Alaska, the thrill and challenge of facing and conquering wilderness and weather? How would I feel to never again stand with a swaying deck beneath my feet? Or hear Dad bellowing fishermen's songs one moment and offering prayers the next? I've been living in Emmet's world and agreeing with everything he suggested. What would Dad think of my becoming a spineless jellyfish?"

"How did your father respond when you announced your engagement?"

Ariel squirmed. "His telegram only said I was twenty-four and should be old enough to choose my mate."

Rebekah grunted. "*Should be old enough* can mean anything. So why did you want to take Emmet to Ketchikan?"

"Dad says you find out what's real when you pit folks against a squall at sea or a blinding snowstorm. Away from civilization people learn to know one another. I asked Emmet to take me home, marry me, and spend our honeymoon there so he could learn who I really am."

"And?"

"He said that even if it wouldn't upset his mother's plans for a Valentine's Day wedding, the last place he intended to spend his honeymoon was in such a godforsaken place. Suddenly life with Emmet yawned before me like a crevasse in a snowfield. 'His' wedding. 'His' honeymoon. Not ours. I couldn't help wondering if God had sent the snowflake to warn me."

Ariel continued. "Anyway, I told Emmet if he wouldn't go with me, I'd go alone. He gave me an I-know-what's-best-for-you smile and reminded me of all the engagement obligations I had in the next few months. He ended by saying he couldn't permit his fiancée to go running off to Alaska. It would cause people to talk."

Aunt Rebekah crossed her arms and scowled. "Pompous donkey. Then what?"

The unexpected epithet generated a fountain of laughter in Ariel. It spilled into the quiet room like a happy waterfall. "I tore the engagement ring off, shoved it into his hand, and said, 'Your fiancée won't go, Emmet. I shall.'"

"Good for you!" Rebekah laughed until tears came. "What did he say?"

"Just that I'd come to my senses soon enough. In the meantime, how could he explain to his mother and their friends that I wasn't wearing my ring?" Ariel hung her head. "I wasn't very nice. I replied, 'Tell them—and the cook—your fisherman's daughter turned into a mermaid and went back to live in the sea.' Emmet was gasping like a salmon out of water when I slipped through the ornate gate between his estate and yours. Aunt Rebekah, the closing *clang* sounded like a toll of freedom from a prison I hadn't realized surrounded me."

For a long moment, only the ponderous tick of the grandfather clock in the corner broke the silence. Then Rebekah said, "So what are you going to do now?"

"Go home and take you with me if you will come," Ariel burst out. "It would be awkward to stay here with the Careys just next door."

"Are you sure you don't just need your winterlude?" Rebekah probed. "Ariel, did you honestly think Emmet could have passed the test, even if he'd agreed to go to Alaska with you?"

She sighed. "I felt it only fair to give him a chance to realize I'm not soft clay from which he can create his ideal woman, undoubtedly a replica of his mother."

"God forbid!" was Rebekah's fervent answer. Then she smiled. "If you feel like that, you must never marry Emmet, for his sake as well as yours. Money and prestige don't bring happiness. Your uncle and I married for love. Even if the riches had never come, we would still have been happy."

"Like Dad and Mother."

Rebekah blinked. "How do you know? Your mother died when you were young."

"Dad told me that when he stands at the wheel of a ship and sails into the sunset or sunrise, he feels her presence. When he comes home at the end of a weary day, he half expects her to come running to meet him." Ariel drew a ragged breath. "That's why he never remarried. With that example, I can't believe I was so blinded by riches and attention as to think I loved Emmet."

Rebekah sniffed again. "Any girl would be flattered by his attention. After all, he's heir to a fortune and the crème de la crème of San Diego society." She hesitated, then asked, "Ariel, did you have no sweethearts in Alaska?"

"Many friends, but only one touched my heart." Ariel stared at her hands. "As children, Jean Thoreau and I vowed to always be together. I was twelve and he was fifteen when his family went away. No one seemed to know why or where. Today while telling Emmet about Ketchikan, I mentioned forget-me-nots."

A poignant feeling of regret and loss went through her. "The last time I saw Jean, he picked a single forget-me-not. He promised to someday come back to me, but I never heard from him again. I pressed the tiny blue flower and put it in my Bible. There are still a few shreds left."

"Was your childhood friend like Emmet?"

"Not at all. He was slim and dark. French Canadian. He could leap like a mountain goat and run like a deer. Dad taught us about boats, to swim, shoot rifles, pistols, bows and arrows. He insisted we learn how to survive if caught in a blizzard or storm at sea. Dad gave us everything we needed to live in a land that's both magnificent and cruel."

"I'm sorry your friend disappeared."

So am I.

"Well, Ariel, I don't intend to be cheated of my year with you."

The troubled girl felt hollow inside. Would Aunt Rebekah insist on keeping her in San Diego for the rest of the appointed time? Ariel bit her lips to hide her disappointment, but the older woman continued.

"I think we had best send a telegram to your father then

arrange for this news clip to appear in tomorrow's *Evening Tribune* under the headline: 'Rebekah Patten to Journey North.'

"Mrs. Rebekah Patten, widow of Frederick Patten, well-known financier, today disclosed her plans to leave San Diego in the height of the winter season for an extended visit to Alaska. Accompanying her is her niece, Ariel Dixon, whose beauty and charm has taken our fair city by storm. Miss Dixon is the daughter of Thomas Dixon, who is highly respected throughout Canada and the entire northwest—the man largely responsible for turning Ketchikan into the Salmon Capital."

Ariel gave an excited squeal. "Do you *mean it*? What will the Careys do?"

"The Careys—and their cook—can go hang!"

The out-of-character comment from her elegant aunt sent Ariel into hysterics. She finally wiped her eyes and asked, "How soon can we go?"

"Tomorrow." Rebekah smirked. "Wealth and position have their usefulness. Besides, if I know Emmet, he will wait a few days for you to come to your senses and realize you are actually giving up him and the Carey fortune before contacting you. By then we'll be long gone." She paused. "It's only fair that he receives word from you before the paper comes out. Write a note, but just say, 'I meant everything I said. Goodbye, Emmet.' Leave it at that."

Chapter 2

Jean Thoreau bounded up the steps of the Dixon home, paused on the wide, covered porch, and stared down the hundred-foot cliff that overlooked Ketchikan. A wave of thankfulness swept through him. How he loved the comfortable, weathered log house! "Lord, I will never tire of looking across Tongass Narrows to the forests of Pennock Island. I love those green carpets edging the salt chuck of the Narrows."

He closed his eyes and breathed in the briny November air. Visions of changing seasons, each unique and treasured, danced through Jean's head. Quaking aspens, whispering secrets in summer, turning gold in autumn, dropping their leaves to shiver in winter. Wild roses, bluebells, and columbine that nodded in the breeze. Forget-me-nots, bluer than the summer skies.

A pang went through him. Would he ever see a forget-me-not without remembering? He fought familiar pain and muttered, "No use crying over what can't be changed." Yet the desire to board the first plane out of Ketchikan and snatch Ariel Dixon from a future foreign to everything she had known and loved threatened to overwhelm him. Why had her father allowed his sister-in-law to take Ariel to the States a few months before Jean came home and hired on as Big Tom's cannery superintendent?

Jean scowled. It had been long enough for the girl to whom he'd remained true to betroth herself, in spite of their vow to always be together. Jean's sense of fair play rose in Ariel's defense.

What could you expect? You were gone for twelve years.

"It wasn't my fault," Jean protested.

"What wasn't your fault?"

Jean gulped and turned. He hadn't heard the door open but Tom Dixon stood in the doorway, grinning like a well-fed husky. The uncrowned salmon king brushed a tawny lock of hair back from his green eyes and waved a yellow piece of paper. The excitement in his face made Jean's heart beat double time.

Tom didn't wait for a reply. "Listen to this:

"TROT OUT THE FATTED CALF *Stop*. COMING HOME *Stop*. BRINGING AUNT REBEKAH *Stop*. WILL SAIL ON. . ."

Ariel, coming home? Jean leaped into the air and let out a bellow that brought Molly, the Indian cook, running. He swung her around until her dark braids bounced. "She's coming home, Molly."

White teeth gleamed in the dark face. "God is good."

A lump rose to Jean's throat. "Yes, but I wonder why she didn't mention her fiancé."

"Pah." Molly waved a dismissive hand. "She will forget him when she comes and finds you are here."

Jean felt he'd been kicked in the gut. He stared at Tom. "All these months, you never told her?"

Tom shrugged his massive shoulders. Deep lines creased his forehead. "By the time you came back, she was already promised."

"She had the right to know," Jean ground out between stiff lips.

"I've told myself that a thousand times," Tom confessed. "The important thing is what to do now." A gleam came into his eyes. "How would you like to fly to Seattle, take care of some business for me there, and sail back up the Inside Passage?"

Jean's heart leaped. "You have a specific date in mind?"

His boss smirked. "Now that you mention it. . .how soon can you pack?"

"Getting up before dawn and standing at the rail won't get us to Ketchikan any sooner," Rebekah Patten acidly observed from her comfortable shipboard berth a few days after she and Ariel had fled from San Diego. But the sparkle in her eyes belied her complaint.

Ariel cocked her head to one side. She planted her hands on her ivory flannel–covered hips, and grinned. "Lazybones miss the best part of the day."

Her aunt scowled. "Lazybones! My dear niece, it isn't yet five o'clock. Even the sun's asleep. I don't remember you rising this early in California."

"That's because I stayed up until all hours." Ariel secured her hair at the nape of her neck. "Auntie, ever since we flew to Seattle it's like I left all my troubles in San Diego." She dropped to the berth in the best accommodations the ship afforded. "How do you like it so far? Isn't Puget Sound grand?"

"I didn't realize it offered such glorious scenery," Rebekah admitted. "All those islands huddled in the water like giant tortoises."

"You haven't seen anything yet," Ariel promised. "Wait until we reach the Inside Passage. It stretches more than one thousand miles, from Seattle to Skagway. Except for one short stretch of open sea, we'll steam between the mainland and a coastline so rugged it resembles the Scandinavian fjords. We may see whales, bears, and other wild animals."

She chuckled. "Ship captains often rely on the echo of the ship's whistle to help them steer a safe course in the narrow places. Fog and sharp turns can catch the unwary off guard." She smiled. "I am so glad you're going with me. I just wish you'd stay with us forever."

"Nonsense. I'm a bossy old woman who'll drive your father to distraction. He's likely to throw me out long before that. Besides, my dear Frederick is buried in San Diego. Still, if Alaska is as grand as you say, I'll come again. Now be on your way so I can get dressed. Good thing we went shopping in Seattle." She shivered. "My San Diego wardrobe wasn't suitable for this colder climate."

Ariel slipped into a warmly lined parka of silvery green and went on deck. At the steamship rail she faced north and reveled in the predawn chill. It seemed incredible that she'd ever considered renouncing Alaska for Emmet. *You'd have been glad to do so if you had really loved him,* her conscience reminded.

"Perhaps, but I don't," she told the friendly stars, glittering white against the night-dark sky. "I'm just thankful I learned in time how little we have in common." Ariel turned toward the east that had swallowed her playmate twelve long years ago. Sadness filled her. Jean Thoreau had never broken a promise. He must be dead.

A long time later, the ship's bell roused her. Ariel smoothed her hair, exchanged the parka for a hand-knit ivory fishermen's sweater, and hurried to the dining room. Aunt Rebekah sat in solitary state at a table set for five; a beaming waiter stood nearby. Ariel seated herself. "What are you doing here all alone?"

"The captain was called away, and passengers evidently eat at a more civilized hour. What will you have?"

"Flannel cakes, a beefsteak—medium rare—fried potatoes, orange juice, and coffee."

"I'll have the same."

Ariel stared. Her aunt never ate a hearty breakfast. Ariel choked and reached for her water glass. It promptly fell over.

"May I?" An amused voice accompanied a slim, tanned hand that snatched a napkin and vainly tried to stop the cascade pouring onto Ariel's lap.

"Thank you, waiter. Will you hold my order, please? I'll have to change."

Rebekah snickered just as the voice said, "You're welcome, but I'm not the waiter."

It yanked Ariel's attention from her soaked skirt to the man who stood beside the table. She stared at the slim, dark-haired man smiling down at her and rubbed her eyes. Was she hallucinating? She sprang to her feet.

"Who, what. . .Jean? *Jean Thoreau?*"

"Hello, Ariel."

Why hadn't she recognized his voice when he first spoke? Ariel fell back into her chair. "I thought you were dead!"

Jean Thoreau's dark eyes shadowed. "I am so sorry. It's a long story—"

Rebekah interrupted. "One that can wait until after breakfast, I'm sure." She held out her hand. "I'm Rebekah Patten, Ariel's aunt. I am glad to meet you, Mr. Thoreau. Won't you join us?"

The smile that had lingered in the back of Ariel's mind for twelve lonely years flashed. "Thank you." Jean seated himself beside Ariel. "I'll get acquainted with your aunt while you change your skirt."

Ariel rose and stumbled to her cabin, still dazed by Jean's Lazarus-like return. Two questions haunted her: *Where had Jean been all this time? How did he happen to be on the very ship bearing her home?*

The questions beat in her brain through an interminable breakfast, making it hard to swallow. At last Aunt Rebekah fixed her gaze on Jean and said, "Now, Mr. Thoreau, if you will be good enough to tell us your story? You seem to be very much alive. In fact, I'd say as Mark Twain did, that the report of your death was greatly exaggerated." Her smug expression reminded Ariel of a Dixon cat who had roused Molly the cook's ire for licking the meringue off a lemon pie meant for company.

"Alive, well, and the superintendent of the Dixon Cove cannery. Tom had errands he wanted done in Seattle but couldn't get away, so he sent me. He said you were sailing on this ship." Jean's musical voice matched his warm smile. He turned to Ariel. "I promised to come back, you know."

She pleated her napkin, hoping he couldn't hear the loud thump of her heart. To her horror, the question that had haunted her for years escaped her lips. "How could you forget me? Us?"

Desolation filled Jean's eyes. "I didn't forget. I thought you had forgotten me. Every day I expected a letter."

"How could we write?" Ariel protested. "No one knew where you had gone or why you left Ketchikan!"

"I know that now. I didn't then."

Aunt Rebekah tapped her fork against her water glass. "Young man, I suggest that you start at the beginning."

A brooding look darkened Jean's face. "Who knows where it began? Perhaps when *ma mère*, my mother, realized her only son had fallen in love with Big Tom Dixon's daughter. She and *mon père*, my father, respected the boss greatly but feared he might feel a trapper's son wasn't good enough for Ariel. They couldn't bear to have my heart broken and prayed it wouldn't happen. When word came from friends who wanted us to move to Nova Scotia, my parents saw it as an answer from God."

Ariel's throat dried. "And so you went."

"*Oui*. I didn't want to leave. When we reached Nova Scotia I wrote to you again and again. I even wrote to your father, asking if you didn't care to correspond. No answer came. A boy's hope dies hard, but eventually our companionship seemed like a dream, except for my promise to return."

Jean's face twisted. "Mon père died shortly after we reached Nova Scotia. Before ma mère died a few months ago, she confessed their fears—and gave me the letters I had written all those years before." The knuckles of his clenched hands showed white. "She said she didn't want to face her Maker bearing the secret of what she had done."

Rebekah leaned forward in her chair. "You mean false pride kept you and Ariel apart?"

"Please do not judge my parents too harshly, Mrs. Patten. Sickness had taken my bothers and sisters. After ma mère's funeral, I headed west, not knowing what I would find. I went straight to your father, Ariel." Jean's white teeth flashed in a broad smile. "Tom and Molly made the Lost Son's homecoming pale by comparison."

"I don't understand," Ariel said. "Why didn't Dad tell me you came back and were running the cannery? He must have known that I. . ." She couldn't go on.

The poignancy in Jean's dark eyes sank deep into Ariel's soul. "By the time I arrived, you were already betrothed."

Chapter 3

Ariel felt as if the breath had been pulled out of her. The next instant, Jean's husky voice cut through her agitation. "The most beautiful words I ever heard were those in your telegram."

Rebekah leaped into the conversation. "Trot out the fatted calf. Stop. Coming home. Stop. Will sail on..." She broke off and laughed. "Mr. Thoreau, I have a feeling we are going to be friends. Good friends."

"Oui."

Ariel's heart ached. Unless she was sadly mistaken, a fifteen-year-old boy's deep feelings had grown into a man's devotion. Jean's expression showed how much he'd suffered. How could she have fallen prey to Emmet's courtship? Thank God for the misplaced snowflake that had brought her to her senses!

"What did Tom say when he heard your story?" Rebekah wanted to know.

Jean's somber expression changed to mirth. "He slammed his fist on the table and bellowed, 'Blast the Thoreau pride!'"

Ariel felt herself relax. "That sounds like Dad. What else?"

"He shook his shaggy head and said my parents evidently did what they felt best, but they had been wrong. Tom had prayed for my return, knowing nothing else could remove the sadness from your eyes, Ariel. He told me I was the son he never had." Jean stopped and cleared his throat. "When he said you were betrothed, I wondered why I had come back until he added that I was an answer to prayer. He needed me as superintendent."

Before Jean could share further revelations, two fishermen

Ariel knew well strode into the dining room and unceremoni-ously seated themselves at the table.

"Ariel Dixon, what's this about you packin' it in and leavin' us?" Carl, a mackinaw-clad giant, demanded. "Is your fee-ann-see too good fer the likes of us?"

"Naw. No Dixon'd pick a pup like that," Swen, similarly clad, asserted.

Ariel felt her face flame. Reluctance to discuss her broken engagement before she could tell Jean the whole story swept over her. She cast an appealing glance at her aunt, wondering what she thought of the free and easy way these men who had dandled Ariel on their knees since babyhood talked.

Rebekah shook her head, as if reading Ariel's mind. "You can trust Ariel's judgment. I can't imagine her going back on old friends or her country."

"Course she wouldn't. Carl's a dunderhead," Swen affirmed.

"Never said she would," Carl quickly put in. Ariel saw his keen gaze fasten on her bare ring finger. "Don't look like the feller reeled her in." He guffawed. "The way I figger, if a gal ain't tagged, it's open season."

Two pairs of blue eyes twinkled and Swen added, "If me and my pard wuzn't fishermen and old enough to be yore daddy, we'd be campin' on your doorstep, Ariel."

The hearty approval made her blink. "Don't forget. Dad's a fisherman too."

"He's the hardworkin'est, slave-drivin'est man in the north. Fair though. Treats everyone the same." Carl grinned across the table at Jean, who had remained silent during the exchange. "Here's another just like him. We put up a bigger pack this year with Jean Thoreau running the cannery than we ever did with Thad Olson bossin' us."

Smile wrinkles creased the corners of Jean's eyes. "I can't take the credit. We not only had a record fish run, but Olson's selling out to the competition gave us an added incentive. Mrs. Patten, these men and others like them kept the fish coming so fast that if Tom hadn't already stocked up on extra cans, we'd have run out halfway through the season! I hope all this talk of fish isn't boring you."

"Not at all." She smirked. "Why don't you and Ariel go do some more catching up? Carl and Swen can entertain me. I imagine they have some exciting fish tales."

Carl let out a war whoop. "Lady, we'll tell you stories that will curl your hair."

"Good. See you later, Ariel. Nice to meet you, Jean." She waved dismissively.

"She c—called you J—Jean," Ariel stuttered when they reached the door.

"Why not? It's my name."

Ariel laughed and caught looks of approval from the three at the table. "You don't understand," she explained after she collected her parka from the stateroom and preceded him up the companionway to the deck. "In all the time I was with Aunt Rebekah in California, I never heard her call someone she had just met by his first name." She felt curiosity rise and overcome her unwillingness to pry. "What did you talk about while I was changing my skirt?"

Jean laid one hand over his heart. "Ah, that must remain our secret." He bowed and crooked his elbow. "Does mademoiselle wish to take a constitutional?"

Ariel slipped her hand under his arm then stood on tiptoe so Jean could hear her over the mournful cries of low-flying gulls. "Did you really miss me?" She saw his face whiten as they walked to a sheltered spot near a lifeboat.

"You will never know how much."

A memory from long ago surfaced in Ariel's mind. A ten-year-old boy with a wicked fishhook imbedded in his hand.

His face had paled then too. Yet he made no outcry when Tom pressed the hook deeper to release its cruel clutch, then removed it with his knife. Ariel remembered how hard she had cried, hot tears that dripped on the wounded hand. Now more tears gushed: tears for the children they had been, the long separation, even for their reunion.

Jean whispered the words he'd spoken years before. "Don't cry, Ariel. It will be all right." He turned her to face him. "I have come back, *chérie*. Is it too late?"

"No." She felt him tremble when he gathered her into his arms. She heard him whisper, "Thank You, God." His lips, cool and slightly salty from ocean spray, touched hers in their first real kiss.

Hundreds of miles lay between them and Ketchikan. Yet Ariel felt she had come home to a familiar, safe harbor after a long and stormy journey.

The tossing waves, deep ravines, silver threads of waterfalls that Ariel had loved since childhood took on new beauty for her in the wonder of a dormant love that sprang to full bloom. No longer did she impatiently wish to reach Ketchikan. From the shelter of her beloved's encircling arm, she beheld again the land of her birth, the land holding her future. She reveled in the knowledge that whatever storm winds blew, God and Jean would be there to protect her. No wonder she had been unable to equate the excitement of being chosen by Emmet Carey to the love she now hugged close! Prayers of thankfulness for being delivered winged up to heaven from her overflowing heart.

Ariel also rejoiced that Aunt Rebekah was outspoken in her approval of Jean. "A real man," she privately announced to Ariel while the two women stood watching a spectacular sunset over the water. Jean had disappeared after telling Ariel she needed time to inform her aunt of the change in nephews. "I hope you have sense to see it."

Ariel hugged her arms across her chest. "I do. I'm going to marry him." She flung her arms wide. "I want to shout it to the heavens."

Rebekah sniffed and said in a passable imitation of Mrs. Carey, "Ree-ah-lly, my deah. Have you no couth? Our family does not shout our feelings to the heavens. Or anywhere else, for that matter. You must learn to conquer your ill-bred habits."

"*Couth?* What kind of word is that?" Ariel demanded when she could stop laughing.

"*Uncouth* is a word, so there should be a *couth*," her aunt informed her.

Ariel gave her an impulsive hug. "You really don't like Mrs. Carey, do you?"

Rebekah's face took on a pious expression. "As a good Christian woman, it's my duty to love everyone. The truth is, I can't abide her. Never could. She's the kind of woman who makes me want to throw something at her smug face. Preferably something that squashes!"

Ariel gaped.

"Close your mouth, my dear. Gawking is dreadfully unbecoming," Rebekah said in her natural voice. "Ariel, I hope you realize how narrowly you escaped settling for second best."

"I do. I would have, if it hadn't been for that snowflake." She couldn't go on.

Rebekah patted her arm. "I can't wait to see your father's face when you tell him about you and Jean, although I suspect he won't be surprised." She grinned mischievously. "How I wish I could be a mouse in the corner when Emmet and his mother discover you threw away the chance to really 'be someone' for love of a French Canadian fish cannery superintendent!"

"You're absolutely gloating over the storm that will break, aren't you?"

"Guilty as charged."

"So am I, especially since I already *am* someone—a special someone loved by God, Dad, Jean—"

"Don't forget me," Rebekah interrupted.

"As if I could." Ariel hugged her again. When she saw moisture fill the older woman's eyes, she realized how deeply Rebekah cared and tactfully changed the subject. "So what do you think of our voyage?"

"Like stepping back in time. It's so unspoiled. I only regret that Frederick and I never came. He would have loved it."

Ariel's gaze followed her aunt's pointing finger to the brilliant star clusters hanging low in the settling dusk. "It's hard to believe even heaven can be lovelier than this. Yet the apostle Paul reminds us that understanding of the things God has prepared for those who love Him has not even entered the heart of man."

"I believe Frederick is there waiting for me to come. That is what sustains me." Rebekah's voice broke, and she walked away.

Ariel didn't follow. Such sacred moments must remain in the locked chambers of the heart. She hugged the knowledge and went to find Jean.

Chapter 4

Ariel rejoiced that the day their ship steamed into Ketchikan, the cloud-dotted heavens smiled, free of the village's legendary rain. "Instruments recorded nearly fifty-four inches for the record month of November 1917," she explained to her aunt, exulting in the crisp, northern air that stung her cheeks. She shaded her eyes against sun sparkles on the water. And against the tears that threatened when she saw her father waiting for her on the dock.

"So you're here," he said, after Ariel disembarked and threw herself into his embrace. He gave her a smile that rivaled the northern lights. "Welcome to Ketchikan, Rebekah. For a while there, I thought we'd lost Ariel."

"Far from it." Rebekah turned her nose up. "My niece changed kayaks in midstream. I am happy to announce that Jean Thoreau has replaced Ariel's former fiancé." Satisfaction oozed from every word. "I couldn't be more pleased."

Ariel saw the wonder, relief, and delight that played tag over her father's rugged features. "Thank God for that." He released Ariel and grasped Jean's hand. "She's yours, son."

"Of all the. . .it was Jean all the time?" Carl hollered from behind Ariel.

"Course it was, dunderhead," Swen called. "Anybody'd know that."

"You didn't, you old barnacle," Carl retorted. Ariel could hear them still arguing as her father ushered Rebekah, Jean, and her into the Dixon family car.

"We have close to four hundred automobiles in Ketchikan," Tom announced. "Also fourteen miles of road." He laughed his powerful, contagious laugh. "Of course, each just stops where the wilderness begins."

Rebekah gasped. "I've never seen the like."

No wonder, Ariel thought. *San Diego has nothing like this short, wide road along the Tongass Narrows' silver curves that winds through hemlocks. Or houses that cling to the side of the mountain.*

"No flowers now, but wait until summer," Tom promised. "You'll stay, right?"

Rebekah's voice showed gratitude for the instant, unquestioning welcome. "Not too long this time, but I'll come back if I may." Ariel watched her aunt crane her neck to see better and rejoiced when Rebekah showed no nervousness as the big car climbed steep, narrow streets until it reached the Dixon home.

Sight of her beloved home made Ariel feel she had been gone for years, not months. She gloated at the contrast between it and the adobe mansions in California. Long and spacious, with weathered shingles of silvery gray, the house blended into a background of ferns and aspens that led to a magnificent forested slope. Far below, Front Street bustled with fishermen and women, native and white, all waiting for the fish run when the canneries opened and offered work. Curio shops and stores, heavily concentrating on fishing supplies, flanked both sides of the street. Ariel's pulse quickened. Fish. The life's blood of Ketchikan.

Rebekah laid her hand on Ariel's. "It's everything you said."

From her position behind her father, Ariel's gaze met his in the rearview mirror. Rich and renowned Rebekah Patten might be, but her present expression showed she was truly a kindred spirit.

To Ariel's great joy, in the days that followed, Rebekah became part of the family and won Molly's friendship. Perched on a high stool in the well-provisioned kitchen, she confessed that she had longed to cook for years but was afraid of offending her servants if she encroached on their territory.

"Frederick inherited them," Rebekah explained. "They depended on us."

Molly's brown face glowed, and Ariel hid a snicker when the cook produced an enveloping apron, handed Rebekah a pan of vegetables, and set her to peeling. "If the Careys could only see you now," Ariel teased.

"I wish they could," her aunt replied. She vigorously beat potatoes with a masher. "I'm having the time of my life. Who needs fancy dress balls and teas with little cookies so small that what doesn't stick in your teeth falls down your front?"

"You're a fraud," Ariel accused when a flush reddened her aunt's cheeks. "All these years, I'll bet you've just been itching to kick over the traces."

"I have. Not that Frederick would have cared. He never kow-towed to anyone." Her face turned somber. "I didn't know how much I wanted to break free after he died until you came, Ariel, fresh and unspoiled as your homeland."

"Why didn't you visit us sooner?" Tom asked.

"I was never invited."

The sadness in her voice pierced Ariel's tender heart. She choked out, "If we'd dreamed you felt this way, Dad and I would have seen to it you came even if we had to kidnap you."

"I wish you had." Rebekah pounded the potatoes again. "No use wasting time on what's done. Now get to the table or these potatoes will be mush."

∽

Ariel couldn't forget the older woman's expression. Late that evening when she and Jean bundled up for a walk, she said, "It is heartbreaking when there is a misunderstanding between those who love each other."

His quick intake of breath sent an arrow of pain into her. His "oui" betrayed the long years of suffering in Nova Scotia. Ariel wrapped her hands around Jean's mackinaw-clad arm. *I will spend the rest of my life making it up to him*, she vowed. *What Emmet called a "winterlude" is actually only a prelude for Jean and me.*

Jean's hand tightened over hers. "What is it, chérie?"

"When can we be married?" Ariel blurted out. By the light of a million stars she saw radiance spring to Jean's face.

"It shall be as your father says, but I hope it can be very soon."

"So do I. I'm not sure how long we can convince Auntie to stay." Foreboding touched her. "Besides, I have a terrible feeling that if we tarry too long something might happen to separate us again."

Jean stopped short, freed his arm from her clutching fingers, and drew her close. "*Non.* Only death can do that."

The shelter of his arms lessened but did not fully dispel Ariel's fears. She cast a glance toward the glittering sky. A favorite psalm came to mind. "*When I consider thy heavens, the work of thy fingers, the moon and the stars, which thou hast ordained; what is man, that thou art mindful of him?*"

A silent prayer followed. *You* are *mindful of us, Lord. Please protect and guide us so we may live for You.* Wrapped in Jean's love and the knowledge that God cared for His own, Ariel felt the shackles of fear that encircled her heart loosen and fall.

Knowing Rebekah was happily ensconced in Molly's kitchen when Ariel wasn't showing her around Ketchikan gave

Ariel the freedom to roam her beloved country during every spare moment.

Rain inevitably came, but nothing dampened Ariel's spirits. While Jean was busy running Dixon Industries during the day, she scooted about in her cabin cruiser, the *Sea Sprite*. Except for having Aunt Rebekah in Ketchikan, Ariel's California odyssey seemed unreal. Emmet receded to little more than a cardboard character in a meaningless, long-ago play. Every day her love for Jean grew stronger. She gazed down the pathway of years ahead and smiled.

Ariel's love of poetry also rekindled. She had only quoted poetry to Emmet once, a passage from James Russell Lowell's *The Vision of Sir Launfal* that both she and her father loved.

"And what is so rare as a day in June?

Then, if ever, come perfect days;

Then Heaven tries the earth if it be in tune,

And over it softly her warm ear lays:

Whether we look, or whether we listen,

We hear life murmur, or see it glisten. . . ."

Emmet had smiled indulgently and said, "You surprise me, little Eskimo. Isn't Robert Service the only poet Alaskans quote? I'd think 'The Shooting of Dan McGrew' or 'The Cremation of Sam McGee' would be more to your father's taste."

His lack of appreciation for the passage that expressed Ariel's deepest feelings about Alaska cut to the quick. "Robert Service worked as a bank clerk in Whitehorse and Dawson and found material for his poetry," she said. "Dad and I appreciate those ballads for what they are. So would you if you'd experienced the hardship and violence of the gold rush to the Yukon in the late 1890s."

"Deliver me." Emmet yawned, obviously bored. "Glad to find out your literary taste includes something higher." He changed the subject to an upcoming tennis match.

Ariel subsided.

Now she berated herself for appearing acquiescent when she had inwardly seethed. The man she had chosen—nay, he had chosen her, and she had been flattered enough to mistake infatuation for love—had never understood. How easy to see through Emmet and his family here in this untamed land. How impossible when surrounded by the dazzle of pomp and ceremony that ordered the Careys' lives!

Chapter 5

Late one afternoon, Ariel and Jean stood on the wide veranda of the Dixon home. Encircled by Jean's sinewy arm, with a curtain of rain that shrouded everything a few feet from the porch, Ariel felt as if no outside forces could touch them.

"Ariel," he said, "you are what the Bible describes as the perfect woman."

A rush of pleasure swept through her. "I am?"

"Yes." Laugh lines crinkled the tanned skin around his velvet-black eyes. " 'Who can find a virtuous woman? for her price is far above rubies.' "

Ariel laughed.

Jean stared at her. "What's funny about my saying my bride-to-be is virtuous?"

"Nothing." But she couldn't control her laughter. "The scripture reminds me of what happened when Aunt Rebekah and I attended church a few weeks ago in San Diego. The elderly minister quoted that verse. The congregation immediately burst out laughing." Ariel wiped her eyes. "The minister's wife sat in the front row. . .and her name was *Ruby*."

"No wonder everyone laughed!"

Ariel's shoulders shook. "The funniest thing was how long it took the minister to realize why his congregation was out of control."

"Speaking of control, why hasn't your former fiancé rushed

to Ketchikan in pursuit of his lady-love?" Jean demanded. "What kind of man is he anyway?"

Ariel bit back the words, *one you could never fathom.* "First, I'm not Emmet's lady-love. What's more, if he wouldn't come with me when we were engaged, why should he come now that we aren't?"

Jean raised his eyebrows and grinned. "From what you've told me about the Careys, they don't easily give up their possessions, and it sounds as if that's what Emmet considered you. He could at least have written." Jean gave a sound of disgust. "It's not like there are a lot of Ariel Dixons in Ketchikan."

"Just one. A girl who is going to marry you, thank God. Not Emmet Carey."

Love replaced the teasing in Jean's expressive eyes. His arm tightened. "Oui. And on that day Jean Thoreau will be the happiest man in all of Alaska."

Ariel stood on tiptoe, kissed him, and said, "The rain has changed to mist. Let's put on boots and oilskins in case it rains again and walk down to the dock."

A few minutes later they started down the zigzag trail that led to town. Ariel loved how the huge evergreen branches from both sides of the well-worn footpath crisscrossed overhead and made the walkway a green tunnel.

Jean took her hand. "Do you remember walking here?"

"It seems like yesterday." She swallowed a sob.

"Don't look back," Jean said in a husky voice. "Remember Lot's wife. I don't want to honeymoon with a pillar of salt."

Ariel blinked. How like Jean to be serious one moment and joking the next!

Just before they turned into the final switchback before reaching town, she paused. The heavy branches overhead offered protection from the dwindling rain. "Jean, something bothers me." She took a deep breath then slowly released it. "You said when you returned to Ketchikan and found I was betrothed, you wondered why you had come back. Then Dad said you were an answer to prayer and he needed you as the cannery superintendent. Carl and Swen showed up before you could explain."

She felt a blush mount from the collar of her oilskin slicker into her cheeks. "I've had other things to think about since then, and what you said slipped to the back of my mind. I do remember Carl bragging that the cannery at Dixon Cove put up a bigger pack this year with you running it than it ever did with Thad Olson as boss. What happened to Thad?"

A dark shadow spread over Jean's face. "He sold out."

Ariel felt like she'd been kicked by an irate moose. "After all his years as superintendent for Dad?"

Jean's face darkened even more. "Your dad said thanking God for my coming back wasn't just idle talk. There was dirty work going on, and he needed me to help fight it. On the eve of what could be the best haul in years, Thad went over to your father's biggest competitor. No replacement was available so late in the season. Tom said he'd take on the superintendent job himself but needed to be out with the fleet."

"Thad Olson? I'd have staked my life on his loyalty!" Ariel cried.

Jean ground his teeth. "They say every man has his price. Evidently Thad did. Anyway, your dad asked if I'd take the job and help put up a record pack." Ariel felt Jean's muscles relax before he added, "I believe it was God's answer to the prayers I'd offered all the way from Nova Scotia to Ketchikan. Even though you were lost to me, I could help your father." He smiled into Ariel's eyes and set her heart fluttering. "I'm glad I stayed."

"So am I," she choked out.

Jean looked troubled. "Thad not only turned traitor. Now he acts like I'm his worst enemy. Maybe he's jealous that we beat him at packing salmon. Or mad because what he did made him mighty unpopular around the docks. On the other hand, he could be feeling guilty for deserting your dad when Tom needed him the most." Jean smiled. "Let's forget Olson and see what's happening on the dock."

"Forgetting Thad's not going to be easy," Ariel warned when they reached the waterfront. "He's up ahead. Shall we turn back or go into a store?"

Jean's eyes flashed. "Non! A Thoreau does not run from trouble, although there should be none. Olson's a blowhard, but unless he's drinking he watches himself when ladies are present."

So much for that, Ariel thought when the big fisherman lurched toward them. He had unmistakably been cozying up to a bottle, probably more than one. The fumes he broadcast made Ariel's nose wrinkle in disgust.

When Thad reached her and Jean, he stopped square in front of them. With a mocking grin, he doffed a disreputable cap and bowed low. "Well, if it ain't the Salmon King's daughter and his high-and-mighty Boy Wonder, all togged out in oilskins and ready to catch a fish." The rasping taunt grated on Ariel's nerves.

"Get out of our way, Olson." Steel laced Jean's voice.

"I don't take orders from the likes of you, Frenchy." To Ariel's horror, Olson swung a hamlike fist, but Jean nimbly stepped aside. The momentum from Thad's swing threw him off balance. He sprawled to the ground amid a roar from the crowd that had quickly gathered.

Thad shot Jean a murderous glare that left Ariel trembling, got to his feet, and stumbled off toward the nearest saloon. When he reached the front doors he bellowed, "This ain't over, Thoreau," then disappeared inside.

Ariel shivered. The menace in Thad's voice confirmed Jean's earlier evaluation. Her fiancé's taking over Thad Olson's job had earned him a bitter enemy. *God, protect Jean*, Ariel silently prayed.

"Shall we continue our tour?" he asked. Not a trace of concern for the threat showed in his voice. But the twitch of a muscle in one cheek betrayed Jean's regret that Ariel had been exposed to the ugly scene.

She valiantly blinked away tears and fears. "Of course. Let's just make sure we don't walk in any dark alleys."

A glimmer of admiration rewarded her efforts. "Good idea. I always have been afraid of dark places." Jean's grin belied his words. Yet in spite of his joking attempt to turn Ariel's mind away from Thad Olson's threat, as they climbed back up the steep hillside, memories of the hate in the drunken fisherman's face lay heavily on her heart.

Chapter 6

Early the next morning Ariel slipped from bed and looked through the window. Not a cloud in sight. So why did the day fail to put a song in her heart and set her spirits soaring the way such a morning normally did?

A mosquito-like whine caught her attention. It turned to the roar of a radial engine when a seaplane swooped overhead and shattered the silence. Ariel grimaced. The noise seemed like a desecration of the peaceful morning. A flock of screeching gulls scattered out of the way along with a flock of ducks. Their beating wings surged to help them escape the landing monster. Ariel watched the aircraft touch down and slow, pushing a wave of green water toward shore. The engine and the huge whirling propeller stopped when the silver pontoons nudged the floating dock. The cabin door opened; the pilot stepped down and began securing the craft.

When no passengers followed, Ariel lost interest. She bathed and donned the ivory flannel outfit Emmet had once told her was unworthy of the Careys. "Why think of them?" she scolded herself. "You've taken yourself and your outfit out of their lives forever." The thought cheered her, and a delicious aroma lured her down the stairs into the kitchen. "I'm hungrier than a bear out of hibernation," she told Molly. "Where's everybody?"

The cook beamed. "On the porch. They watched the seaplane come in." She deftly flipped a row of hotcakes and called,

"Breakfast, everyone."

Rebekah, Tom, and Jean came in sniffing. Jean's smiling, clean-shaven face and the scent of pine surrounding him made Ariel's pulse leap when he took his place beside her and waited for her father to ask a blessing.

"Molly, you are going to be the death of me," Rebekah complained after Tom said amen. "Your cooking is so good I'll look like a walrus when I go home."

Ariel laughed. "Hardly! All the hiking you are doing burns off the extra calories."

"That's good." Her aunt heaped a plate with hotcakes, crisp bacon, and fluffy omelet. "So what are we going to do today?"

"We could—"

Clang. The heavy metal door knocker on the front door cut into Ariel's reply.

Her father's shaggy eyebrows raised, and he slid from his seat. "Now what? Can't a man have a decent breakfast without being interrupted?" He strode from the kitchen, and his heavy footsteps echoed down the hall that led to the front door.

Ariel held her breath. For some unknown reason, the clanging knocker had set her nerves on edge. So did the slam of the front door. She strained to make out the rumble of voices in the hall that faded and died. Dad and the visitor must have gone into the living room. What felt like an eternity later, Tom appeared in the doorway.

"Ariel, Jean, Rebekah, you need to come into the living room. Now."

"Before I finish my breakfast?" Rebekah sounded outraged.

The look on Dad's face stilled Ariel's involuntary protest. What could be so important it couldn't wait until they finished eating? Molly was already scowling. Long experience with the usually good-natured cook had taught Ariel an important lesson: Molly could not abide folks leaving the table before cleaning their plates. Ariel caught Jean's glance—he looked as bewildered as she felt.

Once everyone was seated in the living room, Ariel took stock of the stranger who had disrupted their meal. The tall, silver-haired man wore a leather jacket and high-laced, hiking-style boots. His heavy knit sweater was slightly stained at the neck; a pair of dark glasses hung like a noodle from the V of the sweater. He held a good-sized, brown paper–wrapped package with a firm grip.

"This is Wayne Hunter, the seaplane pilot. He says he has a special delivery for you, Ariel." Tom glowered. "It's from Emmet."

Wayne nodded at the astonished girl. "Miss Dixon, Mr. Carey's orders are to deliver this to you personally then wait while you and Mrs. Patten pack. I can take three passengers plus freight and baggage with me. We'll call a taxi when you're ready to go." He dropped the package in her lap.

Pack? Taxi? Go? "Are you insane?" Ariel demanded.

"I'll wager I know what's in the package," Rebekah said. "Open it, Ariel."

The bewildered girl glared at the package as if it were a hungry wolf waiting to attack. "How dare Emmet send me a gift? Open it, Auntie, if you like. I won't."

"Gladly." Rebekah snatched the package and tore off layer after layer of wrapping paper. A wooden box appeared. More wrapping paper. Then a small velvet box. She pressed the spring. The box opened.

The Carey heirloom betrothal ring in all its glory glittered from a satin nest.

Ariel heard Jean's intake of breath and turned toward him. He looked as if he had been struck. Rage at Emmet mingled with compassion for the man she loved. The ring surpassed anything Jean would ever be able to afford. "Get it out of my sight," Ariel told Rebekah. "It's too heavy. All I want is a plain gold band like Dad gave Mother."

"Thank you, chérie." Jean's husky voice and the relief in his face sank deep into Ariel's heart.

"It will have to go back," her father announced. A vein pulsed in his forehead. He glared at Wayne. "What was Carey thinking? And what do you mean, wait while Ariel and Rebekah pack?"

The obviously embarrassed pilot turned red as he replied, "Mr. Carey said there was a note in the package that would explain."

Rebekah caught up the wrappings and unearthed a small envelope. "So, let's see what the young whippersnapper has to say." She ignored Ariel's muttered "who cares" and ripped open the envelope. A curious smile crossed her face. "Listen to this:

"Dear Ariel:

"Stop acting like a child and put the ring on your finger where it belongs. Mother is frantic, and we are running out of excuses for your absence. The pilot will fly you down the inside waterway of British Columbia to the docks at Lake Union in Seattle. Reservations are already made from there for you to return to San Diego on a commercial plane. Emmet.

"Of all the unmitigated gall!" Rebekah started to crumple the note then smoothed it out. "Tom, get me something to write with." He grabbed a stubby pencil from his shirt pocket and handed it to her.

Too shocked to speak, Ariel stared at her aunt. *What is she up to?*

Rebekah turned the note over, wrote, stopped to chuckle, and wrote some more. A few moments later, Ariel saw a gleam of triumph in her face. "As folks here say, this will settle Mr. High-and-Mighty's hash."

"What did you write?" Ariel's father demanded.

"Why, Tom, do you think a lady like me would be anything but polite?" She ignored his sputter and began to read:

"My dear Mr. Carey,

"You are evidently under the mistaken impression that Miss Ariel Dixon will renew her engagement. She will not. This will be the second time she returns your ring. Should you be foolhardy enough to send it again, we shall immediately arrange to have it sold. The local Pioneers of Alaska, which provides funds to help the widows and orphans of fishermen who lose their lives at sea, will certainly be overwhelmed by your generous contribution.

"Signed, Thomas Dixon and Rebekah Patten."

In the stunned silence that followed, Rebekah stuffed the note back in its envelope and buried the ring box in its original wrappings. Her eyes twinkled when she handed it to the gaping pilot. "I trust this is safe with you. Emmet Carey and his mother would never permit the ring out of their sight unless they knew whoever handled it would guard it with his life."

A grin lightened Wayne Hunter's craggy face. "You're right about that, ma'am," he drawled. "I've flown for them before, so they know I'm trustworthy. I also happen to know the ring is insured for enough to buy a good share of most of the salmon canneries in Alaska." He stuffed the package inside his worn leather jacket.

Thunderstruck, Ariel couldn't move. Not so her father. He let out a *whoop* that rang from the rafters. It brought Molly running from the kitchen when the others joined in, including the pilot. "It's all right, Molly. A little squall, but it's over now."

The cook planted her hands on her hips and challenged, "Come eat your new breakfast. I threw the cold food out."

Tom patted her shoulder. "Thank you, Molly. Wayne, will you join us?"

"Sorry. If someone will call a taxi, I'll be on my way. The one that brought me here wouldn't wait."

Before long the *chug-chug* of a taxi laboring up the hill gave way to the grinding screech of brakes. When the pilot glanced out the window, Ariel said, "I'll show you to the door." They walked down the hall and stepped onto the porch. Ariel frowned. "I don't envy you when Emmet finds out you failed to carry out your mission."

"Failed?" His keen gaze bored into her. "I delivered the ring. I'm sure kidnapping is outlawed in Ketchikan as well as elsewhere." The laugh wrinkles around Wayne's eyes and mouth deepened.

"Congratulations, miss, on escaping marriage with a stuffed shirt. By the way, the dark-haired young man inside appears more than willing to replace your California fiancé. He looks at you the way I look at my Marie."

"Yes." She shook the pilot's hand. "Safe journey."

"And good fortune to you, miss." He saluted her with two fingers to the brim of his hat and marched down the steps to the huffing taxi.

Ariel watched him go. The multitude of emotions she had experienced in the past hour threatened to overwhelm her. Heedless of the chilly air, she huddled in a chair and allowed the peace of her home to gradually do its healing work. A warm blanket fell over her. "It really is all right," a mellow voice assured from behind her. "Even when we can't understand, we have the promise that all things work together for good to those who love God."

Tears threatened. Ariel reached for Jean's strong hand. His fingers clasped hers. "I know, but Emmet must have spent a fortune to get that ring here and me back there—all because he *and his mother* are running out of excuses for my absence!"

Jean's smile went a long way toward settling her down. But when he said, "Hmmm. Seems like I told you he wasn't one to give up a possession," she pulled her hand free.

"If you ever call me that again, I'll scream."

"Come here, Ariel," Jean raised her from the chair and held her close. "You will never be a possession to me. You will be my companion, my beloved wife."

She nestled in his arms. *Jean speaks wisely*, she thought. God's in His heaven and Emmet is far away. Everything really is all right.

Chapter 7

A few mornings later, Ariel awoke to lazy white flakes drifting from a leaden sky. She donned her parka just after dawn and ran outside to catch snowflakes on her tongue, the way she had done as a child. She waved to Rebekah, who stood just inside the shining window, smiling and shaking her head. Supreme happiness filled Ariel. *Thank You, God. You are so good.*

To her chagrin, the snow continued just long enough to winter-coat trees and shrubs, gateposts and streets, but soon melted. "Too bad," Rebekah mourned at breakfast. Ariel noticed how sunlight glinted on the nicely laid table and danced in her aunt's silver-shot hair. "I wish it had snowed a lot more."

"We will probably need to take you to Juneau for that," Jean teased. "Ketchikan normally gets less than three feet of snow per winter."

"Maybe this time it will be different," Rebekah replied. "As long as I'm in Alaska playing Ketchikanite, I'd like to get snowed in at least once." She cocked her head toward Jean. "Well, if we can't have a blizzard, how about a wedding? You *are* going to marry this girl of yours while I'm still here, aren't you?"

Ariel felt herself redden but felt Jean's strong fingers lace with hers under cover of the starched tablecloth still warm from Molly's iron. "Christmas Eve, if it's all right with my girl." He smiled at Ariel, and her heart gave a happy little bounce.

"No better time," Tom approved. He placed both wool

plaid–covered wrists on the table and leaned forward. "Have you two decided about a honeymoon?"

Ariel hesitated. "Not really."

"You could always go to California," Rebekah wickedly suggested. "I could stay here and you could camp out at my place. Of course, there's always the neighbor factor to take into account." Muffled laughter came from behind the napkin she quickly placed over her mouth when Ariel glared at her.

Tom's *haw haw* almost drowned out Jean and Ariel's emphatic, unanimous, "No thanks!" He laughed until tears came. "So where *do* you want to go?"

Ariel took a deep breath and slowly expelled it. Did she dare speak out, say what lay deep in her heart? "The cannery at Dixon Cove."

Tom stroked his chin. "Not a bad idea. No one's there this time of year. You'd have peace and privacy. The shack's weather-proof." Little motes in the eyes so like his daughter's sparkled.

Rebekah gasped. "They're spending their honeymoon in a *shack?*"

"Don't let him plague you, Auntie." Ariel patted Rebekah's arm with her free hand. "We have a smaller version of this place for use during the canning season. Two bedrooms. Fully equipped and some distance from the cannery. A huge fireplace and a magnificent view." Her heart thumped at the thought. How many happy hours she and Jean had spent at Dixon Cove! Spending her honeymoon there would be perfect.

Her aunt snorted. "How do you know it's fit for human occupation?"

"We check periodically," Tom assured her. "It's a good idea, though, to take a run down and make sure everything's in order. It's only fifty miles. Jean, I can spare you tomorrow. Better go while the weather permits." He chuckled. "Should Rebekah's longed-for blizzard come, you'll have to change your plans, but it doesn't look like she'll get her wish soon." He took a final sip of steaming coffee and stood.

"Thanks, Tom. Great idea. Aunt Rebekah, you can go with us," Jean promised. "You'll love Dixon Cove, cannery and all." His eyes gleamed. "We'll make a Ketchikanite, as you call us, out of you yet."

Rebekah beamed at him. "I can hardly wait!"

∽

Ariel awakened the next morning and bounded out of bed. Sun sparkled on the smooth water far below. The perfect day for Jean and her to show the aunt she loved Dixon Cove. "Thank You, Lord." Heart filled to overflowing, she made ready for the day and ran downstairs caroling,

> "This is my Father's world,
> And to my listening ears
> All nature sings, and round me rings
> The music of the spheres.
> This is my Father's world,
> I rest me in the thought
> Of rocks and trees, of skies and seas,
> His hand the wonders wrought."

Ariel began the second verse and stepped into the kitchen. Her father and aunt sat at the table, and Molly hovered nearby. The expression on their faces cut short Ariel's song of praise. "What's the matter?" One hand flew to her throat. "Where's Jean? Nothing's wrong with him, is there?"

Tom shook his head. "No, but I'm sorry to say your aunt's a bit under the weather."

"I woke up with a stupid sore throat," Rebekah croaked. "Fine thing. I don't have time to get sick."

"I fix." Molly poured steaming water into a large cup and added honey and lemon juice. "You drink."

"Thank you, Molly." Rebekah sipped the brew then said, "Dixon Cove doesn't appeal to me right now as much as a day curled up on the couch with Molly looking after me. Ariel, you and Jean don't need to wait. Go while the weather is nice. You can take me another time. If not now, when I come back next summer. Staying here means I may stop this cold before it develops into something more serious."

"That's right," Tom approved.

Ariel tried to hide her disappointment. "Are you sure?"

Jean stepped into the kitchen, eyes sparkling. "Sure of what?"

"Aunt Rebekah's not feeling well, but she wants us to go ahead with the trip to Dixon Cove," Ariel explained. "Dad agrees with her."

Regret filled Jean's expressive eyes. "I'm sorry, Rebekah, but thanks for understanding. We need to make the most of a good day."

"So, go along with you and do whatever you have to do to get ready," she ordered.

"Yes," Ariel said. "We've had precaution drilled into us since we were toddlers."

"I've already checked the cabin cruiser to see what's on board," her father said. "All you need to add is more food, fresh water, extra blankets, and medical supplies. You'll be all set."

"My goodness! Are they heading for Seattle?" Rebekah exclaimed while Jean and Ariel piled the provisions by the front door.

"No, but this country demands that we be ready for the unexpected," Ariel said.

"You wouldn't go if you thought there was danger, would you?" Rebekah peered out the window. "There's no chance of a storm with that kind of sky, is there?"

Jean shook his head. "You wouldn't think so, but we don't take chances." He smiled at her with a sweetness that showed Ariel he had come to love her aunt.

A kaleidoscope of emotions swept over Rebekah's face. "What if you get caught out overnight?" Her face flamed. "Won't there be gossip?"

Tom gave Rebekah a reassuring look. "Not at all. Folks up here know how sudden a squall can appear or fog roll in so thick that a boat's running lights aren't much help. Besides, Ariel's reputation is such that anyone who casts a slur on her has a lot more folks to deal with than Jean and me." He grinned. "Especially Carl and Swen."

An hour later Ariel boarded the *Sea Sprite*. She thrilled to the simple joy of being alive and with Jean. From the shelter of his strong arm, she waved a bright scarf in farewell to her father, who stood on the dock. Arms crossed, he waved back. A mist came to Ariel's eyes and a lump to her throat. What memories did seeing her with Jean steering with one hand and holding her in the crook of his other arm bring back? So had Dad sailed with her mother during the too-short years they'd had together.

Ariel and Jean made the run south from Ketchikan to Dixon Cove in record time. "You'll want to stay in Ketchikan for Christmas, won't you?" Jean asked. He sounded hesitant. "I know what it means for you to be with Tom."

Ariel blinked at his thoughtfulness. "It would be wonderful." A new thought struck her. "My goodness, aren't we a couple of silly snow geese! We haven't talked about where we're going to live. Will it be with Dad and Molly?"

Jean shook his dark head. A melodious laugh rang over the water. "My dear girl, the fine young man you plan to marry is the proud owner of a mansion. Well, not a mansion, but a comfortable home not far from your father's."

"Really? Where? When did you get it? Why didn't you tell me?"

His face blazed with joy. "When I came back, I learned your father had purchased my family's home shortly after we moved. I bought it from him."

Ariel caught her breath. "I never knew that." She wrinkled her forehead, trying to remember. "For a long time I wouldn't go near the place. I knew I'd cry. When I finally went, the emptiness hurt me." She laid a hand over her heart. "It was even worse when a new family moved in. If I thought about it at all, I suppose I accepted they owned it. Instead, they must have rented it from Dad." She rested her chin on her hand. "I wonder why he bought it. Or why he didn't sell it during all these long years?"

Jean's awe-filled voice sounded choked. "Your dad told me that deep in his heart he always felt I'd come back." He swung the cabin cruiser toward the dock at Dixon Cove. "Tom added he hoped I would be single. . .and come before you had chosen your life companion."

Chapter 8

Ariel felt tears crowd behind her eyelids. "Dad said that? He never told me."

A brooding look crept into Jean's face. "He wouldn't trespass behind the wall you set up, even when he saw you look east a hundred times. If only my parents had told me sooner why they took me away!"

Ariel's heart echoed the wish, but she patted his hand and said, "I wish they had. Yet perhaps we wouldn't appreciate our love as much if we hadn't come so close to losing it." She leaned against his shoulder and laughed shakily. "Now, Mr. Jean Thoreau, you are stuck with me for the rest of our lives. That is, if you'll unwrap Molly's sandwiches before I starve to death!" She felt regret float away on a cloud of healing laughter.

Fed and happy, Ariel inspected the "honeymoon house," as Jean called it, with him at her heels. After he started a blaze in the big fireplace that soon chased away the winter chill, he took her in his arms.

"I love you, Ariel. *Lioness of God*. Will you defend me like the mighty beast from which your name is taken defends its young?"

"After all these years you remembered!" Ariel felt a wellspring of happiness rise within her and she looked straight into his smiling face. "I will defend you to the death, my Jean. A beautiful name that reminds us *God is gracious*. He truly is."

"He will always be Head of our household," Jean vowed in a low voice. "We will teach our sons and daughters about Him from the time they lie in the cradle my father carved for me, his firstborn."

Ariel clutched his arm. "Jean, should God choose not to bless us with children, will you still love me?"

"How can you ask?" His dark eyes flashed fire, the way she remembered from years before when she questioned him on a sensitive point. "Have I not been faithful for twelve long, lonely years?"

"More so than I." Tears clogged her throat.

"Forgive me, chérie." He caught her close. "If you had not believed yourself forgotten by the boy who left you, neither Emmet Carey nor any other man would have caught your fancy. I believe your heart has always been mine."

"It has, even when I didn't know it," she whispered. Doubts fled, and his tender kiss forever sealed the question of whether Jean had forgiven her temporary defection.

Snuggled in the crook of his arm and the familiar cushions of the comfortable sofa before the fire, Ariel fell to dreaming. She didn't rouse until a burned-through log snapped and sent a shower of red-gold sparks up the chimney. Then she glanced out the window, freed herself from Jean's protective embrace, and leaped to her feet.

"What's the matter, chérie?"

Unable to speak, Ariel raced to the window and pointed through the clear glass. Long experience had taught her only too well how northern skies jealously demand complete and undivided attention, especially in winter. And that storms delight in swooping down on the unwary. How could she and Jean have been so caught up in making plans for the future that they hadn't noticed the tendrils of gray-velvet fog creeping from the horizon toward the "honeymoon house"?

Jean sprang from the couch, sprinted to the window, and echoed Ariel's thoughts. "How could I have been so careless? Come. Perhaps we can beat the storm."

"Don't blame yourself," Ariel told him, ignoring the uneasy feeling that crept over her. "Just because I've been in California doesn't excuse me for not watching. Besides, it isn't that bad." Yet even as she spoke the tendrils thickened.

A shadow darkened Jean's face. "Ariel, I have a bad feeling about this. No one can predict how fast the fog's moving or how quick it will reach us. We're better off here than halfway back to Ketchikan. We can't depend on finding shelter the way we once could. A new clement has surfaced, one that laughs at the Law of the North. Carl and Swen told me last winter they got caught in a sudden squall. They fought their way to shore on a small island that had a shack always stocked for emergencies. It wasn't." The succinct words fell like stones into Ariel's heart. "Someone had robbed the cache. Fish pirates, or maybe a fugitive. Carl and Swen had enough food aboard ship to see them through, but they would have been in bad trouble if they'd lost their boat or the storm had gone on for several days."

Ariel felt hot Alaskan blood rise to her face. "A thief up here is as bad as a murderer," she exploded. "Anyone who steals a cache will have to answer to both the law and God." She stared over the waves that reflected the gunmetal skies. "You're right. It would be foolish to attempt a run toward home. Let's pack in what we need from the *Sea Sprite* while we can still see her. As Dad said, these things happen."

By the time they finished carrying their supplies and extra blankets to the house, the fog had rolled in like a juggernaut. Smokelike trails became a solid bank that obliterated sea, sky, and even the well-secured *Sea Sprite*, adding to Ariel's growing concern. She and Jean staggered under the weight of an enormous log and heaved it into the fireplace, making flames roar up the chimney. He also started fires in the small woodstoves in both bedrooms.

Ariel put a kettle of water to boil on the enormous kitchen woodstove and warmed bedding in front of the living room fireplace then made up their beds. When she returned to the kitchen and Jean, who had obligingly offered to start supper, she forced a laugh and commented, "This is deluxe camping out."

He turned from a skillet of sizzling bacon. To Ariel's surprise, he didn't join in her laughter. After a long moment he said, "Ariel, you know you'll be as safe with me here as though I were your father."

Her mouth fell open. "Of course, Jean. There was no need for you to say that."

"Oui." He smiled and turned the bacon slices, leaving Ariel to thank God for the integrity of his big, wonderful heart.

They spent a happy evening discussing a multitude of things. Their Christmas Eve wedding. How they'd return to Dixon Cove Christmas afternoon. How terribly Ariel missed not being in Alaska for the previous summer's fish run and canning season. They talked of excursions, always in the north. "I want to visit or revisit every inch of Alaska," Ariel declared. "I can hardly wait to get on snowshoes and skis, perhaps even train and enter a dogsled race, although not the Iditarod."

Jean's dark eyes gleamed. "Not without me!" Teasing gave way to the poignant expression that hinted of depths waiting to be explored. "God willing, we shall have many years to do all the things you mention and more." When he kissed her good night at her bedroom door, he promised, "Next time we'll be together."

In perfect love and trust, Ariel gazed into his face. "I know." The look he gave her remained in her dreams long after she fell asleep.

To Ariel's relief, which she saw reflected in Jean's face the next morning, the capricious fog soon fled before a brisk wind that sprang up shortly after a pallid winter sun appeared. Only a few festoons remained, hanging like the gray moss that beards giant trees in the endless northern forests. Jean and Ariel made short work of breakfast and packing. Their return trip to Ketchikan proved uneventful. When they arrived, a dozen lounging men, Carl and Swen among them, lounged on the dock.

"Morning," Jean sang out.

A hateful laugh sounded from one of the men who stood back of the others. Ariel recognized Thad Olson. She thought of his confrontation with Jean a few days before and shuddered. His expression shouted that more trouble lay ahead.

Her father's former cannery superintendent elbowed his way through the crowd and sneered, "Come far?"

"From Dixon Cove," Jean briefly explained. "Fog caught us yesterday afternoon." He docked the *Sea Sprite* as skillfully as Emmet Carey parallel-parked his fancy car.

"Shut up, Olson, you're drunk," Swen bawled. Face anger-black, he took a step toward Thad with Carl at his heels. A murmur of approval swept through the crowd.

Ariel swallowed. Hard. She had seen a few dock fights, and the mood of the moment boded well for a full-scale brawl.

"Not so drunk I can't see what's plain to be seen," Thad gloated, an evil look creeping over his face. "And I shore ain't seen no fog. Have the rest of you fellers?" He shot Jean a venomous look even more insulting than his taunt.

Jean sprang to the dock, but not fast enough.

Thud. A mighty splash closely followed Swen's blow. Olson's heavy body hit the water. He bobbed to the surface, bellowing like an enraged polar bear and cursing at the top of his lungs.

"Shut your dirty trap, or I'll finish what my pard started," Carl bellowed. Swen nodded, nursing his skinned knuckles.

"If he can't, the rest of us will," a burly fisherman threatened. "No one talks that way about Ariel. Jean Thoreau either. If they say there was fog at Dixon Cove, there was fog. Olson, either you haul yourself out of the water and apologize or be on the next steamer. We ain't forgot how you walked out on us on the eve of last year's run."

A low, menacing murmur went through the crowd. Men surged forward.

"Wait!" Ariel stepped to the dock. "He's drunk and not worth listening to." She cast Olson a withering glance that brought dull red to his face. His unexpected bath had evidently sobered him up enough to sense danger, for he struggled to shore, grumbled, "Sorry," and shambled away.

"Thanks, boys." Jean put his arm around Ariel. She rejoiced when his smile shone white in his lean, tanned face. "I guess some folks just judge everyone by themselves. By the way, you're all invited to a wedding come Christmas Eve. Ariel and—"

"That isn't necessary," a haughty voice cut in. "Such a small service doesn't require that kind of reward."

Jean's fingers bit into Ariel's shoulders. He took an involuntary step backward. "Who are you?" he hoarsely demanded over the top of her head. "What right do you have to say who shall or shall not come to the wedding?"

"Every right in the world," the stranger said. "I am Emmet Carey, Miss Dixon's fiancé. Now if you will excuse us, we have a previous engagement."

Chapter 9

Ariel couldn't believe her ears. Emmet here? Impossible! She had thought Aunt Rebekah's curt message would penetrate even his tough skin.

"Want we should dunk him too, Ariel?" Swen offered.

"Yeah, give it to him, the stuck-up swell," a loyal Dixon employee called.

Ariel tore herself free from Jean's grip and whirled. It wasn't a nightmare. Emmet Carey stood a few feet away, perfectly turned out and wearing the blackest frown she had ever seen cutting deep lines between his brows. "What are you doing here?" she demanded, her voice colder and more jagged than broken icicles.

Emmet stroked his smooth-shaven chin. "I think my telegram explained sufficiently. I do not intend to engage in a lengthy explanation in front of these men or this buccaneer who has the audacity to lay hands on your person." He glared at Jean.

"Wot's he talkin' about?" Carl wanted to know.

"Beats me." Swen scratched his head with a long, callused finger. "But we're standin' by in case she needs us."

Ariel ignored them. "I received no telegram." Never in her life had she been angrier. She glanced at Jean. To her amazement, not a trace of anger flickered in his eyes, and amusement lurked in their depths. What a contrast between the self-important Californian in all his sartorial glory and Jean, carelessly clad, with a crimson kerchief at his neck. A laugh rumbled deep in Jean's throat then bubbled out like lava from a volcano. Ariel recognized it as the laugh of a conqueror, a man who refused to allow lesser mortals to drag him to their level.

The next moment, Ariel's laughter ran out like a silver chime and aligned her alongside those with whom she had grown up. "This buccaneer's name is Jean Thoreau, the man I'm going to marry," she announced.

When Emmet only crossed his arms and glared, Ariel repeated, "I am going to marry Jean."

The fishermen cheered. All but the intruder joined in the thunder of congratulations. When the crowd at last fell silent, Emmet raised his chin and said dismissively, "I will speak with you at the home of your father. Your aunt will talk reason into you." He turned on his heel and marched toward a waiting taxi. Carl, the irrepressible, fell in a few paces behind him in a ludicrous caricature of Emmet's walk. It set the watching crowd roaring again.

Jean cocked an eyebrow. "Shall we beard the lion in his den?"

"Yes, but it isn't going to be fun!" Ariel bit her lip. An unpleasant interview lay before them. Yet why should it be? She had broken her engagement to Emmet before she knew Jean Thoreau was still alive. She owed her former suitor nothing. *Father, give me the wisdom to handle this.* Peace returned, and a reassuring grin from Jean when they climbed the path to the Dixon home helped immeasurably.

Armed with prayer in one hand and love for Jean in the other, Ariel smiled and entered her home. Her heightened awareness made the living room look like the stage setting for a melodrama. Her father relaxed in a chair. Rebekah lay in her nest of blankets. Molly's brown face peered in from the kitchen. Emmet paced the floor with military precision, now and then stumbling over the giant bearskin rug before the fireplace. Ariel could feel Jean's breath on her neck from where he stood behind her.

"Here you are at last," Emmet snapped. "Ariel, before you explain your actions, I suggest you read this. Aloud, if you like, since it hasn't been opened."

"We aren't in the habit of opening messages not addressed to us," Tom growled.

Ariel felt anger spurt but opened the yellow telegram and read,

"You win *Stop*. Arrive by plane tomorrow *Stop*. Find priest or missionary to marry us *Stop*. Won't affect Mother's arrangements *Stop*. Real wedding Valentine's Day, as planned *Stop*. Have gone to great expense and inconvenience because of your stubbornness."

Priest? Missionary? Mirth bubbled inside Ariel like coffee threatening to boil over, but she swallowed hard. Was Emmet so ignorant of Alaska he thought the only ministers available were the traveling priests and missionaries of gold rush days? She threw the paper to the floor. "I can't understand why you came at such expense and inconvenience. I made it clear in California that I didn't intend to marry you. No, don't leave," she ordered when the others moved restlessly. "Emmet has drawn you all into this. You have a right to know the end of it."

If Emmet heard her, he gave no sign except to stop pacing. "The end will be when we get out of this accursed country and back to civilization. Can you imagine how I felt, finding you the reason for a brawl by a bunch of louts?" He shuddered and rolled his eyes. "I considered bringing Mother with me. Thank God, I did not. She would never tolerate such a scene."

A quick movement brought Jean to Ariel's side. She clasped his muscled arm and squeezed a silent warning. His arm slowly relaxed under her touch, and he said, "Those so-called louts would defend Ariel's honor to the death." Although spoken softly, the words dropped into the hushed room like ice crystals.

"If Ariel had been here waiting for me, where she should

have been, there'd have been no need for such a degrading performance," Emmet flared. "Neither would she be the subject of gossip."

Like a bolt of lightning, Ariel knew what to do. *Thank You, Lord.* "The important thing is not what others think, Emmet. Do you believe Jean and I are guilty of wrongdoing, even in the slightest degree?"

Dull color suffused his patrician face. "Are you *mad*? Of course not! No woman in her right mind would risk losing the Carey fortune by besmirching her reputation with such an escapade." He drew himself to his fullest imposing height. "Anyone can see Thoreau's in love with you. I trust it's enough for him to keep mum." He shrugged. "Anyway, it's a long way from Ketchikan to San Diego."

Ariel's father leaped from his chair in a mighty bound. "That will be enough, you insolent pup. Concerning my daughter *and son*…" He shot a glance toward Jean, whose arm remained imprisoned by Ariel's strong grip. "Their actions are beyond reproach. Yours aren't. Clear out of here before I forget I'm a God-fearing, peace-loving man and throw you out!"

"I'll help," Rebekah volunteered in a voice that showed she meant what she said.

Ariel wanted to cheer. She bit her lip to keep from howling at the look on Emmet's face. He whipped toward Rebekah, clearly aghast at high treason from the one person present he'd obviously counted on as his chief ally. His mouth flopped like a beached whale. No words came.

Not so with Ariel. Jean's laughing question from the day before rang in her ears, as loud as if he had just spoken. *"Ariel. Lioness of God. Will you defend me like the mighty beast from which your name is taken defends its young?"* Her vow: *"I will defend you to the death."* The first chance to keep that vow had come.

Ariel released Jean's arm and stepped in front of him. She

leaned back against his strong chest, both arms outspread to keep him from attacking Emmet. She felt his heart beat, the great heart that so easily shed insults to himself but gave no quarter for those aimed at her.

"Thanks, Dad. You too, Aunt Rebekah, but I'll handle this." Exaltation filled her. "Emmet, Jean Thoreau is farther removed from the tawdry world in which men and women dally with the sacred things of life until they slip into infidelity than Ketchikan from California. Jean would die before uttering one word or committing one act that would cast reproach on my name."

"Well, bravo for him." The red in Emmet's face receded to pallor, but his sct jaw showed he refused to bow to the inevitable. The next instant, he abandoned his sarcasm and donned the boyish, winning smile that had once set Ariel's heart aflutter. "This place has mesmerized you, Ariel. Think. What has this fisherman to offer, compared with my wealth and—and love?" The word slipped out as if reluctant to drop from his lips. "I do love you, you know."

Anger fled. Pity filled Ariel's tender heart. It stilled the accusations that hovered on her tongue, truths she had fully intended to hurl against his arrogance. Jean's love for her was pure and selfless, enduring, akin to God's love for the world. Emmet based his love on her outward appearance, how well she would fit into his world, the children she would bear to follow in his footsteps. A rare flash of insight told her the futility of trying to make Emmet understand.

"Forgive me for not knowing my own feelings," Ariel impulsively said. "If I had, all this unpleasantness would have been avoided."

"You actually *care* for this man?" Emmet challenged.

"With all my heart." Ariel turned to Jean, who magnificently rose to the occasion and extended his hand to Emmet. "I loved him as a child but thought him dead all these long years." She held her breath. Would the breeding and good sportsmanship ingrained in Emmet since childhood be strong enough for him to finally believe any girl in her right mind would turn down a Carey for a French Canadian fisherman?

Emmet ignored Jean's outstretched hand. His jaw set in the stubborn line Ariel knew so well, face darker than the storm clouds that often plagued Ketchikan. His hands clenched. A tiny muscle twitched in his cheek. After what felt like a lifetime, he looked at his watch, the same watch he had worn the day the errant snowflake came to San Diego and freed Ariel from prison bars she hadn't known surrounded her.

"I believe my pilot can still reach Vancouver if we start now." Emmet squared his shoulders, gave a stiff nod, and marched out the door.

Ariel realized the nod was the only outward sign of Emmet admitting defeat that she would ever get. *I can be thankful for even this small token. It truly means he is out of my life forever.* A flash of discernment brought a new thought: *Perhaps that small nod indicates a crack in the Carey shell of pride. If so, there may be hope for Emmet to someday find happiness with another young woman. I just thank God it won't be me!*

When Emmet's footfalls across the wide veranda and down the steps ceased, Aunt Rebekah cleared her throat and announced in a good-riddance voice, "That's that. Now let's talk about the wedding."

Chapter 10

Every passing hour erased a little more of Emmet's visit from Ariel's mind. To her relief, Thad Olson had also disappeared. "Gossip has it he decided to spend the rest of the winter elsewhere," Carl reported.

Swen echoed Aunt Rebekah's unspoken thought. "Good riddance."

Ariel appreciated her faithful friends refraining from questioning Emmet's short stay in Ketchikan even though she saw curiosity in their weather-beaten faces. Their unusual tact made her laugh.

December scurried toward the 24th in a mixture of weather: rain and wind, occasional light snow, and brilliant winter days that set Ariel's heart singing. She had refused Rebekah's offer of a complete trousseau. "I have everything I need, even a wedding dress. Remember that gorgeous ivory silk from San Diego?"

"Are you sure you don't want white, beaded with pearls?" Rebekah asked.

"Jean likes me in ivory." Ariel smoothed the soft flannel of her favorite outfit.

"Then ivory it shall be." Mist crept into Rebekah's eyes. Ariel suspected her aunt was remembering the day she became wife to her beloved Frederick.

"Most everyone in Ketchikan wants to come," Tom complained at one point. "What are we going to do with them?"

"Hold the wedding in the biggest hall in town and invite 'em all," Rebekah advised. "Ariel and Jean are part of this town. Folks deserve to be at their wedding." She sniffed. "You're not sending out engraved invitations with admittance cards, are you?"

Tom raised his hands into the air at her suggestion. Ariel giggled but sobered when she saw a wary look in Jean's eyes.

"I know you don't regret giving up Emmet, but are there any twinges over the lack of fuss and feathers?" he whispered when they were alone.

"Not a single twinge." She happily leaned against his shoulder. "I'm right where I belong. Besides, I do have the fuss and feathers. Auntie fusses over the details and Molly's giving us a patchwork quilt with a pattern of wild geese flying. She made it years ago and put it away for me." Ariel shook her head and another giggle erupted. "Can you imagine the heir to the house of Carey sleeping under a handmade patchwork quilt? You don't mind that it was originally meant for a different groom?"

"Who says it was?" Jean looked mysterious. "Molly had never heard of Emmet Carey when she made the quilt. Maybe, like your father, she thought I'd come back someday." His black eyes twinkled. "She always did have a spot in her heart for me warmer than her big cookstove!"

Ariel opened her eyes wide and pretended amazement. "That big?"

"Oui, chérie." A slow smile tilted the corners of his lips upward, followed by a look of pure mischief. "We will have to be careful or she will spoil our little Ariel and Jean when they come."

Ariel felt hot color surge into her face. She fled, pursued by Jean's boyish laughter.

☙❧

Early on Christmas Eve, Ariel stood in the darkened alcove at the back of the hall chosen as the only place big enough in town to hold her wedding guests. Her heart did a staccato beat, so loud those present must surely hear when she started forward up the aisle with her father. It was almost time. Any minute Jean and the white-haired minister who had known her since childhood would step to the front of the room.

"I intend to remember every detail of tonight," Ariel told herself. Her hand shook as she slid the heavy curtain of her hiding place back a few inches so she could see. She breathed deep, loving the pungent smell of hemlock and pine branches tied with scarlet ribbons that pervaded the air.

Her fascinated gaze rested on candles by the score, casting their soft light on faces of many hues. She stifled merriment. What would Emmet, his mother, and their cook think of the wide variety of clothing displayed? Outdated dress suits and once-elegant gowns rubbed shoulders with plaid mackinaws and soft chamois shirts. Yet San Diego in all its splendor could not begin to compete as far as Ariel was concerned.

The curtain was pushed aside and her father held out his arm. "Ready?"

"Yes."

A little frown appeared on his broad forehead. "No regrets, Ariel?"

She thought of her long years of heartache, not knowing where Jean had gone and why he had not kept his promise to return. Of the fool's gold glitter from a world in which she could have never been a part, while real love waited for her just around a bend in life's road. Of spilling water on the ship's table and an amused voice saying, "I'm not the waiter." Most of all, at the joy when she looked into the beloved face of the one she had thought lost to her forever.

Ariel looked into her father's rugged face. "It's been a long, hard road, Dad, but no regrets. Weeping truly endured for a night. Now God has replaced it with joy."

Her father's smile sank deep into her heart. "Come." He held out his arm.

Pulse pounding, Ariel took it and stepped out of the alcove. One look at Jean, resplendent in a new dark suit and wearing the pride of possession, quieted her nerves. Jean, with whom she would continue the love story that had begun years ago. Step by step she went forward, increasing her pace until her father whispered, "No need to rush, Ariel. Jean isn't going anywhere."

"At least not without me," she returned then wished she hadn't. The last thing she needed was for Dad to let out a loud *haw haw*. Thankfully, he only grunted and led her to Jean.

"Who gives this woman to be married?" the minister asked.

"Rebekah Patten and I do," Tom declared.

A ripple of surprise ran through the room. Ariel sneaked a glance at her aunt. Face wreathed in smiles, she nodded and dabbed at her eyes with a lace-edged handkerchief. Ariel choked up then concentrated on the service.

"Do you take this woman...?"

"Do you take this man...?"

A circlet of gold slipped onto Ariel's ring finger. No memory of the ostentatious diamond ring she once wore rose to spoil the moment.

"What God has joined together, let no man put asunder. You may kiss your bride."

Ariel turned to Jean as a sunflower to the sun. His lips pressed hers in a promise as binding as the wedding vows. Ariel returned his kiss amid loud clapping, followed by a stentorian roar she knew came from her old friend Carl.

"By mighty, now that's what I call a weddin'."

"Amen to that," Swen chimed in.

"Not exactly the way I'd put it," Jean murmured when they turned from the minister to face Ketchikan and the future as Mr.

and Mrs. Jean Thoreau. "But close enough. Hold out your left hand again."

Ariel obeyed. Her heart thumped when Jean slipped a second ring on her finger. A curiously carved stone of Alaskan jade, translucent and holding all the mystery of the land from which it came rested in a simple golden setting.

All through the toasts—drunk by many Ariel suspected longed for something stronger than fruit punch but stoutly insisted was nectar itself—Ariel gloated over her wonderful ring. It caught and reflected the shimmering candlelight, turning it into a rainbow on her finger. Yet she wasn't so absorbed that she failed to notice how several of her father's bachelor associates including Carl and Swen cast wistful glances at Aunt Rebekah, resplendent in gray taffeta.

At last Rebekah announced, "Thank you all for coming. I'm sure you want to get home and spend the rest of Christmas Eve with your families. Tom, my coat, please." She led a general exodus toward the front door, giving Ariel the opportunity to slip out the back into the gently falling snow.

Ariel's heart fluttered when Jean caught her in his arms at the door and ran with her to the brand-new red Ford V-8 parked behind the building, motor running. "Wedding present from Tom and Rebekah," he whispered, tucking warm robes around her. "Wife, don't think we're going to be accepting such gifts in the future. We'll make our own way." He kissed her then hurried around the car and hopped behind the wheel. "Good. No one's seen us. Besides," he laughed gleefully, "they won't recognize us if they do."

A short drive up the narrow, winding streets Ariel loved brought them to the Thoreau home. Lamplight flickered in a window, as if dancing for joy. Jean parked the car then came around to open her door. "Tears, Ariel?"

For a moment, past misery dimmed the brightness of her

wedding day. "It's just that for so long I couldn't stand to come here," she choked out. "I missed you so much."

"I know." Jean caught her close, blankets and all. The soft swish of light snow falling like a curtain whispered sweeter in Ariel's ears than the finest symphony when Jean carried her across the wide porch and inside. "Welcome home, wife." He set her on her feet, shoved the door shut, and bent his dark head. His lips felt cool against her own but soon warmed her even more than the blaze in the fireplace.

At last Jean released her and unwound the enveloping wraps. He knelt and held out his hands. Ariel joined him, her wedding dress an ivory billow on the wolf-skin pelt in front of the fire. Jean took her hands in his. "We dedicate our life together to Thee, oh God, who has brought us home."

Ariel could only brokenly whisper, "Amen." She raised her bowed head and looked into the dark gaze that promised future happiness. Tomorrow, they would go to church and celebrate the birth of the Savior. Tomorrow, God and the weather permitting, they would board the *Sea Sprite* and sail to Dixon Cove.

But tonight she thanked God that a thousand snowflakes fell, shutting them away in their own private world for a brief and hallowed winterlude.

Colleen L. Reece learned to read by kerosene lamplight near her Darrington, Washington, home that was once a one-room schoolhouse where her mother taught all eight grades! Love for God and family outweighed the lack of modern conveniences and became the basis for many of Colleen's 150+ books. Her "refuse to compromise" stance has helped sell six million+ copies and spread the good news of salvation through Christ.

Colleen is best known for helping to launch Heartsong Presents Book Club in 992 and was twice named Favorite Author in reader polls. In 1998, she and Tracie Peterson were the first authors inducted into the Heartsong Hall of Fame.

Colleen's creed: *Help make the world a better place because she lived.*

Christmas Bounty

by MaryLu Tyndall

Chapter 1

August 1855
Santa Barbara, California

What kind of God would allow children to go hungry?

Caroline Moreau jingled the few coins left in her purse and gazed over the colorful assortment of fruits and vegetables displayed across the vendor's cart.

"Mama." Her son, Philippe, called to her from the next stall, where he pointed to a hunk of raw beef—enough to feed them for a week. Shooing flies away from the display, the Mexican butcher cast her a toothless grin. "You buy, señora. Good for growing boy." She wondered whether the man ever got to enjoy the meat he sold, for he was no doubt just a farm worker employed by a rich ranchero. Regardless, her mouth watered at the sight. It had been months since she and the children had enjoyed meat for supper.

"Please, Mama." A stiff ocean breeze tossed her eight-year-old son's brown hair across his forehead while blue eyes alight with hope tugged on her heart.

What she wouldn't give to satisfy that hope, but she had only enough money for a few vegetables and a sack of beans.

"Not today, Philippe." Frowning, the boy dragged himself back to stand beside her while Abilene, her youngest, tugged on her skirts and pulled the thumb from her mouth. "I'm hungry, Mama."

"I know, *ma chère*." Caroline felt like weeping. Instead, she raised her chin and spoke to the vendor. "A red pepper, one onion, two tomatoes, and a bulb of garlic, please." At least that would give the beans a different flavor from last week. She glanced down at the despair tugging on her children's faces and added, "And twenty-five cents worth of cherries."

Abilene cheered, while a tiny smile wiped the frown from Philippe's lips. "For dessert," Caroline said, drawing them both close.

After gathering her purchases, Caroline scurried among the throng that mobbed the busy public square, still amazed—even after living in the California coastal town for nearly three years—at the vast diversity of people inhabiting Santa Barbara. Spanish dons, attired in black embroidered coats and high-crested hats, strolled the streets with ladies in multilayered skirts, colorful silk scarves, and long, braided hair. Beside them, servants held fringed parasols to protect them from the sun. Mexican vendors and shop owners abounded, dressed in plain trousers and colorful *sarapes* with wide sombreros on their heads. A cowboy tipped his hat at Caroline and smiled, while the chink of coins drew her gaze to a group of gold miners exiting the bank, where, no doubt, they'd converted their gold dust into money. Facing forward, she nearly bumped into a monk. He barely acknowledged her before proceeding with his brown cowl dragging in the dirt and a Chumash Indian following on his heels.

Turning left on Bath Street, Caroline headed toward the coast, where she'd left her buckboard. The crash of waves soon drowned out the clamor of the town as sand replaced dirt, and the glory of the sea spread out before them. Sparkling ribbons of silver-crested azure waves spanned to the horizon where a thick band of fog rose like the misty walls of a fortress. When the sun set, those walls would roll in and cover everything in town just like the many hoodlums who would roll down from their hide-outs in the hills to enjoy the nighttime pleasures of Santa Barbara.

The California coast was so different from New Orleans where she'd grown up. There the steamy tidewaters had been filled with all manner of shrimp, oysters, crawfish, and crabs. Here the water was icy and wild, like the city itself, and filled with kelp forests, sea lions, otters, and whales.

She drew in a deep breath of the salty breeze and allowed the wind to tear through her hair. With it came the sense of freedom she so craved but had not felt since her husband died six months ago. Shielding her eyes against the sun, she spotted a ship anchored offshore. Could it finally be the packet bringing mail to Santa Barbara? She'd sent a post home several months ago, informing her family of her dire situation, but still no response had come. But no, this ship was much smaller than the normal paddle-wheel steamship that brought the mail.

Regardless, she must get the children home before the sun sank into the sea. Santa Barbara was not a safe town at night, especially not for women and children. Though she'd heard the city hadn't always been like that. Before the Americans arrived, the Spanish had kept it orderly and civilized, built a mission, and introduced culture. But all that had crumbled when America won the territory in 1847 and cowboys, fortune hunters, and gold miners had flooded the city. Because the town employed so few law officers, mayhem ruled, not only the streets, but the country-side as well. Every week for the past two months, vigilantes had attacked her vineyard, stealing valuable farm equipment, burning grapevines, and even striking her foreman unconscious for several hours. Caroline had spent many a sleepless night worrying for her children's safety.

"Hear ye! Hear ye!" a man shouted first in English and then in Spanish from down shore. Caroline glanced up to see a crowd forming around a wooden scaffold. No doubt some poor criminal was being hanged. Most likely a horse thief or highwayman. At least they had caught one of them. Turning, she started toward her buckboard.

"Mama, can we go see?" Philippe asked, running beside her.

"No. We should not see such things."

"But it's a hanging, Mama!"

"Precisely why we are not going, Philippe."

"Don't you want to see who it is?" He scratched his head as if he couldn't make sense of her attitude.

"No."

Abilene plucked out her thumb. "Me neither," she said.

"There you have it." Caroline smiled. "Two against one."

"Ah, that doesn't count. You're girls. Boys like to see hangings."

"Not civilized boys, Philippe, of which you are one."

Lowering his chin, he slogged beside her, kicking sand as he went and slowly falling behind.

"Hurry along, children. I have dinner to make. You can help me, Philippe. Would you like that? I'll let you build the fire in the stove." Surely that would cheer the boy up.

When he didn't answer, she turned around to see him speeding down the sandy street heading straight for the scaffold.

"Oh, *bon sang!*" Growling, Caroline spun around and darted after him, dragging poor Abilene behind. But her son was quick. He got his speed from his father, along with his mulish disposition! The boy disappeared into the burgeoning crowd as the sheriff began listing the man's crimes.

"I, Samuel Portland, magistrate of Santa Barbara, do hereby charge you, Dante Vega, with the following crimes: thievery, drunkenness, licentiousness. . ."

Halting at the edge of the crowd, Caroline peered through the swaying bodies for a sign of her Philippe.

"Forgery, cheating at cards. . ."

Caroline pressed through the mob.

"Making a lewd suggestion to a lady," the man continued, causing some ladies to gasp. "And piracy."

"Hang him! Hang him!" someone shouted.

"Cuelgalo a el!" others repeated in Spanish, stirring the crowd

into a frenzy. Even a few of the ladies joined in.

"What does 'hang' mean?" Abilene asked.

"Nothing." Caroline drew her daughter close, glad the little girl was too short to see what was happening.

Caroline, however, had a full view of the man who had committed all those horrid crimes as a masked executioner escorted him up the steps of the scaffold to a waiting noose. Dark hair jostled over the collar of his open brown shirt. A red velvet sash was tied about his waist, while baggy black trousers fed into thick boots that clacked up each wooden tread of his death march. He glanced toward the crowd. Her heart froze. She'd never forget a face like his. Nor his imposing figure. The only thing that was missing was the sword and pistols he had kept stuffed in a thick leather belt—now conspicuously absent from his chest. Yes, she'd know him anywhere. Particularly when his eyes now reached through the crowd and locked upon hers. Coffee-colored eyes, if she remembered. Eyes that—against her best efforts—had once made her insides melt.

Eyes that had assessed her with impunity above a devious grin, while he and his crew had plundered the ship that had brought her and her husband, François, to Santa Barbara.

"What have you to say regarding these crimes?" the magistrate asked him.

The villain pulled his gaze from her and faced the portly man. "I am innocent, of course!" His baritone voice bore a slight Spanish accent, while a boyish grin elicited chuckles from the crowd. "On what evidence do you charge me, señor?"

One man pointed toward the ship in the bay. "On the evidence of your ship, you vile pirate!"

"My ship? It has done nothing wrong. As for myself, I was coming ashore to purchase supplies."

The eloquence of his speech surprised Caroline. Certainly not what she expected from a pirate.

"Purchase? You mean steal!" another man yelled.

"And then murder us all in our beds," someone added.

The pirate snapped hair from his face. "I had no such intentions, I assure you."

One of the wealthy ranchers stepped forward, adjusted his embroidered vest, and nodded toward the pirate. "This bandito robbed me of my money and my wife of her jewels when we sailed from San Diego to Santa Barbara three years ago." He glanced over the crowd and huffed. "And he even propositioned my poor wife. She has never quite recovered from his lewd suggestions."

The pirate shrugged with a grin.

"I was there as well," another man shouted. "I can vouch for what Señor Lucero says. This man boarded our ship and looted all the passengers."

Caroline could very well add her testimony to the others, for she had been on that same ship. But her experience had been quite different. This pirate—this Dante Vega—had done her and her husband no harm. In fact, quite the opposite. He had hidden them away in their stateroom and forbidden his men entrance. Not only that, but he had not taken their money or any of their possessions. Nor had he frightened the children. In fact, he seemed quite intent on keeping the little ones safe. Caroline could make no sense of it, though at the time she had thanked God for giving them favor in the cullion's sight.

"Therefore," the magistrate shouted, bringing her back to the present, "as judge of the court of Santa Barbara, I deem that you shall be hanged by the neck until you are dead."

The executioner slipped the noose over Dante's head. Still, his eyes held no fear as he faced the magistrate. "Is there no mercy to be found in this hellish mockery of a court, sir?"

"No mercy for pirates," the potbellied magistrate spat back. "Unless "—he grinned and scanned the mob—"according to our law, one of these ladies agrees to marry you. Make a decent man out of you." His jovial tone spoke of the lunacy of the statement.

Laughter swept through the crowd. Caroline's heart thrashed like a storm at sea. This man had obviously not come here to pirate. In fact, for all she knew, he'd given up the trade and had become an honest man. And she needed a man. A strong man. A man who knew how to fight. Someone to protect her and her children from vigilantes and help her workers harvest the grapes. If not, they would lose everything, their wine, their grapes, and eventually their land.

And her husband's dream.

"Very well." The magistrate gave a nod to the executioner to pull the lever.

Hoisting Abilene in her arms, Caroline plowed through the crowd, ignoring the gasps and moans, and stood before the scaffold.

"I'll marry him!"

Chapter 2

Dante couldn't believe his luck. If there *was* a God, He must be looking out for Dante. Though why, he couldn't imagine. Dante had broken every one of His commandments—at least the ones his mom had pounded into him as a child. Yet, to not only save his neck but give him a beautiful wife. . . Well, perhaps Dante should rethink his rejection of religion as a guilt-ridden cult of greedy hypocrites. Still, the woman was an American. And Dante hated Americans. He'd spent the last seven years plundering American ships along the California coast—beautiful shores and golden rolling hills that had once belonged to Mexico. And would belong to her again, if Dante had his way. Perhaps it was for the best that the lady was his enemy. That way he wouldn't feel the least bit guilty when he took what he wanted from her, repaired his ship, and sailed away.

His new wife had not spoken a word to him after the ceremony except to say they'd discuss terms later. *Terms?* He smiled. The only terms he was interested in was sharing this lovely's bed for a night or two and then pilfering her goods.

She snapped the reins, urging the horse forward down Delavina Street. Wisps of hair the color of the sun trickled from beneath her straw hat, drawing his gaze to a neck as graceful as the lady herself. A blue gown, bordered in lace tightened around a tiny waist then flowed down to her mud-caked ankle boots. Though her hands were small and delicate, rosy cheeks and glowing skin revealed that she didn't shy away from the sun like so many American ladies. Eyes as green as sea kelp glanced his way. He swallowed. Why hadn't this beauty been snatched up by one of the wealthy ranchers in town?

The wagon dipped into a hole, creaking and groaning and nearly sending Dante over the side. The children giggled behind him. He could feel their little eyes boring into his back and glanced over his shoulder. Wide, innocent grins met his gaze. Handsome children. But then he always did like children. They were so honest and pure before the harsh realities of the world tainted them—taught them to lie and steal and cheat their way through life.

Because in the end, it was every man, *or woman,* for themselves.

A salty breeze stirred the sycamores and bay laurels lining the street as they jostled past several adobe homes and a few wooden ones, a warehouse, a string of shops, and a Baptist church, of all things. Not something he'd expected to see in this nefarious town. In the distance, final rays of the setting sun swept over the hills bordering the city on the east and then shimmered off the white mission with its stark belfries shooting into the sky.

Jerking the reins, the lady turned down Micheltorena Street, crossed over a bridge, and headed beneath an arched sign that read MOREAU WINERY. Row after row of vines, heavy with grapes, spanned out from the dirt road like spokes in a wheel. In the distance, an adobe home with a red-tiled roof nestled among the golden hills. Not only had he married a beautiful woman, but a rich one as well! Things were looking up, indeed.

"Are you a real pirate?" the little boy asked Dante as they stepped into the cool interior of the home. The lady ushered in the little girl and set a satchel atop a wooden table.

"That's not a polite question, Philippe." She removed her bonnet and turned to face her son.

"But Mama, that's what the other man said."

"Forgive my son, Señor Vega. If you would care to sit?" She gestured toward a stuffed sofa in the corner, but Dante had trouble taking his eyes off her. Ringlets of gold framed a face that would stop a thousand ships. Yet there was something familiar about her. He would never forget a woman possessing such beauty.

She must have seen the desire in his eyes, for she drew a ragged breath and lifted her chin. "These are my children, Philippe and Abilene."

"Nice to meet you, señor." The young boy reached out his hand and gave Dante's a firm shake. The little girl, a mass of red curls surrounding a freckled nose and green eyes, peeked at him from within the folds of her mother's skirts.

Now he remembered them. The beautiful señora, her adorable children, and her spindly whiffet of a husband, who had been too cowardly to defend them from pirates. "Thank you for saving me from the noose, Señora. . .Señora. . ."

"Moreau. Señora Caroline Moreau. And you are welcome." She inched backward toward a rack of rifles hanging on the wall. "But your life comes at a cost."

"I have no doubt." Dante snorted as he glanced around the room. A rug covered the redbrick floor while white-washed adobe walls boasted tapestries, brass sconces, and oil paintings. A piano sat in one corner, an olive-green sofa in another, and next to the beautiful señora stood an oak dining table. Open french doors framed in yellow velvet curtains led to a veranda overlooking the vineyard, while arched openings on either side of the room led to additional chambers. Perhaps there were more valuable items elsewhere, for there certainly wasn't anything worth stealing here.

"They were going to hang you, señor." Philippe's eyes widened.

"Indeed, they were," Dante replied with a smile.

"What's 'hang,' Mama?" The little girl, still clinging to her mother's skirts, pulled the thumb from her mouth to ask.

"Never mind that now, ma chère. Philippe, please take your

sister and go fetch some water from the creek. I wish to speak to Señor Vega alone."

"Ah, Mama," the boy complained, but one stern look from his mother made him grab his sister and slog out the door.

Turning, she plucked a rifle from the rack, spun back around, and aimed it at Dante's heart.

∽

Caroline judged the distance between her and the pirate. A good fifteen feet. Time enough to shoot him before he charged her. Oh, bon sang, what had she done? Why did she always rush into things before considering the consequences?

Before the pirate could do whatever evil deed his salacious gaze bespoke, Caroline cocked the rifle. "I know how to use this."

He chuckled and rubbed his dark bristled chin. "Yet it makes no sense why you would save me from the noose only to shoot me."

"Regardless, I *will* shoot you if you try anything untoward."

"Untoward?" He took a step in her direction, his dark eyes twinkling with mischief. "Now, why would you presume such a thing?"

"I know that look in a man's eyes."

He took another step toward her.

"Stay where you are." Her hand trembled, sending the barrel of the gun oscillating over his chest—a very muscular chest that peeked at her from within his open-necked shirt.

Stopping, he shook his head with a snort. "You marry a known pirate, bring him into your home, and you expect him to act like one of the monks from your mission?"

"I expect him to be grateful for his life."

"I *am* grateful." He stepped closer, his boots clacking on the brick floor. "Let me show you how much." He reached for her, his eyes flashing. Before she could react, he jerked the gun from her hands. "You've no need for this, señora." He unloaded it and set it down on the table. "I have no intention of hurting you or your children."

Heart crashing against her ribs, Caroline backed away from him. He towered at least a foot above her, all muscle and man, and she knew he could do whatever he wanted. But the look in those coffee-colored eyes made her almost believe what he said. Almost.

"Don't point a gun at me again, señora." A breeze brought his scent of sweat and the sea to her nose, a briny aroma not all too unpleasant. He gestured for her to move away from the rifles. She did. Over to the piano out of his reach. He raked back his slick dark hair and stared at her. "Why bring me here if you fear me?"

"Because you were kind to me once," she said.

He nodded.

"So, you remember?"

"You are a hard lady to forget, señora." One side of his lips quirked as his eyes roved over her yet again.

She hugged herself, trying to hide from his gaze. "Why did you help us? On the ship. Why did you protect us?"

He rubbed the back of his neck and stared out the open french doors where the sun stole the last of the light. "My men would have. . ." He hesitated and faced her. "Let's just say they would have sorely used you, and then. . .well, a white woman of your beauty would bring a great price down south."

A sour taste climbed up Caroline's throat. She had always longed for freedom. She had wanted to live life outside the strictures of her wealthy family back in New Orleans. And so, against their will, she had married François, a penniless Frenchman with a dream of producing the best wine in America. But she hadn't realized that freedom came with a price: hard work, uncertainty, scarcity, and worst of all danger—danger to herself and to her precious children and finally, death to her husband.

"And the little ones," the pirate added. "I could not tolerate their innocence stolen at so young an age."

So the man had some kindness in his heart, after all. Perhaps she hadn't been completely wrong about him. "That is why I chose you, Señor Pirate."

"Where is your husband?" he asked. "The man you were traveling with."

"Dead. Trampled by a horse." Only six months ago, but sometimes it felt like a lifetime.

"I'm sorry." There was genuine sympathy in his voice. He pulled a chair from the table and sat down, leaning forward on his knees. "What is it you want from me, Señora Moreau?"

"Protection."

His brows rose. "From what?"

Philippe's laughter drifted in from the window. "I'll explain later, señor, when the children are asleep. But for now, I want your promise that you won't steal from us or hurt us."

"I already told you I would do you no harm. Besides"—his sultry grin returned—"why would I hurt my own wife?"

There he went again, looking at her as if she were a sweet beignet served up on a platter. Though her insides trembled, she forced authority into her voice. "Wife in name only, Señor Pirate. There will be no marital relations between us."

∽

Though the woman held herself sturdy, Dante sensed the terror storming through her. No marital relations? That would be impossible with a woman like her. He'd intended to tell her just that when the children returned, sloshing water from a bucket they fought over between them. With her head held high, Señora Moreau grabbed the pail and left the room, dragging her children with her. Within moments, the sizzle of a stove sounded, followed by the scent of garlic, and Dante made himself comfortable on the sofa, looking forward to his first home-cooked meal in years. Whatever the reasons the lady had brought him here, it couldn't hurt to stay for a night of good food and a warm bed. Especially if he shared that bed with her. Plus, it would give him a chance to scour the place for any valuables he could use to redeem his ship from the city council.

Dinner consisted of a meager portion of beans and bread—hardly enough to satisfy the children, let alone a grown man—making Dante wonder at his first assessment of their wealth. Nevertheless, he was about to shove a forkful into his mouth when the lady shot him an accusing glance and asked Philippe to bless the food. The young boy gladly complied, lifting up a prayer of thanks so sincere it would make a priest rejoice.

It made Dante uncomfortable.

Still, the simple fare was delicious. And the company even more enjoyable as the children prattled on about their day helping some man named Sisquoc tend the grapes. The little girl, Abilene, never took her eyes off Dante, even as she partook of her meal. The adoring, curious way she looked at him made his insides feel funny. He gave her a playful wink, finally eliciting a grin in return. Philippe, on the other hand, boldly asked Dante question after question about how he got caught and how many ships he had plundered and whether he had killed anyone.

Señora Moreau, barely touching the small portion she'd served herself, chastised her son and apologized to Dante, but he shrugged it off. "Curiosity is a good thing in a lad."

"He is much too curious about the wrong things." She gave her son a look of reprimand, but embedded in her eyes was a love Dante had never seen before. His own mother had done quite a bit of chastising but had omitted the loving part.

After supper the children happily assisted their mother clearing the table and helping to clean the dishes. So much giggling poured from the kitchen that Dante wandered to the door and leaned on the post, watching the three of them smiling and laughing as they worked together. An unusual sadness swamped him. He harbored no such memories of his childhood. No laughter, no smiles, no warm embraces.

Dante should leave. Go back to the harsh, cruel world where he belonged. There was nothing for him here. He could join one of the many games of faro downtown and win enough to get his ship back in a matter of months. But curiosity kept him in place. That and the way the little girl now stared at him after the dishes had been done and they all sat together in the main room—as if he were her best gift at Christmas. She no longer clung to her mother's skirts but instead even dared to take a seat beside him on the sofa.

Señora Moreau brought out a small bowl of cherries for them to share and coffee for Dante. He'd prefer something stronger. Much stronger if he was to combat the odd sensations flowing through him. Especially when Abilene slid her tiny hand in his and looked up at him with those innocent green eyes and said, "Are you my new papa?"

Red blossomed on Señora Moreau's cheeks as she drew the little girl away from Dante and set her on her lap. "No, Abilene. Señor Vega is only staying a short while."

"Ah, Mama." Philippe plopped a cherry in his mouth. "Can't we keep him?"

∽

"I saved your life, señor. In return I need protection. Only until the grapes are harvested in a few months." With the children finally abed, Señora Moreau had invited Dante out onto the veranda. She gripped the railing and stared over the shadowy fields where grapevines reached for the dark sky like multiclawed monsters.

Dante slipped beside her. "A few months, señora? I don't—"

"We've been attacked four times so far," she interrupted,

desperation creeping into her voice. "Equipment stolen, grapes destroyed. I'm starting to fear for our lives."

Lantern light flickered across her back, sparkling over a loose tendril of hair, but her face was lost to him in the shadows. She smelled of sunshine and sweet cherries, and it took everything in him not to lower his nose to her silky hair for a deeper whiff.

"Who is attacking you?" he asked. "And for what purpose?"

She released a heavy sigh. "I have my suspicions, but I don't know for sure. Let's just say there are many men in town who don't believe a woman should be running a vineyard and who would love to possess it themselves."

Dante would agree with that. American women were spoiled, selfish, fickle, and manipulative. Despite her beauty, this particular woman before him was no exception. She had saved him for her own selfish purpose and was now manipulating him into doing her bidding. That she hailed from money was obvious by her manners and speech. That she stared down her haughty nose at others was evident. But that she stubbornly forced herself into a man's world would be her undoing.

"Why not sell the place and go back to wherever you came from?"

She spun to face him, indignant. "Because this vineyard is my husband's dream. For François's sake, I will not give up now."

Pig-headed woman! Dante huffed and glanced into the shadows.

"After the harvest, you are free to go, Señor Pirate, with no further obligation to me and the children. It is a good bargain. Your life for three months of work. During which time you'll have a roof over your head and food in your belly."

"Listen, señora. I know nothing about grapes or wine or farming. I am a sailor, a privateer."

"You don't need to know anything about a vineyard. I simply need your protection. Fighting is something you are skilled at I presume?" Her voice was sarcastic.

He cocked his head with a frown. "You can hire fighters."

"In case you haven't noticed." Her luscious lips grew tight. "I have no money. Nor will I have any until last year's wine is ready to sell and this year's harvest comes in."

He rubbed the back of his neck. "I appreciate you saving me, I do. But I am not the marrying kind, señora. I have a ship to redeem. And when it is back in my possession, I intend to sail away and never return to this waste of a town again."

"Back to pirating?" she quipped.

"You call it pirating. I call it fighting for land stolen from my country."

"From *your* country? You aren't Mexican. Your accent and speech betray you."

"My father is Mexican, señora. And California was ours until the arrogance of America trampled my people." He tightened his grip on the railing as thoughts of his father filled his mind, igniting his ire.

"California was won in war. And if that wasn't enough, my country paid Mexico for the land as well."

Dante's blood simmered at the American's lies. He faced her.

"Fifteen million for the disputed territory," she added. A flicker of fear crossed her eyes when they met his. She backed away. "Or perhaps your government did not inform its people of that fact."

She bumped into the post.

He approached her. "All Americans lie."

Her chest rose and fell, but she lifted her chin and met his gaze. "All people lie, Señor Pirate. But I speak the truth."

Whether she spoke the truth or not, he wanted to kiss her. He wanted to drag her into the bedroom and take what was his right as a husband. Instead, he allowed his anger to grow. Jerking back, he leapt down the steps and stormed into the night.

Five hours later and well into his cups, Dante sat in a saloon that smelled of sweat and spirits. He'd seen several of his crew, including his friend and first mate, Berilo Diaz, who informed him the men were happy to enjoy their time ashore until Dante could redeem the ship. An endeavor he was well on his way to achieve. He'd already won ten dollars at faro and was about to win more from a group of goose-brained miners when whispered threats from a nearby table pricked his ears. As a captain, he'd honed his listening skills for any mention of mutiny or rebellion. This time he heard only snippets over the clamor of fiddle and laughter and cursing that filled the room: *fire*, *rifles*, *run off*, and the word that sent icicles down his spine, *Moreau*.

The men finished their drinks and rose from the table, scraping back chairs and grabbing guns as they made for the door, grins of anticipation on their faces. Six of them, from Dante's count. Six armed men attacking Señora Moreau's vineyard. She and the children wouldn't stand a chance.

Chapter 3

Caroline woke with a start, perspiration covering her body. A breeze stirred the gauze curtains of her open window, casting ghoulish shadows etched in moonlight onto her ceiling. Every creak of the house, every rustle of leaves outside her window, the distant howl of a coyote—all jerked her from her semiconscious state. Ever since that foul pirate, Dante Vega, had stormed off in a rage, her nerves had refused to unwind. She knew he didn't want to be here. She could tell he hated Americans. But she'd seen something in his eyes during dinner and later with the children—a deep yearning, some kindness, even. Or perhaps she was only deluding herself. A man like him felt no obligation to repay her for saving his life. A man like him thought only of himself. And Caroline's impetuousness had once again caused her to make a huge mistake.

A horse let out a frightened whinny. Gunshots cracked the air! Caroline leapt from bed, her heart spinning in her chest. Tossing a robe over her shoulders, she darted to the gun rack in the main parlor and grabbed two of the loaded ones as another gunshot thundered across the valley.

Philippe ran into the room, rubbing his eyes. "Mama, what is it?"

"Philippe, take Abilene and go to your hiding place. Stay there until I tell you." She didn't have time to ensure he obeyed as laughter and the pounding of horse hooves drew her outside. She crept onto the veranda, peering across the vineyard, rifle raised and ready. Torches—at least seven—bobbed up and down in the distance, heading her way.

Sisquoc, her foreman, appeared out of the shadows, fear in his eyes and a gun in his hands. She was surprised the aged Chumash stayed on with her in the face of so much danger. "They try to set barn on fire, señora. I shoot and scare them, but they keep coming."

"Did you wake the others?"

"Yes. And they got guns. Two guard barn, and here is Diego and Manuel." He gestured toward two men, one who positioned himself behind the watering trough and the other behind an old wagon.

All four of her workers. One Chumash and three Mexican. None of whom could hit a beached whale from two feet away. If the vigilantes succeeded in setting the barn on fire, she'd lose her horse, her milk cow, chickens, hay, and most of her farm equipment. And possibly even her wine stored in the cellar beneath. "Get the animals out of the barn, Sisquoc. I'll hold them off."

He cast her a worried look but ran off to do her bidding. She forced her trembling legs to descend the stairs, one by one, and walk onto the path to intercept the attackers. Cocking her rifle, she raised it to shoulder height, waiting until they materialized out of the shadows and she could hear their voices bragging about their impending victory.

"That's far enough!" she shouted. "Any closer and I'll blow your heads off!" Her muscles strained beneath the weight of the rifle.

The men laughed—coarse belly laughs as if she'd told a joke. Still, they came, their torchlight twisting their features into maniacal threads of light and dark. "Now looky here. If it ain't the mistress of the vineyard herself. Hello there, pretty!" They stopped some twenty feet before her, each one of them eyeing her up and down and licking his lips as if she were one of their trollops from the saloon.

Blood pounded in Caroline's ears. Her knees began to wobble. But she must remain strong. For her children. "You will leave my vineyard at once, or I swear I'll shoot!"

Again they laughed. A cow lowed, and out of the corner of her eye she saw Sisquoc leading the animals from the barn.

"Don't matter 'bout your animals, señora; we will still burn it down. And your grapes too."

"But not before I shoot one of you dead," she replied, anger crowding out her fear. "You go back and tell your boss that he's never going to get my land."

"Mama!" Abilene's voice spun her around. A man dragged her precious girl out of the house with one hand while Philippe squirmed in the other. Caroline's breath abandoned her. Gasping, she pointed the rifle at the man, even as several of the men behind her cocked their guns in response. Philippe kicked the villain in the shin. He howled and bent over to rub his leg. "You ill-bred *mocoso!*" he shouted, while her brave son attempted to tug his sister from the man's grip. With a heavy hand, the man knocked the boy aside and sent him sprawling onto the dirt.

Terror gripped Caroline. *No, Lord, not my children. Please protect my children.* She gripped the rifle tighter as it swayed over the man's frame. Her finger hovered over the trigger, desperate to shoot, longing to save her children. But she feared to hit Abilene.

"Put down your gun, señora, and tell your men to do the same, or ol' Pedro will have to hurt *los niños.*"

Pinned within the man's harsh grip, Abilene's teary eyes reached out to Caroline. Blood rushed to her head. She grew faint. With one hand raised, she slowly lowered her rifle and called for her men to do the same.

The ominous crack of a gun thundered across the valley. The man holding Abilene let out an ear-piercing howl. Releasing the girl, he stumbled backward and gripped his shoulder. Caroline dove and scooped Abilene in her arms before searching for Philippe in the shadows. Shouts and curses rumbled behind her. More shots split the night sky. Grabbing both children, she spun around, intending to take them into the house when another shot struck one of the vigilantes. He slid from his horse to the ground with a thud. Two of the others began shooting into the darkness, while the rest scattered for cover. Gun smoke bit Caroline's nose and throat.

She scanned the darkness but could see none of her men. Could *they* be the ones shooting? Another shot exploded. Ducking, she hurried the children into the house and ordered them to crouch behind the table. Outside a *thwack* and a grunt sounded. She peered around the open door to see a man strike one of the vigilantes across the jaw with the butt of his rifle then shove the other one down with his boot. A third one already lay prostrate in the dirt. She couldn't make out her rescuer's face in the darkness. But moonlight gleamed off the knife in his hand. Caroline's breath stopped. He tossed the blade with precision. It met its mark, and another villain dropped to his knees before falling face-first to the ground.

A barrage of shots peppered the area. Grabbing a pistol and rifle from the dirt, the man darted behind the water trough and returned fire. A groan of agony rose in the distance. Movement to her right caught Caroline's gaze. The man who had held her children was starting to rise. Dashing into the kitchen, she grabbed a frying pan, and before she could consider the wisdom of her action, she rushed toward the man and slammed it over his head. The *thunk* of iron on a skull sent bile into her throat, but the man once again returned to the dirt. She glanced toward her rescuer, lit by a shaft of moonlight. It was Dante Vega, the pirate!

And he was smiling at her.

More shots sent her racing back into the house. But after she ensured her children were safe, curiosity kept her peering out the door. An eerie silence invaded the vile scene, made all the more spooky by smoke spiraling from torches abandoned to the dirt. A cold sweat snaked down Caroline's back. Crouched behind the water trough, the pirate remained so still, she feared he was dead. But then one of the villains fired, giving him a target, and he shot back. A howl spoke well for his aim.

"We can do this all night, amigos!" he yelled. "I've already shot five of you. Come on out, and let's finish this!"

Silence again. One of the men left his hiding place among the vines and sped toward the house. Gripping her throat, Caroline thought to warn Dante. But he'd already seen him. With precise aim, he followed him with the barrel of his pistol and fired. The man stumbled forward like a broken wheel on a wagon before tumbling to the dirt.

Cursing floated on the wind, soon joined by the sound of a horse galloping away.

Dante rose to his feet and rubbed the back of his neck as casually as if he'd just been working in the fields. Slowly, one by one Caroline's farm workers, including Sisquoc, came out from hiding, rifles in hand.

"You, you." Dante pointed at two of the closest men. "Go check the perimeter. Make sure no one else is coming."

Sisquoc quickly translated into Spanish, and the men sped off.

"And you two." Dante gestured toward the remaining men. "Tie up these injured men, set them on their horses, and send them on their way."

Sisquoc translated again, and Dante gripped the old man's shoulder. "Thank you, friend. Can you make sure the man who galloped away has indeed left?"

The old Chumash Indian nodded and without hesitation obeyed Dante's orders. On shaky legs, Caroline went to fetch her children. Abilene flew into her arms, but Philippe darted past her and out the door before she could stop him.

"Golly, Señor Vega!" The boy glanced at the injured men who were being hoisted up by the workers. "Did you knock out all of these men by yourself?"

Dante glanced toward Caroline. "I had a little help from your mother." The look in his eyes nearly stole her remaining breath. It was more than admiration. It was a knowing look, an intimate look that bespoke a long acquaintance. Or perhaps the moonlight played tricks on her. Abilene's sobs drew her attention, and she tightened her embrace on the little girl. "It's all right now, ma chère, we are safe."

"Because Señor Vega shot all the *bandidos*, Mama!" Philippe exclaimed. "*Parbleu!* Did you see?"

"Yes, Philippe. And we are very grateful to you, señor."

Kneeling by the trough, Dante scooped water and splashed it over his head then stood, raking back his dark hair. "I don't think they'll bother you for a while, Señora Moreau." He ascended the steps and stood beside her. The sting of gunpowder and danger hovered around him.

Abilene, still hiccupping with sobs, lifted her head from Caroline's shoulder and reached out for the man. Without hesitation, he took her in his arms. "You are safe, little one." Though Caroline had said the same thing just moments before, there was something assuring in his deep voice, a soothing confidence that caused Abilene to immediately stop crying, heave a deep sigh, stick her thumb in her mouth, and settle onto his shoulder.

If Caroline hadn't seen it with her own eyes, she never would have believed it possible that her shy, frightened little girl would allow anyone to hold her, especially a stranger. A pirate! Yet, as she watched him wrap his thick arms around Abilene and whisper assurances into her ear, Caroline suddenly longed to trade places with her daughter. Ever since François had died, she'd lived in a constant state of fear and uncertainty. How lovely it would be to feel protected and safe. If only for a moment.

∽

Caroline woke before dawn with visions of Dante—the pirate—holding Abilene affectionately in his arms. For some reason, it caused an odd sensation within her—not at all an unpleasant one. After stirring the coals in the stove and putting on some water, she drew a cloak about her and made her way through the morning fog to François's grave beneath a large oak in the middle of the vineyard he had loved so much. Though François had adored his children, he'd rarely showed affection—to them or to her. He was a dreamer, a man with a thousand ideas buzzing through his head—so many, he rarely allowed real life to intrude. A brilliant, innovative man who would have made the best wine this side of the Mississippi just as he said he would.

If he hadn't died.

Fog enshrouded the scene with a ghostly white and sent a chill down her spine.

"Dear Lord, thank You for sending Señor Vega to save us last night. Thank You for all You provide. But please, please help us. I don't know what to do. I don't know how—"

A twig cracked. Gasping, Caroline spun around. Señor Vega materialized out of the mist, his dark eyes smiling at her. "I didn't mean to startle you."

She faced forward, embarrassed that he'd heard her praying.

"I saw you leave the house and worried."

"I'm quite all right, as you can see, Señor Pirate." She snapped her gaze to his. "I thought you'd gone back to town."

He ran a hand through his hair. "I slept in the barn just in case those men returned."

The sentiment sent her emotions whirling. "When you stormed off last night after supper, I assumed you were gone for good."

"Do you want me gone for good?" His eyes held a playful glint, yet his tone was serious.

"I've already told you what I want, señor." She returned her gaze to the grave.

∞

"What was he like?" Dante knew he shouldn't ask, but he could not reconcile the man he remembered from the ship with a man who would have won the heart of such a woman. A woman who had stood her ground, rifle in hand, against seven well-armed men. He'd never seen the likes of it. Especially not from a proper lady who'd obviously benefited from an education only wealth could provide. When he'd heard the shots and seen her in such danger, a foreign sense of terror had screeched through him. He couldn't remember ever being so angry or so afraid—even on his crew's most dauntless raids.

Fingers of fog slithered over the wooden cross marking the grave.

"He was a good man," she finally said. "Wise. Creative. He had wonderful dreams for his life."

"Yet he seemed unwilling to stand up for you when we raided your ship."

"He was not a violent man like you, señor," she spat. "He was a gentle man. A man of peace."

"Peace or not, if I had a wife like you and children like your little ones, I'd fight to the death to keep you safe." Hanging his head, he silently cursed himself. Why had he said that? Why was he feeling this way toward an American?

She stared at him as if he'd told her he intended to become a monk.

"Why did you marry him?" He nodded toward the grave.

"You are too bold, Señor Pirate." She shifted away from him and hugged herself. Creamy mist swirled about her, coating her cheeks with glitter. "I loved him, of course." Her tone was curt. "Why else does a woman marry a man?"

Dante chuckled. "Apparently for protection."

Even through the fog, Dante saw her face redden. She shifted her shoes over the gravel and let out a sigh. "I mean a *real* marriage." She flattened her lips. "Besides, I wouldn't have risked defying my father's wishes and losing my family's favor if I hadn't loved François."

Then why did she sound like she was trying to convince herself of that fact? Dante rubbed his chin. "So, let me guess. Your father finally refused one of his precious daughter's requests? And you went and had your way regardless."

"You know nothing of me, pirate!" Blazing eyes snapped his way. "You are an insolent brute, señor."

He grinned. "I agree. But I speak the truth, don't I? You hail from money—one of those long-standing families out east, I'm guessing. And from your accent, somewhere near New Orleans. My bet is you ran away with this François to escape the strict rule of your parents."

She pursed her lips and huffed. "You may think what you wish." Moments passed before she swung a suspicious gaze his way. "But what of you, Señor Pirate? You are obviously schooled here in America, not in Mexico."

"Harvard, in fact."

"A Harvard-educated pirate?" She laughed.

"Privateer, señora, if you please." He grinned.

"Whatever you call it." She waved a hand through the air, stirring the fog into a whirl. "You must have had an American mother, a wealthy one, since you seem to find success so disdainful."

Dante narrowed his eyes. The woman was not only beautiful but smart. "I abhor neither success nor wealth but rather what they both do to people."

She studied him with those green eyes of hers—the color of a tropical sea. The fire went out of them, replaced by understanding. "Your mother was cruel to you." It was both a statement and a question.

Dante tightened his jaw. He wanted neither understanding nor sympathy. Especially not from an American. All he wanted from this woman was the means to redeem his ship from the city. "If you wish to know, perhaps you should ask the God to whom you were praying a moment ago."

She jerked her gaze back to the grave. "How dare you spy on me!"

"I'm curious, señora, why an intelligent woman like yourself believes that God actually cares about our troubles."

"Of course He cares! How can you say such a thing?"

"If He cares so much for you, why are you speaking to a husband six feet under? Why do you barely have enough to eat? Why is your vineyard being attacked?"

Her chest began to heave like a sail catching the wind. "I insist you leave at once, Señor Pirate. I don't want an American-hating, atheist thief around my children."

He smiled, dipped his head, and turned to leave. "You should have thought of that before you married me."

Chapter 4

Philippe's laughter drew Caroline to the kitchen window where she brushed aside the gauze curtains and gaped at the sight before her. Dante and her son sat on a bench in the shade of a tree, their heads bent together over a long, coiled rope. On the ground lay several knots tied in other pieces of rope—unusual knots, the likes of which she'd never seen. The pirate's husky voice came to her on the wind, confident, kind, and patient as he taught her son how to tie what she assumed were ship knots.

"You try it now, Philippe," he said, handing the boy the rope.

Caroline stiffened, waiting to see if her son failed in his attempt. The poor boy had already suffered enough beneath his father's neglect. Caroline would not allow any man to wound her son's tender confidence with more rejections or rebukes.

Philippe finished and held up the rope, but then he shook his head. "It's not right, is it?"

"No." Dante took it. "But it's almost right. Here, let me show you again. These knots are not easy to learn." He slowly slid the rope through loops and circles, while Philippe watched with more focus than Caroline had ever seen from the boy.

This time Philippe tied the knot correctly, his blue eyes gazing up at Dante in expectation and pride.

"Well done!" the pirate exclaimed, tousling the boy's hair. "We'll make a sailor out of you yet."

Philippe beamed, and Caroline's heart filled to near bursting with joy for her son. Slipping from the window, she returned to clean the final dishes after breakfast, her mind awhirl with the events of the past few weeks. Despite her insisting that Dante leave, the stubborn man had stayed on. At first she'd been worried at his intentions and also that he'd get used to a roof over his head and cooked meals and then never leave. The last thing she needed was another mouth to feed. Yet, not only had the pirate behaved as a perfect gentleman, but he had actually assisted Sisquoc in tending the grapes, feeding the livestock, and irrigating the land. He'd even fixed a broken wheel on their wagon and replaced a few tiles on the roof.

He took his meals with her and the children and seemed to actually enjoy their time together. But every night after supper he headed downtown. Some nights when she couldn't sleep, she heard him stumble into the barn well after two in the morning. Oddly, even though she kept a pistol beneath her pillow as a defense against *him*, she felt safer when he returned.

They'd not spoken privately since that morning by François's grave, but that was for the best. Not that she was looking for a husband, but this particular one possessed all the wrong qualities: he hated Americans and America, he didn't believe in God, he was often rude and ill-mannered, he drank and gambled. And worst of all—lest she forget by his civilized behavior—he was a thief and a pirate! Bon sang, she shouldn't even be thinking of him this way at all. Tossing down her towel, she stormed from the kitchen. If she had a thimble of brains, she shouldn't even allow such a man around her children. He'd told her more than once that as soon as he redeemed his ship, he would leave.

And the way Philippe was starting to look up to the man, she knew her son would suffer. Not to mention Abilene, who also seemed to have developed an affection for the pirate. Ensuring the little girl still played contently on the sofa, Caroline marched onto the veranda. "Come, Philippe. We are going into town."

"Ah, Mama, but Señor Vega is teaching me to tie sailor knots."

"I need you to come with me, Philippe. Now." She kept her voice stern.

The boy scowled and handed the rope to the pirate. Dante stood and faced her. "Something has upset you, Señora Moreau?"

"Of course not. I simply need to purchase supplies."

"Then I will go with you."

"There is no need."

"Nevertheless, you married me for protection. And protect you I shall. Since I am not permitted any other privileges of the sacred union." He winked above a disarming grin.

"If you consider protecting us a privilege, I am happy for it, señor." Clutching her skirts, she spun around before he could see the red creeping up her face. Infuriating man! She wasn't a woman to blush easily, but this pirate seemed to know just what to say. And just how to look at her—as if she were a precious gem he longed to touch.

After a brief argument, she allowed him to take the reins and drive them into town, and within minutes, Dante parked the buckboard near the public square. After helping them down, he guided them through throngs of donkeys, carts, horses, and people to the vendor stalls and booths. The smell of human sweat and animal dung joined the briny scent of the sea and the sweet perfume of fresh flowers in a dichotomy of odors as they passed carts stuffed with all manner of dry goods, fruit, meat, fresh flowers, objets d'art from the East, furniture, and rugs.

"Mama!" Philippe called, luring her to where he stood before a leather shop, a whip in hand. "Can I have one?" His expectant gaze met hers, and she'd give anything to be able to see his smile grow larger, but the price read $2.50. And $2.50 would feed them for a month.

"Not this time, Philippe," she said, hoping to placate him with a smile, but the disappointment on his face broke her heart.

Dante gripped the braided leather rope and nodded his approval. "Every young boy needs a whip."

Caroline chastised the pirate with her eyes.

"But not every boy gets what he wants when there's food to buy," he instantly corrected. "A man needs to earn these things on his own." He placed the whip back in the cart, and Philippe's scowl faded as he nodded his understanding.

"Mama." Abilene tugged on Caroline's skirts and pointed to a booth filled with dolls of all kinds: some made of cornhusk, some wood, some wax, some cloth, and some porcelain—all dressed in lavish gowns. Before Caroline could divert her daughter's attention, the little girl darted to the cart and shyly brushed her fingers over a doll perched up front, a porcelain beauty with long ringlets of black hair, a satin ruffled gown, pearls around her neck, and a feathered bonnet.

"A beautiful doll for a beautiful señorita!" the vendor said as Caroline approached.

But another two-dollar price tag caused her heart to sink. She'd not been able to buy the children anything special in years. Not even for Christmas. To her rescue yet again, Dante swept the little girl in his arms and diverted her attention to a woman in the next booth who was weaving straw hats.

While the children watched the woman, Caroline slid beside Dante. "My children are not the type to ask for such expensive gifts, señor. I do not know what has come over them." Even as she said it, her eyes landed on a bonnet in the millinery behind the booth. It was fashioned of sheer gauze embroidered in gold thread and embellished with pink silk bows. She fingered her own plain bonnet with its frayed edges and torn ribbons and felt the pirate's intense gaze on her. Flustered, she turned away. "Come, children, we have shopping to do."

He smiled, handed her Abilene, and dipped his head. "I must go to the council to discover the redemption price for my ship, señora. I will meet you later." And off he went with that confident gait of his, drawing the eyes of more than one female in the plaza.

Caroline huffed. Some protector he was. But she didn't need protection in the daylight, not with all the people milling about and the vendors and cantinas and shops filling the square. Gathering her children close, she found the things she needed: soap, beans or *frijoles* as they were called here, oil for lanterns, and oranges. Now, to check on the price of fresh fish. The fish monger, however, spoke no English and insisted on arguing with her over the price. They bartered back and forth until Caroline's frustration was near bursting. Stealing herself for her final offer, she glanced down to ensure her children were still beside her.

But they were gone. She scanned the market square. They were nowhere in sight!

"Philippe! Abilene!" Caroline shoved her way through the crowd, her heart pinched tight. How could she have let them out of her sight? *Oh, Father in heaven, please help me find them.* Desperation dizzied her as she pressed through the throng, shouting their names. Finally, she spotted her son's mop of brown hair and Abilene's red curls across the plaza. They sat in a café under the shade of an awning, eating as if they hadn't nearly put their mother in an early grave.

Furious, she marched toward them, intending to *first* take them in her embrace and *next* to give them a scolding they wouldn't soon forget. Before she could reach them, a man drew close and placed two cups next to their plates and then lifted his gaze to hers. A slick smile tugged on lips below a thin mustache. He straightened his gold-fringed black vest and shifted his boots over the ground. The chirping of his spurs grated her nerves. Gray streaked across the dark hair circling his handsome face. Deep-set eyes she had never trusted met hers. Domingo Casimiro de Iago.

"Señora Moreau." He bowed elegantly. "I am sorry to have alarmed you, but when I saw your children in the square, I couldn't help but offer them a *fardelejo*. I know how much they love the Spanish pastry."

"Mama, this is so good!" Abilene glanced up at Caroline, crumbs dancing on her lips.

"Thank you, Señor Casimiro!" Philippe beamed from ear to ear while he shoved another forkful of the almond-filled pastry into his mouth.

Trying to contain her fury, Caroline drew Señor Casimiro aside, noting as she did that several of his men lingered just outside the café, watching them from beneath sombreros.

"Señor Casimiro," she began.

"You may call me Domingo, *por favor*, señora."

"Señor Casimiro, while I appreciate you buying my children treats, I must protest you doing so without my permission. They are my children, and I should decide what and when they eat."

"Ah, but they are only los niños, señora, and you know how much I adore them." His smile was sickly sweet.

Did she? He had told her more than once, yet she'd never seen him actually speak to them except with trifling flatteries such as "what a good boy" and "what a beautiful girl."

He leaned toward her, smelling of Spanish cologne and spicy mustache oil. "I know you cannot afford such treats, señora. Why not allow the children to enjoy?"

She took a step back. "Again, I thank you for your generosity, but in the future, I would prefer you ask me. And my finances are none of your affair."

"But I would like to make them my affair, as you say, señora. I would like to wipe away all of your troubles. A beautiful woman like you shouldn't have to worry about such matters."

Acid welled in her belly. Ever since François had died, the wealthy don had not hid his interest in her, nor stopped pursuing her—even in light of her continual rebuffs. Certainly marrying the man would solve all her problems. She'd live on the largest ranchero outside the city, have a bevy of servants attending her every need and tutors for her children. But something in the man's eyes caused her insides to squirm. Something in his arrogant demeanor made her realize she'd lose the freedom she'd grown to love. Still, she would marry the pompous man for her children's sake, for them to have a better chance at life, if only she didn't catch the flickers of dismissal in his eyes when he looked their way.

"Perhaps you have not heard, señor, but I am newly married." She glanced at her children still enjoying their pastry then up at the don whose face had tightened into thin lines.

"A pirate, I am told, señora. What were you thinking?" Though his voice was still sweet, one side of his lips twitched.

"I saved a man from the noose."

"A villain who deserved such a death. Or perhaps it is his warmth at night that pleases you." He raked her with his gaze.

"How dare you, señor?" She raised her hand to slap him, but he caught it. The veneer of civility shattered from his face, replaced by a sinister glower. Clutching her arm—a bit too tightly—he led her off the porch to the side of the café. "Do you think such a villain will stay with you? *Estúpido!* He will take what he wants and leave."

"You're hurting me!" She raised her voice, hoping passersby would notice and come to her rescue, but even the few who glanced up didn't dare to confront the most powerful man in town.

"How could you marry a thief, a villain, a man of no consequence, no wealth, while you dare to shun me?"

"Let go of me!" Though she tried to hold them at bay, tears filled her eyes.

Señor Casimiro's men gathered close, forming a barricade around them.

"Mama!" Philippe's voice rose above the crowd.

Hot sun seared her skin. Perspiration beaded on her forehead and neck as the men's boots stirred dust in her face.

"Please let me go to my children," she sobbed, coughing.

"I will, señora, I will. But not until we come to an understanding. If you insist—"

She kicked him with all her strength. Howling, he leapt back. Her thrust hadn't landed where she'd hoped. Instead of incapacitating him, she'd only infuriated him. Raising his hand, he slapped her across the face.

The sting radiated from her cheek down her neck.

"Mama, where are you?" Abilene whimpered.

Caroline tugged against the man's grip.

"I have been kind to you, señora. But my patience will soon come to an end. When your pirate lover leaves you, and you have nothing to feed your little ones, you will come to me then. You give this pirate everything now, but you will soon be mine. *And* your precious vineyard."

Chapter 5

"She will never be yours, señor!" Dante gripped the man by his gold-embroidered collar and tossed him away from Caroline. Señor Casimiro stumbled backward, his expression brimming with shock and fury. He reached for his pistol. Dante kicked it from his hand then leveled his own weapon on the don's advancing men. One of them seemed familiar, his shock of light hair a beacon among so many brown-haired men. He walked with a limp as eyes bent on revenge pierced Dante. These were the men who had attacked Caroline's vineyard. And this popinjay was their boss.

Philippe, a weeping Abilene in hand, pushed through the growing crowd and ran to Dante. He nudged the children toward their mother and took a stance before them. Not that he could stop all these men by himself. But he would die trying. More than anything, he hated when the strong picked on the weak. As his mother had done to him his entire childhood.

"Call off your men, señor. I've already proven able to beat them. Or will you now attack women and children in the light of day?"

"I know not what you mean, *pirate*." The Spaniard spat as he rose to his feet and brushed dust from his clothes.

"I think you do."

"This was only a misunderstanding. One which you would do well to stay out of." He plucked his hat from the dirt and eyed

Dante with disdain. "Señora Moreau and I were merely discussing her future. Nothing more."

"A future which required your hand striking her face?"

"Disrespect from women must be dealt with, or it will grow like a cancer. Surely you agree?"

"I do not." Dante scanned the men waiting for one word from their boss to pummel him. But a crowd formed around the altercation, and he doubted the don wanted his reputation soiled. Dante glared at him. "Stay away from Señora Moreau and her children."

"Of course. I mean them no harm." The Spaniard slipped on his hat and dipped a bow toward Caroline. "When this pirate is through with you, señora, you know where I am."

∞

Caroline would like to tell the man that even if he lived in a golden palace, she'd never seek him out, but she didn't want to cause more trouble and upset Abilene, who still clung to her chest as tight as a barnacle to a ship, her thumb stuck in her mouth.

Philippe, however, spit after the men as they and Señor Casimiro sauntered away. "Hush, Philippe." She held him back, lest he try something else. Her son, where did he get such courage? Certainly not from his father. Trying to settle the pounding of her heart, Caroline drew a deep breath as Señor Vega turned to face them. Once again he had saved their lives. Once again he had stood up against overwhelming odds when he could have run. Why? The look she now saw in his eyes made her forget he was a rogue, a thief. And that he'd soon leave. It was a look of concern, protection, and even affection. But that couldn't be.

Steeling herself against the longing rising within her, she thanked him politely and started on her way, but Abilene reached toward the man. The pirate took her in his embrace, her red curls tumbling over his brown open shirt, her tiny hands reaching around his neck and gripping his collar as she nuzzled her head beneath his chin. He rubbed her back and glanced down at Philippe, who stared at him with awe. "You were very brave, Philippe," he said, patting the lad on the back.

"I was?" The young boy's eyes flashed. "If I'd had a pistol, Señor Vega, I'd have taken care of them all!"

"No, you wouldn't have, Philippe," Caroline said sharply, still trying to recover from her daughter's complete trust in this pirate. "And you won't have a gun until you're fully grown."

The excitement fled from Philippe's face, but it couldn't be helped. She would not have this pirate influencing her son to become a fighter like he was.

After gathering the supplies she'd dropped, Caroline followed Dante back to the buckboard, ignoring the curious eyes of the townspeople staring at the enigma who was both a family man and a pirate. She couldn't agree more, for she was having just as much difficulty associating the two. At the moment, however, she was thankful for both. Her arm still throbbed from where Don Casimiro had clutched her, and a shiver ran through her at the thought of the horrid man. If Dante had not come when he did. . . Well, it was best not to think of it. For now, he sat beside her on the driver's perch—so close their legs almost touched. Yet she felt safe. Very safe.

He snapped the reins, and within moments the sea came into view. A sheen of dark blue spanned to the fog bank on the horizon as waves tumbled ashore in a foamy dance. The same ship she'd seen two weeks ago rocked in the choppy waters.

"Is that your ship, Señor Pirate?" A blast of wind nearly tore off her bonnet, and she held it in place.

He pulled the horse to a halt and gazed out to sea, the longing in his eyes confirming what Señor Casimiro had said. This man would leave. He would sail back out to sea where he belonged. But what did she care? As long as he stayed through the harvest as he'd promised.

"The *Bounty*," he finally answered.

"How much is the council charging to redeem her?"

"More than I have." He smiled, but his eyes remained on the ship.

"You miss being at sea," she stated rather than asked.

He said nothing.

"Can I come aboard your ship?" Philippe poked his head between them from behind.

"Now, Philippe, that's not polite to ask. And besides, when Señor Vega gets his ship back, he won't want children running about on deck."

"But I won't run, and I can tie knots now and help."

Dante smiled down at the boy. "You would make a great sailor, Philippe."

Abilene pulled out her thumb. "Me too. I can learn knots. And I can clean floors. Mama lets me help at home."

"We can all become pirates!" Philippe shouted, beaming.

"We are not becoming pirates!" Caroline said with horror as Dante chuckled and snapped the reins.

∞

Dante dabbed a moist cloth on the edge of Caroline's lip, where a bruise had formed from Señor Casimiro's strike. Supper was over, and after several stories were told and prayers were said, the children had finally fallen asleep. Prayers, bah! Even after her harrowing day, the lady had still thanked God for His love and protection. Now, as they sat on the veranda under the light of a single lantern and a full moon, Dante finally did what he'd been longing to do all evening—tend to the lady's wound. He hadn't been sure she would allow his touch, but when he'd brought the bowl of water and a cloth onto the veranda, she hadn't flinched like she usually did when he drew near.

"I'm sorry he hurt you." Dante forced down an anger that, even now, threatened to send him over to this don's estate and teach the man chivalry. He'd been searching the plaza for Caroline and the children when he'd seen her kick the brute. Even with several armed men surrounding her. What bravery! What pluck! Then, when the man had slapped her, Dante's blood had boiled.

She closed her eyes to his touch and let out a sigh. A cool breeze stirred the loose curls at her neck. "Do you truly believe he's responsible for the attacks on my vineyard?"

"I recognized one of his men. *Si*, he's the one, all right."

"He is one of the wealthiest dons in the city. His family came here in 1815, hailing from royalty in Spain, they say. What does he want with me?"

Dante raised a brow at her naïveté.

Even in the dim light, he saw the lady blush. "But until today he's always been polite, even kind to me. Complimentary."

"Of course he's polite. Has it been so long since a man courted you?"

"In truth, yes." A little smile graced her lips. "Yet attacking my vineyard is hardly a path to my heart."

"I don't believe your heart is his goal, señora. Just a means to an end." He dipped the cloth in the water and dabbed her lips again. The blood was gone and the cut was small, but Dante didn't want to stop. She smelled of lilacs and fresh bread, and her closed eyes afforded him a chance to study her delicate features: the slight upturn of her nose, the curve of her chin, the sweep of thick lashes resting on her cheeks.

"I can hardly believe it of him," she said.

Leaning closer to get a whiff of her hair, he pressed the cloth to her mouth once again.

"Ouch." She opened her eyes.

"Apologies." Dante withdrew. "He won't give up. You need

protection. A group of farmhands to defend you."

"Or just one pirate." She smiled, but then it slipped away. "But you will leave soon."

Dante could not deny it. He was not a man meant to be land-locked. The sea called to him day and night. He longed to be back aboard his ship, free again to travel where he wanted, to seek his fortune, make a difference for Mexico.

"Thank you." She scooted away from him. "I cannot afford to pay more men. But God will provide. He always has."

Dante flattened his lips. "You are safe now because of me and not this God of yours."

"But He sent you to us, did He not?" She smiled then gazed up at the starlit sky as if she were looking at the Almighty Himself. Faith settled like a peaceful stream in her green eyes, and Dante felt a stirring of envy. What would it be like to have a Father who was all-powerful and who truly loved you? One on whom you could depend, one who would never disappoint or leave you.

She must have read his thoughts, for she laid a hand on his. "Where is your father, Señor Vega?"

"In Mexico. Veracruz. He runs a merchant business."

"So, that is how he met your American mother? In his travels?"

He nodded, uncomfortable with the turn of the conversation. "Si, in Boston."

"Then why were you raised in America?"

Dante dropped the cloth in the bowl. "My mother's family had fallen on hard times, and her marriage to my father supplied much-needed wealth. An arranged marriage. After the wedding, she refused to move to Mexico. Then, when I was born, she used the excuse of wanting the best education for her son." He stared at the wooden porch beside his boots as anger smoldered in his heart. Dante had been a mistake, an unfortunate product of a loveless marriage.

"But your father didn't move to America?"

"No. His business, his life, was in Mexico. I hardly ever saw him. Once a year, perhaps. My mother's family was very powerful."

"I'm so sorry."

Dante rose and walked to the railing. "It was for the best. He didn't turn out to be much of a father. After I left Harvard, I traveled to Mexico to be with him, but he disapproved of my idea of privateering. Vehemently disapproved." He snorted. "Told me no son of his would ever be a pirate."

"Then, why become one, Dante?"

The sound of his Christian name on her lips brought him around. The look in her eyes made him continue his tale.

"America had taken everything from me, my childhood, my father, my national identity. And then they took my homeland. I couldn't understand why my father wouldn't do something about it. I was as disappointed in him as he was in me, I suppose. Yet suddenly I was a man without a home. Neither my father nor my mother wanted me. In the end, it was the sea that gave me a home, a life, a purpose."

"So, you truly believe in this cause of yours? Provoking American ships for Mexico?" Disapproval laced her tone.

"We all have our causes, señora. You have this vineyard, this dream of your husband's. I have my revenge."

"But yours will lead to death."

He chuckled. "Perhaps. But it seems yours might as well." Turning, he gripped the railing and gazed over the dark vineyard. "Is your husband's dream worth dying for, señora? Don't you have any dreams of your own?"

∽

Dreams? Caroline had never asked herself that question. When she'd lived with her parents, their dreams had been hers. After she married François, his dream took their place. Now she supposed all she wanted was a good life for her children. A good home.

Someday perhaps, a loving husband. And the freedom to make her own choices. Rising, she slid beside him. "My dream is for my children, Señor Vega."

A breeze blew his black hair behind him. "I liked it when you called me Dante."

She had liked it too. Too much. It sounded right on her lips. Not the name of a pirate, but the name of a man who was kind and good, albeit a bit wounded by life.

"If you dream for a good life for your children, Caroline, you must keep them safe. I know men like Señor Casimiro. They strive for things they cannot have. He will not give up. Not even with me here."

She hadn't thought about that. The danger she was putting this man in. Before, it hadn't really mattered. He owed her for saving his life. But now the thought of him being killed caused her insides to clench. "I have put you in danger."

"I don't fear him. I fear for you." His eyes were lost to her in the shadows, but his sincerity thickened the air between them. "You must have protection, Caroline," he added.

"God will protect us."

"Blast it all!" He huffed and rubbed the back of his neck. "What has this God of yours done for you?"

Caroline lifted her chin. "He gave me a husband and two beautiful children, a vineyard, wine in the barrels, my freedom, hope for a future. And He brought us you. I'd say He's done quite a bit."

"You speak of Him as if you know Him."

"I do. You can too, Dante."

"No thanks." He leaned against the post. "My mother showed me what God was like. I had my share of punishments for not obeying Him."

Caroline's chest grew heavy at his statement. "Your mother was wrong. God is not a set of restrictions and rules. He's a father,

He's a friend. He's a savior. And He wants to help you with your life."

She could feel his gaze pierce her. "You make me want to believe that," he said.

"Then do." She stepped toward him.

"This is what I believe." Lifting a finger, he ran the back of it over her cheek. "You are the most precious woman I've ever met. Brave, kind, caring, a good mother—so unlike my own." His touch sent a prickling feeling down to her toes. What was wrong with her? His gaze dropped to her lips, and he swallowed. Was he thinking of kissing her? Her breath came fast. Her world began to spin. His scent of leather and earth swirled beneath her nose like a heady perfume. Then his lips met hers in a soft caress so at odds with the rough pirate. She knew she should stop him, but when he wrapped his arms around her and drew her close, drinking her in like a desperate man, her knees reduced to mush, and she wilted against him.

A coyote howled in the distance, a cow lowed, and a breeze stirred the leaves on a nearby tree, but nothing seemed real to her except the man who held her so protectively. The kiss was sweet, deep, and went on far too long. Another second and she'd be lost to him forever.

She pushed away, stepped back, and turned her back to him. How could she have done such a thing? Was she some hussy to kiss a man she hardly knew? "Forgive me."

She could hear his heavy breathing, his deep groan as if someone had stolen his last meal. "No need to be ashamed, Caroline," he finally breathed out. "We are married, after all."

"You are married to the sea, Señor Vega, not to me. And I insist you never touch me again."

Chapter 6

With a hand to her aching back, Caroline stepped onto the veranda and drew in a deep breath. She'd spent the morning scrubbing floors and kneading bread and longed for a glimpse of her children. She knew they fared well. Their laughter had serenaded her during her chores, but now as she scanned the vineyard all she saw were clusters of nearly ripe grapes hanging from vines like plump plums from trees. From the taste and feel of the few grapes she'd sampled yesterday, it may only be another two weeks before Sisquoc and the crew could start harvesting the fruit—a late harvest this year due to their unusually cool summer. Of course, after they picked the grapes, the men would press them and then place the strained juice in jugs to ferment for days before transferring it to oak barrels in the cellar to cure for next year's batch of wine. Good thing she already had a buyer for the wine from last year's harvest. She'd been testing it and adding water to top it off just like her husband had instructed her, and hopefully, it would meet the standards of her buyer, a merchant who intended to sell it to another merchant in New York. Things were looking up, indeed.

To say this past month had been one of the happiest in her life seemed a betrayal to both herself and François. To her husband because, even though she'd kept her distance from Dante, just having the pirate around—hearing his confident voice, watching him with her children, and exchanging pleasantries over their meals together—had made her far happier than she'd ever been in the intimacies of her marriage to François. And it was a betrayal to her own sentiments because she allowed them to grow for a man who would soon be gone.

Taking her heart—and she feared her children's hearts—with him.

But how could she have held her heart at bay? How could she ask her children not to follow Dante around, not to speak with him, not to crawl into his lap and receive his embrace, when she'd give anything to be able to do that herself?

Dante stepped into view, carrying Abilene in one arm and an ax in the other hand. Philippe strutted by his side, chattering like a magpie. Caroline smiled. She couldn't help but smile. Though they'd not shared a private moment since their kiss—she'd made sure of that—Dante had never faltered in his care of her and her children. He'd worked side by side with Sisquoc and the other men tending the grapes, he'd repaired a hole in the barn and cared for the chickens and the cow, he'd periodically rode along the perimeter of the property to ensure all was well, and he'd even assisted in hauling water from the creek. The Chumash foreman liked him, as did the other workers, and they readily obeyed his orders. He was a leader of men. A hard worker. Kindhearted. A good man. And a gentleman. Despite his occasional suggestive teasing and the desire in his eyes, he had not once pressed her for marital privileges.

He set Abilene down on the bench, stuck the ax in a stump, and pulled his shirt over his head. Noon sun gleamed on his bronze skin and rippled like sunlit waves over the muscles in his back and forearms. Philippe removed his shirt too, tossed it aside just like Dante had done, and beamed up at the pirate with pride.

As if sensing her eyes on him, Dante turned around, giving her a glimpse of the molded muscles of his chest and stomach. He smiled and waved. Heat expanded out from her belly until it flooded every inch of her. Still, she could not turn her eyes away. She returned his smile.

No doubt a man like him had been with many women—could have any woman he wanted. Why, then, did he stay with her? Surely it wasn't the roof over his head. He slept in the barn. Nor the scant meals she served when, instead of beans, he could purchase a steak downtown. What other reason could keep him here other than the one that made her heart soar—the one that made her want to run to him and beg him to stay.

She huffed. She'd become a dreamer like François. The pirate was just being kind. Perhaps he liked playing the hero to the damsel in distress. Perhaps he enjoyed the adoration of her children. That must be it, for night after night he continued his treks downtown, where she'd heard he'd drained the pockets of many of the drunken gamblers. He was only biding his time until he could redeem his ship and leave. Still, she would cherish the moments she had with him, for he had proven himself a good man. A worthy man.

"I'm teaching your son how to chop wood," he shouted.

Fear buzzed through her, and taking a step forward, she opened her mouth to tell him that it was far too dangerous, but he held up a hand and chuckled. "I know, señora. I'll be careful. He's using a smaller ax."

Philippe hefted the small blade and stood bare chested beside Dante. "Please, Mama! I'm not a little baby anymore."

Abilene nodded her approval from the bench. Where was the thumb that was normally in her mouth—that had been in her mouth since her father had died?

Outnumbered, Caroline finally nodded her consent, but stood there for several more minutes watching the muscles roll across Dante's back and arms while he raised the ax and chopped wood. Periodically, he'd set aside smaller branches on another hewn stump for Philippe to hack. The boy picked up instruction well, and assured that he was in good hands, Caroline decided it was best if she got back to work before she made a fool of herself gawking at the man like an innocent maiden—imprinting his image on her mind so she'd never forget him. Not that she could ever forget a man like Dante Vega.

∽

Taking her children's hands in hers, Caroline gestured for them to bow their heads while she thanked God for the food. On one side of Dante, Abilene slipped her tiny hand into his, while across the table, Philippe stretched his arm to grab his other. Dante's eyes moistened, but he kept them open while Caroline prayed. She spoke with such honesty and sincerity and genuine thanks, as if she were speaking to someone sitting beside her, some generous benefactor who provided for all their needs. It baffled Dante. She was so grateful for so little, while his mother had been disappointed with so much. His mother's prayers had been rote, austere, recited. Empty. But this beautiful señora's prayers touched a place deep in his heart, a longing to believe in something more than himself.

The prayer ended, and they all enjoyed a supper of home-baked bread, frijoles with eggs, and squash from the garden. Though the food was slight—barely filling half of Dante's belly—the joy and satisfaction filling his heart more than made up for it. At their request, he entertained the children with fanciful tales of sea storms and mermaids as they oscillated between oohing and aahing and giggling until tears flowed down their cheeks. All the while, Caroline ate and watched, casting him an occasional smile, despite the sorrow he sensed lingering about her. She'd been aloof since their kiss. He'd chastised himself more than once for taking such liberties with a lady like Caroline. But she'd been so beautiful in the moonlight, so easy to talk to, he'd been unable to resist. She'd not mentioned it since, nor had she allowed them to be alone.

Which was for the best. The way Dante was feeling—like he could find no joy in life aside from seeing her smile—he doubted he could resist her. And he must. A lady like Caroline would never settle for a scoundrel—*should* never settle for a scoundrel like him. No, she deserved a gentleman, someone with education and fortune and culture, a godly man who shared her faith. Someone who would raise her children right, not prune them to be pirates and ne'er-do-wells. Based on her offish behavior, she'd no doubt come to the same conclusion and was looking forward to him leaving after the harvest.

Which is why he intended to enjoy his remaining time with the Moreaus. But with each passing day, it grew harder and harder. This was *true* family. The family he never had. The family he never thought existed. The affection, the care and unity between mother and children, never failed to put a lump in his throat. The gentle way she scolded her children, always in love and with purpose, caused anger to well at his own childhood. But the look of trust and adoration in the children's eyes, and sometimes in Caroline's, when they looked at him made him want to give up the sea and become a husband and a father. Almost.

Later that night, after playing a game of jackstraws with the children, Dante headed to the barn as was his custom, not trusting himself to be alone with the lady after she put Philippe and Abilene to bed. He grabbed his rifle and strolled among the grapevines, ensuring all was well. The sweet scent of grapes and rich earth joined the salty brine of a sea that called to him from the distance with each mighty crash of its waves. Fog rolled in, masking the moonlight and muffling each tread of his boots, making them sound hollow. Like his soul.

A scream pierced the night. A child's scream! Terror gripped every nerve as he dashed for the house, burst inside, and made for Abilene's bedchamber. A single candle cast flickering light over

Caroline holding her sobbing daughter.

"What happened? Is she hurt?" Dante dashed to the other side of the bed.

Caroline rocked Abilene back and forth. "Just a nightmare." Concern moistened her eyes. "She's had them since François died." The little girl's body shook as she glanced up, her face hidden beneath a web of auburn curls, and reached for him. Emotion clogging his throat, Dante swallowed her up in his arms and kissed the top of her head. "Just a bad dream, pumpkin. All is well. You are safe." Her sobbing stopped, and she melted against him as if she trusted him to protect her forever.

Caroline, her golden hair tumbling to her waist, gazed at him with such appreciation, it brought moisture to his eyes. *Moisture!* He lowered his chin to sit atop Abilene's head and forced back his tears, ashamed.

Pirates didn't cry.

He sat there holding the precious girl until slowly Abilene's tight little body relaxed and she drifted to sleep. Setting her down on her pillow, he brushed curls from her face. She moaned in her sleep, peeked at him through slitted eyes, and said, "Thank you, Papa," before her breathing deepened and she drifted off again.

Overcome with emotion, Dante rose from the bed and backed into the shadows, lest Caroline see his weakness. She stood and approached him. Her night robe clung to curves not normally revealed by her gowns. Her lips were red and puffy, her eyes shimmering.

And worst of all, they were alone.

"I don't know how to thank you, Dante. You have such a way with the children." She smelled of lilacs and life and hope. Candlelight haloed her in shimmering gold, making her look like the angel she was—an angel sent to rescue the wayward pirate.

He wanted her. He wanted to make her happy. He wanted to love and protect her and be a father to her children.

Instead, he grabbed his rifle and dashed from the room.

Two hours later, Dante was on his fifth mug of ale and his third game of faro. The more he drank, the more he seemed to win. And the more his heart ached. He cursed himself for growing soft. Since he'd been a child, he'd prided himself on being able to control his emotions. When his mother had ignored him, belittled him, punished him unfairly, and finally sent him away to school, he'd kept it all inside, never allowing her to see his pain.

But this woman and her children. They had bewitched him. A plague on all women! For they truly possessed the power to destroy men—just like his mother had done to his father.

"*Capitán!*" A shout brought his attention from his cards to Berilo, his first mate, sitting down at a table beside his. "Do you win much?"

Tossing down his cards, Dante bowed out of the game, grabbed his mug of ale, and joined his friend. Two scantily dressed women sashayed up to the table. Berilo welcomed one onto his lap, but Dante waved the other away. Women were a curse. And besides, Caroline had ruined him forever to anyone but her.

Berilo showered kisses over the trollop's neck until she giggled and slapped him playfully. "When do you get the ship back, Capitán? The men grow restless."

"More than likely it is their pockets that are empty." Dante snorted.

"Si. That is true. But they are anxious for the fight."

Dante frowned and sipped his drink. Anxious to fight? Somewhere in the past few months, he'd lost that desire. But he would get it back. He *had* to get it back.

"Go get us drinks." Berilo flipped the woman two coins and slapped her behind as she sped off, smiling.

Dante leaned back in his chair. "If I continue to win, I'll have enough to redeem the ship in a month." And his obligation to help with the harvest would be completed by then as well. Then he would leave. Leave behind the only family he'd ever known. But it was for the best. For him *and* for them.

"Let us drink to redeeming the *Bounty!*" Berilo took one of the two mugs the woman plunked on the table and slid the other to Dante.

"To the *Bounty!*" Dante raised his mug. "And to leaving this paltry town!"

They continued to toast everything from Mexico, to freedom, to the sea, to whiskey, to loose women, to frijoles, until the world spun around him. Stumbling home, Dante intended to tell Caroline that she could no longer trap him with her feminine wiles or her children's adoring smiles.

He burst into her bedchamber, squinting against the darkness.

Shrieking, she tossed back her covers and leapt from her bed, grabbed her robe, and held it to her throat. "What are you doing, Dante? Get out of my chamber at once!"

Chapter 7

"I have something to say to you." Dante's intimidating form stepped into a shaft of moonlight. Dark hair brushed his shoulders as he teetered where he stood.

"In the middle of the night?" Flinging on her robe, Caroline groped for a match on her bed stand, and after lighting the lamp, turned toward him. "Are you injured?"

Lantern light flickered over his handsome face as he studied her with an intensity that should have frightened her. But it didn't. Perhaps she was a fool, but she trusted Dante Vega. With her life.

"No," he replied, rubbing his stubbled jaw. He leaned one hand on the bed frame for support.

She inched closer and touched his arm. "Ill?" Surely that must be it from the way he seemed unable to stand straight.

"No," he replied.

The smell of alcohol stung her nose. "You've been drinking!" Releasing him, she backed away.

"I have, señora. It is what pirates do. Or hadn't you heard?" He huffed and crossed his arms over his thick chest as if proud of the fact. "And I've come to tell you. . .to tell you. . .that I'll not allow you and those. . .children of yours to weasel your way into my heart and trick me into"—he waved a hand through the air—"staying in this house with your good cooking and charming family and your. . ."

Caroline's face grew hot. "How dare you insinuate such a thing? We. . .I am not tricking you!"

He wobbled and took a step toward her, leveling a finger toward her face. "Then, stop being so kind and patient and gentle and"—withdrawing his finger, he rubbed his temple as if it ached—"absolutely wonderful. I'm not falling for it."

Her anger dissipated beneath his compliments, no matter their drunken delivery. "You're making a fool of yourself, Señor Pirate. I suggest you go back to the barn and sleep it off." She attempted to turn him around and shove him toward the door, but even in his besotted condition, she couldn't budge him.

He chuckled. "You call me Señor Pirate when you're cross with me."

"Then you have no doubt as to my current disposition." She managed to turn him to face the door. "Nor that my anger will only rise if you do not leave immediately."

"And one more thing." He spun back around. "Tell your children to stop calling me Papa. I am not their papa, and I will never be." Though his tone was harsh, the look in his eyes spoke otherwise. Was the moisture she saw there from emotion or alcohol? He stepped toward her and gently fingered a lock of her hair. "And stop being so beautiful." His voice softened. "With your gold spun hair and sea-green eyes and skin a man longs to touch." He ran the back of his fingers over her cheek.

Why, when he'd burst into her bedroom, shouting and accusing her of tricking him, did his touch feel so good? Stirring a longing in her she'd never felt before, not even with François. "I'll do my best Señor Vega to not be so appealing," she breathed out in a whisper.

"Impossible." He huffed, dropping his hand to his side.

"Let's get you to bed, Señor Pirate."

He grinned, his gaze shifting to her tousled covers.

"To the barn I meant." Shaking her head, she grabbed his

hand and started for the door.

He pulled her to him, pressed her against his chest, and wrapped her in his thick arms. He smelled of leather and ale and the sea, and she settled her head against his shirt. Despite his drinking, despite his intrusion in her bedchamber, she felt safe in his arms.

For the first time in many years.

A shout and a crackling sound drew them apart. Dante darted to the window. In the distance, yellow flames reached for the sky.

"My grapes!" Caroline threw a hand to her mouth. "The vineyard is on fire!"

Dante instantly sobered. "Stay here. Protect the children," he shouted before storming off.

But she couldn't stay. Not when her livelihood, her very survival, was at stake. Instead, she got dressed as quickly as she could, roused the children, instructed Philippe to stay with Abilene on the veranda, and then sped into the darkness. But it wasn't dark anymore. Fires had sprung up in every direction. Red flames licked the sky, casting a hellish glow over the entire vineyard. Where had they come from? Smoke burned her nose. Men sped past, hoisting buckets of water from the creek. First Sisquoc then Manuel, Diego, and finally Dante, who ordered her back in the house. Clutching her skirts, she grabbed a bucket to assist them. She would not stand by and do nothing.

The sound of rifle shots exploded over the crackle of flames. *Pop! Pop! Pop!* Halting, she spun around. The men crouched to the ground as more shots thundered. One zipped past her ear. Fury started its own fire in her belly. Señor Casimiro! It had to be him and his men. He would not burn her out! She would not let him! Dropping her bucket, she started for the house to get a rifle. Dante hid behind a large grapevine and returned fire, gesturing for the other men to stay low. But what did it matter? Half her vineyard was aflame. Flames she could feel from where she stood as heat seared her in rolling waves, bringing with it the sting of smoke and the sour scent of burning grapes. Halting before her house, she stared benumbed at the sight of everything she'd worked so hard to achieve devoured in an instant.

"Get in the house!" Dante shouted, his voice muffled by the roar of the fire. But she couldn't seem to move. How would she support her children now? What would happen to them?

In the blur of heat and haze of smoke, she saw Dante running for her.

A shot fired. He clutched his shoulder, stumbled, and fell to the dirt.

∽

Blackness as thick as coal surrounded Dante. Someone was hammering. *Thunk! Thunk! Thunk!* The vibration sent piercing pain through his head. He tried to rub it away but couldn't move his arms. *Make the pain stop. Oh God, make the pain stop.*

"Will he live, Doctor?" The words were distant and muddled yet distinctively Caroline's.

"Yes. He'll recover in time. A quarter inch to the right and I'd be saying something different, but with lots of rest, your husband will be back on his feet in a month, maybe less."

Light tried to penetrate the darkness. It failed. Dante was swept back into the night.

Sometime later—an eternity or only a moment, he didn't know—he heard Caroline praying by his bedside, pleading with her God for Dante's healing, thanking God that he lived. Oddly, it brought him comfort. Other moments came and went like scattered dreams. Children's laughter, sunlight, darkness, someone spooning broth into his mouth, a weight on his chest. Pain that sent him back into the darkness. Heat. . .fire. . .why was it so hot? His mouth felt full of cotton. His head spun. Someone held his hand, caressed his skin. A kiss on his cheek. He smiled and fell back asleep.

Thoughts came alive in his mind. Instead of drifting atop a nebulous mist, they landed on reason, where they stirred more thoughts to life. Sounds alighted on his ears. Children's voices, Caroline singing, birds chirping. The smell of smoke filled his nose. *The vineyard!*

He pried his eyes open and blinked to focus. The wooden ceiling beams of a bedchamber came into view. He lowered his gaze to a pair of walnut Victorian chairs then to the matching wardrobe and over to the lacy covering atop the dresser, the glass candlesticks, bottles of perfume, jars of cream, and the brush and comb lying before a framed mirror. Definitely a lady's bedchamber. He pressed a hand against his chest and groaned.

"You're awake." Caroline entered the room, rubbing her hands on an apron, and dropped beside him, smiling.

"How long?" His voice came out scratchy.

"Four days. You had a fever." Taking a cool cloth, she mopped his brow. He tried to move. Pain rumbled through his shoulder.

"You're not going anywhere, Dante. You've been shot and you need your rest." She propped the pillows up behind him then took a glass from the table and held it to his lips. He hated being coddled, but the water tasted so good.

He wiped his mouth. Even that small effort pained his chest. "The vineyard?"

She sat back with a sigh and looked out the window. "Burnt to the ground."

"I'm sorry."

"It's not your fault."

"Yes it is. If I hadn't been drinking, maybe I would have seen the men coming, stopped them before they set fire to the grapes."

"You don't know that." She leaned forward and took his hand in hers. "Besides, you saved my life." Sunlight glittered on spirals of golden hair framing a face that looked drawn and tired.

"I got shot is what I did, and that does you no good."

"It certainly didn't." She arched an accusing brow. "I and the children have been worried to tears over you."

"You have?" No one had ever worried about him before. Not even his own mother. Emotion burned in his throat. "Thank you for caring for me."

She smiled. "My pleasure, Dante."

"What will you do?" he asked.

"What can I do? I'll sell the wine I have, start a new crop with the few vines that remain, and"—she sat back with a sigh—"pray."

"Why not just sell the land and go back home?"

She rose and made her way to the window. "I promised François on his deathbed that I'd keep the land, raise his grapes, and make the wine he dreamed of making his entire life."

"He was a fool to ask you that. To put you and his children in jeopardy."

She shrugged. "How could I deny a dying man his one request?"

Dante could not believe the selfishness of this man. "What of next year when you have no wine to sell?"

"I will learn a trade." She hugged herself. "We will trust God to take care of us."

Dante ground his teeth together. "You're a stubborn woman, Caroline. I don't know whether your faith in God is commendable or crazy."

"He has never let us down. There's a verse in the Bible that says, 'I have been young, and now am old; yet have I not seen the righteous forsaken, nor his seed begging bread.'"

Dante snorted. "I'd rather do things my way. As soon as I am well, this Señor Casimiro will pay for what he's done."

"No, please." She turned, worry lining her face. "You cannot fight a man like him. He is too powerful."

"Perhaps not alone, but you forget, I still have a crew in town.

And by now they will be itching for a fight."

"Then it will never end. And more people will get hurt." She sat beside him and took his hand again, pleading. "Leave it to God, Dante."

He was about to respond that he didn't trust God to right wrongs when Philippe and Abilene skipped into the room. Their faces lit when they saw him, and making a mad dash, they both leapt onto the bed. Philippe perched beside him, while Abilene tossed her arms about Dante's neck. His shoulder throbbed beneath her weight, but it was worth the pain for the love these precious children lavished upon him.

∽

Dante hated being bedridden. He'd always been a man of action, strong, capable, able to do anything he put his mind to with wit and vigor. But he'd never been shot so close to his heart, and the wound took its toll on his strength. It also took its toll on the way he looked at things. Facing one's eternity had a way of making a man think. And he had plenty of time to do that while he recovered.

Caroline and the kids entertained him well enough: they played card games, Philippe practiced his reading, Abilene regaled him with made-up stories, and Caroline spent countless hours talking with him. He cherished those moments the most, listening to her soothing voice, her pleasant laugh, watching the adorable way her nose scrunched when she disagreed with him, the sparkle in her green eyes when she teased him, the shy looks of affection that made his heart leap.

At night she'd read to him from the Bible, stories of adventure, romance, and war—exciting tales he never dreamed were to be found in such a holy book. With every inflection of her voice, with every tear of joy that slid from her eye, he knew she believed every word she read. Words from a God who loved His creation more than anything, who wanted the best for them and agonized when they chose a path that caused them pain. Words from a God who, when all else failed, sent His own Son to redeem people from the depths of hell.

Words that woke a deep hunger within Dante.

One night, after all had gone to sleep, he called out to this God of hers, expecting nothing but silence in response to a man like him. But instead, a glow ignited in his heart. It spread to his limbs in a tingle that brought a chuckle to his throat. Wind stirred the curtains, and though the night was foggy, silvery light spun ribbons of glitter through the room. And a voice sounded from deep within him. *"I love you, son. You are home now."*

Dante drifted to sleep, comforted by a Father he'd never known, but One who was here to stay. He'd also made up his mind on another important matter. If Caroline would have him, he would forsake the sea, stay with her and the children, and become the man she needed him to be.

Chapter 8

"It's only a week until Christmas, Mama." Abilene bounced up and down on the sofa as Caroline gathered her children close after supper.

"Yes it is." She smiled. "A very special time of year."

Philippe tugged from his mother's grip. "Will Santa bring us presents?"

Caroline's chest grew heavy. Children should have gifts at Christmas, but for two years now, hers would have none. "Christmas is not about gifts. It's about the birth of God's Son, Jesus. He is our greatest gift."

Abilene seemed to ponder this a moment. "I think He would want us to get other gifts too. Don't you think so, Mama?"

Caroline *could* purchase gifts. She'd sold the wine to Mr. Norsen, the merchant who already had a buyer in New York. Heaven be praised, he'd been quite pleased with the quality of the merlot. But she must save the money to provide food and other necessities for the next year when they had no wine to sell. "I'm sure he would, ma chère, but sometimes"—she hesitated, asking God for the best answer—"God gives gifts to children who have more need of them. We have everything we need, don't we?"

Both Abilene and Philippe nodded, though she sensed their disappointment. A disappointment she shared, for she wished more than anything she could afford something this year. Still, she felt guilty for even thinking such a thing. God had more than blessed them. They had a home, food, and each other. And most of all, Dante was nearly recovered. Why, he'd even been eating supper at the table with them the past week. His color had returned, along with his sarcasm and wit. She smiled. And even better, he seemed different somehow. Not so restless—at peace, happier. She could not understand it, would not allow her heart to hope. For a man like Dante would never be happy landlocked and burdened with the responsibility of a family. No, she must steel herself to accept that once he was fully recovered and had enough money, he'd set sail and leave them behind.

"Can we get a tree to decorate, Mama?" Philippe asked.

"Of course. And we'll pop corn and make beautiful ornaments. Won't that be fun?"

Abilene's eyes sparkled. "And we can make fruitcake too."

Caroline kissed her daughter's forehead. "Indeed."

"And your mother can read *A Christmas Carol* to us all." Dante's voice brought Caroline's gaze up to see him leaning against the frame of the open french door. He'd gone outside after supper to check the perimeter, and she hadn't heard him return. His brown shirt, open at the collar, flapped in the incoming breeze, revealing the bandage covering his wound. His black hair was pulled back in a tie. Leather boots led up to thick thighs that seemed not the slightest bit weakened by his illness.

And she thought him the handsomest man she'd ever seen. Would he really stay for Christmas? Part of her desperately wanted him to, part of her feared that if he did, her heart—and her children's hearts—would be forever lost to him.

After spending an enjoyable evening with her and the children, Dante, for the first time, helped her tuck them into bed, embracing each one, listening to their prayers, and kissing their foreheads. Once back in the parlor, he sat on the sofa and held out a hand for Caroline.

"Will you pray with me, Caroline?"

She blinked. "Did you say *pray*?"

"I did." He grinned.

"Do you mean that you want me to pray *for* you?"

"No." He took both her hands in his and pulled her down beside him. "Please allow me to pray for you and the children."

Shocked, elated, and ignoring the hope rising within her, she nodded and bowed her head. His prayer was awkward, cumbersome, and disjointed, but it was the most beautiful prayer she'd ever heard. He asked for God's protection over her and the children, for Him to provide for them during the lean years. He asked for good health, joy, and peace to flood their lives. By the end, tears trickled down her cheeks. "You believe in God now?" She squeezed his hands, his face blurry in her vision.

He brushed the moisture from her cheeks. "I do. Because of you. I gave my life to Jesus a week ago."

Joy bubbled up in her throat. "Oh Dante, I'm so glad!"

"And He has already shown me so much." He smiled.

Unable to control herself, she flung her arms around his neck and hugged him tight. "This is wonderful!" She withdrew and kissed his cheek. An innocent kiss of joy that sparked something deeper in his eyes. He eased a curl behind her ear, drinking her in with his gaze. A gaze that finally settled on her lips. He swallowed, brushed fingers over her cheek, then leaned in and kissed her. This time there was no shout, no rifle shots, no fire to stop them. This time she didn't care. She wanted to give herself to this man. Her husband.

But then he would leave and break her heart.

He swept her in his arms, carried her to her bedchamber, and set her down on the bed. Against everything within her, she moved to the edge and stood. He drew her close and kissed her again.

"I can't," she whispered against his cheek.

He cupped her face and met her gaze. "Do you love me?"

"With all my heart."

"Then believe I love you too. And I promise I'm not going anywhere. I will never leave you."

At that moment, with the adoring way he gazed at her, the gentleness of his touch, she *did* believe him. God help her, she did.

Later that night, Caroline snuggled beside Dante with her head on his chest and listened to the beat of his heart. Steady, strong, just like the man himself. He brushed fingers through her hair, drew her closer, and kissed her forehead. "I love you so much, Caroline. I never thought it possible I could be this happy."

"Are you truly happy?" She propped her chin on his chest to look at him.

He ran a finger over her bare shoulder and down her arm. "You are everything any man would ever want."

"But what of your ship, the sea? How could you be happy as a farmer? You'll be miserable." Fear battled her newfound joy—fear and sorrow. Yet love demanded the best for those in its embrace.

"With you, señora? Only a fool would be miserable."

"Are you still planning on redeeming your ship?"

"I believe the good Lord would frown on my career as a pirate." A chuckle rumbled through his chest.

"But there are legal vocations upon the sea."

Releasing a heavy sigh, he gazed into the dark room, and she knew he thought of his ship and the sea. But then his eyes snapped back to hers, and he smiled. "We need my winnings for the vineyard. To survive until we can produce more grapes."

"But—"

He pressed a finger on her lips. "That's my final decision, wife. Doesn't the Good Book say you must obey your husband?"

"I suddenly regret reading you that section." She pouted.

He brushed a curl from her face then leaned forward and kissed her. Deeply. "Any more regrets?"

"Not when you kiss me like that."

"I can do so much better than that." He winked and swallowed her up in an embrace.

∽

The twitter of birds drew Caroline from her deep slumber. She pried one eye open to see shafts of sunlight swirling dust into glittering eddies as memories of the most wonderful night she'd ever experienced filled her heart and soul to near bursting. She stretched her hand across the mattress, anticipating the feel of hard muscle but found only air. Opening her other eye, she sat up, drawing the sheet to cover herself. Dante was gone.

A momentary prick of fear quickly dissolved when she realized he'd no doubt gotten up early to tend the animals or chop wood or start the fire in the stove or do any of the various chores he'd been so diligent to perform.

An hour later, storm clouds gobbled up the sun, while a fierce wind tore over the vineyard. And Dante was still nowhere to be found. He hadn't even come in for breakfast. Sisquoc hadn't seen him, nor had any of the other workers. No matter. If anyone could take care of himself, it was Dante. He was probably on some errand in town. In fact, she had an errand of her own to run—one she was most excited about.

A gust burst into the house, swirling in leaves and knocking over a candlestick on the table. With the children's help, she closed and latched all the doors and windows and waited until the wind settled. It finally did after lunch as the blaring sun resumed its reign, sweeping away clouds and sparkling over the moist grass.

Putting on her best gown, she gathered the children and headed to see Judge Albert Packard, whose vineyard bordered hers on the south. She'd made up her mind even before speaking with Dante last night what she would do, and even now as the horse plodded along on the muddy road, excitement made her as giddy as a child at Christmas.

"What are we doing, Mama?" Philippe asked from his spot beside her on the driver's perch.

"We are going to get Dante a Christmas present."

"We are?" Abilene's smile was as wide as the sea.

Caroline nodded. *And he's going to love it.* She expected her children to mention the gifts they wanted for themselves but was quite pleased when they seemed more excited at doing something nice for Dante.

"Is he going to be our papa?" Abilene asked.

Caroline smiled, wondering if she should tell them yet, but thought since it was nearly Christmas, it would make a nice gift. "Yes, he is."

"Yay!" Philippe shouted. "He's the best Christmas gift of all, Mama."

Wiping tears of joy from her face, she halted the buckboard before Judge Packard's home, and with her children in tow, she knocked on the door.

The man was thrilled at her proposition, and within an hour he had summoned the city commissioner—a personal friend of his—along with the clerk of records to complete the transaction.

The deed of trust was exchanged for money the judge had in a safe on his property, and just like that, she had sold François's vineyard.

Though sorrow tugged at her heart at betraying him, she felt a great deal of satisfaction that Señor Casimiro would never get his hands on the property. Or on her. She also could hardly wait to see the look in Dante's eyes when she presented him with her gift.

The surprise, the twinkle of delight, the thankfulness. . .the love.

Yet, as she drove up the pathway to their home, she drew a shaky breath. In a few days, they'd have no place to live. She was relying completely on a man—a pirate—whom she'd only met four months ago. And that pirate still wasn't home. Nor did he come home that evening. Worry began to fester in her soul like a cancer, keeping her up all night. First thing in the morning, she hitched up the buckboard and took the children into town. There was something she had to do anyway, and it would give her a chance to ask whether anyone had seen Dante.

First stop was the City Council's office. She halted at the clerk's desk, Philippe and Abilene by her side. The spectacled man finally glanced up from his paperwork, his smile widening at the sight of her. "Ah, Mrs. Moreau. What may I do for you?"

Opening her reticule, she drew out a stack of bills then another and another and set them proudly on the desk. "I wish to redeem the *Bounty*, sir."

For a moment, he merely gaped at the bills, but then he slowly lifted his confused gaze to hers. "The pirate's ship?"

"That's the one."

"He's my papa now," Abilene announced proudly.

Offering the girl a look of concern, the man shook his head. "But he already redeemed it."

"Who?"

"Señor Vega. Yesterday morning, I believe." He stood, removed his spectacles, and walked to the window to look out. "Yes, and it appears he's already set sail."

Numb, Caroline could barely move her feet, let alone thank the man, grab her children, and leave. She managed to get outside, where the sea breeze could revive her before she fainted like some weak-hearted female.

"Why did Dante set sail, Mama?" Philippe asked. "I'm going to go see." Before she could stop him, he sped around the corner of the building.

"Bon sang," she muttered and hoisted Abilene in her arms to follow him.

"Mama, where is Papa?" Abilene asked, her voice teetering on the edge of tears.

"I don't know, but I'm sure he's safe." She forced strength into her own wobbling voice. That wobbling sped to her legs when she caught up with Philippe and followed his gaze offshore to the spot where the *Bounty* had been anchored. Setting Abilene down before she dropped her, Caroline knelt to gather her children close.

"Where did he go, Mama?" Philippe asked.

"I told you it was foolish to trust a rogue like Señor Vega." The familiar voice scraped down her spine. She stood and faced Señor Casimiro, fingering his pointed beard beneath a grin of victory.

"I'm sure there is an explanation for his departure," she returned. "Not that it is any of your affair."

He snorted. "I assure you. There *is* an explanation. My man overheard him down at the saloon telling his first mate that he got what he came for and he was itching to return to piracy." He grinned. "What did he finally get from you, señora? Shall I wager a guess?"

Chapter 9

Christmas Eve

Caroline stood on the shore, one hand holding Abilene's, the other Philippe's, while their trunks were stacked on sand beside them. All they had left in the world was stuffed in those portmanteaus. All except her heart, which was out on the sea being devoured by a man she'd never see again. Fog as thick as the heaviness in her soul crowded around them, muffling the sounds of crashing waves and embedding a chill in her bones. A chill she hadn't been able to get rid of the past two days. She'd spent them in a benumbed haze of conflicting emotions that threatened to bury her in the dirt beside François.

Where she no doubt belonged for her stupidity.

Still, she had done her best to remain strong for the children, to put on a happy face and spout hopeful words of their future. But every time either of them began to cry about Dante, she unavoidably joined them. Now they stood forlornly gazing at the steamer ship that would take them to the port of Los Angeles, where they'd catch a larger ship that would escort them around Cape Horn and up to New Orleans. Though she still hadn't heard from her family, Caroline held on to the hope that they would forgive her and take her and the children in.

If not, she didn't know what she'd do. The money she'd procured from the sale of the vineyard wouldn't last forever. And she couldn't very well marry another man when she was still legally joined to Dante.

Soon the small boat returned, her trunks were loaded, and a sailor carried the children through the crashing surf into the wobbly craft. Caroline turned to glance at Santa Barbara, her home for the past three years, but the gray shroud hid it from view. Just as well. She had very few pleasant memories of the place. A squab, round man who reeked of fish assisted her into the boat, and once she was seated, he shoved off from shore, leapt in, and along with two other men, plunged oars into the foamy wavelets.

Tears burned in her eyes as the sight of the steamer brought thoughts of another ship to mind. A two-masted pirate ship that had once sat majestically in these waters.

All of Dante's kindness, his hard work in the vineyard, his protection, his risking his life for them, his goodness to her kids, his compliments and charm, even his supposed encounter with God, all had been a ploy to get in her bed. She could come up with no other explanation. Yet why go to such trouble when he could have any of the many women who haunted the saloons downtown? Perhaps he'd grown bored with wayward women. Perhaps Caroline had presented a challenge for a man who possessed no scruples and needed to pass the time while he earned back his ship. Why else would he leave town the day after they'd consummated their marriage? The tears flowed freely now, and she pounded her fist on her knee. How could she have been so stupid? So utterly and completely gullible. When she knew better! He was a *pirate*!

And worst of all, she'd allowed her children to become attached to him, had stood by and watched as he broke their hearts and shoved another wedge of bitterness and mistrust into their innocent souls. Some mother she was.

As the ship loomed larger, Caroline quickly dried her eyes. It would do no good to have her children see her agony. Perhaps the excitement of the voyage would help them forget the man who said he'd be their papa. Perhaps it would help her forget the man who'd said he'd never leave her.

She doubted it.

Once their trunks had been hauled below to a cabin, Caroline gathered the children and stood at the railing, watching the other passengers come aboard, along with crates and barrels of goods to be sold down the coast. The fog bank had already begun to roll out to sea, allowing sunlight to christen certain sections of town. Like the mission that now gleamed white on the hill in the distance—a beacon of goodness in a city gone mad with debauchery.

Soon, all was brought aboard, and as passengers and crew milled about the deck, the captain shouted orders to weigh anchor.

Philippe tugged on her skirts. "Mama."

"Yes, Philippe." Her gaze remained on town, memorizing the streets and homes, the red tile and adobe of some, the wooden walls of others, the pastureland and cattle, the churches with steeples, and the many vineyards lining the hills.

"Mama!" His voice heightened in excitement.

No doubt a sea lion had surfaced to play among the waves.

Abilene plucked out her thumb—having returned to the bad habit after Dante left—and pointed. "It's Papa's ship!"

Caroline snapped her gaze to the sea where the *Bounty* sped toward them, all sails to the wind. She rubbed her eyes, expecting it to be gone when she opened them again. But the crew had seen it too.

"Captain, a brig heading our way off the starboard side," one of them said.

"Blast it all! What could they want?" the captain replied, scope in hand. "I have a schedule to keep."

Within minutes, the *Bounty* lowered sails and halted expertly alongside the steamer, some twenty yards away. Dante Vega, looking more like a pirate than he ever had, hailed the ship through a speaking cone and requested an audience. Without awaiting a reply, he ordered a boat lowered, climbed down into it, along with a few of his men, and with white flag raised, began rowing toward them.

"Papa is coming for us!" Abilene squealed with glee.

"Told you he didn't leave us." Philippe crossed arms over his chest.

The captain, a young, barrel-chested man approached. "Do you know this man?"

Caroline could hardly find her voice. "He's my husband," she mumbled out.

"Your husband? Well, he's delaying me! What does he want?"

A very good question. As she watched him and two of his crew row toward them, a battalion of emotions raged within her: anger, hope, love.

"This is ludicrous," the captain said as he marched away. "I must be under way. Raise topsails, Mr. Blaney."

"Captain." Caroline swung about. "Please, just a moment more, I beg you."

Whether it was her pleading tone or the look in her eyes, the gruff man finally relented and belayed his last order. "You have one minute, lady."

The boat thudded against the hull, and Caroline leaned over the railing to see Dante gazing up at her, his hair flailing around him, and a look of shock on his face. "What are you doing, Caroline?"

"I'm taking the children home to New Orleans. What else would I be doing?"

"Why? What about the vineyard?"

"Where did you go?"

"Hi, Papa!" Abilene waved down at him.

"Hi, pumpkin. Hi, Philippe." He waved and smiled.

"Where did you go?" Caroline demanded.

"I went to Los Angeles. Did you get my note?"

"What note?"

"I left it on the table with a candlestick on top."

Caroline shook her head, only then remembering the storm that had come up suddenly the morning Dante had left. Was it possible the paper had blown out the window before she'd closed up the house? "I never saw it."

Crewmen and passengers lined the railing with interest.

Dante raked a hand through his hair. "You must have thought"—his voice trailed off as he shook his head—"and then my ship was gone."

"What was I to think when the day after"—she hesitated, heat flooding her cheeks—"the day after you promised to stay, you redeem your ship and sail away?"

"I didn't redeem my ship," he shouted up. "I sold it."

"Do you take me for a fool? It is right there!" She pointed behind him.

"I sold it to my first mate on the condition he let me borrow it for a short trip to Los Angeles."

"You expect me to believe you sold the most precious thing in the world to you?"

"You are the most precious thing in the world to me."

One lady at the railing sighed with delight.

And though Caroline longed to join her, she couldn't. Not yet. "Why did you go to Los Angeles?"

His lips flattened. "A surprise. Please, Caroline, I love you. Come with me. Berilo will take us wherever we want."

"I don't believe you."

"I meant what I said that night. I won't ever leave you. I'm here, aren't I?"

"Ah, go with the poor fellow," one man beside her said.

A lady passenger brought a handkerchief to her eye.

"Mama." Abilene jerked on her skirts again. "I want to go with Papa."

"Lady," the captain said. "Your minute is up. I must be under way."

"At least come down here and talk about it," Dante pleaded.

But if she went down, she'd never get back up. Her heart said to go, but her heart had been wrong more often than not.

"Lady, I beg you, please relieve the man of his suffering," a man dressed in a posh suit said, looking at his watch.

Before she could stop him, Philippe swung both legs over the railing, grabbed ahold of a dangling rope, and made his way down to Dante's waiting arms.

"Philippe!" *Oh, that boy!* "Captain, do you have a rope ladder?"

"Aye." He snapped his fingers and a crewman grabbed one that was already tied to the bulwarks and tossed it over the railing.

"Abilene, hold on to my neck and don't let go." She hoisted the girl in her arms and slowly made her way down. The scratchy rope bit into her palms. The ship rocked. The ladder swayed. Abilene's harried breathing filled Caroline's ears as the girl's grip tightened on her neck. "It's all right, ma chère." But it wasn't all right. Caroline glanced down at the boat bouncing in choppy waters at least ten yards below them. And froze.

"Hold on," Dante shouted. "I'm coming to get you."

Hungry water lapped against the hull, reaching for Caroline. She could do this. She didn't need to be carried like some child. A wavelet struck. The ship careened, groaning, and the ladder slapped the hull. Pain throbbed through her fingers. Her sweaty palms slid on the rope. Her foot slipped, and she knew it was all over. She and Abilene would plunge into the icy water and drown before anyone could save them.

But instead of water, she fell against Dante's thick chest. He wrapped one arm around her and Abilene and inched down the ladder, his warm breath wafting over her neck. "I've got you. Now and forever."

Later that night as the *Bounty* rose and plunged through the ebony sea, Dante brought Caroline, Philippe, and Abilene on the foredeck where they could sit and watch the stars.

"There's so many of them!" Caroline exclaimed with delight as she tossed blankets over the children.

"And they all twinkle!" Abilene added, plopping to the deck.

"Look at that one." Caroline took a seat beside Dante on a crate and pointed to a particularly bright one in the eastern sky.

Philippe tightened the blanket around his neck. "Is that the star that led the wise man to baby Jesus?"

Dante threw a coat over Caroline's shoulders. "It must be. It's Christmas Eve, isn't it?"

"Will it lead *us* to Him, Mama?" Abilene asked.

"No need," Dante answered. "He already lives in our hearts, pumpkin. And He will never leave."

The ship careened over a wave, spraying them with a chilled mist. The children gripped the deck and laughed then settled to gaze back up at the stars.

Caroline's eyes met his, so full of love and admiration, he gulped down emotion before he made a fool of himself. "You sold your vineyard to redeem my ship." Dante still could not believe it. "That was all you had."

"It was to be your Christmas gift." She gave a lopsided smile and reached for his hand. "But you sold your ship. I can't believe you sold it. It was so important to you."

"How else could I provide for my family, save the vineyard, and"—he raised his voice so the children could hear—"buy Christmas gifts?"

"Christmas gifts!" Both squealed and turned around.

Grabbing the sack he'd brought on board, Dante untied the rope, feeling a bit like Santa Claus himself. "What have we here?" He pulled out a porcelain doll dressed in a lustrous silk gown and gave it to Abilene.

For a moment, she merely stared at it, her eyes wide and

sparkling like the stars above. Then she took it in her arms and embraced it like it was her own child. "I love it, Papa!"

His heart near bursting, he peered into the sack again. "Now, what is this?" He pulled out a leather whip and handed it to Philippe.

"Wow" was all Philippe said as he grabbed the whip and began to unravel it. "Thanks! Mama, look at this!"

"But you must keep it coiled on the ship," Dante said. "I'll teach you how to use it when we reach land." Philippe nodded, and Dante gave Caroline a reassuring glance. "It will be okay."

"Merry Christmas, Papa!" Both children said as they began playing with their gifts.

"Merry Christmas," he replied.

"There's something else in your bag." Caroline's voice was teasing as she pointed to the sack.

"Is there?" He scratched his head and peeked inside. "I do believe you're right." Reaching in, he pulled out a box containing a bonnet, the latest fashion from Paris and quite popular among high-society ladies—or so he'd been told by the woman at the millinery.

And apparently—if the look on Caroline's face was any indication—she'd been right.

"Oh Dante." She opened the box and caressed the silk ribbon, seeming about to cry. "I can't believe you bought this for me. And here I thought you'd abandoned us." She dabbed the corner of her eye.

Placing a finger beneath her chin, he raised her eyes to his and placed a gentle kiss on her lips. "Never."

Their gazes held for several seconds, several magical seconds, during which Dante thanked God for such a precious woman and vowed to make her happy the rest of his days.

"Where are we going, Papa?" Philippe looked up from fingering his whip.

Dante shrugged. "I thought perhaps Veracruz to see my father. He has a merchant business he's been begging me to join. That is, Señora Vega, if you'll come with me?" He brought Caroline's hand to his lips for a kiss.

"Señor Pirate, I will follow you anywhere."

MaryLu Tyndall, a Christy Award finalist and bestselling author of the Legacy of the King's Pirates series, is known for her adventurous historical romances filled with deep spiritual themes. She holds a degree in math and worked as a software engineer for fifteen years before testing the waters as a writer. MaryLu currently writes full time and makes her home on the California coast with her husband, six kids, and four cats. Her passion is to write page-turning, romantic adventures that not only entertain but open people's eyes to their God-given potential. MaryLu is a member of American Christian Fiction Writers and Romance Writers of America.

The Gold Rush Christmas

by Michelle Ule

Dedication

For the adventurers who sailed to Alaska with me:
Robert, Christopher, Jonathan, Nicholas, and Devin;
and for the one still awaiting adventure:
Michael

I sent messengers unto them, saying, I am doing a great work,
so that I cannot come down: why should the work cease,
whilst I leave it, and come down to you?
Nehemiah 6:3

Chapter 1

August 1897
Port Orchard, Washington

"Here's the last quilt." Samantha Harris brushed tears from her eyes and tossed her heavy gold braid over her shoulder.

Mrs. Parker sighed as she folded the wedding ring quilt into the final crate. "I remember your dear mother stitching the quilts on the veranda. She tucked a prayer for your future husband and Peter's future wife into each stitch. I'm sorry she'll never learn who they are."

Peter grinned. "I'm sure Samantha can find a husband in Alaska territory."

"I'm hunting for Pa, not a husband."

"Maybe you'll find both." Peter set her indigo carpetbag with the luggage. "Alaska's a land of golden opportunities. We're throwing off civilization's shackles and sailing to a territory of unlimited prospects. I'm ready to go."

Mrs. Parker frowned. "You're like your father—never satisfied. You've always wanted to be somewhere else. How your mother fretted over your rash schemes."

Samantha glanced at her twin as she set her father's carved candlesticks on the quilt. She stuffed in the last two feather pillows, sprinkled dried lavender on top, and spread a clean sheet over them. Peter nailed on the lid. The Parkers would store their few remaining possessions.

"Look how your sister taught at the Port Orchard School the last three years. She never complained about taking care of your mother while your father. . ." Mrs. Parker hesitated.

"Shared the Gospel with the Indians?" Samantha grabbed the heavy crate, which also contained her mother's cherished china, and carried it to the door with Peter's help. She heard the Parkers' horse clopping up the road with a cart.

"I don't know what she saw in your father. An itinerant preacher who itched to preach to ruffians even after Port Orchard became civilized. He got his travels, but your mother paid a pretty penny for them. She wouldn't approve of your taking Samantha off to the wilderness. You should be ashamed of yourself, Peter Harris."

"I'll return next year to attend the University of Washington." Samantha hoped her brother's promises and her mother's dream would come true. "But we need to find Pa first."

Reverend Parker entered carrying four Bibles under his arm and gripping a letter in his hand. He scowled at Peter. "Muscular Christianity sounds like your idea."

"Sir?"

"You challenged Miles, didn't you? You told him to abandon his books for action. Are these not your words?"

Peter stood at attention. Samantha froze.

"According to this, my son left seminary just short of his ordination exams." Reverend Parker shook the letter. "He wants to explore his faith in practical ways and take his chances in the Klondike goldfields. He's headed to Alaska, and we are not to discourage him, only pray." Reverend Parker offered the Bibles. "If so, he'll need these extra Bibles."

Mrs. Parker gasped.

Samantha advanced on her brother. "Did you invite him to come with us?"

"Miles wants to be a preacher. Miners have spiritual needs. I told him Alaska could prove his calling to ministry." Peter set the Bibles with their luggage.

"You talked Miles into going to Alaska? He's. . ." She chose her word carefully. "He's clumsy!"

Reverend Parker read aloud. "Don't try to stop me. I prayed and believe this is God's direction for my life right now. I love you. Tell Peter and Samantha I will see them in the north."

"Where would he obtain the money?" Mrs. Parker clutched her throat.

Reverend Parker examined the letter. "He borrowed funds from a friend. Miles purchased his provisions in Seattle and mailed this letter from the docks before he sailed."

"Sailed?" his mother cried. "Who would have loaned him so much money?"

Samantha squelched the urge to strike Peter. "You didn't!"

Samantha watched two men lift her mother's prized pump organ onto the cart. She gulped a sob as she recalled Mama singing and playing hymns, particularly on nights when they missed Pa.

Peter cleared his throat. "That's done. Let's say goodbye to Mother." They walked up the dirt road to the cemetery.

"What were you thinking inviting Miles?"

"How could we go on an adventure and not take our third musketeer? We need him."

Samantha sighed. "You know what he's been like the last couple years. He'll propose again."

Peter snorted. "He loves you. You just don't appreciate him."

Samantha swatted at Queen Anne's lace. "His head is so full of God—not that there's anything wrong with loving the Lord—he misses obvious things. Alaska could kill him." When they were growing up, pudgy, bespectacled Miles was always falling out of trees, getting stung by bees, or tripping over his own feet.

Peter stopped. "He's shorter than you. That's the real reason you turned him down."

She stomped her foot. "That's not true."

"You're six feet tall, Sam. Your chances of finding a guy tall enough to suit you are slim."

"I'm five-eleven and a half."

He laughed. "You're still taller than most men. But maybe giants like us live in Alaska."

Samantha shut her eyes and counted to ten, like Mama always advised. She lowered her voice to soften her anger. "You told me we sold our household goods to pay our way on the steamship and for our supplies. I signed over my bank account to cover unexpected travel incidentals. Are my savings funding Miles's trip?"

Her high-spirited brother turned his blue eyes away. The cheekbones above his beard turned pink.

She smelled the damp Washington soil and the decaying rot of soggy plants as the summer day dwindled to dusk. "Please tell me the truth."

"I promised to find Pa," Peter said. "Once we find him, you can stay with him through the winter and Miles and I will go to the Klondike. I'll reimburse you. You'll only lose one year. I've waited my whole life for an adventure beyond this little town. If I had to sit at that desk in the lumber mill one more day I'd go crazy."

"We couldn't have survived without your hard work." She patted his arm. "But why does Miles have to come?"

Peter unlatched the squeaky cemetery gate. "I can't prospect alone, and I trust him. Besides, the Klondikers will hear the Gospel if he's with me. I'll work and he'll preach. Pa will like that. Don't worry. We've always saved Miles before. We'll do it again. We need him. I promise he'll be safe with me."

They pushed past the overgrown phlox to their mother's fresh grave. Thin grass blades poked through the ruddy earth around the beloved azalea Samantha had transplanted from their garden.

Could so much have changed in only a month?

Peter's shoulders shook. "She'd be proud of us—you'll see. Mother wanted us to spend more time with Pa. It's our job to tell him about her passing. We'll find him."

Samantha let the tears flow. How often had Mama warned Samantha to use her head and curb Peter's fancies? How many times had Mama told her to watch out for bookish Miles?

"I'll do my best to trust you, Peter," she sniffed. "I'll try to be thankful Miles is with us, because it means the Parkers will be on their knees. We'll need their prayers."

Peter brushed leaves off the grave. "Mother would like that."

Samantha pressed her lips together and stared at the head-stone. She wasn't so sure.

Would Mama have approved of anything about this scheme?

Chapter 2

Seattle docks

Miles Parker shoved the bowler hat down over his forehead, only to have it pop up again. He should cut off the fair curls his mother liked so much. They got unruly and made him look like a tall child instead of the man he wanted to be.

Miles corrected his thinking. He was a twenty-one-year-old man voyaging to uncharted lands. Alaska's adventures would prove he was a man that women, particularly Samantha, could admire.

Miles was counting on it.

He peered over the hordes swarming Seattle's docks, searching for the towering Harris twins. When Peter sent the money and the packing list last week, he'd ordered Miles to supervise the purchase and loading of their provisions onto the steamship *Alki*.

Miles spent the first dime at the Seattle Hardware Company on *Facts for Klondikers*. He knew the booklet would more than repay them with gained insight. In addition, the outfitters Coopers and Levy had suggested several items. Figuring it better to be safe than sorry, Miles added snow glasses and cozy knitted hats.

Miles checked his coat pockets. His extra pair of spectacles remained secure. His small New Testament rode, as always, in his breast pocket close to his heart.

"Excuse me, sirs." Miles lifted his hat to the scowling faces of gold-fevered men.

When they didn't budge, Miles gently pushed through the crowd with his broad shoulders. Two men resisted, so he put on his charming smile.

"What's your rush?" one growled.

"I have a ticket." He'd learned that speaking slowly in a cordial tone worked better for him than belligerence.

The crowd parted.

Miles watched stevedores hauling cargo onto the *Alki*. The ship creaked against the quay as travelers crossed the gangplank to board. He could hear the frantic barking dogs, bleating sheep, and neighing horses that would spend the six-day journey in the ship's hold.

A whiff of coal-fired smoke mixed with the tangy sea air and press of humanity. He straightened and his heart skipped a beat when he saw Samantha.

Miles waved his bowler and whistled their childhood signal. Samantha turned in his direction. Peter grasped her elbow and pulled a cart behind them loaded with baggage. Samantha didn't need help, but it always pleased Miles when Peter recognized his sister was a young woman and not merely a shorter version of himself.

"Everything on board?" Peter demanded.

Miles ignored him. "Hello, Samantha. I bet you're surprised to see me."

"That doesn't half express my thoughts," Samantha murmured. "Peter said you purchased our equipment?"

"Yes. I bought everything on Peter's list. My research suggested beefing up on antiscurvy items, so I purchased four bottles of lime juice. They loaded our provisions on the ship this morning."

"What research?" Peter stepped closer.

Miles held up *Facts for Klondikers*.

"I figured I'd ask men who've been to Alaska before," Peter said.

"Sourdoughs? An excellent idea. I suspect, however, most of the voyagers on the *Alki* will be Argonauts; that's another name for folks headed to the goldfields."

"I've heard that." Samantha elbowed the man behind her. "This crowd is rough."

Miles tapped his chin, the old sign for the musketeers to bow close. "I haven't seen many gentlewomen boarding. I'm concerned about the people Samantha will encounter."

"What do you mean?" Peter asked.

Samantha frowned. "I can take care of myself."

"Certainly." Her lilac scent reminded him of home. "You're strong and resourceful, but desperate times may require desperate measures."

Samantha's sigh dismissed him, but Miles continued. "Where's Samantha supposed to sleep? I've seen few women except"—he leaned toward Peter—"the wrong type."

Peter had always been the most cunning of the three. Miles watched him consider his sister, taller than most of the other passengers, and the surly men around them. He met Miles's eyes. "Should we disguise her?"

"You can't be serious." Samantha stepped back. "We're adults, not kids playing *Twelfth Night*. You want me to masquerade as a man?"

Peter nodded. "We need to decide now, before we embark."

"It's for your own good," Miles explained. "You can sleep between us on deck if they think you're a boy. We can protect you."

Samantha looked down her nose at him, but Miles didn't flinch. He was used to it.

"We need to cut her hair, and she can wear my clothes. I've got a change in my carpetbag." Peter ignored her protests. "It's only until we get to Alaska. Then you can put your corset on again."

Samantha reached for her blond knot. "Pa called my hair a crown of golden glory. How can I cut it off?"

Miles winced at the threat to Samantha's splendid hair, but he steeled himself. "There's not much time."

"Let's go. I'll use my knife. Watch our luggage." Peter seized his sister's arm and dragged her toward a nearby building.

Smoke belched from the forward smokestack, and the throng grew more restless. The twins returned with Peter's expression stiff and Samantha's eyes red. Her hair stuck out in pitiful tufts, and Peter's clothes hung on her.

Loss pricked Miles. When he had suggested Peter leave Samantha behind, his oldest friend refused. "We've always said all for one—we can't leave her behind. Sam's yearned for Pa since the day he left. Besides, the trip will keep her mind off losing Mother."

What did Miles know about missing a parent? His parents had fussed over him his entire life. He'd agreed to go with Peter just to keep an eye on Samantha.

Miles removed his bowler. "Wear this, Samantha."

"It's Sam," Peter said.

In Peter's tightly belted pants with the hems rolled up four inches, her angular frame resembled that of an adolescent boy. Sam grabbed the hat. If no one looked too closely, she would pass.

"Give me your necklace," Peter commanded.

Sam clutched the carved cross around her neck. "Pa made this. I never take it off."

"Do you see any other men wearing necklaces?"

Sam turned away to remove the chain. Miles patted her arm. "Time to board."

Peter led the way, hauling their personal baggage. Miles slung his blanket roll across his shoulders and toted a rust-colored carpetbag crammed with saltine crackers, ginger root, and other soothing food in case seasickness struck. Growing up, the trio had sailed a small boat in Sinclair Inlet with Mr. Harris. Miles never had a problem, but Samantha's stomach was another story.

The *Alki* had large open deck areas front and back with passenger cabins two stories high in the center. Travelers bustled about arranging their gear into a space to call home for the voyage. The Port Orchard trio found a spot on top behind the smokestack near the lifeboats. Peter pointed at Miles. "Pray for clear weather or we'll get wet."

"We grew up in the Pacific Northwest. I think we can handle rain." He put cheer in his voice to encourage them.

Sam stared west toward home and the summer snow-topped Olympic Mountains. She fidgeted with something in her pocket. Miles tapped the bowler. "What're you thinking, Sam?"

She pulled out the bulky golden braid Peter loved to tug but Miles feared to touch. She smoothed it between her hands. "I just want to find my father."

Chapter 3

Inland Passage

Miles fussed about arranging things and defending their spot against interloping Argonauts. When Peter invited her to watch the ship cast off, Samantha shook her head. She felt hollow and assaulted, too drained by recent events to budge.

A horn blasted for departure. Hoarse voices shouted, "Alaska, Alaska!" but Samantha covered her ears and face to forget the milling crowds, rumbling engines, and squalling sea birds. Her grieving heart longed for a home now lost and a cherished mother whose voice she'd never hear again.

Mama would be horrified at their recent actions. They'd sold their possessions, abandoned Port Orchard, bought steamship tickets, chopped off Samantha's hair, and now she wore Peter's clothes. But what choices did she have? Mama was dead. Pa was missing. Peter had spent her savings. Until he earned more money, she had neither home nor future.

All Samantha had was hope she'd see her father again. Two years was a long time not to hear Pa's warm voice reading the Bible. She yearned for his calm reminders that Jesus loved her and God had a good plan for her life.

But where was Pa? He'd sent the last letter in June from somewhere near Skagway, explaining he missed them but had important work to finish by Christmas. He'd come home then. Mama had read the letter aloud. "Remember how God sent Nehemiah to help his people? Pa is doing the same thing."

Mama had folded the pages carefully, coughed into her handkerchief, and found solace in her Bible, as always. Peter had paced and run his hands through his hair, his frustration barely contained.

Samantha craved Pa's strong arms. With her mother dead, she needed his comfort. Surely he would understand the trip, her shorn hair, and Peter's ambitious plans.

She took a deep breath and told herself to appreciate the freedom of not wearing a pinching corset. Her disguise depended on her ability to behave like her brother. She willed herself to act manlike. Perhaps she should spit or scratch.

Or order someone to do something he didn't want to do.

Peter returned. "You shouldn't be mooning up here. This is a turning point in your life. Everything will be different from now on."

"What if I didn't want my life to change?"

"You don't have a choice, Sam. The past is gone. This is your new life. Are you going to embrace it or sulk?"

Peter's eyes danced with excitement, and he brimmed with confidence.

Miles tripped up, his hair curling above his ears like a toddler. His round cheeks already looked sunburned above his scraggly beard. "Just like when we were kids, Sam, and played three musketeers. One for all, all for one."

She really looked at him for the first time. "When did you start growing whiskers?"

"As soon as I heard about the trip." He hooked his scholar's tweed jacket over his shoulder and played his jovial role. "We should eat in shifts, one of us guarding our spot. You two go first."

Samantha wasn't hungry, but she stepped over the neighbor sprawling beside their gear and followed Peter down the steep stairway. They skirted the outside cabins to a line at the dining hall on the back end of the ship. "Best get the eats while they're hot," mumbled the Sourdough in front of them.

They waited an hour before space opened at a long table. Distracted white-coated stewards passed metal plates and flung cutlery before sliding large bowls of grub—the obvious description of the food—before them.

Her nose prickled at the sour smell of boiled cabbage and a slab of unrecognizable meat, but she ate it. Peter handed her a chunk of bread, she drank a mug of water, and then the stewards evicted them to make room for other diners.

"I'll relieve Miles. Do you want to explore?" Peter asked.

"Yes." Samantha squeezed past Klondikers clogging the interior hallway between the staterooms. Belongings spilled out narrow doorways.

"I paid for a double berth," a dandy bristled. "Who are all these other people?"

The harried steward consulted a paper. "We've got too many people on board. Two hundred travelers need beds."

"Six men are in here. I want my money back."

The steward eyed him. "We could sell your berthing space ten times over. Are you sure?"

The man swore and shoved in.

Three doors down a woman in a low-cut emerald dress leaned against the wall. "Hiya, honey, are you going to Alaska?"

Sam jumped. "Me?"

"Sure thing." The woman drew a scarlet fingernail along Sam's cheek. "You're kind of young to be traveling alone. You looking for a place to stay?"

"No. I want the toilet."

The woman shook her silky black hair. "They call it the 'head' on a ship, honey. Though why a boy would need our head I don't know." She peered closer. "Or do I? It's the last door on the left. If you need privacy to change, come here. There's no room for modesty on a ship like this."

After using the cramped and nose-wrinkling head, Sam returned to the top deck. Miles, full of details and holding a booklet, was lecturing to the men camped around them.

"The *Alki* is 215 feet long and can make up to ten knots an hour. She's a powerful beauty." Miles patted the white lifeboat beside him. No one asked any questions.

Sam pushed a carpetbag out of the way when Miles joined her beside their luggage. "The food's awful, but you should eat."

"Soon enough. I haven't had a chance to tell you how sorry I am about your mother."

Miles had missed the funeral. He'd been so busy at seminary, she hadn't seen him since Christmas. "Thanks."

He ducked his head. "Mrs. Harris was always kind. She wrote every week like clockwork."

"Really?"

"She sent encouraging notes, telling me to stay true to the calling God had placed on my heart and assuring me of her prayers."

Sam rocked back. "I had no idea."

"Your pa left her behind because she was too delicate and refined for the frontier, but she had a missionary spirit." Miles raised his chin. "I hope to have a wife like her someday, a woman who will support me no matter how hard a life God sends."

Sam shuddered and put up her hands. "Don't ask."

"This is not a proposal, Sam." He emphasized her nickname. "I'm just saying your mother understood personal sacrifice for the spread of the Gospel. I admired her."

"Thank you. How do you know so much about the ship?"

He jabbed her forearm like she was a boy. "I always do my research."

Samantha sighed. "Do you know what you're getting into?"

"Yes. How about you?"
Peter wouldn't lead the musketeers into danger, would he?
"I'm not sure."
That's what scared her the most.

Chapter 4

At sea along the
Inland Passage

Other than crossing Puget Sound on his way to the Seattle seminary, Miles had never been outside of Port Orchard. He leaned on the ship's railing, entranced by the views. They journeyed among small islands covered in evergreens, ocean birds whirling in the skies, and a variety of logging or fishing boats.

He relished the sharp ocean air. When the ship sailed close enough to land, he could smell cedar and rotting kelp on the beach. When they hit a wave, he tasted salty spray. So far the weather had been dry and sunny, just as he'd prayed.

As the *Alki* steamed north, they passed Indian families digging clams and fishing. Too bad the ship's cook didn't do the same. The fare plopped onto the crowded tables often made the passengers gag. Miles ate it only to keep hunger at bay.

Beside him, a miserable Sam hung over the railing. She paid no attention to the scenery as she heaved over the side. Miles coaxed her to sip water and nibble soda crackers, but nothing stayed down. Even the ginger root didn't help.

Peter joined them. "Seen any killer whales?"

Sam groaned.

Miles shaded his eyes with *Facts for Klondikers*. "Scientists call them orcas."

Peter lifted an eyebrow. "Do you know everything, Miles?"

"I read up on the flora and fauna. I wanted to know what I would see."

Peter leaned on the railing. "What else do you know?"

Miles consulted his pamphlet. "As soon as we reach the end of Vancouver Island, we'll be out of sheltered water. The seas can be fierce in Queen Charlotte's Sound."

Sam moaned.

Miles dared to pat her back. "Come below. Maybe they'll serve broth today."

Normally Sam shied away, but this time she slumped against him. "I need the head."

Leaving Peter behind, Miles helped her downstairs, conscious they didn't look very manly. At the bottom, they met Faye, a saucy brunette who licked her lips into a lascivious smile. "How's our *boy* doing?"

Sam ducked her head and held her stomach.

"You men ready for some real entertainment yet?"

"Join us tonight," Miles said. "I'm preaching from the book of John."

"Not likely. But if either one of you needs a soft bed, we could find room in our berth. Especially for this one whose voice hasn't dropped."

"No thanks," Miles muttered.

Faye laughed after them.

∽

Miles watched Sam choke down the bean swill. The warm broth revived her, and she raised her head to study the jam-packed dining area. "I've never seen women dressed like that before." She nodded in Faye's direction. "Is she wearing face paint?"

Miles adjusted his glasses. "Possibly."

"She's very friendly."

He concentrated on his food. "But in need of the Gospel."

Sam peered at him. "Your whiskers are growing. It becomes you."

He smoothed the stubble on his chin and didn't try to hide his smile.

Two-dozen Argonauts lounged against their bags smoking pungent cigars and playing cards when he opened his study Bible that evening. Miles recited John 1:10–12 from his heart.

"He was in the world, and the world was made by him, and the world knew him not. He came unto his own, and his own received him not. But as many as received him, to them gave he power to become the sons of God, even to them that believe on his name."

"Preach it, brother," hiccupped a man brandishing a brown bottle.

Two women sat on a lifeboat swinging their legs. A half-dozen Klondikers huddled nearby, trying to make conversation. Few people seemed to be paying attention. Miles continued. The Word of God did not return void, even if they pretended otherwise.

No one asked questions when he finished his sermon, so he returned to their section of the deck. Sam slept wrapped in a blanket with her carpetbag as pillow.

Peter held up his thumb. "Good job. Your father would be pleased."

"Yours too, I hope. He must preach to people like this." Miles gestured to the groups of motley men.

"Probably. He's always liked savages and rough characters. Pa said they recognized their need for a savior better than civilized folks. He knows how to talk in ways they can understand. That's why he went to Alaska."

Miles was always confused when Peter spoke about his father. Miles knew his friend loved and missed Donald Harris, but underlying bitterness always tainted his words. "Do you think he meant to be gone so long?"

Peter shrugged. "He was doing a good work and could not come back. That's what Mother always said. Maybe he lost track of time. Maybe he forgot his son would like to see the world too. He always said he'd send for me when the time was right. He needs me now and I'm coming, even if he doesn't know it."

"Any more thoughts on the plan? What'll we do first?"

Peter stared at the stars prickling the twilight. "I've been talking with the Sourdoughs."

Miles nodded.

"There's good money to be made hauling other people's cargo over the pass. I think we should do that. We can ask around for Pa while we're working so I can repay Sam faster."

"Do you think it'll take long to find your pa?" Miles asked.

"Who knows? He could be anywhere."

Miles spoke slowly. "If we found him right off, Sam could see him and then sail home. But where would she live?"

"She'll want to stay with Pa for a while. If she decided to return, I figure your folks would take her in until classes start at the university. Sam wanted out of Port Orchard too." Peter snickered. "Her idea about college made Mother happy and gave her a respectable way to leave. Me, I'd rather not spend my life indoors. Sam's more like you, wanting to teach and help people."

A window of hope opened in his heart. "I appreciate your advice. I need to spend time in the world before I can minister to it. If I only know people like me, how will I understand how to help those not like me?"

Peter squeezed Miles's shoulder. "You're a good man. Thanks for coming. This adventure wouldn't feel right without you and Sam. I'm going to walk around the ship before bedtime."

"All for one," Miles murmured as the boldest person he knew

hopped lightly over the men sleeping on deck.

But then Peter's words penetrated.

"What do you mean 'repay' Sam?"

Peter had disappeared.

Chapter 5

At sea

When the *Alki* entered the Queen Charlotte Straits, Samantha thought she would lose her mind as well as her stomach over the roiling, rocking, rolling waves.

On day five, however, she opened her eyes to a bright morning and felt weak but no longer nauseated. "I think I'm going to live."

Miles closed his Bible. "You've finally got your sea legs. You'll be fine the rest of the trip."

"Promise?"

He cocked his head as if listening to something. "Yes. I brought you a cup of tea. It may still be warm."

Samantha held the thick mug to her nose and inhaled the thin spicy scent. Before she sipped, she frowned. "What's on your face?"

Miles's fingers went to his left cheekbone. "Nothing."

"Did one of those women *kiss* you?"

He rubbed the red mark into his flushed skin. "I don't want to talk about it. Peter will be back soon. Let's eat."

Samantha swallowed the tasteless, lumpy porridge in the congested dining area and felt almost alert for the first time. Faye noticed the difference when they met her in the companionway.

"You're looking better, honey. Maybe a kiss will do you good too."

As Miles recoiled, Sam shook her head. "No thanks."

Faye's enveloping perfume improved the moldy hallway. "Lover boy there may be too innocent to know," the woman murmured, "but you're not fooling us. Your face is too smooth and your voice and movements aren't masculine. Be careful. Men on this ship need to be tamed or manipulated."

Sam stuttered. "I don't know what you mean."

Faye's lips twitched and her drop earrings danced. "A real man would've slugged me. Let me help." She kissed Sam's cheek. "Leave it there and the Klondikers will be envious, not suspicious."

Laughter followed Sam and Miles's hasty exit.

Upon return to their encampment, Samantha took in the scenery. The air smelled of ocean brine and promise. Icy blue and white glaciers glowed pink in the morning sun. Miles joined her at the railing where Sam pointed to a log sculpture on a nearby beach. "What's that?"

"A totem pole. The Indians use them to tell stories and remember their myths." He shuddered. "Savages."

"But those are the type of people my father serves," Sam said.

Miles blinked. "You're right. But don't you wonder if he might have served God better by staying with his family?"

Sam said nothing. Mama never allowed traitorous thoughts.

Miles tossed his head the way he always did when anxious. "I've seen several on shore. Pretty impressive carving."

"Maybe Pa went to the Indians." Sam reached for her missing necklace. "He likes to carve. Have I missed anything else?"

"Natives paddling long canoes and golden eagles soaring to the sun. Enormous trees and spectacular mountains. If I never pick up a nugget of gold, I'll still feel I've gotten rich from this trip." Miles removed his steel-framed glasses and rubbed the lenses clean.

He looked taller, somehow, in his torn and rumpled clothing. Sam fingered a tear in the sleeve of his denim shirt. "What happened here?"

"I ripped it on a nail."

"Any other mishaps?"

He looked sideways. "Be careful around our neighbors. Most don't like me." He squinted at the sun. "I don't have your father's way with rough men."

Samantha should have expected problems. "What happened?"

"They're tired of being on board. I've knocked things over, spilled drinks, kicked luggage, the usual."

She nodded, fluffed her dusty wool blanket, and stretched it over their bags to air. "There hasn't been any rain. Peter must be pleased with your prayers. Where is he?"

Miles put on his glasses. "I research in books. Peter picks up information from people. He's been learning about Alaska from Sourdoughs. We'll be in Skagway tomorrow."

"Wouldn't you love to see Pa standing on the dock?"

Miles stared at her. "Yeah."

She didn't remember him being so focused; Miles had always been the bumbling musketeer. Confused by his intensity, she gestured at the area. "Look at this disorder. I need a broom."

The Klondiker next door scowled when she pushed the carpetbags aside. "Watch what you're doing, kid."

"I'm sorry."

"I mean it," he bellowed.

She suppressed a chuckle. He sounded like one of her eight-year-old students. "I apologize. I'd like to straighten up."

The man clambered to his feet. "Watch yourself. We don't need you sweeping anything onto our luggage. You can't stand the stink, go home to your mama."

Sam trembled and dropped her chin toward the deck. If she didn't look at him, maybe he'd leave her alone.

"Hey! I'm talking to you."

She stood tall and clenched her fists. He was half a foot shorter. "I'm trying to be a good neighbor."

"I don't like your lip."

Miles spoke in a slow, reasonable voice. "Leave her alone."

A crowd moved in their direction.

"Yeah, *her*. That's a good one A regular pansy, this kid."

Samantha turned her cheek.

"Will you look at that?" He sneered. "The little boy got himself a kiss." He grabbed Sam's arm. "Look at me when I'm talking to you."

Butterflies stormed her gut while she located her classroom voice. "I beg your pardon, sir. I assumed you were speaking to another."

His foul breath forced her backward. "Speaking to another? He talks like a schoolmarm. You need some toughening up before you hit the north. Spending time with the sporting women is a good start, but don't bring their marks up here to torment us. You need a lesson."

His fist struck Sam's jaw with a sharp pain that snapped her head and sent her reeling against the luggage.

Miles lunged, but others beat him to the man. Shoving, kicking, yelling, and the smack of fists turned the top deck into a brawl. Three men tripped over Sam. Wooden boxes scattered, along with luggage, blankets, and the dirty flotsam from a week on a crowded ship.

Sam crunched herself into a cowering ball. Peter yanked her away.

Two sailors blew shrill whistles and broke up the fight. Miles's glasses were askew, his lip bled, and he panted with rage. His shirt had lost a sleeve.

"Miles got into a fight?" Peter snickered.

"A Klondiker hit me." Sam rubbed her throbbing jaw.

"Which one?"

She shook her head. "It doesn't matter. We're supposed to turn the other cheek."

"Not on the frontier. Turning the other cheek is a good way to get killed."

"What do you mean?"

Peter's eyebrows drew together. "Alaska's far rougher than I imagined. You better stay a man as long as possible."

"What will Pa think?"

"He'd want you safe."

Sam touched the remains of Faye's kiss. The task might be harder than her brother thought.

Chapter 6

Skagway,
Alaska Territory

Miles's body ached from the fistfight, but the physical pain wasn't as bad as his disappointment when he first saw Skagway's scraggly tents and half-finished buildings.

Ragged mountains marched to the sea at the head of the Lynn Canal and towered above the narrow Skagway River delta. The canal continued northwest through another channel between imposing peaks and ended at Dyea, where travelers could climb the arduous Chilkoot Pass to the Yukon's Klondike River goldfields.

Miles looked from his information pamphlet to the scenery when the *Alki* anchored well offshore. "No dock?"

"No." Peter pointed to log rafts headed their way. "We'll unload onto those shallow barges and transfer ashore."

"I'm glad I'm wearing trousers," Sam said. "It'll be easier to climb a rope ladder without worrying about a skirt."

"Be thankful you're not livestock. They have to swim ashore." Peter strapped the blanket roll onto his carpetbag. "Let's go."

They met Faye, teasing and rosy, at the ladder. "I've got my pretty knickers on, boys, so enjoy the sight." She tossed her bag to a stevedore and winked at Sam. "Go before me, honey. I figure I can trust you."

Sam dropped her baggage onto the barge, grabbed the ladder, and climbed over the side. Faye's full silk skirts slapped Sam's face as Faye maneuvered down. Miles followed, careful to avoid squashing the sporting woman's feathered hat.

The ship's stevedores and anxious Argonauts manhandled crates onto the barge, rocking it with every load. Overhead slings swung out from the deck and dropped screaming horses into the cold water with a thunderous splash. One Argonaut jumped in with them, climbed onto a frantic steed, and urged the herd toward land.

Sam steadied herself on the bouncing deck. "Oh no! The poor horses. What kind of a place is this? Why is Pa here?"

Miles faced the cluster of tents and shacks nestled along the shoreline. Behind them, a black-green spruce forest separated the hamlet from rugged mountains. Miles swallowed. This adventure might be more dangerous than he had pictured at his seminary desk. *Facts for Klondikers* hadn't mentioned Skagway's brooding and forlorn setting.

"Isn't this great?" Peter and two stevedores pushed off from the steamship and poled the barge toward land.

They ran aground in the stinking mudflats ten feet off-shore. Argonauts shoved crates toward the rocky beach. Miles slipped into heart-stabbing icy water up to his hips. The shoals lapped to Peter's thighs as he cheerfully hauled their goods to land.

A soaked Sam sloshed up to them. "I couldn't decide what to do, and that Faye pushed me in."

Miles's face felt hot as soon as he saw her, and he peeled off his jacket. "You better wear this."

She glanced down, gasped, and thrust her arms into the heavy sleeves. *Facts for Klondikers* fell from the coat pocket and floated away before Miles could grab it.

"The sporting woman needs help," Miles muttered. Faye waved from the nearly empty barge.

Peter snorted. "Do you want to carry her ashore or shall I? Sam, grab those barrels. I bet they're hers."

Miles and Sam wrestled the barrels ashore, panting from the effort. Peter arrived with a flutter of Faye's skirts and giggles. He retreated before she could bestow another florid kiss.

"Welcome to Skagway. You gents want to store your goods?" A small man wearing a friendly smile and a preacher's collar stuck out his hand.

"Thanks." Miles reached to shake.

"We'll be fine." Peter stepped between them. "Sam, you guard our gear while we scout a tent site."

"Try east." The preacher pointed toward the edge of town.

"Thanks." Peter picked up two carpetbags and jerked his head north. Miles followed.

Men milled around a row of tents surrounded by stacks of wooden crates. Pounding hammers and scratching saws made a deafening noise. The air smelled of cedar. "Is it wise to leave Sam alone with the gear?"

"Wiser than leaving you," Peter said. "She's suspicious by nature and you're not."

"He was being helpful." Miles shifted a wet canvas bag from one arm to the next. "It's important to be polite when entering a new community."

"Did you notice the goons behind him?"

Miles spun around. The "preacher" stalked the waterfront greeting Argonauts, shadowed by ruffians wearing heavy revolvers. Sam scowled and paced around their boxes, arms folded tight across her chest. Faye, he noticed, had found men to carry her luggage as she sashayed toward the business district.

"We can't leave her alone. I'll wait with Samantha and not speak to a soul."

"Fine. I'll mark a spot at the end of this street." Peter indicated an area near the forest. "We'll haul everything ourselves."

"Deal." Miles spied a wooden shack beyond the tents. "Hey, we can send a telegram home to let them know we arrived." He gulped. "Five dollars is a lot of money, but it will ease my mother's worry."

"Telegraph? Here?" Peter peered at the building and frowned. "Do you see any telegraph wires?"

"No." Miles's jaw dropped. "That's dishonest."

"Assume everyone wants to steal our money," Peter said. "Sourdoughs say there are two types of people in Skagway: the skinned and the skinners. We've landed in a lawless town on the edge of nowhere."

Miles trudged toward the beach. How could Peter discern people's motives so much better than he could?

Barges continued moving toward shore. The *Alki* steamed a plume of smoke as she rode at anchor, an insignificant piece of civilization against the dramatic Alaskan backdrop. Dozens of horses shook themselves dry on the rocky beach as Argonauts organized their soaked possessions. The thin sunshine provided little warmth, and a chill blew from the high mountains. Miles shivered in his wet clothes, but Sam needed his jacket more.

At the water's edge, Sam ignored the fast-talking men who addressed her. With her lanky frame and Miles's bowler pulled low over her ears, it took sharp eyes to see her feminine features. Indeed, as she kicked at boxes and spat, she reminded Miles of Peter.

Certainly she'd behaved more manly than Miles.

Miles reached for a barrel when he joined her. "Peter says we shouldn't trust anybody."

"He's right," Sam said. "See him waving? He must have found a spot."

They shuffled their goods a quarter mile down the muddy path. When they finally got everything moved, Peter pried open a crate and pulled out a heavy canvas tent.

Miles read the directions while Sam and Peter erected it.

Peter pulled out another tent.

"Why two?"

He felt his face grow hot. "We're not kids anymore. I thought Samantha needed privacy."

Peter turned to his sister. "Will you be comfortable in a tent by yourself?"

Sam stopped pounding stakes to push the hat off her face. "As long as you two are next to me, yes. If we find Pa, I may not be here long anyway. When can we start looking?"

Peter shuffled his feet. "I'll make inquiries tomorrow when I look for work."

"Work?" Sam frowned.

"I figure to kill two birds with one stone: hunt for Pa and earn money. The people who got rich during the California gold rush were the folks who sold to the forty-niners. We'll ask around for Pa, but if we carry freight over the White Pass at the same time, we can earn hard cash."

"I came to find Pa. He's the only reason I'm here."

Peter picked up the white canvas and motioned for Miles to stretch his end over the tent poles. "We'll start tomorrow."

Miles had trouble falling asleep after a week rocking on the *Alki*. Peter snoozed soundly beside him, but Miles eventually got up and pushed out the tent flap. A full moon rose over the mountains, and muffled voices rumbled from nearby tents. A bonfire lit the beach, and music called from Broadway, a mere block away. An owl hooted, and Miles looked up, amazed at the splendid stars filling the sky.

"The heavens declare the glory of God," he whispered.

"And the firmament declares His handiwork." Samantha stepped from her tent. "You're not sleeping."

He could see her clearly in the moonlight, her chopped hair sticking up in all directions. The left side of her face was swollen, and Miles's muscles tensed remembering the fight. At least she looked more feminine in a white nightgown.

Nightgown.

"Why are you dressed like that? What if someone sees you?"

She scratched at the remains of her hair. "It felt so good to get out of Peter's dirty clothes after a week, I didn't think. I'll go in the tent."

"It's more prudent." Miles hated to see her go.

"You're right." Samantha sighed. "Thank you. I appreciate how you watched out for me on the ship."

"I'll always defend you."

Samantha touched the cut on his cheek. "Good night."

Miles smiled. He could sleep now.

Except he tripped on the stake peg and toppled Samantha's tent.

"Oh Miles!" Samantha groaned. "Forget what I said."

They re-erected her tent in silence and returned to bed.

But Miles lay awake most of the night. Why had he thought Samantha would treat him any differently in Alaska?

Chapter 7

Skagway
September 1897

"You want me to do what?" Sam dropped the frying pan.

"Packing freight is the fastest way to prosperity," Peter said. "We'll split the jobs three ways in a rotation. One of us will stay in town to rest and hunt for Pa. The other two will haul goods to the pass for the Klondikers."

"I can't manage horses or mules. Why don't we look for Pa first? Once we find him, you can go on your way," Sam said.

"Even if we found him, there's no money to return you to Washington." Peter uncharacteristically twisted his hat in his hands.

Sam gaped at Miles. "You spent all my money?"

"Peter told me to spend it all to outfit us. I'd have been more careful if I'd known it was your savings." He picked up the frying pan.

Peter patted the money belt he wore under his shirt. "All we have left is here. Thirty dollars. It might pay your way if we begged the steamship captain, but then what? What would you live on?"

The betrayal stabbed all the way to her spine. Three years of teaching hooligans in a small Port Orchard classroom had been transformed into the crated goods stacked around them. Tents, clothing, food, and equipment were the physical remains of her college dream. She didn't care if she was supposed to be a young man, she let them see her eyes pool with tears. What would Mama have said?

"The packers driving horse teams make twenty-five dollars a day. With all three of us working, we can earn a lot of money in no time. Then when we find Pa, you can decide what you want to do." Peter's voice rang with his traditional confidence.

Sam snatched the frying pan and slammed it against a crate. Peter could not keep making life-changing decisions for her. "I came to find Pa, nothing else."

"We'll ask around for him. The sooner we get jobs, though, the sooner you'll have your money. Deal?"

"No. I came to find Pa. We need to look for him."

"We'll ask around today. Somebody must know something about him, since he sent a letter from here," Peter said. "But we've got to act quickly if we're going to work. People want to get over the pass before winter. Now's the time to haul goods."

"You can't just keep making decisions without discussing them with us. All for one and one for all means we discuss what we're going to do before one of us just decides. Isn't that right, Miles?"

He put up his hands. "I'm here to support both of you. But we do need to look for your father."

"We're going to look for him," Peter said. "But we're going to look for work too. Sam needs her money back."

Did she have a choice? It burned that she had to agree, but his argument made sense yet again. "Miles, you need to pray we find Pa soon. I don't trust Peter. He's probably made some other bargain with God."

"Maybe we should eat," Miles said.

Miles read the directions for constructing the camp stove and then dropped most of the pieces in the mud trying to set it up. Peter got the metal contraption burning hot within minutes. Samantha mixed flour, soda, and water to make flapjacks. They drank boiling coffee with condensed milk as sweetener, secured their possessions, and then explored Skagway.

The town crackled with activity. Argonauts organized their possessions and argued among themselves. Whiskered Klondikers with determined faces packed heavy loads to Broadway, turned north, and headed up the Skagway River to White Pass. Grim men plodded the rutted muddy road, leading sickly nags overburdened with goods.

The sawmill at the water's edge shrieked out planks in a cloud of pungent cedar sawdust. Barking dogs and the jingling reins of pack animals livened the chilly morning. Samantha watched three young women enter a two-story building with a steep-pitched roof. Lace curtains hung in the upper windows. Faye leaned out to shout hello.

"Don't look at her," Miles said. "We don't want people to think we're acquainted with her type of woman."

Peter squinted in the sunlight. "They say Doc Runnalls handles the mail. Let's see if he knows anything about Pa."

They picked their way along the mucky street lined with new buildings to a hovel marked MAIL OFFICE. "He's the closest thing we got to a postmaster," a grizzled Sourdough explained. "He meets the steamers when they come into port and hands off the mail. Twenty-five cents a letter—expensive."

"Harris?" The bespectacled doctor shook his head. "Don't know the name."

"He's a missionary, a big man like my brother," Sam said. "Pa sent a letter in June saying he was headed this way to finish a job."

"Haven't seen many missionaries in Skagway. It's too crude and lawless with people mostly passing through. A fellow they call Peg Leg lives down the canal with some Tlingits, but I never heard his real name or if he's a missionary."

"That wouldn't be him," Peter said. "Pa's a strong man. He's been traveling well-nigh two years. He's got both his legs."

Runnalls shrugged. "Soapy Smith might know him. He'll be at his saloon."

When they reached the saloon, which reeked of cheap liquor even on the boardwalk, Samantha noticed the shorefront minister entering ahead of them. Peter set his jaw. "Take Miles's wallet and stay outside, Sam."

She stuck the wallet and her hand into the trousers' front pocket and leaned against the building in a casual manlike way. Four women flounced by wearing colorful dresses and heavily fringed silk shawls. She stared after their saucy confidence.

"No luck," Miles said when the two men rejoined her. "They offered to hire us to haul freight, but we turned them down. We'll check with more reputable packers."

"This Soapy Smith controls the town." Peter put on his hat. "Stay away from him and his con men."

When Sam described the fancy women, Peter drew his eyebrows together. "This is a dangerous place. Keep to yourself."

"How will I find Pa without talking to people?"

"Do you think Pa would know sporting women and con men?"

Samantha had not seen her father in two years. She had no idea.

∽

Peter and Miles left before dawn the next morning. They would lead a string of pack mules six miles to Liarsville at the base of White Pass and return to Skagway late in the afternoon. "I'll try to get back early." Miles wore worry lines across his forehead. "I'll go with you to ask around for your pa then. Don't go near anyone who looks threatening."

Sam shook her head. "Folks see me as a boy. I'll be safe. Help Peter find his fortune."

"It's not like that," he began, but Sam turned away.

She asked at the lumber mill if they'd heard of Donald Harris or seen a very tall man with fair hair starting to thin. No one had.

Sam rubbed her hands as she tramped toward the business district. Would Pa still have hair? Two years in a cold climate might have changed him.

She stopped in the shops lining Broadway: a real estate investment office, a hardware store, and a mercantile. Mr. Brown at the mercantile looked through a ledger he kept behind the counter. "No Harris listed. If he's been in the store, he must have paid cash. Sorry, sonny."

She steered clear of the pool hall and passed four men throwing dice against the jail.

The door burst open at a saloon, and a black-goateed man tossed out a native. "Don't come back."

The mahogany-skinned man rolled in the dirt and moaned. Sam stepped toward him. "Do you need help?"

He groaned in a tongue she didn't understand, shook her off, and crept away on hands and knees. Giggles sounded from a neighboring window. "You can help me, honey," shouted a fleshy woman dressed in a loose wrapper.

Sam cringed and headed north.

By the time she'd reached the end of the street, Sam had no leads on her father and a disgust with the town. Was no one honorable?

"Hey there, boy, do you want a job?"

A petite woman wearing a flour sack tied around her waist beckoned from a rough log hut. A placard reading RESTAURANT hung over the entry. "I need someone to wash dishes. I'll pay two bits."

The woman ushered Sam into a crowded room where a pot of water boiled on the stove. "Start there. I've got an hour before customers return. I'm Mollie."

A plank table with crude benches ran the width of the

restaurant. Mollie pushed stray hairs off her face with her fore-arm and returned to chopping onions, chattering the entire time.

"You a *cheechako*? I'm a newcomer too. I got here last week, and Reverend Dickey found me this job working for Mr. Brown who owns the mercantile. You headed to the Klondike?" Her blade never stopped moving. "Once you finish, I'll pay you to peel potatoes."

Sam kept her head down, not trusting her voice.

"How old are you?" Mollie asked. "Fifteen, sixteen?"

"Yeah."

Mollie showed Sam how to keep track of the bread baking in the tiny ten-inch-square oven. "Do you know how to cook flap-jacks? We'll need filling when the stew runs out."

"Yes ma'am."

Men trooped in when the friendly bread aroma seeped from the cabin. Sam fried flapjacks while Mollie served food, collected money, joshed with the Argonauts, and made everyone feel at home. By the time they scraped the last of the stew from the pot, they'd fed three-dozen men.

Mollie jingled the coins in her pocket, pushed the hair out of her eyes, and bustled to the stove. "You got yourself a job if you'll come back tomorrow at dawn."

"Yes ma'am. I will."

Mollie laughed. "What's your real name, sweetie? Since we'll be working together, I'd like to make sure you're a girl."

"Samantha Harris." Sam felt her face flush.

"It's hard to be a single woman in this town," Mollie said. "Maybe I should dress as a man. Do you think I can fool anyone?"

With her curly hair, sparkling eyes, trim shape, and small hands, Mollie was all female. It took a tall, spare figure like Sam's hiding in men's clothing to stride through the town without concern.

Sam grinned. "No one would mistake your fair sex."

Mollie held out her hand. "Your secret is safe with me."

They shook on it.

Sam whistled as she walked to her tent after work, hands in her pockets. She could make her own plans. Peter didn't dictate her life. She'd find Pa without him.

Chapter 8

White Pass and Skagway
October 1897

Miles hated freighting work.

Everything about the job disgusted him.

The vulgar, arrogant men desperate for riches. The abused horses forced to carry overweight loads. The glacial Skagway River he sloshed into several times a day. The fear he might stumble off the narrow trail into canyons spiked with boulders. The interminable hours of waiting when the foul path backed up because something far ahead had broken or fallen and blocked traffic.

The change in Peter over the last six weeks bothered him even more.

Always craving adventure and excitement, Peter now had a bad case of gold fever. He strapped on his snow glasses and went to work every morning with determination. While Miles appreciated Peter's resolve to repay Samantha, his single-minded fervor for every cent was troubling.

"Everyone has a price, and these Argonauts need to pay for what they're getting," Peter explained during one of their waits. The hard labor, long hours, and frigid wind had pared down their features, giving Peter a golden wolfish look. Miles had taken in his belt two notches, and his shirts felt tight across the shoulders.

"Why does it always have to be about money? Is it necessary to charge for every service?" Miles preferred to include minor assists in his daily fee, but Peter debited everything and expected a tip as well.

"Yes. It's a brutal world, and traveling to the Yukon to prospect for gold in the Klondike River isn't going to be easy on them."

"What about us?" Miles asked. "How will we manage?"

Peter raised his jacket lapels and tugged the knit cap over his ears. The mule beside him shifted, and Peter adjusted its load. The line of Klondikers ahead grumbled and kicked at rocks.

"Don't you feel stronger? You climb this pass without wheezing now. You needed to get into shape before our hard work begins."

Miles removed his glasses and fished out his red calico kerchief to polish the lenses. "This has been training for me?"

Peter poked him. "Your fat's gone and your endurance is much improved. We've got money in our pockets and information. We'll be ready to hike over the pass for ourselves soon."

Miles replaced his glasses and pulled out his pocket New Testament. If they got too delayed, he liked to walk along the pack line offering to read encouraging scripture. He held out the book to Peter. "Do you want to read today?"

"I'll manage the animals so you can." Peter rubbed his mule's nose. "The way packers treat these poor animals is the worst part of this job. I'm glad Sam isn't here. She couldn't handle the violence."

Miles agreed. The restaurant job kept her safe and warm, though he wondered at the wisdom of two women serving food to strange men. Of course, no one knew Sam was a woman. He shook his head. He couldn't imagine how men could be so blind. Every time he looked at her, his heart raced.

He opened his New Testament and reread the note she'd slipped him that morning: "I thank my God, making mention of thee always in my prayers."

Miles kissed the note. He'd cherish Philemon 1:4 forever.

Miles and Peter usually only hauled freight to Liarsville, where they cached the goods for Klondikers to pick up later.

They often managed two trips a day. That day, however, they were going higher, and Miles worried about leaving Sam alone in the unguarded tent overnight. "Do you think she'll be okay?"

"For the ninth time, yes. I left her the gun, and she's a better shot than you anyway. If she gets scared, she can stay with Mollie."

"Not if she's a boy." Miles brushed a snowflake off his nose.

Peter shrugged. "With the new preacher setting up a church, I think she'll transform into respectable Samantha soon."

"Which will make Skagway even more dangerous for her. Why won't you help her look for your father? She's visited every tent and shack in town. It's not safe. She's talking about hiking outside of town to look, and that's plain foolish."

"I ask everyone I see. The weather's turning bad, and he hasn't come into town. I don't know where he is. Runnalls hasn't gotten any mail."

"What about that Peg Leg living with the Tlingits? Why don't you check him out?"

Peter snorted. "My father would have said something in his letter if he'd been injured. Besides, Runnalls says it's a four-hour hike in good weather if you can find someone to guide you. There's no reason to risk our lives and lose two days of hauling fees without anything more to go on."

"So you have made inquiries?"

"I'm trying to be pragmatic. If I don't get my hopes up, I can better cope if we never find him." Peter slapped at the thickening snowflakes.

Miles's heart sank. He'd been afraid of the same thing. But what about Sam's feelings? How could he protect her from the inevitable? "Have I earned enough money yet? I'd like to stay in town."

"Sam can take care of herself. You don't need to protect her." Peter tugged the mule forward.

Miles shook his head. "No. Skagway's dangerous. I'll ask for a job at the mercantile for the winter. I'd like to help build the new church anyway."

"Suit yourself. You won't make as much money."

The snowflakes gusted. Miles tucked his scarf over his beard and thought of Sam's desperate searching. "Money isn't everything."

∽

"I'm glad you're working in town," Sam said as she picked up supplies for the restaurant.

Miles nodded. He ate every meal at the restaurant and stayed into the evening with the two women. "The job is better, and I get to see you more."

She hesitated before leaning over the mercantile counter to whisper, "It makes me feel safer knowing you're nearby."

Before Miles could respond, Sam spun around and exited. He watched her try to walk like a man on the boardwalk and chuckled. She couldn't fool him, no matter what she wore.

Miles battled guilt every morning he sat on a stool beside a crackling stove while Peter hauled the trail alone. Snow covered the ground now, and dark clouds often loomed over the narrow Skagway valley. He watched the sky every afternoon, wondering what would happen to those on the trail in a blizzard.

Peter insisted he'd charge more.

Miles prayed more.

Whenever a Sourdough entered to make a purchase, Miles asked if he knew Donald Harris. No one recognized the name. One or two had heard rumors, but most thought missionaries lived farther down the west side of Lynn Canal in Haines. One Tlingit tribe southeast of Skagway hosted a *skokum*, but no one knew his real name.

"Old man," explained a Tlingit in broken English who had come in to buy cornmeal. "No hair, bad leg, round belly." His description didn't match the robust skokum—man—Miles knew from childhood.

From his seat in the warm mercantile, Miles daily witnessed Alaska's heartbreak. If he hadn't lost *Facts for Klondikers*, he would have burned it in disgust. No words could have prepared him for Skagway. He saw Argonauts scrambling to land their possessions on shore. He watched Soapy Smith's gang fleece newcomers and the mostly futile attempts by responsible citizens to intervene. Packs of abandoned dogs roamed town fighting over food scraps.

The most troubling residents were the sporting women.

Flocks arrived on every steamship, fancy women wearing elaborate hairstyles and paint on their pretty faces. They pranced up slushy Broadway to the two-story houses across the street. He seldom saw them leave, and indignation fired his soul. Why would a woman choose a life of degradation?

In the doorway, Mr. Brown sniffed as the women strolled past swinging their hips. "We're trying to build a civilized town, and those women are bad elements. As a minister, you should steer clear of them."

"I'm not ordained yet," Miles reminded him. He tried not to think of the women and what they did in the house across the street.

"You're close enough for this town." Mr. Brown left for the waterfront to claim supplies sent on the most recent steamship.

Miles stepped to the shelves to rearrange the stock. The door opened and Faye entered wearing a sweet-scented silk shawl over a blazing blue dress. "I've wanted to stop in and say hello, honey, but old sourpuss wouldn't let me through the door."

"How may I help you?" Miles looked past her, hoping no one would peer in the window.

"I've come for Pear's Soap. This climate affects my complexion."

She sounded stiff, and he glanced out the corner of his eye. Dimples of irritation appeared on either side of her pursed ruby lips. "Are you too proud to take my cash?"

"I'll check our supply."

"You're looking good, preacher man. I'm surprised working in this store could cause such a change in your physique."

He found a bar of Pear's Soap and laid it on the counter, still not looking at her.

"Where's young Sam these days? She's not bulked up like you, is she?"

Startled, Miles finally met her eye. "No. She's working up the street with Mollie."

Faye's eyes shocked wide open and her voice shrilled. "What do you mean up the street? I thought you were a God-fearing man. Which crib? I should slap you." Her face flushed with rage.

Horror dawned. "She's not working—" Miles couldn't say the words. "She and Mollie run a restaurant." He pushed the soap across the counter. "Ten cents."

Faye lifted her chin. "Is she still dressing as a boy?"

He nodded.

"Keep her that way. The men in this town can't be trusted." She dropped a coin from her crimson velvet bag and picked up the soap. Faye swept to the door and paused. "You, preacher man, should pay more attention to how Jesus treated sinners and Pharisees."

The door shut behind her with a soft click.

Chapter 9

November brought snowdrifts and ice to the Skagway waterfront, while the pass became nearly impossible to traverse. Sam
watched men trudge by the restaurant each day. Were they all as
determined as Peter with his chapped red skin and thick beard?
How long could they go on?

"Until they close the pass," Peter said. "Then they'll shift to
the Chilkoot."

"Will you hunt for Pa then?" Sam stirred the oatmeal on the
restaurant stove. She prepared him a hot breakfast every morning
to guard against the arctic conditions.

"I've been asking. No news."

Sam splatted oatmeal into a bowl and thrust it at her brother.
"What about the outlying areas? We're practically snowed in
here—when will you visit the natives?"

"It's not that easy, Sam." Peter stared at his breakfast.

"Only because you haven't looked." Fury vied with despair.
To give her hands something to do, she passed the coffeepot to
Miles.

He shook his head. "No word at the mercantile either."

"Christmas is coming." She tried to steady her voice. Peter
never responded well to anger. "He said he had a project to finish
up here and then he'd come home. Where is he?"

"Is Christmas significant?" Mollie returned the coffeepot to
the hot stove.

Sam slumped at the table, chin in hand. "Pa loves Christmas. He thinks Jesus' birth is the best way to explain God coming to earth and being accessible to all."

"True." Miles picked up his spoon.

"I don't think we're going to hear from him by Christmas." Peter stretched his arm across the table to take her hand. "You need to face facts, Sam. I don't think he's coming back."

All the air disappeared from her chest, and the frozen chill of fear that had haunted her stabbed Sam's soul. "Is that why you haven't looked for him? You think he's dead?"

"Everyone knows we're looking for him. You torment Runnalls about the mail every other day. You buttonhole every native you see. I don't have to go to the outlying areas. Everyone in Alaska knows Mollie's assistant Sam is looking for his father." He pushed back from the table and reached for his knit cap.

"What are we going to do?" Sam crossed her arms tight against her body and tried not to whimper.

"I'm going to haul over the pass. Another couple weeks of this and I'll have enough to send you back to Washington. You can go to school in the spring." He stuffed a loaf of bread into his pack and banged out the door, taking her hopes and unanswered questions with him.

Miles cleared away the remains of breakfast. Sam stared at nothing, trying to slow her breathing and absorb Peter's words. Mollie took her knife to the onions and began to chop. They worked in silence for a time before Miles slid in beside her and took her hands.

"Peter doesn't know everything. He's just as scared as you are. All he can do is take care of you as best he can."

Sam nodded. She knew that.

"You've got to have faith," Mollie said. "Maybe your father's working so hard he hasn't needed to come to town. Maybe he'll hear of the church being built and want to come see it even if he can't get home. It'll be finished by Christmas."

"We can't give up hope," Miles agreed. "Anything can happen."

"I just want to see Pa again." Sam put her head on the table. "I'm not giving up before Christmas."

❧

Mollie had sailed to Skagway on the same ship as the Reverend R. M. Dickey, and they were fast friends. Caught up by the reverend's enthusiastic vision, the civilized townspeople had banded together to construct a church building. Funds had come from all walks of life: Sourdoughs, businessmen, packers, even Soapy Smith. Mollie kept a jar at the restaurant and encouraged customers to donate tips for the lumber and nails.

Mollie, Samantha, and Miles volunteered to help the effort. The women made coffee and served sandwiches, but after Miles split a board, hammered his thumb, and nearly fell off the roof, Pastor Dickey asked him to teach a small Bible study. Samantha agreed with the preacher's carefully chosen words: "Let's build the congregation while we construct God's house. God can better use Miles's Bible skills in a less physical way."

Mollie offered the restaurant as a meeting place with Mr. Brown's approval. "Sam and I can listen to the lessons while we clean up."

Sam loved the lectures. Miles had learned a lot at the seminary. His teaching blew a glow of pride into her heart.

Miles began every meeting with prayer for Donald Harris. He asked each student if he'd heard the name. No one ever had, but the fact others knew to look for him eased Sam's worry. She announced a prize to the men who bundled into the restaurant: "If you find my father, I'll praise God and make you an apple pie."

On the evenings they finished kitchen duties early, Sam and Mollie helped the students locate and read passages from Miles's extra Bibles. Sam assisted men writing letters home. Miles shared information about the Klondike goldfields he had gleaned while doing research and from working at the mercantile.

"You must be pleased folks want to learn about the Bible," Mollie said one night after the students left.

"You're the reason the men come, Mollie." Miles adjusted his glasses. "How many marriage proposals did you get today?"

"Two serious, three fake. What do you suppose will happen when Sam reveals her true identity?"

"The class will double." Miles held out her coat. Sam slipped her arms into the sleeves.

"How much longer can you get away with your disguise?" Miles murmured.

Mollie laughed. "Good question."

"When the church is finished, I will worship God as a lady." Sam put on Miles's old bowler hat.

"Then the real trouble will begin." He buttoned up his parka.

Mollie saw them out.

The cold night air hit their faces like a chisel. Sam took Miles's arm, and they huddled together on their walk home.

"Do you like Mollie?" Sam asked.

Miles nodded. "She's the finest person I've met here."

During their months in Skagway, the town had taken on a more established look. Buildings now stood on either side of Mollie's restaurant, and while the rutted frozen streets were dark, the snow reflected enough light that they could see. "Mollie's talking about opening her own restaurant at the top of the pass," Samantha said.

"Do you want to go with her?" Miles stepped carefully; he'd tripped the night before and sprawled facedown into a drift.

"No. Listening and helping you makes me miss teaching. If anything, I'd like to start a school. There's enough children in town." She squeezed his arm. "Your work on the trail gave you practical applications for your lessons. Some men may come to admire Mollie, but you're telling stories about God they want to hear. You're a good teacher."

Miles clutched the Bibles to his chest. "Thank you," he whispered. "Your words mean a great deal."

She leaned closer. Miles no longer acted like the bungling boy she'd grown up with. "The beard makes you look distinguished."

He smiled. "Will I look proper enough to escort you to church soon?"

Sam laughed. "Only if you wear your bowler."

As they turned off the boardwalk, a shadow scurried from behind a two-story house. "Are you one of the preachers?"

"He is." Sam dropped her hand. She'd forgotten about her disguise in the dark street.

"Please, sir, I need help." The woman's voice wavered. "I want out, and they're after me. Can you take me somewhere safe?"

Miles stiffened. "Who's after you?"

"Please," she coughed. "They'll beat me. I have nowhere to go."

Two figures loomed. Sam plucked off her hat and pushed it on the frail woman's head. She took the woman's arm and dragged her in the direction of their tents two rows away. The neighboring tents glowed from the lanterns inside, leaving a cool whiteness gleaming on the snowbank. "What's your name? How can we help you?"

"Lucy." She shivered. "They're coming for me. I know they are."

Sam opened the tent flap. The woman trembled. "I can't go in there."

Miles stopped. "She's right, Sam, your reputation will suffer."

Two brutes ran up. "You've got something that belongs to us." The taller one reached for Lucy.

"Pretty strange doings," the shorter man said. "You fancy yourself a preacher, and here you're taking a sporting girl to your tent."

"You can't take her if she doesn't want to go!" Sam put her

hand on Lucy's arm.

"You don't think so?" The big man shoved her. Sam fell against Miles, and the two stumbled against the tent. The men dragged a screaming Lucy down the street.

The bowler hat rolled to a stop beside Sam, who struggled to catch her breath.

"I'm so sorry. Did they hurt you?" Miles held her close. "We'll find Lucy and help her. I'm here, and I won't leave you. I'll keep you safe."

As she nestled against him, Samantha knew she didn't want to be manly anymore.

Chapter 10

December

The respectable citizens of Skagway completed Union Church a week before Christmas. True to her word, Samantha put away her nickname, returned Peter's borrowed clothes, cinched up her corset, and swept into church wearing a woolen skirt. Mollie had trimmed her ragged hair straight across. She held her chin high, and male heads turned as she and Peter took seats in the third row.

Mollie hugged her. "You're beautiful. We'll have even longer lines outside the restaurant today."

Miles figured she was right.

Samantha seemed oblivious to the stares as she focused on Reverend Dickey's words. She sang the hymns and Christmas carols with her pleasing soprano. Men clustered about her after the service, and Samantha brushed them off with a lighthearted, "Time for work."

When she caught Miles's eye, Samantha winked.

As they exited the church, Peter pulled Miles aside. "The pass will close after the next snowstorm. Hauling is finished here until spring."

Miles nodded. "We need to find better quarters for the winter. Will you hunt for your father now?"

"There's plenty of packing work on the Chilkoot Trail," Peter said through cracked lips. "I figure two more weeks and I'll have enough money for Sam's college in the spring. It won't be everything I owe her, but enough to start. I'm going to head over there."

"She wants to find your father. Why don't you help her?" Miles couldn't keep the annoyance out of his voice.

"He was coming to the Skagway River area. Here we are. No one's heard of him. Your parents haven't forwarded a letter. He probably wandered off and couldn't be bothered to write, if he's even alive."

"You can't break Sam's heart." Miles sighed.

"Her heart's going to be broken when he doesn't turn up by Christmas. I'll talk to her tonight."

"How can you abandon her?" Miles demanded. "Especially if your father is dead. When are you coming back?"

Peter's hand came down on his shoulder. "You'll be here. I figure she can bunk with Mollie. Can you winter in your store until we've got enough money to head to the Klondike?"

Miles had already gotten permission. "I'll give you my earnings. Skip the Chilkoot and do a thorough search for your father."

Peter shook his head. "I'm counting on your pay to see us through the next year."

Miles should have thought of that.

Mollie had invited the men to spend the day in the relatively warm restaurant. When they arrived, they found Mollie in tears and Samantha indignant.

"We have to do something about this town. Mollie saw a woman she knew from home working as a sporting woman. It was Lucy. When we tried to talk to her, Soapy Smith's gang threatened us."

"Did they recognize you?" Miles had feared this.

"What does it matter? Lucy's the one in trouble." Samantha paced the cramped room.

Miles removed his gloves. "Do you know which house she's in?"

"No. She wants to escape, and they've snagged her twice now." Samantha tripped on her long skirt. "She's ill."

Mollie reached for a knife. "I'll chop onions while we think of something to do."

Peter shook his head. Miles had no ideas. Samantha kneaded the bread dough with vengeance and stuffed it into pans for the oven.

Night fell around four o'clock. Just before the dinner rush, Faye entered. "Is this where Mollie lives?"

"What do you want?" Miles stood up.

"I'm looking for Mollie. Lucy over at the house is sick and needs help."

The sporting woman who had sailed from Seattle didn't look confident or saucy anymore. Her dull hair slumped. Her face paint no longer precisely outlined her lips. Powder to cover the circles under Faye's eyes accentuated her weariness. Miles felt a tug of pity, which he quickly covered with bravado.

"Why don't you take care of her?"

Long, blackened lashes blinked twice. "She wants Mollie."

"Mollie's busy," Peter said.

Faye pressed her lips together and glared at Miles. "What if Lucy's dying and wants a preacher man? Will you come?"

He frowned.

"How can you not go?" Samantha whispered.

"I'm not ordained," he muttered.

"Go."

Mollie grabbed her coat. "Peter, will you stay and help Samantha feed the men? Miles can fill in until Reverend Dickey can come. Let's go."

Miles carried his Bible and tried to estimate the damage to his reputation as he followed Mollie and Faye past Soapy Smith's pool hall and the mercantile. He shuddered as they entered the two-story establishment reeking of cheap perfume and filled spittoons. Faye led them down a gloomy hallway into a tiny room. Lucy lay coughing on an iron cot.

Mollie knelt at the bedside and ran her hand across Lucy's perspiring forehead. "We're here, little one," she crooned. "Miles will read you the stories."

How could he not?

By the light of a small wax candle, he read the Gospel of John, assuring Lucy of God's love for her and willingness to forgive her sins. The woman coughed and panted, but her eyes focused on Miles.

Mollie straightened the bedclothes, wiped Lucy's brow with a damp cloth, and tried to coax liquid into her. Faye stopped in periodically with broth for the woman, but it soon became apparent Lucy wouldn't survive long. When Reverend Dickey arrived, Miles had reached a contentment about sitting with her he could not explain.

Lucy's face softened, relaxed, and slid into peace as Reverend Dickey pronounced absolution over her soul. Miles stood in a corner to watch. And so he remained when the young woman passed into eternity, taking a surprisingly sympathetic piece of his heart with her.

Two days later, Reverend Dickey hosted Lucy's funeral at Union Church over the objections of many in his fledgling congregation. Disgruntled townspeople stayed away.

With no flowers available in snowy Skagway, Samantha used Miles's buck knife to cut evergreen boughs and bunches of red berries. He helped carry them to the church and followed her decorating directions, hanging the boughs along the wall.

When they finished, the new church smelled of pine and winterberries.

Miles centered a Bible on the plain wooden altar.

"Christmas is coming." Samantha squeezed her eyes shut. "Dare I ask to see my father for Christmas?"

He couldn't help himself. Miles stretched his arms to her, and Samantha went into them, trembling. "I'm starting to lose hope we'll find him, and then I don't know what I'll do. What good was it to come here?"

Miles rubbed circles on her back and kissed her hair. "You've made this church and this town a better place by your presence. Don't you know that?"

She nodded against his chest, and he continued. "Your hard work enables Peter to climb the pass every day with pockets full of food. Your voice cheers discouraged men. Your contributions have put together a church in a lawless place. You've made a difference here. I thank God for your presence."

"We couldn't have managed without you." Samantha rested her cheek on his shoulder. "You've been patient with Peter, helped build this church, and you've protected me. I don't know what I'd do if I lost you too."

He closed his eyes to let her words sink in. Maybe coming to Alaska was proving his calling in more than one way.

"There's more to be done." Samantha broke away. "I need to help."

At ten o'clock, Miles, Peter, and two Sourdoughs carried in Lucy's plain cedar casket. Reverend Dickey waited near the altar at the foot of an elaborately carved cross three Tlingit natives had delivered to the church that morning.

Almost every sporting woman in Skagway, close to fifty in number, filled the pews. Samantha, Miles, Peter, and Mollie sat in the front row, singing the funeral hymns in full voice. Miles leaned forward in professional respect when Reverend Dickey challenged the mourners.

"Dear sisters," he said, "listen to this invitation from Jesus. 'Come unto Me all ye that are weary.' You are weary of the life you have been living. Leave it. It holds nothing for you but sorrow, suffering, and shame. Jesus received Mary Magdalene. He said to another who had been led into sin, 'Neither do I condemn you—go and sin no more.'"

The women wailed so loudly the hair on Miles's arms stood up.

After Reverend Dickey pronounced the benediction, Miles set his old bowler on his head and slipped outside. His soul churned, and he needed to calm down. Was it possible sporting women could repent after just one sermon?

He walked along the shore, his boots crunching on sand and rocks mixed with ice, where he saw Captain O'Brien, a steamship captain, conversing with a Sourdough named Jim.

"What's the news, Mr. Parker?"

Miles described Lucy's funeral, still astonished at Reverend Dickey's invitation for the women to give up the sporting life.

The captain spoke slowly. "Do you think any of them will do it?"

"How could they? They have no place to go," Miles said.

"Go to the church and tell them I have plenty of room on my ship tomorrow. I'll take anyone who wants to return to Seattle for free. It won't cost them a cent."

Miles's mouth dropped open. Here, he thought, was true Christianity—seeing a need and responding to it. Hope flared, but he shook his head. "What good will that do? They've no money. They'll have to return to the same way of life in Seattle."

"No they won't," Jim said. "I already found my bonanza. I'll give Captain O'Brien money to cover all their needs."

The men shook hands. Miles retraced his steps, his soul reeling.

Two doors from the church, a gang of Soapy Smith's men leaned against a building and glared at him. Three held clubs.

He straightened his shoulders and took a deep breath. Would he be able to help the sporting women escape Skagway's thugs?

Chapter 11

Samantha and Mollie brewed tea and served biscuits to the sorrowful women. A dozen wept while others touched dainty handkerchiefs to their damp eyes and sniffed.

Miles burst through the door waving his arms. Samantha set down the teapot and hurried to him. His ruddy face and flashing eyes made him look confident and in charge, taller.

Mollie joined them as he described Captain O'Brien's offer to Reverend Dickey. Mollie clapped her hands. "God is using you! Thanks be to God!"

Samantha felt a stab of jealousy. Why didn't she say that?

Reverend Dickey climbed onto a pew. "For those women interested in a fresh start, Captain O'Brien will take you to Seattle tomorrow for free. Anyone who wants to take him up on the offer, come tell me."

Thirty women gathered around Reverend Dickey, burbling with excitement. Samantha and Mollie hugged each other. "Lucy will not have died in vain if these women escape," Mollie exclaimed.

Miles joined them. "A little problem. They want their possessions and are afraid to retrieve them." He rubbed his full-bearded chin. "Soapy Smith's gang won't like this."

Samantha surveyed the room. "What can we do?"

"Where's Peter?"

"He went to the tent."

Miles blew out his breath. "Reverend Dickey is making a list of what each woman wants from her room. I'll get the lists and then go for the marshal and Peter. We can't do this without their help."

"I'm coming with you." Samantha put on her cloak when Miles had the list and followed him out.

"It's not safe. You've already been assaulted by these men. You saw with Lucy what they've done to the sporting women. Stay here at church." Miles marched down the street.

"One for all, Miles. I want to help you." Happiness bubbled inside her, and she took his arm. "We'll do this together."

Six of Soapy's men loitered outside a pool hall. The scowls on their hairy faces made her stomach curl. Samantha shivered.

Miles slowed his steps and patted her hand. "Let's not make them suspicious."

"Okay." She kissed his cheek.

"Samantha!"

"A good distraction, right? Keep walking."

Snowflakes swirled and dreary clouds threatened more as they entered the hovel that housed official Skagway justice. The marshal sprawled in a chair leaned against the wall, a potbellied stove emitting toasty heat.

When Miles described the situation, the marshal's chair thudded forward. "Are you out of your mind? Don't you know Soapy's income depends on these women turning over their earnings to him? He and his men won't give them up without a fight. I can't do this."

"How can you not?" Miles asked.

Samantha's heart soared with Miles's confidence. But she also remembered how her body ached from the skirmish over Lucy. How could they thwart the thugs outside?

"What kind of preacher man are you?" the marshal grumbled. "This is going to cause me no end of trouble, but I'll do it if the church folks will back me."

"We'll need God's help to be successful. Let's pray. Then I'll send Samantha for her giant brother. Round up some men, and we'll meet you at Mollie's restaurant."

"Our boy has grown up." Peter laughed when Samantha told him of Miles's plan.

"Why do you say things like that?" Samantha demanded. "You belittle him. He's taken a principled stand and is facing real danger for the good of these women. You have no reason to make fun of him."

Peter's eyebrows went up, and he crossed his arms over his chest. "Are you finally recognizing Miles's value?"

"One for all and all for one," Samantha retorted. "I'm changing my clothes."

"Why?"

"I'm going with you."

Peter blocked her exit. "No you're not. This isn't safe. The sporting women houses are no place for my sister."

She narrowed her eyes. "I'm not going as your sister. I'm going as Sam, your brother. Besides, you know I'm a better shot than Miles."

They met the marshal and half a dozen deputies at Mollie's restaurant. Miles sighed when he saw Sam dressed in her brother's clothes. "I suppose you had to come along, but you'll stay with Peter and me."

The marshal divided them into three squads, gave each group a list, and directed them to the church when done. "Soapy's gang knows something's up, but let's keep them confused as long as possible. As soon as we've got everything, we'll escort the women to the ship. They'll be safe there."

Miles led Peter and Sam to the house on Broadway across from the mercantile. They stepped into a wallpapered parlor stuffy with horsehair furniture and Victorian furbelows. The cloying scent made Sam wrinkle her nose.

A squat man with a plug mustache tromped down the stairs. "The girls are out. Only Faye's here. You'll have to take your turn."

"May we see Faye?" Sam asked. Miles displayed the list.

"I can't let you go through their things," the man sputtered. "Does Soapy know about this?"

"I'll handle them, Billy." Faye glided downstairs. Red eyes sagged in her gaunt face.

"Soapy's not going to like it," Billy growled.

"Follow me, Sam. The other two should stay below." Faye led Sam to the first door at the top of the stairs. "We have to work fast. Let me see the list."

Faye stripped the dingy pillowcase off the bed and rummaged through the plain bureau to find what the woman wanted. Sam examined the cramped, windowless room: dresses and a worn silk wrapper hung on nails. Face paint littered the bureau top, and a small round mirror hung above. A wooden chair draped with clothing and a pair of overturned boots on the floor gave the room color and texture. The rumpled bed linens needed to be washed.

Sam turned away. The whole room reeked of a cheap sadness that suggested endless tears.

Seven women's names were on the list. Faye went through their possessions while Sam carried the pillowcases and tried not to react to the grim living situations. Most of the women in this house would travel to Seattle. Sam stopped at the last door where a window faced the street. "Is this your room? What are you bringing?"

Faye's shoulders slumped. "I'm not coming."

"Why not? This is your chance. They'll help you start over. You don't have to live like this."

Faye closed her eyes a moment and then straightened. Her

voice turned sassy, and she stretched her lips into a confident smile. "I came north for the Klondike. Skagway is a stopping off point before I cross the pass and make my fortune come spring. I'll turn civilized when I've got a big enough poke to buy me a big house in Seattle with a water view. You got to stay focused, Sam, to get what you want."

"No." Sam shook her head. "This isn't what you want."

Faye's eyes narrowed. "It's what I want today, missy, and it's my business. You need to decide what's important to you. That preacher man loves you. Ask yourself what you want, and then choose how you'll live. Time for you to go."

Was Faye right? Could Samantha choose how she wanted to live her life? Had her presence in Skagway really helped others as Miles said? If she never found Pa, would this trip still have been worthwhile?

Sam followed Faye's swaying hips and clicking high heels back down the hall. At the stairs, Faye pointed. "Go. Tell my girls goodbye. Don't come back."

Samantha considered Faye one long moment and then hurried downstairs. She handed the pillowcases to Peter and Miles. Billy gnawed the end of a moldy cigar.

"Remember," Miles told him. "You don't need to stay in this life either."

"Get out of here." The man stood back from the open doorway. "I ain't seen nothing."

Across the street, a bearded man wearing a suit with a bolo tie pushed a black Stetson off his forehead. He ambled over to greet them in the middle of Broadway.

"Good afternoon, Mr. Smith," Miles said.

Samantha turned wide eyes to Peter. He silenced her with a look and braced his shoulders. Sam followed suit, scrunching her face into a snarl.

"What have we got here, preacher man?" Soapy Smith

drawled around a pungent cigar. "Ransacking the home of honest citizens?"

A low mutter rose from the boardwalk where four brutes glared.

Miles pushed his glasses higher on his nose. "No sir, just picking up some items for friends. You'll excuse me, but we're wanted at the church."

"I don't think so. Step into my parlor, I'd like to have a word with you. Your boys are welcome to join us if they leave their weapons at the bar." Smith removed the cigar from his mouth and breathed smoke.

Sam prayed for wisdom.

Miles waited long enough for Soapy's men to grow restless. His blond curls stuck out from under his bowler hat. "I'm sorry, sir, but I'm doing a good work, and I can't go into your parlor. We're needed at the church."

Soapy Smith dropped his cigar into the slush. "I helped build that church. They can wait for you."

"We appreciate your monetary contribution, but we must be gone. Good day, sir." Miles turned to walk away.

"Soapy! Come quick," shouted a man running down Broadway. "They're stealing our girls."

Smith and his men took off, and the three musketeers hastened to Union Church. They handed the pillowcases to their owners and sat down. The frazzled marshal and his deputies burst through the doors an hour later, their arms full of women's finery and bags. A dozen townspeople followed.

The marshal rubbed his lined forehead. "I may need to get on that ship myself. Soapy's mighty riled. You should consider leaving town for a while, preacher man. He pulled a gun on me."

"How did you get away?" Reverend Dickey asked.

The marshal nodded toward the townspeople. "They came up

and took our side. Someone shot into the air, and Soapy's men scattered."

Miles smiled. "God protects those doing His work."

Mr. Brown from the mercantile joined them. "Soapy's outside with his men, but they don't like the numbers. More folks are headed this way. I knew if enough people went to church, those thugs would back down. We licked 'em today."

Once the women obtained their possessions, Reverend Dickey offered a prayer. As the afternoon waned toward sunset and flurries filled the air, dozens of church members escorted the women to the shore. They cheered as the majority of Skagway's sporting women climbed aboard a barge.

"That Soapy's nothing but a bully," screamed a woman as they cast off. "Goodbye and good riddance!"

"Without the Lord's help we never could have accomplished this," Miles said.

Sam hugged him. "The Lord's help and you being in the right place at the right time. I'm so proud of you."

His eyes shone. "I'll take another one of those."

Peter intervened. "No you won't. It's time for me to shake your hand. I'm proud of you too."

The enormous mountains loomed to the west across the gray canal, aloof and frozen in surprise. Three women fluttered handkerchiefs when they reached the steamship. Samantha's soul soared. Even if they never found Pa, something good had come of their time in Skagway, and Miles had instigated it.

Doc Runnalls crunched across the snowy shoreline carrying the canvas mailbag.

Miles reached into his coat pocket. "With all the excitement this morning, I forgot to give you my letter." He handed it to the mailman with two bits for postage.

Runnalls examined the envelope. "What's this town? Port Orchard, Washington?"

"Yes. We're from there."

"How very curious. I've got another letter for Port Orchard, brought in this morning." Runnalls noticed Samantha. "What's your name again, sonny?"

"I'm Samantha Harris from Port Orchard."

"Samantha? You don't look like a Samantha to me." Runnalls dug through the mailbag and extracted a discolored envelope. "This is for a Mrs. Mary Harris of Port Orchard, Washington."

"My mother. She's dead. That's why we're here."

"Dead?" He held out the cheap envelope. "If she's dead, I believe I can pass this on to her next of kin."

Samantha gasped at the slashing scrawl. "Where did this letter come from?"

"The Tlingits brought it with the cross for the church this morning. Peg Leg sent it. I hope it's the news you've wanted." Runnalls cleared his throat. "I need to get the mailbag to the steamship."

Samantha ripped open the envelope. "Pa's alive!"

Chapter 12

South of Skagway

Miles and Peter huddled around Samantha as she read the letter aloud.

> *My darling, what I feared has come to pass. I must ask you to send my son. I need Peter to help me. Only his young strength and manhood can bring me home to you.*
>
> *Dr. Harry Runnalls of Skagway, Alaska Territory, has a letter giving directions on how to find me. If Peter will come, Dr. Runnalls will help him. If you do not have the funds, go to the good John Parker. I know my brother in Christ will lend Peter the money he needs.*
>
> *Bestow a kiss on Samantha's crown of golden glory. The good work is finished. I pray I will see you all soon. I will not be there in time this year, but Merry Christmas.*
>
>

Your loving husband,
Donald Harris

Samantha's eyes shone as she clutched the letter to her chest. Miles watched Peter blink rapidly and swallow.

When he got control of himself, Peter whooped and spun his sister around. "I knew it. Pa needed us."

Samantha laughed when he put her down. She stroked her still golden, but not much of a crown, hair. "I knew he'd be disappointed Peter chopped off my hair."

"You cut it for good reason," Miles said. "He won't care."

Dr. Runnalls returned. "I take it you have good news."

"The best," Samantha said.

Peter indicated the letter. "It says you've got directions for how to find Pa."

Dr. Runnalls shouldered his bag. "Come up to the office."

A blizzard blew in during the night and shut down White Pass for the rest of the winter. While Miles sought time off from the mercantile, Peter scoured the waterfront looking for someone to guide them down the southeast side of the canal. Samantha could scarcely wait to find the village Donald Harris indicated in the letter left with Runnalls, but Tlingits rarely visited Skagway.

December 24 dawned clear and cold. A Tlingit Indian hiked into town that morning on a beach trail. After picking up mail and several items from the mercantile, he agreed to escort them to his village and Peg Leg.

The trio stowed clothes, bedrolls, and foodstuffs into packs and followed him.

The small dark man in a thick bearskin coat walked briskly along the rocky shoreline. A bone-chilling wind blew off the water, and sea spray soaked them more than once. They scrambled over driftwood and boulders, grateful for low tide.

Miles was thankful for the days spent on the trail; he had no trouble keeping up.

"Why Peg Leg?" Samantha asked as she dodged a sudden wave.

Peter and Miles didn't know. Their guide spoke only broken English.

When she struggled in her long skirts over large boulders and nearly slipped, Miles held out his hand. She took it and did not let go, even when the path smoothed. Peter raised an eyebrow but said nothing.

Miles's heart thumped with optimism. "Are you looking forward to returning to Washington?"

Samantha tripped on a piece of driftwood. "I don't know."

He hated to say it, but he needed to know her plans. "You probably can begin in the second semester, only one term late."

She bit her lip. "But I don't feel like I'm done in Skagway. How can I leave now, when there's talk of a school?"

Miles stopped. "You would stay to teach school? I thought you didn't like this town."

"Things have changed since Lucy's funeral. People are different. Did you notice the children at church? I can be useful in Skagway. I can't stay by myself, but with Mama gone, maybe Pa won't want to go back to Port Orchard."

Miles tucked her hand under his elbow. His blood pounded in his ears all the way down the coast as he contemplated how to tell her of his own change in heart.

Two hours later, the winter night and rising tide were nearly upon them when they reached a river mouth. Three native lodges sprawled three hundred yards from the shore. Canoes were beached high above the surf line. A pack of barking mongrels rushed to greet them.

Their guide led them to the first house—a long cedar-planked building with a peaked roof covered in bark. They pushed through a door into a great room smelling of smoke and close living. Four decorated corner posts held up the roof, and the floor was dug down in the middle, providing earthen seating around a central fire. Wooden partitions to divide the area into sleeping compartments lined the walls. The fire in the center and two kerosene lanterns provided dim light.

Twenty people startled at their entry, and the deerskin-clad women recoiled in surprise, calling their children to them. An elderly man stepped forward and addressed them in the sliding guttural Tlingit language.

When Miles, Peter, and Samantha removed their wraps, the chief laughed. "I think you speak English. *Tillicum*"—he motioned to a seated man smoothing a totem pole in the far corner.

"Papa," Samantha cried, starting forward. Her brother followed.

"Peter? Samantha?" Donald Harris's deep voice cracked. "But I just sent the letter. How are you here so soon?"

"We've been in Skagway looking for you." Samantha fell at his feet.

Miles blinked back tears.

Donald sat on a skin-covered box with one leg stretched before him, a carved crutch at his feet. His big hands shook as he embraced the twins. His bare head, now shaved bald, shone in the firelight, and his coarse beard was white. The hearty man who had led the trio on hikes and taught them about the outdoors years before looked diminished in the longhouse.

The natives around Miles gabbled in a language he could not understand. Possessions filled the room, fishing gear hung on the walls, and the families obviously were preparing a meal. Their trail guide slipped away, leaving Miles towering over the Tlingit families. Peter looked like a giant.

Donald ruffled his hands along Samantha's head with a chuckle. "Your crowning glory is shorn these days. Did you think to find riches in your golden hair?"

"Peter and Miles thought I would be safer if I blended in with the Klondikers. I've been wearing trousers and pretending to be a man."

"Your mother agreed to a disguise?" Donald laughed.

The twins shared a glance.

"That's why we're here, Pa." Peter took his father's hands. "Mother died in June. We've been in Skagway since August looking for you."

Donald's joy crumbled. "Mary's dead?"

His distress caught the ear of the natives. The elder who had greeted them stepped closer, and a nearby woman moaned. Miles scanned the room; all the Tlingits watched Donald, waiting. For what?

The man buried his face in his hands. "Tell me."

Samantha recounted her mother's illness, the hours spent reading the Bible, the moments of her death. Peter described the decision to close up the house and head north. "We needed to find you."

Donald's shoulders shook, and Samantha hugged him. Peter completed the circle, and the three cried together.

At their tears, the Tlingits murmured a low sympathy. Miles went to his friends. Peter pulled him into the wide embrace too.

There in a native house on the edge of nowhere, the civilized, cultured, devout Mary Harris's death was fully mourned by those who loved her best.

∽

Donald opened his watch and gazed at a photograph of his wife while the native women served them dried salmon and tea. Miles chewed on the salted smoked fish. Sips of spruce tea cleared his sinuses.

"This is not what I expected," Donald finally said. "She never wrote of illness. Mary's refinement had no place in Alaska, which is why she stayed behind. She argued she would get in the way of God's work and slow me down. She always sent me without her."

"But you wanted to return to Port Orchard." Peter leaned forward. "That's what you said in the letter."

Donald gestured to his leg. "I broke it right after I wrote in June. I can't walk without a crutch. I finished my task—the totem—and I wanted to see my family. But now Mary's gone."

"You have us, Pa," Samantha said. "And Miles."

Donald scrutinized him. "Ah, Miles. How did you escape your mother?"

Miles set his jaw. "I sent my parents a letter and said I was leaving. Here I am."

The Tlingit chief joined them around the fire. Behind them, the families prepared their meals, settled their children to sleep, and murmured among themselves. A log shifted on the fire, and the light danced. With his stomach full and his body finally warm, Miles should have relaxed, but Donald's steady gaze held a challenge. He smoothed his beard and mustache.

Samantha rubbed Miles's arm. "He's done very well, Pa."

Donald noted her movement. "Were you ordained?"

"No sir. I finished my coursework but missed ordination. The missions board members laid hands on me before I left and charged me to preach the Gospel."

His questioner's right eyebrow went up just like Peter's. "Have you done so?"

"He has," Samantha declared. "He preached to the Sourdoughs and sporting women on the ship. He read his Bible to packers on White Pass. He nearly killed himself building the church, and then he started teaching Bible study in the restaurant."

She gazed at him with shining eyes. Miles's heart hammered. "He's the one who instigated the sporting women leaving Skagway, and then he took on Soapy Smith when we collected their belongings. The town has seen God in action ever since Miles arrived."

Peter slapped. Miles on the back. "Miles bought our provisions. He's watched out for Sam. We never could have made this trip without him. 'All for one,' we always said, but it's really been all Miles for us."

Donald smiled. "The Tlingits like nothing better than a good story. My three musketeers have all grown up. I'd like to hear about your adventures."

They told their story long into the night.

Chapter 13

Tlingit Village
Christmas

Samantha woke the next morning fully clothed but wrapped in a blanket beside the banked fire.

Peter and her father snored softly while the Tlingits moved quietly about their chores. Miles's bedroll lay folded in a neat pile. Samantha stretched, pulled on her boots and coat, and headed outside.

Dawn took a long time coming in the December north, and at the shoreline she saw a broad-shouldered man wearing a misshapen bowler hat watching the waves. He stepped backward as a roller slipped far up the beach and bumped into a driftwood log.

She sighed, but he stepped nimbly over it and laughed.

Pa was right. Miles had changed.

So had Samantha's opinion of him. She went to her childhood friend with a shyness she'd never felt before.

"Merry Christmas." He put his arm around her shoulders to protect her when a gust of frigid air threatened to knock them over.

"The same to you."

"I wonder if mistletoe grows here."

Samantha tilted her head. "Why?"

"After what you said to your father last night, I'd like to kiss you." The cold wind blew ruddiness into his face.

Satisfaction swelled from deep within. "We don't need

mistletoe. I'd be honored to kiss you."

His brow wrinkled. "Do you mean it?"

"I do."

He considered her. The water crashed; a shorebird scooted past. The village dogs barked, and a curl of cedar smoke reminded her breakfast would be ready soon.

She held her breath.

"What happens next, Sam?" Miles asked in a husky voice.

"Pa will tell the Christmas story."

"Will you stay in Alaska?"

She gazed toward the jagged white mountains across the canal. "Mollie is taking her restaurant to the top of the pass in the spring. You and Peter are headed to the Klondike."

"I'm not going to the Klondike." Miles pushed at the driftwood with his heavy boot. "I feel like your pa. He stayed because of the work he believed God called him to do. Reverend Dickey heads over the Chilkoot soon. He means to start a church in Dawson."

"Will you take his place?"

"Only if I don't have to minister alone. I'm not as strong as your father and mother."

Her lips parted. She moved within a breath of a kiss but stopped when she heard rocks shift on the beach.

Peter jogged up. "Happy Christmas. You need to come inside. Pa's going to explain his totem pole. Hey. What's happening here?"

Miles gazed a rueful moment longer and then tapped Samantha's chin. "Everything."

They made their way back to the longhouse, shucked off their wraps, then joined the clan seated around the central fire hearth. Babies cuddled on their mothers' laps, small children played at their feet, and the men stood behind. Donald leaned on his carved crutch beside a blond totem, the scent of freshly cut wood still in the air. The trio found spots beside the fire.

"I came to you a year ago," Donald said. "You asked me to tell more about the good news other missionaries brought. It has been an honor to read the scriptures and to teach some of you to read. But not all can read the words, and so for this Christmas, I did what missionaries asked me to do when I came: I've carved a totem so you can remember God and how He came to earth to live with His people."

Samantha's father spoke in simple English with a young interpreter by his side, but the way he communicated with the native people filled her with pride. They wanted to hear the story of the Creator who sent His Son to teach them about love and how to know Him better. The contrast between the "savages" in a wooden longhouse hungering for the Christmas story and the thugs controlling Skagway couldn't have been plainer.

Her father pointed to the top figure on the totem. "Raven is the emissary of the great Chief of Heavens who holds the Christmas star."

"Raven is a sort of an angel here, but he often is a joker," Miles whispered.

Peter nudged her. "Trust Miles to have done his homework, even on native tribes."

In the past, she would have laughed with her brother at Miles's need for research, but that day Samantha thought about how thorough Miles had been in his preparations. He not only learned about the Alaskan country before he left his books at the seminary, but he investigated the beliefs of people he expected to meet.

She smiled to herself, however, realizing how he had miscalculated on the sporting women.

"Joseph is the wood carver who led Mary on a journey to Bethlehem. Here I've represented him by a man holding a canoe paddle." Donald pointed midway up the totem at a mother and child. "Many people came to the potlatch where the powerful chief wanted to display his wealth. Mary gave birth to the baby Jesus at the gathering."

Samantha took Miles's hand. He had provisioned their trip and made sure they had what they needed. He worked the pass with her brother, but he came back to Skagway to watch over her. Because he loved her.

Just like that, she knew what she wanted.

"The bear lives in a cave, or a manger," Donald explained, "and the keepers of the fish trap, the men who tended animals, proclaimed the good news. The chief beneath them is one of the three wise men who brought gifts to the newborn king."

Miles brought his talents to worship his God in Skagway. He tried to build the church but then got correctly diverted to teach instead. Samantha shook herself—she needed to pay attention to her father's story, not think about Miles.

The bottom two characters were the frog, symbolizing the angel who appeared to Joseph in his dream, and the upside-down chief, symbolizing evil King Herod who was outwitted by the angel.

Samantha told Miles, "You were the angel who outwitted Soapy Smith."

Peter and Miles both laughed.

Donald blessed his congregation and hummed the opening bars of "Joy to the World." Men in leggings, women in deerskin, children, and the Americans from Port Orchard put their hands into the air and sang.

Worshipping God, Samantha reflected, could be done anywhere with anyone who believed.

Salmon, seafood, dried berries, and more spruce tea made up the natives' Christmas potlatch. Her father brightened when Samantha pulled dried apple turnovers from her backpack, along with sourdough to make flapjacks.

The women crowded to watch as Samantha greased the skillet with salt pork and poured in the batter. "I've learned a lot at the restaurant."

"She has," Peter agreed. "Her cooking is almost edible now."

When she made a fist in his direction, her brother put up his hands. "You're not Sam anymore. You're a real woman. Act like one."

Miles and her father shrugged together.

The four sat by the fire after the Tlingits had their fill of flapjacks, and they ate their meal on tin plates. They drank coffee from metal mugs and reminisced about Christmases past eaten on china plates.

"What happens to you now?" Donald asked when they finished their meal.

"We'll take you back with us tomorrow." Peter stretched his feet toward the fire. "You're crippled, and you're a long way from civilization. Samantha will travel home with you from Skagway."

They watched the fire crackle in a companionable silence.

"I've been thinking and praying since last night," Donald finally said. "I've not lived in a town or a house for two years. It won't hurt me to stay with these people now that Mary's gone."

Peter shook his head. "With these simple natives?"

Donald looked around the longhouse and smiled. "They're the most honest people I've met in Alaska. I can continue teaching them to read and to understand the scriptures, and I can help them deal with the white men. It's a good work for someone like me."

Samantha kissed him. "I think Pa should stay here."

"Without us?" Peter shook his head.

"With people who care about him and whom he loves,"

Samantha said. "He's needed here. We have our own lives now."

Peter pulled a small canvas bag out of his money belt. "Fine. Here's most of the money I owe you. Now you can return to Washington and go to college."

Samantha touched the rough, dirty pouch. "Where is my home? Washington or Skagway?"

Miles moved closer.

"You can't live in Skagway by yourself. It's not safe. Take the money." Peter held out the bag.

Miles took her hand. "She doesn't have to be alone. I'm not going over the pass with you, Peter. I'm staying in Skagway. The two of you dragged me into a ministry I never dreamed of at seminary. Samantha made me confront evil with good because she saw the need in the sporting women's hearts. Now the town has built a church and needs men to preach the Gospel. That's a harvest richer than Klondike gold and one I mean to pursue."

"You're not going with me to the Klondike?"

"No."

"Surely you've met others you can travel with," Samantha said.

"Yes." Peter looked troubled. "But I don't trust anyone like I do Miles. I thought I'd do the heavy work while he could minister to the miners, just like we did on the trail. I'm not a preacher. I can't do that."

"Here we have it." Donald clasped his son by both shoulders. "I've prayed you would embrace the man God created you to be. You don't have to be a missionary to serve God. Your desire to go to the Klondike could be for gold. But maybe it's really an adventure for a young man who stayed with his mother and sister far longer than he wanted so his father could do a good work. This is your time, Peter. Go into the world and follow where God is leading you. You have my blessing."

"Do you want to come with me, Sam?" her twin asked.

Samantha stood. "I love you, Peter, but it's time we went our own ways. I don't want to go to the Klondike. I've found what I want here."

The Tlingits hummed. Her father stirred the fire. Miles stood beside her and tilted her chin toward him. "We're both doing a good work in Skagway. Will you marry me so we can serve the town together?"

Samantha gazed into his eyes a long moment. "Wait a minute." She looked him up and down. "Have you grown, Miles? How tall are you?"

"Six feet. Why?"

Peter burst into laughter.

"I would love to marry you," Samantha said. "Pa can do the honors."

"What does my height have to do with it?"

Samantha hugged him. "Absolutely nothing."

Donald stood to pronounce a benediction. "Mary was proud of all three of you, but today your plans complete her dreams and prayers."

He faced his son. "I know how thankful she was you stayed in Port Orchard. You go to the Klondike with her blessing and mine."

Donald smiled at Samantha. "She would have rejoiced that you finally learned you don't have to live in Peter's shadow. She wanted you to choose what is important for your own life."

He shook Miles's hand. "Mary prayed long for your calling, Miles, and would have been even more grateful you stood by your friends and gave them the opportunity to find themselves." He caressed Samantha's cheek. "I think you've got the best end of this deal."

Donald gathered the three into another hug. "Mary, I am sure, is rejoicing with the angels right now. Peter will have his adventure, and today we'll have a wedding. Anything else?"

Miles smiled at Samantha. "May I kiss my bride?"

Samantha looked up at him. "Yes."

Historical Notes

While Miles and the Harris family are fictional characters, the story of the sporting women's exodus from Skagway after hearing Reverend R. W. Dickey's funeral sermon is true. Steamship captain O'Brien met Dickey on the beach after the service and volunteered to take the sporting women back to Seattle at no cost. Sourdough Jim contributed one thousand dollars to cover their costs. Mollie Walsh knew "Lucy," and Mollie set up a restaurant at the top of White Pass in the spring of 1898.

The Christmas totem pole described in *The Gold Rush Christmas* was carved by Reverend David Fison of Alaska in 1987. I used the concept with his permission and my thanks. You can see a photo of it at my website: www.michelleule.com.

Michelle Ule is the author of six bestselling novellas, two novels, and a biography of Mrs. Oswald Chambers. Married to a now retired submarine officer whom she followed all over the world, she lives with her family in northern California. You can learn more about her at www .michelleule.com.

More Christmas Romance Collections!

Christmas Next Door

Visit an Old West Texas town where a mysterious benefactor leaves gifts each Christmas, but also where four pairs of neighbors battle over hearsay, secrets, and mysteries. Even as romantic tensions increase, love seems beyond reach. Can their problems bring them closer to share in the generous spirit of the season?

Paperback / 978-1-64352-167-1 / $14.99